ROYAL SPY INSTITUTE

2

FIVE & CHANCE

Copyright © 2024 by Elise Hennessy

All rights reserved.

No part of this book may be reproduced in any form or by any electronic or mechanical means, including information storage and retrieval systems, without written permission from the author, except for the use of brief quotations in a book review. This book may not be redistributed to others for commercial or noncommercial purposes.

This novel is entirely a work of fiction. The names, characters and incidents portrayed in it are the work of the author's imagination. Any resemblance to actual persons, living or dead, events or localities is entirely coincidental.

Flutterbye Trail Press
797 Sam Bass Road #2541
Round Rock, TX 78681

First edition

Editing by Red Loop Editing
Cover Design by Black Bird Book Covers
Chapter Art by Etheric Tales
Printed Interior Design by Enchanting Covers
Published by Flutterbye Trail Press

ISBN: 978-1-954582-22-4 (E-book)
ISBN: 978-1-954582-25-5 (Paperback)
ISBN: 978-1-954582-26-2 (Hardback)

Feedback: Encounter a problem with this book? Let us know at elisehennessyauthor@gmail.com

BOOKS BY ELISE HENNESSY

Books in the Altare World

GRYPHON RIDER ACADEMY
Second Chance
Chosen
Storm Front
Wild Flight
Gryphon Rider Academy Omnibus 1: Books 1-4

ROYAL SPY INSTITUTE
The Crown Heist
Five & Chance

Also by Elise Hennessy

BLOOD LEGACY SERIES
Dream Walker
The Winter Key
Queen's Return
Court of Illusions

Shadow Dance
Rule the Night
Dhampir's Wish
Blood Curse
Blood Legacy: The Complete Series

ROYAL SPY INSTITUTE 2

FIVE & CHANCE

ELISE HENNESSY

CHAPTER 1

SUMMER SPYING

THE CONNERY ESTATE was pretty in the late afternoon light, boasting the perfect beauty that belonged on a painting. Its bricks were even and clean, and bright pops of blooming flowers flanked the carefully maintained gardens. I stood at the railing of a ferry as it glided into Luccal's port and observed the estate as the ship floated past it.

Carmen rested her weight on her elbows next to me, her gaze on my face rather than the estate. "Well?" she asked pointedly.

The tall girl simmered with barely restrained energy and no immediate outlet. Give her an opponent, and she would acquaint them with her fists, no problem. Tell her we're on a mission for a summer extracurricular—a fancy way of saying *for fun*, I'd learned—project, and at a key observational moment, she would stare at me like she wanted me to turn my brain inside out and sift through my thoughts.

"It's good we know folk who know folk," I said.

She raised an unimpressed brow back. "That's all?"

I simply nodded. The someones who'd first built the estate had pushed it back from the beach far enough to give it a fence perimeter. The third-floor balcony had a guard to dissuade any would-be thieves from sneaking in from the back.

For all that it was a pretty building, it also had roofing tiles arranged in the patterns of two different spells. The first was a slipping trap, a classic. The second took me a moment longer to recognize since it was unusual to see an amplification spell on a roof. The pattern was too big and complicated, but some mage had pulled off a miracle and made it fit. With its power twined with the slipping trap, there would be no climbable surface on the Connery estate from the outside.

Considering one of us was supposed to squeeze into a suite on the third floor, it wasn't ideal. Thus, it was lucky Margot still exchanged letters with a former maid of hers who was willing to leave a door unlocked tonight. Margot treated "the help" like friends, even after her sudden departure from the estate, and this was the result.

If I were brave enough to offer Carmen a critique, I'd have told her she should've looked for herself and tried to understand everything I'd just learned from one long glance. But I could picture her scoffing and saying, "That's what you're for, pipsqueak," so I didn't bother.

Instead, I said, "Wanna get Margot? I'll watch our stuff."

Though she grumbled that I could send my mouse to do it, she left. I probably could've trusted the job to Chance, but since we'd boarded, I'd spotted at least two ship cats, lean hunters who'd make a snack of my beloved carpenter mouse. He was napping in my pocket, his pointed head hanging off the side, since my belt with its special pouch for him was secured in one of my bags. I'd hidden him under the hem of my blouse, as we hadn't wanted to draw attention.

Margot wouldn't be saying a word until nightfall. Her noblewoman's accent was just as conspicuous as my utility belt, and I was missing both things. Margot tended to chatter to fill the air, talking for the sake of there being no silence. My anxiously spinning mind could've used less quiet. My eyelid twitched, betraying my inner turmoil.

It was the moments before something big that were the worst. Everything that could go wrong looped in my head, as it always did. If my little sister, Jackie, were here, she'd take my hand and remind me that this was my kind of magic. I'd know what to do to avoid all the bad endings swirling through my thoughts. It was uncomfortable, but few successful operations began in a place of ease.

We had to do this right for Margot.

Plus, she was tossing some clorets to Carmen and me for helping. I'd be lying if I said I wasn't doing it for the money, too.

WE DISEMBARKED from the ferry and settled our things in an inn room. From there, I spoke more freely about what we were up against. Spread on the battered wood table was a map Margot had made of the estate from memory across three sheets of parchment, one per floor. I moved around a button, a needle, and a perfectly round metal sphere to represent us, until Chance nudged the latter into motion and scampered after it off the edge of the table.

Rolling my eyes with a warm smile, I said, "Ya get the idea."

"Which one was I again?" Carmen asked, picking up the needle and testing its point. "Ow."

I tried not to release an annoyed sound. She wasn't paying attention at all, was she? "The button. You're the lookout," I said.

"Lame," she muttered.

Margot sniffed. "If you see my cousin walking around after dark, you have my full permission to punch him."

"Was he the one with the drifting hands…" she began to ask.

"He was," Margot confirmed.

Carmen's expression grew stormy, and she punched her palm.

Margot kept fidgeting with her hair, gingerly brushing it over her shoulder. We'd made her the opposite of what she usually was. The prim noblewoman with her cute blonde curls and preference for pastel outfits was now covered in a layer of dust and grease and changed into dark, shoddy clothes. She'd applied the cosmetics herself to put hollows under her eyes and add a hint of age to her corners.

The hope was that, if her uncle's family or a less friendly staff member saw her tonight, they wouldn't realize Margot had left the capital and RSI to break in to her former home. With Vance stuck inside RSI until further notice, we'd had to disguise her the old-fashioned way.

Hopefully, Carmen did not encounter Margot's cousin, let alone punch him. This plan was a "no violence" kind of plan, where we got in and out without detection. But I also didn't say that to Carmen.

"How long will you need to copy the records?" I asked.

To have our outing during the summer break approved, we'd had to provide some benefit to the Spymaster. Miss Barrios had suggested we do some spying while we were here. It was apparently common practice. The Crown maintained a stream of information on many people—including Baron Connery—and we would be updating the Crown's copy of his financial ledgers going back to a specific date eight months ago.

We were officially running a *spy operation*, not a heist.

"A couple hours at most, darling. That should give you plenty of time," Margot said.

I nodded with a slight flare of confidence in my gut. I was used to counting down my time in minutes, not hours. We were playing to our strengths and splitting tasks tonight. To be more accurate as to the nature of our mission, Margot was spying, I was stealing, and Carmen was helping us both.

Now, if only the feeling of self-assurance could last. We had to wait until the dark of night, a period punctuated by my pacing, Carmen napping, and Margot playing fetch with Chance. At some point, she'd traded a ball of yarn that resisted being thrown far for a small sphere with an elastic bounce that he eagerly chased.

Occasionally, I'd whisper a possibility we hadn't discussed earlier to Margot, who had a quick answer for most things. She got tired after a while and handed me Chance's toy, going to the other bed in the room to lie down and cover her face with a pillow.

"Are you going to have the energy to help me tonight?" I asked Chance after giving the ball a toss.

He returned and dropped it at my feet, tilting his head with rounded ears perked. There was a spot of white behind them, but otherwise, his fur was a solid brown. As a carpenter mouse, he had extra digits that acted like thumbs, which he flexed as he stood straight and reached for me, his sign that he wanted to be picked up.

I bent and offered my palm, holding him close to my face. "Yes yes! Plenty energy for spying," he squeaked.

I understood him without trouble since he was my Linked companion. The downsides to that was that he still had a small voice to go with his tiny body and obviously lived his life at thrice the speed I did. He spoke in a rush and teased me sometimes for doing things the "slow human" way.

"Good mouse. Sweet mouse." I petted his silky fur as I cooed over him. He bobbled his little head happily.

With him in hand, I didn't pace. I knew my role and what I was good at when it was literally in my palm. I was going on four years of being Mouse, so named in my old street gang for being small, sneaky, and unassuming.

When it was time to move, I placed Chance on my shoulder and woke my friends. After Margot adjusted her outfit and checked her makeup, we left out the inn's back door and took a quiet backstreet route to the Connery estate. It was pitch-black nighttime, our way dimly lit from the streetlamps on the main road. The constant gusts off the ocean smelled of salt and days-old fish, turning my stomach.

It felt off not to have a cloak blowing behind me. I'd taken to wearing one to conceal the heavy utility belt I'd brought to this operation, loaded with pouches of helpful knickknacks and tools. After months of creative lifting around RSI, I'd assembled a kit of items to answer most any situation.

I fiddled with my belt, counting each loop and the pouch, tool, or satchel that went with it. It was large and reversible, with one side being solid leather and the reverse side sporting two smaller belts sewn into the leather for me to secure double the number of items on my person. Though Fariq teased me for carrying around "junk," he'd bought the belt for me after observing my habits. I missed him a lot as we approached the silent front face of the Connery estate. He had chosen to stay in Kaiamear and start his apprenticeship early rather than join us, his straitlaced way of looking away from our impending mission.

I wasn't used to entering through the front of a building I intended to rob, but Margot strode ahead of us confidently and turned the knob. It opened, left unlocked as promised. She held it at an angle for me to head inside first.

Margot had already shared that the home defense magic in the estate was twined with a deadbolt on the front door. As long as we didn't lock it into place, there would be no alarms or active traps needing to be disarmed. I could preserve the few precious pinches of crimson desda powder I carried for a different night's work.

I tiptoed within and scouted for light or movement. Shadows obscured any details of the upper floors and the end of the first-floor hallway. There was a kitchen to my right, still fragrant with savory smells. Out of old habit, I pinched my nose so my belly wouldn't rumble.

As I scuttled my way to the first-floor office and set Chance on the carpet, I passed several pieces of art and sculptures I barely gave a glance to. One of the first rules of thieving was to not get dazzled by the surroundings.

That done, I went back to the door and motioned for my friends to join me. Margot went to the office and opened the door. The three of us peeked inside together, and I reached around the jamb to offer my palm to Chance, who'd slipped underneath the door and unlocked it for us. All was quiet so far.

Nodding toward me, Margot slipped into the office. A few moments later, dim light from a lit candle floated under the door. I glanced over at Carmen, who jerked her head for me to get going, and she followed me as I headed for the stairs. We kept our ears perked for the sound of movement.

I sweated. This was the most precarious part of the plan. For all Carmen boasted that she could take out any guard with one properly placed strike—and I believed her—there was always a chance we'd be taken by surprise. Most guards roamed on a set schedule, but humans weren't clocks. The Connerys' guard could be bored by this point and choose to walk their route early rather than wait for the next chime of the evening bells.

We heard nothing by the time we scaled to the third floor and inspected what we could in the dark. The door out to the balcony was a solid sheet of glass, an expensive touch to the pretty, perfect building. Its clear surface gave us a view through it to the other side.

"Where's the guard?" Carmen hissed.

My eyes narrowed. I'd seen a man standing there on the ferry ride earlier, but he was not at his post tonight.

For a moment, I thought like Baron Connery. He believed the downstairs door was locked when he went to bed tonight, knowing the only entrances to the estate were the ground-level doors. I'd counted no less than four magelights with alarm spells so far, each floating harmlessly with the home defense magic deactivated. But the baron didn't know that; he thought his home was shut and safe. No need to pay a hired hand to intimidate calm air.

Could it be that easy?

"There ain't a guard. Go stand watch," I whispered.

Her brows rose, but she didn't argue, creeping back down the stairs. We'd agreed that, if we were caught, Margot would need Carmen's help more than I would.

Even if I was the one sneaking into her old room, the one she was fairly sure now belonged to her handsy cousin. *Musty devils,* she may have sweetened the pot by paying for our carriage rides, meals, and the new pair of slippers that helped me sneak silently down the hall, but I still didn't want to do this and risk his hands finding me.

Think of the challenge and the reward, not what could happen, I reminded myself.

Chance looked up at my face from my palm, one ear swiveling. If we weren't sneaking, he'd ask, "Why scared?" Little wonders weren't supposed to make Links strong enough for us to share emotions, but he always seemed to pick up on mine when they were strong. Likewise, I could tell he was concerned when he lifted a tiny fist and offered it to me.

I bumped fists with him gently and kissed his side to reassure him before I placed him before the door to Margot's old room. He slid himself underneath it, just to reappear after a few moments with his paws raised. Picking him back up, I held him to my ear so he could squeak quietly, "Somebody there snore loud."

Well, at least the cousin snored. That gave me an audible clue as to whether he was awake. I nodded and put Chance back down, swallowing my nerves. It was so quiet that I'd heard the soft slide and click of the lock when he twisted it open. I dragged the door open and cringed when it creaked.

Someone inside the room snorted in their sleep, followed by several long seconds of quiet. I only opened the door further when he snored again. When the opening was big enough for me to slip through, I did and left the door ajar to keep it from creaking a second time.

The drapes were drawn, the famed "best view in Luccal," according to Margot, blocked out for the evening. I crouched low and moved along the edges of the room, finding the foot of the bed with some help from the cousin's snoring. My nose wrinkled; his feet stuck out from the covers, and they were musty.

I dared to summon a pinprick of light, cupping the ring I spun with my thumb. Spymaster Manny had given it to me for a job well done, and I was eager to finally use it during a mission. Since I'd spun it slowly, an ember of red light appeared down its center. I used it to see the outline of the man's feet and the arm and skewed comforter hanging off the side of the bed.

He slept on, unknowing of the Mouse sliding under his bedframe. It was smooth until my hips stuck, and I decided that was good enough. I counted planks with my fingertips. *One, two, three…four.* Ever so slowly, I eased the false board loose and lifted it, finding a square hole of darkness just where Margot said it would be.

I could hear her accented voice in my head as I used the board to shield the light of my ring and inspected the contents of her old hiding place. "Before my uncle's family could sell everything my parents owned that wasn't bolted down, I hid the small valuables. I squirreled away my mother's pearls, some documents and bills of sale, and all the loose clorets that could fit in my little hidey hole. And because they tossed me out on my ear so abruptly, they're still there."

"Under the bed?" I'd asked in disbelief.

"Yes," she'd answered proudly.

Musty devils. Margot didn't have a criminal bone in her body. Under a bed was the first place anyone thought to hide their valuables.

Thankfully, her stash was still here, in all its messy glory. I reached for my belt and unclipped the satchel at my hip. Using my fingertips, I navigated the feeling of paper, boxes of various sizes, and the cool, rounded corners of stacks of clorets.

One coin fell with a metallic *clink*. My heartbeat doubled, throbbing in my ears as the snoring cut off. He shifted above me, his weight dipping the mattress. Pursing my lips, I prepared to give Chance the signal that would send him scurrying to Carmen to summon some backup.

The cousin rolled over and yawned, smacking his lips. I listened with my eyelid twitching until a small snore cut through the night air. *Just take it slow. Margot needs time anyway.*

Those loose clorets were going to be the noisiest part, so I saved them for last. I lifted box after box from the stash and stacked them big to small in the satchel until they filled about half of it. Well, if it wasn't a big enough bag, a couple of pouches on my belt had room for some coins. Anything else there wasn't room for would have to be left behind forever.

I kept my fingers moving with painstaking care and held my breath every time the cousin seemed to stop breathing. He really needed to see a Tulari healer about his snoring; it didn't sound pleasant. The documents were easy enough to slip into a side pocket. Some of them might be worth more than all the clorets in this hole, but in the dark, they were folded and shoved anywhere they could fit.

I told myself I didn't need to lift all the clorets, but I hadn't been raised to leave money behind. Granted, I hadn't been raised much at all, except by the gang sibling I thought might be my father, Thylacine.

Don't get greedy now, Heather. She's rich enough, he would say if he knew about this mission.

I apologized to him in my head and started digging out all the coins. As I suspected, not all of them fit in the satchel, so I started opening pouches and stuffing clorets in them. A lot of clorets fit in Chance's special pouch, and I made a note to clean away the metal stink of the money later for him.

Miraculously, I cleared out the stash completely. While I hadn't been counting time as strictly as I usually did, it'd been at least an hour. Maybe Margot was done and we could still get a decent nap in before catching a different ferry ride to Daramaine tomorrow morning.

I buttoned the satchel and pushed it out from under the bed. It immediately fell onto its side with the unmistakable sound of sliding coins. My belly clenched in fright.

"Huh? What was that?" The cousin sat up.

If he woke a magelight, I was caught. I made a soft click out of the corner of my mouth and hoped Chance hadn't fallen asleep waiting for me.

In the meantime, I grabbed the satchel with my legs and dragged it with me as I wiggled my way under the bed completely. I scarcely dared to breathe after he clapped and warm light suffused the room. His feet hit the ground, along with an extra section of comforter.

I curled in on myself as tight as possible and watched him circle around. *Don't look under the bed. Don't look under the bed...*

"Could've sworn," he was muttering, sounding only half awake.

His feet turned. For a moment, I thought he was going to go back to sleep, but then he muttered a curse and headed for the door I'd left ajar.

I covered my face, exasperated with myself. This was much worse than having to work around some creaky hinges.

Of course, that was the moment Carmen barreled through the opening. I knew that gleam of eagerness on her face, excited for a fight. She was on the cousin before he could react, and her fist flew straight for his jaw.

His heavy body fell with a choked sound. Carmen caught his arm at the last moment and lowered him to the ground quietly. I peered out from behind the comforter after a few moments, during which he was still. "Guess you was right. Only took one punch," I whispered.

Carmen seemed a little disappointed when she looked down at me. "*Were* right," she said absently.

I rolled my eyes but accepted the correction for what it was. The old, lazy gang speech came out more when I was in the mindset of a sneak, and it was a little embarrassing.

Ducking under the bed again, I made sure to close the hidey hole before emerging from the foot of the bed. Carmen and I exchanged a glance over the unconscious body lying on the floor. "Well, let's get him sorted," I said.

"You want to tuck him in?" Carmen hissed in disbelief.

"Naw. But he'll wake up tomorrow with a heck of a bruise and no sign of us being here," I whispered. "Maybe he'll think it was just a bad dream."

We got to arranging him as he'd been when I came in. "Margot's done, by the way. We were waiting for you," she said.

"Really?"

"You took *forever*."

I shrugged. Once he was positioned right, with his hand hanging and everything, I said, "Least you got to punch him."

She smirked. "Yeah, better than listening to Margot. She's furious." She motioned for us to go, and I followed her to the door, an expression of bafflement crossing my face. Margot, angry? I don't think I'd ever seen it.

At the doorway, I turned and clapped, plunging the scene of the crime into darkness. As I eased the door closed behind us, I whispered, "Would you lock it right quick, Chance?"

I pictured how hopelessly confused Margot's cousin was going to be tomorrow morning when he couldn't find any evidence of our break-in and smirked.

CHAPTER 2
MASTERY

An angry Margot turned out to be just as talkative as a happy Margot. She was just a bit more shrill. Once we were safely in a carriage heading south, she recited monetary figures without referring to the copy of the baron's finances. I assumed that was because she'd already read it front, back, and front again until the numbers were burned into her mind.

Carmen attempted to dull the sharpness of how little she cared about the finer details of the Connery family's money. I joined her in looking attentive, though my head was empty, boggled after the first few numbers and Margot not explaining the long litany of expenses.

Inevitably, she grew teary and snapped open her pink lace fan, flipping it toward her face. "They spent all of my dowry and more," she concluded. "The *absolute gall* of those charlatans. They're bankrupt. Worse, they're debtors!" A delicate shudder ran through her body. "My father kept the books balanced as baron, but then my uncle's family just…just sweeps in and sells everything of worth! And then spends it on such frivolities. Can you believe it?"

I sighed with some relief, glad to hear her sum up why she was so upset. I'd be angry too if folk who were meant to be loving family spent what was mine. "Sorry, Margot. At least you don't have nothing anymore. You—" My lips formed *was*, but I paused for a small moment and reminded myself to speak properly. "—were smart enough to hide all this from them."

I gestured down at the satchel I'd stuffed with her stash. Next to it was a sack we'd bought to store all the loose clorets. It made my fingertips tingle to be so close to it. My cut of the job was inside once we took the time to count it all.

Margot had offered both of us five percent of the loose clorets, promising it would be worth our time...and it certainly was. My gaze kept straying to the sack, betraying how eager I was to hold my new wealth.

I'd never had more than a few clorets to rub together before arriving at RSI. Having money that was *mine* was a novelty. When I was a part of Jace's Menagerie, my cut of any profitable job was always handed to the man I used to call my uncle. The Spymaster had revealed that Jace was little more than a handler for my gang siblings and me, collecting our profits to hoard like a dragon of old.

My hands balled into fists. By keeping us hungry and telling us every completed job and each pilfered valuable we presented to him might be the tipping point to ensure Jace's Menagerie survived the winter, he'd created a cloret farm. A spinning wheel of coin dropping into his mouth. I'd lived that desperation once, and what he'd done to my family—my former gang siblings—was evil.

Margot had long replied to me, but it was Carmen's elbow to my side that woke me from my thought spiral. I flinched away from the contact. "Sorry, what?" I asked.

The noblewoman answered with more patience than I deserved. "I said it's a pittance compared to what I had, but it *is* better than nothing."

A pittance, right. I rubbed my arm, keenly aware that wasn't the word I would use.

"'Sides, you can always join my family," I said with a shy smile.

I expected Margot to scoff and call that offer a trifle too. She closed her fan and tapped her chin with its edge. "Hmm. What animal do you think I would be?"

"A fancy-bred cat," I said immediately. *Cute, fluffy, pampered, and declawed.*

"Oh, like a dolly cat?" Margot lit up and launched into a cheerful chatter. "My good friend adopted a dolly cat when we were younger. Did you know they really do go limp with happiness when you pick them up and pet them? He was the sweetest cat, and his fur was like velvet. If I was in any place to adopt a cat, a dolly would be my number one choice of companion. Well, as long as she was well mannered enough not to chase Chance."

My carpenter mouse made a squeak of thanks from somewhere around our feet.

Well, that cinches it. She's Dolly or Dolly Cat now. I meant to figure out what kind of animal each of my crew represented. At one point, I'd been responsible for naming my younger family members when they turned ten. A lot of personality quirks can be likened back to animals.

Carmen blinked a few times before saying in a demanding tone, "What's *my* animal, then?"

I answered her just as quickly. "A kheneas."

I flushed with happiness when she grinned and pumped her fist. "One of those birds that kick rozash. Yeah! That's exactly what I am," she exclaimed.

"It sure is." I'd figured this out a long time ago. She'd reminded me of a kheneas bird without a flock. While she had the energy of a predator, she'd always been a touch vulnerable at RSI, separated from her gym, family, and the friends she'd made while practicing her fighting style, Tosh Zorena. But I kept those additional observations to myself as well.

Now, if only it were this easy to name the animal that

represented Fariq. Vance could only be a chameleon, even though that seemed incredibly mundane for someone with formshifting magic. But Fariq...I was genuinely stumped, since there was no animal out in nature who was smart and generous like him.

To my relief, the naming of their animals had lightened the mood in the carriage for the rest of the journey back to Kaiamear. Margot still gazed out the window occasionally, lost in her own thoughts and frowning hard enough for a line to appear between her brows. If there were any fresh troubles in her head, she kept them buttoned up for now.

WE MADE a quick stop in Kaiamear to debrief at RSI. Margot stayed to work her job at her employment agency, while Carmen and I got ready to set off on another mission. Not that I was an actual spy or all that important, but I was Carmen's first trainee in the art of Tosh Zorena, and that was a big deal to her. She'd gotten permission to visit her gym in Zoreen and asked me to come with her.

If *asked* resembled her demanding I go too and me meekly saying, "Okay."

The round trip to Zoreen and back would occupy the rest of our summer break, and I was disappointed my request for Jackie to come along was denied. But before I left, I checked in with her and heard all about the fun she was having.

The RSI kids who actually liked Theater class were putting on a production, and Jackie was helping. As she described the backdrops she'd helped paint and the lines she'd helped some of the cast remember, a bit of life flared back into her amber eyes. To my great relief, she was already healing from her ordeal at the hands of Springfield and Jace.

I asked her a few questions before I left, learning Miss

Barrios was making sure Jackie was occupied with a task or activity every day. She was looking after my sister in my absence, which I appreciated so much. When my family came flooding into RSI a few months ago, Miss Barrios took on the responsibility of being our mentor, otherwise known as a Big Sister.

It was a lot of extra work for the Tulari secretary, but after sharing that she was Foxglove, a former teen thief from our side of Kaiamear, she'd become family, too. Jackie called her Miss Fox, and the rest of my siblings were apparently doing the same.

Once I was convinced my sister was thriving at RSI, I got into the carriage to Zoreen without complaint. The ride south was quiet without Margot, who could get Carmen and me to talk. Without her, there wasn't much for us to say, other than discussing the general rules and oddities of her gym.

Carmen had me reciting the creed of Tosh Zorena in no time, though. "Effort. Control. Respect. Honor. Purpose." Those five words encircled the symbol centered on the leather band she held. I hadn't seen it since she'd retrieved it from her father's things, and she handled it with uncharacteristic delicacy. Since her father and uncle had passed during the Storm Front War, the band had passed to her, the eldest direct descendant of Tosh Montes.

It meant she was a master of the art, despite her age. Our mission was for us both to gain more knowledge of the fighting style. Carmen needed to polish the skills that would make her a true master, and I, as her first trainee, had to learn fast and make her look good in the eyes of her people.

As I recited the long version of the creed, Carmen nodded with each sentence. "I will be attentive and learn to the best of my ability. Anything I learn, I will not misuse on those weaker than myself. My elders, those senior to me, and all masters of the art have earned my respect. My word is honorable and true. And my purpose to learn is self-discipline and self-defense."

"Good," she said. "You'll be reciting that every training session, so don't forget it."

I shifted in discomfort, earning a raised brow. "What if one of those things isn't true? Of myself, I mean," I asked her.

"Then you're not a master of Tosh Zorena," she answered. Any pride she wore in my perfect repetition of the creed vanished, and she frowned at some place over my shoulder. "Try to make it true while we're there, pipsqueak. It'll be less than a fortnight of pretending."

Her expression worried me more than the invitation to lie. In the moment, I couldn't shake the thought that Carmen was talking to herself instead of me. I had experience in pretending to be honest my whole life whilst being anything but. What was she really worried about?

I didn't see any reason for her to be concerned when we arrived at her gym and a group welcomed her "home" heartily. There were hugs and playful punches and even one boy who grabbed Carmen in what I could only describe as an affectionate headlock. I kept a safe distance from any touching and waited.

Carmen had made it clear that I had to wait to be introduced by her, which was fine by me. I liked watching her soak in the attention and start to smile, a rare glimpse of happiness when most days, she woke up angry, and that'd been happening more frequently after her father's passing.

Gym life continued behind them, marked by the pounding of drums, the shouts of those practicing on the mats, and the smell of sweat and aromatic starry jasmine. The building was more like a temple, with its front and back walls resembling rectangular holes. Its insides were elongated and lofty, and on a nice day like today, dozens of shutters were open to the breeze and the vines of starry jasmine covering the walls.

I sneezed into my shoulder. At the sudden noise, Carmen

seemed to remember I was there. "Everyone, this is Heather." She gave me a look full of meaning. *Don't mess this up for me,* she said without saying. "She's my first trainee."

There was a noticeable shift in the air at her words. The eight or so people who'd rushed to greet Carmen now all inspected me. My eyelid twitched to be under such sudden, intense scrutiny. "Um…hi," I said faintly.

A woman old enough to be Carmen's mother cleared her throat. She, like everyone except Carmen and me, was dressed in a pair of loose pants and a shirt that fit tight to her torso. Her feet were bare, and her dark hair was nearly as short as my friend's. "Hello, Heather. I am Larisa Venton, one of the masters in residence." She eyed me with a look like there was a question lingering on her tongue.

"She can recite the creed already," Carmen put in.

I took that as my cue and did so, drawing a few approving nods.

"We're ready to train, Master Venton," Carmen added.

She raised a brow, a pointed look that echoed all the strong stares I'd gotten from Carmen in the past. "Not dressed like that. Let's get you both a place to stay, and then we'll talk about training."

The tall girl didn't even mutter a complaint as we followed Master Venton out of the front of the gym and looped around it. More people trained on the back lawn, sparring in the grass or an arena of hard-packed dirt. Behind them was a cluster of apartments, and we went to the closest building. "Masters have permanent housing here, so you both will stay for free, of course," the older woman explained. "Heather, that's quite fortunate. Most trainees pay to stay here so they can live, eat, and breathe Tosh Zorena to immerse themselves in the art for as long as they can afford it."

"Do you have to live here to learn?" I asked. The three hundred clorets I'd worked hard to earn felt heavier on my belt. I was glad I wouldn't have to spend any of them.

"No, but it certainly helps. I'm sure Carmen's told you the regimen requires utmost dedication."

I just had to know Carmen to realize how much effort it took to learn Tosh Zorena. She made fighting look like a graceful dance. That kind of ease had to take endless amounts of practice. I simply said, "Yes, ma'am" and held in a gulp.

These next couple of weeks were going to hurt.

I'D HAD an aversion to touch for a long time. In Jace's Menagerie, they often partnered a kid like me with older, more experienced folk from Springfield's gang. No one questioned if they snuck pinches or feels. Most of the women looked the other way, even if they'd grown up with the same treatment. We all had to learn our own ways of dealing with it, and my methods involved being slippery and keeping a safe distance from all folk.

But in a spar and the heat of the moment, I could wrestle with someone on the ground without feeling my skin crawl. My heart would beat hard with excitement, and I wanted the thrill of victory. Carmen always sought opponents who could challenge her, and I finally understood why.

I also realized that they didn't partner someone like me with someone like her. We were on two different tiers of knowledge. So, instead of being embarrassed every time I mustered up the nerve to step on the mat, I squared off against opponents of my knowledge level, most of whom were younger than me. That didn't give me any size advantage since I was still built like a sneak, but at least I could practice stances and blocking until my limbs felt twice their weight. I was glad we all wore padding for protection. Otherwise, I'd be covered in more bruises than I already was from repeatedly hitting the ground.

And when I was too sore or too embarrassed over a loss to fight, I had my pick of the drums set across one side of the mats close to the wall. Those who weren't actively sparring set the beat for those who were. Elderly Master Essor would sit in a comfortable chair and beat the largest drum front and center for the rest of us to echo. We'd talk when I perched next to him.

Well, he'd talk, and I'd listen. Trainees had uncomfortable pads to kneel on, but I endured it to listen a little longer. Most of the time, he gave me pointers on what to do better in my next spar.

But sometimes, he'd direct my attention across the mats, occasionally to other young trainees executing maneuvers I'd struggled with and other times to what Carmen was doing as she trained hard with other masters. "Your friend is struggling with her focus," he said.

Today, it was Master Venton who had Carmen on her belly, an arm around her neck and a knee pressed to the small of her back, holding my friend down until she tapped out. She got up and went for a drink of water with a frustrated puff of breath.

"She's got a lot going on, sir," I said in an undertone.

"I imagine so," he said vaguely. "Speed up now. We're putting the gym to sleep."

We played at a faster pace together, and the trainees sped up their movements to match. One-two-three-four, one-two-three-four. Carmen returned to the mat.

"Mastery is a difficult mantle to wear," Master Essor commented. "There are expectations of perfection."

I glanced at him askance. There was some meaning he wanted me to take from that, but it would not be as easy as him telling me outright. Adults loved this game and were especially pleased if a kid like me figured it out.

Well, Master Essor was going to be disappointed; I wasn't

bright like that. "You should get back to the mat," he said after a prolonged moment.

Nodding, I returned to sparring and did my best to learn. That part of the creed, I could handle. For Carmen, I made my best effort to make her look good. I ended up on my rear end a lot, but sometimes, my opponents did too. Even someone small like me could target joints and slip out of holds.

It was toward the end of our stay when Carmen discovered one of my big weaknesses. We would spar once a day, our last bout before we called it quits and went into Zoreen for a meal and sometimes a show.

For this bout, we'd gone around in a couple circles, with me blocking and deflecting her hits, backing away as she bore down. "Hit me," she demanded.

I punched, and instead of brushing it off, she let it connect with her shoulder. "You call that a punch?" she scoffed. "C'mon, pipsqueak. Hit me!"

She purposefully gave me an opening to spin and kick the padding over her ribs. The momentum was there, but the force wasn't, something that drew an ugly scowl on her face. "I said, *hit me!*"

"I...I don't want to," I said in an undertone.

I was great at dodging, deflecting, blocking, and diverting, but I'd finally gotten to the point where I was expected to hit back. And Carmen was a friend. More than that, someone whose animal I'd named, practically family.

Her footwork faltered, and she came to a halt in the middle of the mat. Panting, she planted her fists on her hips. "You don't want to," she repeated, sounding baffled.

"I don't want to hurt you," I said, stopping too.

Her gaze unfocused, her lips moving. For once, it was her eyelid that twitched. "You're not going to hurt me. It's okay," she said.

"No, it's not. You're my friend," I replied, drawing my shoulders in when the familiar spark of anger ignited in her expression, along with that more vulnerable, pleading something.

"Just…pretend a little more. It's time for your birthday fight anyway." She put her fingers to her lips and whistled.

My *what*? I'd lost track of the days, apparently. On the ride to Zoreen, I'd tentatively told her I'd be fourteen soon, but it wasn't a big deal, really. She'd said her gym celebrated birthdays with something special.

I should've realized it was a fight! A crowd of trainees formed around us with eager smiles. "Everyone, we have a birthday today!" Carmen announced to hoots and pumped fists. Master Essor rapidly tapped his drum. "Heather here is fourteen. You know what that means."

The older, more experienced trainees hung back or took up the drums too, playing a steady beat, while the kids I'd been sparring with pressed forward with their hands raised. Carmen numbered them off grandly, one to thirteen, while I looked on with ever widening eyes. "And fourteen," my friend said, slapping herself on the chest. "Go!"

Number one stepped forward, and I automatically fell into a defensive stance, arms upraised. He came at me slowly, circling around, while the other numbered off kids bounced on their heels. When I blocked his quick jab, he acted more thrown off than such a simple move should've made him. I threw him to the ground with that momentum, and he stayed there with an exaggerated groan of pain. Master Essor hit the drums definitively with my victory.

The second kid stepped up, still bouncing on her heels. "It's an honor to face the great master… What was your last name again?" she asked.

I didn't have one and gave her a confused look. "Wasn't it Mouse?" she asked, then added in an undertone. "On your birthday, you're the strongest kid in the gym. Have fun with it!"

Oh, wow. I should've picked that up after tossing the first boy to the ground and him letting me. I broke into a grin, realizing why everyone else was so excited about this. We exchanged exaggerated blows before I left her on the ground too, and she loudly proclaimed, "Master Mouse has felled me!"

From there, I picked up momentum, littering the mats with fallen foes bemoaning their fate of crossing "Master Mouse." The biggest drum sounded deeply with each of my strikes, adding drama and heft to them.

After nearly a fortnight of sweating, falling, and scraping myself back up to earn Carmen's rare approval, it felt good to be the undisputed victor and have others take my too-gentle punches and kicks like the blows they were meant to be.

At the end of the line, I faced Carmen again, who waited with her arms up in front of her, weight shifted on her back leg. She lifted one side of her lips in a smirk. "Let's try this again. Hit me!" she exclaimed.

She deflected my first blow with a lightning-fast push, her forearm to my wrist. Her answering attack could've been made by a snail, her bladed hand chopping in a telegraphed motion toward the space where my shoulder and neck met. I pushed the move aside like she had with me.

Much as she wanted me to hit her, she made me work for it harder than my other opponents. She caught my leg when I tried to kick her and slipped out of my grasp for easy throws, but she didn't end the fight with her usual force and ease.

"Last opponent is the hardest?" I huffed out.

"Yeah," she said, barely winded. "This year is a fight you haven't won yet. How are you going to handle it, pipsqueak?"

My brows fell, forming a determined face. For one perfect moment, her world and mine met in a perfect eclipse of values. Every year had been a fight I'd won, sometimes eked out by a knuckle length. But now I was fourteen and, for once, fed, strong, and overall happy with where I'd ended up after one terribly botched heist.

I could take on this year and win. All I had to do was hit the representation of it, Carmen, in a way she didn't expect. We circled, and she gestured for me to bring it on. My heart thudded in my ears, and my face ached a bit... I was smiling, just as thrilled as she always was for a fight.

We exchanged another couple sets of blows. She defended herself like a master, but she was also beginning to anticipate the order I performed each move. I was predictable—punch, throw, disengage, kick. But there was one thing I hadn't tried yet. As she pulled her arm free from an attempted throw and moved to right her balance, I hooked my foot around her ankle and pulled.

She stumbled, but there was a glimmer of pride in her gaze, and she dipped her chin toward me in an unspoken *I'll give you that one.* She made herself fall with one last definitive thump of the drums. "Happy birthday, Master Mouse," she said.

The gym erupted in calls of happy birthday and other well wishes. I blushed under the attention or just flushed from the exertion, but as I looked around and lifted a hand in thanks, I felt I understood Carmen better. More specifically, why she'd want to stay here and train her days away.

Unless something changed to pull her from RSI, though, neither of us could stay. But I sure wanted to visit again someday to become a real master.

CHAPTER 3

INTERMEDIATE

After my busy summer, returning to RSI and donning the uniform felt a lot like stepping backward. All the momentum I'd gathered and the progress I'd earned had led me right back to the structure and rigidity of school life.

Not that it was a bad thing. This school, with its carefully created public image as the Radcliffe-Stone Institute for Troubled Youth, had freed me from my old gang and admitted my siblings when they had nowhere else to go. They would teach us espionage here and, even if we proved less than capable at spy craft, would also offer us apprenticeships in the city so we could earn an honest living.

Those facts simply didn't stop me from hating school, especially *difficult* school, and by the way the headmaster was talking to the group of intermediate teams, this year would be more challenging than the last by far.

We were in the cafeteria, seated with plates of snacks and our new schedules. My friends and I ringed one of the smaller tables and looked around like wary prey at the pack of semi-familiar faces that surrounded us.

Even though we were promoted into the intermediate group months before summer break, we were meeting most of our new peers and being mixed into their classes starting today. We'd had to become older and more experienced to be educated at a higher level and upgrade our bracelets to the next tier.

Headmaster Arthur Radcliffe—not his real name, though I didn't know him by any other—was speaking at the front of the cafeteria next to a few instructors. "Your intermediate years start with individuals assigned into specific tracks. In your time here, your teachers have observed your strengths. From here on out, you will receive targeted education to hone your gifts to a fine edge."

Next to me, Fariq perked up. He'd been listening with an expression of complete focus, hanging on every word the headmaster said.

On my other side, Carmen placed a pointedly displeased slant back on her mouth. Her leanly muscled body coiled up tensely, her hands tightly clenched into fists on the table. "Like this place can hone anything about me," she muttered.

"Maybe if you applied yourself," drawled Vance. He wore his usual face, the perfectly symmetrical one with a shock of blondish-brown hair. Using his formshifting magic, he'd hidden the Tulari spell circle that otherwise took up the space where his left eyebrow would be. He had also erased the ugly snake tattoo on the side of his neck, hiding that he'd once been a member of the nearly mythical gang of Tulari mages, Morashi Venom, and survived the attentions of their cruel leader.

"You're one to talk." She gave him a look that would have most folk backing down.

Not Vance, though. He'd always matched Carmen's level of predator energy. I don't think she'd ever intimidate him, since she was nowhere near as frightening as Madam Morashi.

He lifted and flexed his hand, showing the copper bracelet around his wrist. The unbroken circle denoted he was on tier zero, not allowed to leave RSI at all. Miss Barrios placed the runes of a tracking spell on the bracelet just in case he managed to escape the school anyway. "At least you have the choice to leave," he said.

Fariq flashed an irritated glance over at them. "Be silent. This is important," he put in.

To my surprise, they hushed up. I'd stopped paying attention too and huffed an annoyed sigh at myself. The headmaster was talking about rankings and acknowledging the current top intermediate team, Davit's Day. They received a short round of applause from most of the cafeteria, while my crew remained quiet. None of us wanted to clap for those bullies.

"What'd he say about tracks?" I asked Fariq in an undertone.

He turned my class schedule and pointed to the name on the top left. *Sasha Barrios*. "They are categorized by the main instructor. Better to talk about any classes you have in common with others in front of younger students without them noticing anything unusual."

Though I'd gotten used to the cadence of Fariq's Lithosian accent and understood him perfectly fine, he still earned a couple glances from the teams sitting closest to us. We'd been at war with the desert kingdom of Lithos for longer than I'd been the Mouse, but despite how he talked, he was Altarian and here to learn. While most of us had committed some kind of crime to earn our place at RSI, it seemed all Fariq had done was be born to a family that didn't speak Altarian.

"But Miss Barrios is the secretary?" he asked, narrowing his eyes at my schedule. "She teaches two of your classes this year."

She had her name listed under Agility and Craft during the middle of the day. I lifted a shoulder. "Foxglove," I said as if that explained it. I'd once eavesdropped on a teacher saying that Miss Barrios had "claimed me day one." I was finally going to see what that meant.

He nodded and turned his attention back to the headmaster. I took the hint and did the same. "Those of you who are new to the intermediate classes this year will receive a bracelet upgrade to tier two. If you've already received this upgrade, show a neighboring team what symbol they'll receive."

A girl from a nearby table paraded around wrist-first, showing off a symbol that rested on top of her cuff-like bracelet. A pair of crossed keys only as long as a knuckle length.

"You will understand what this symbol and others mean in Language class. Until then, you won't want to flash it at people around the city. You never know what you'll accidentally agree to." The headmaster chuckled at his own joke, while most of the kids looked at him blankly. "Until then, welcome back to RSI. Remember that tomorrow, classes start with syllabus day. You have the rest of today to meet with your mentors and settle your things. If you need your bracelet upgraded to tier two, stay, but everyone else is dismissed."

A little over half the teams filed out. My brows lifted slightly as I took in a few of the faces that passed by my crew's table. There were several in their last year, eighteen-year-olds still stuck at the intermediate level. Even the members of Davit's Day, so proud of their spot at the top of the intermediate board, were in their late teens. Davit smirked at Fariq and me on his way by, gaze lighting with challenge.

So, his grudge was going to continue. I didn't mind. I acted like everything was normal for a few minutes, sitting quietly as we waited for Miss Barrios to come around to our table with her wand. Only when I was sure Davit hadn't noticed my fingers in his coin pouch did I open my fist and count out the four measly clorets I'd stolen.

Davit should've learned that things tended to appear or

disappear from his pockets around me. One of his teammates had figured it out last year and carried fake clorets, especially on those days when he decided to shove me into a wall.

Oh well. Davit would help me save up enough money to buy my friend something nice. I'd accepted the belt from Fariq but felt a sense of debt. He was getting a useful and well-made item in return soon, and I was going to buy it for him honestly so he wouldn't think he needed to give it back.

There was a small tug on my pants. Chance stood on my boot, chattering quietly and paws upraising. I lifted him up in my palm. "I hide chain for you," he said.

"Somewhere no one will find it?" I asked to be sure.

"No one find! Humans never look in place."

He swiped at an ear, starting to groom himself. That was usually the signal that he was done talking about something. "And will you be able to find it again?" I confirmed.

"Yes yes," he promised. After we bumped fists, he scampered up my arm to perch on my shoulder to groom himself in earnest.

Spymaster Manny had given me the Eye of Acuity with very specific instructions. *"I want you to keep this safe. Don't let it leave RSI."* It was my ticket out of the school if I decided it was time to leave. All I had to do was return it to the family I'd originally stolen it from, the Gladbecks.

But Madam Morashi desired the magical necklace enough to kill for it, implying that she would steal it from the Gladbeck mansion again once it was returned. I was doing them a favor by holding on to it.

We were still waiting, so I slipped the opal pendant out of Chance's pouch on my belt, where I'd stashed it for safekeeping. It was the eye of the Eye of Acuity, a milky gem cut in beautiful facets that gleamed in the daylight. It was set in a disc of gold with fancy filigree around the edges and an empty hoop waiting for a chain or cord. Though it was an enchanted opal, I hadn't gotten it to do anything special yet.

It'd once been on a big gold chain, something a man would wear. That's what Chance had hidden, since I was too paranoid to put it in Margot's jewelry box or even the deposit box she was renting at the bank for all the valuables we'd recently lifted from the Connery estate. Technically, I was still doing what the Spymaster instructed. The Eye of Acuity was here in RSI. Well, most of it.

When Cartier had betrayed me for this piece of jewelry, he'd said, *"You just tell it what y'wanna see and look inside it to see that thing."* That was most definitely not how the magic worked. I'd tried it. A lot.

Yet I kept trying, just in case the magic wanted to humor my attempts. "Show me the Spymaster," I murmured, then brought the pendant to one eye while closing the other one. All I saw was a white rock with a hint of an orange gleam in my field of vision.

Disappointed, I glared at the pretty and useless thing. Vance was watching me across the table, looking thoughtful. "Is that what I think it is?" he asked.

"Possibly."

His eyes narrowed at my cagey answer. "Can I see it?" he pressed.

Most folk wouldn't trust Vance if they understood who he'd once worked for. As far as he knew, he was the first member of Morashi Venom to be caught by the Crown. He wasn't allowed to leave the school until he squealed every detail he could about the gang. Yet he'd experienced a brief period of freedom last year.

The one to set him free…was me. I'd burned his first tier-zero bracelet off his wrist with desda powder and figured he'd betray me and return to his old life. Yet he'd returned with a magical contract that we'd destroyed together and did everything he could to help save my sister. He wasn't a part of Morashi Venom anymore; he was crew, and that meant he'd earned my trust, even with the Eye of Acuity.

I passed him the pendant, and he tilted it this way and that. Multicolored sparks played over his face. He pitched his voice low so only our table would hear. "You know, it's not wise to bark orders at a tool of power."

I rolled my eyes. "Do you know how it works?" I asked.

"Not a clue. All I know is that there's a corerune etched on this thing somewhere, which means it has a trigger phrase," he said.

"A what?" Carmen asked what I was thinking.

Margot had her fan flicked out, speaking in a low tone behind its flapping edge. "Well, no wonder it's so danged expensive," she breathed. "It's a true family artifact."

Vance nodded in agreement. "Only crafter-class Tulari can make tools of power with a corerune, a personal symbol they can manifest on one object. Most tools of power are weapons. Think about the Sword of Altare. Or maybe you've heard of the staff Starfall, wielded by the Hero of Altare who can throw comets with it."

The staff sounded incredible. All I knew was that the Sword of Altare was as old as our nation and first wielded by King Altare himself. It now sat in a cage of solid glass under a constant vigilant watch. Even thieves as legendary as Morashi Venom would find it next to impossible to steal it. Not that anyone *should*, when the sword's curse spelled the doom of anyone who attempted to take it from the royal family.

"Anyway, there was probably a Gladbeck way, way, *way* back in the family line that was a crafter-class Tulari. He or she put their corerune on this"—he shook the pendant, rattling the hoop—"and now it won't work for any of us unless we figure out the trigger phrase."

"Couldn't you just wiggle your fingers over it and get the phrase?" Carmen asked, unimpressed.

He put a hand to his chest, mock offended. "I do not *wiggle*—"

An adult woman's voice spoke over his. "Perhaps I could assist?"

Miss Barrios had made her way to our table in her preferred manner. Silently. She was tall and moved like a sleek wildcat, a predator in her prime. The blue Tulari mark on the brown skin of her cheek was stretched from her customary smile.

I nearly startled out of my seat, my eyelid twitching as I thought through our recent conversation. Odds were good that she'd heard most of it.

I'd learned my lesson in trusting her last year. Anything we planned, she'd know about, whether we were honest and told her or she had to rely on her magic to eavesdrop on us. Even though she was now mentor to dozens of my siblings, I didn't doubt she'd find the time to keep tabs on us.

Vance met my eye, and I nodded. He handed her the pendant. "It's some fancy magic thing that needs a phrase to work," I summarized.

"Interesting. I will look into it." She pocketed the pendant, and my heart just about dove right out of my chest. If she were anyone else, I'd make sure I lifted it back out of her pocket before she left.

Seeing my expression, she added, "You're going to get it back. I just need to work a spell on it. Just like I need to see your bracelets."

She's giving it back. Stop jumping to conclusions, I said harshly in my head.

We all presented our wrists, including Vance. Miss Barrios flicked her hand dismissively at him. "You're still on probation. As you're *well* aware."

He snapped his fingers. "Darn."

One by one, she placed the new mark on the rest of our bracelets using her wand. She worked on my bracelet last. "I'm going to be in a couple classes you teach," I ventured.

She flashed a warm look my way. "That's right. You're

finally getting into the good stuff, and I get the privilege of teaching it to you," she said. "Some of your siblings would be great fits for your track as well. I just hope they realize what kind of school they're in."

For a moment, she let those words sit in the air. It was that game again, where she waited for me to discover their hidden meaning. "Just remember your oath, Heather. You're bound to say nothing about RSI's secrets until your siblings take the same oath. But…you can always hint."

With that advice, she finished working her magic on my bracelet. It was a leather strip with a metal clasp, something I picked because it wasn't showy or sparkly like the jewelry most of my peers selected. No one would think to steal it from me.

The top now sported an etching of the pair of crossed keys. I'd read the headmaster's meaning earlier, that this mark had a purpose for those around the city. The school had just claimed me further, marked me as a spy candidate to those who knew what to look for.

But the headmaster hadn't told us directly that was why we wore RSI's crossed keys on something a little more permanent than our uniforms. How interesting. The mind games were already starting.

CHAPTER 4

SYLLABUS DAY

THE NEWEST KIDS and those still on tier zero had orientation last. All they knew was that they were at a reform school, so the message they received probably wasn't warm and welcoming.

I waited in the hall for Jackie and the rest of my siblings to emerge, seated on the ground with my knees up to prop my journal. Fariq sat next to me in a similar pose; Vance, Margot, and Carmen had left to do other things until dinnertime.

Fariq and I had matching welcome letters from the headmaster, written in code. I was thankful it was a straightforward cypher. I still struggled with reading on a good day, and adding in jumbled-up words was a great way to fry my mind.

On the other hand, Fariq was an attentive member of the language club with Miss Liang, which meant at some point, he'd learned how to do this for fun. He'd already written out an alphabet with the cypher unscrambled above it. We consulted it together as he translated the front side into Altarian and I did the same with the shorter message on the back.

After we'd finished, Fariq looked at both sides and then

asked me to read it out loud to him. I did so slowly, nervous I'd mispronounce something. "Dear intermediate students, welcome back to another year at the Royal Spy Institute. Once you read this message, you are to sign the bottom of it to show that you translated it properly and turn it in to the main instructor of your track. To earn full marks on this assignment, do this task by the end of syllabus day."

"Do not give our translation to Carmen," Fariq said, eyeing me sternly. "Let her figure it out for herself."

I wondered for a moment how he knew I was already planning on doing that. Otherwise, Carmen wouldn't bother and would fail her first assignment.

"Right," I said, then continued reading the letter aloud. "Congratulations on making it this far. We have seen promise in every student who makes it to the intermediate level, but now it is up to you to prove that you have what it takes to serve our great nation. You will be tested thoroughly during this upcoming year. It is the Spymaster's hope that you rise to the challenges ahead.

"That being stated, do not fear failure. The res…ressilent…"

Fariq leaned over to look at the word I was stumbling over. "Resilient," he whispered.

I nodded. "Resilient candidate who falls and gets back up again is worth far more to us than those who never engage in trials out of fear of hardship. This is where we see the difference between candidates who are moldable and those who are merely getting by.

"Do not forget that you strengthen yourself to support your team. You will find that this year will test the bonds of your group. Show us that your team can remain strong despite other demands on your time and efforts to earn the Spymaster's regard."

I couldn't help the queasy roll of nerves in my belly the

more I read. Headmaster Radcliffe wasn't one to exaggerate. Only the best teams—made of the strongest individuals— would advance from here. And judging by how many older teens were still intermediate level, this could be where my crew stopped, destined to be informants rather than spies.

I read the last paragraph with reluctance, knowing it would change Five & Chance's dynamic the most. "The main instructor of your track has your full schedule, including the whereabouts of your new apprenticeship and the days you will attend to it. Do not be surprised if you work every day of the week, between your schooling and your apprenticeship. Leisure time is a reward, not an expectation."

Fariq eyed my expression. "If you enjoy the work, it's like you're not working at all," he said. He'd already told me that his apprenticeship with the Builder Guild was great fun over the summer. For once, he'd been around like-minded personalities, other people who could marvel over his journal and know what they were really looking at.

My friend, who diagrammed and built miniature models of drawbridges and other innovations, now had a job where he could contribute to making real things. Sure, as an apprentice, he was learning about the creation of "component parts" and "manufacturing," but he'd still been noticed for his type of intelligence.

"Hopefully I enjoy my apprenticeship too," I mumbled. I flipped to my translation of the back of the headmaster's letter, the three extra credit challenges for this year. After reading them to Fariq, I added, "They don't make a lot of sense."

1. Use Uncommon to make contact with five people outside of RSI.

2. Steal a key to the city.

3. Impress the Spymaster.

What was Uncommon? Where was I supposed to find a key to the entire city?

I scowled at the paper in frustration. Completing these challenges wouldn't just help my team pass our classes. If we did well with them, we'd be promoted to advanced and then up to full-time spy work. There was nothing I wanted more than to have Five & Chance earn a spot as a spy team.

He lifted his shoulders. "Same as last year. We figured them out over time. They were part of what the school wanted us to learn."

I nodded reluctantly in agreement, since I wouldn't have gone out of my way to learn how to code a message or assumed the elusive Spymaster frequented RSI at all if it weren't for the challenges. Judging by how difficult this year was promising to be, we would need to figure out these extra credit opportunities through what we were taught and turn over every loose stone until we discovered what might "impress" Manny.

Last year, with the crown heist, we'd gained our promotion to intermediate without realizing how important it was. I'd given little thought to my future before I came to RSI, believing I would find a job in Springfield's gang once I aged out of being a sneak. To be able to use my talents as a spy instead was my dream. And the only way to do it was to continue climbing the ranks in RSI and gaining the Spymaster's favor.

We sat in companionable silence until the new kids were finally released from the cafeteria. My siblings weren't technically *new*-new, but most of them hadn't realized the truth about RSI yet. The older kids, like Ram and Dexis, would be out of RSI and into their apprenticeships by the end of the school year. No one was hinting at them too hard since they didn't have time to work up the ranks and become true spy candidates.

Others, like my true sister, Jackie, were simply too young. She'd only just turned ten a few months ago and was amongst the smallest kids exiting the orientation. "I'll see you later," I said to Fariq. He smiled and left, probably going to the innovation workshop to continue with one of his projects.

Jackie cast a wary glance around before coming over for a hug. "Hi, Gryph. How did it go?" I asked.

I'd named her after a feligryph for being sweet, fierce, and unexpected. Though she doubted she was any of those things, I thought she would show those characteristics in time. She just needed more time to recover and adapt to her new life.

Right now, she resembled a smaller version of me, shoulders hunched, eyes constantly on the move for carefully hidden danger. Crowds made her skin break into gooseflesh, which made this hallway a less than ideal place to stand. I took her hand and tugged her toward Hawthorne Hall, where the girls' dorms were. Her breathing evened out in the quieter space.

"Y'sure about this school?" she asked.

"Yeah. It's better than anything else out there," I said.

She fidgeted with her copper bracelet. She hadn't gotten much more of a fundamental school education than I had, but since she was only ten, I hoped the instructors could shape her into an even better spy than I might become. Once she figured out RSI's front, she would understand why I was so desperate for her to come here.

"They said I was assigned to be friends with a boy and attend all my classes with him," she admitted. "He's not a brother; he's someone who just got here."

I bit my lip, unhappy for her but unsurprised she had a male partner. If she was going to be a spy one day, she would have to work with men. But she wasn't a spy yet. Whoever had made this decision needed to know it was too soon to push her.

"I'll talk to Miss Fox," I promised her.

Miss Barrios was busy adjusting bracelets into the evening and had mouthed "later" when I tried to get her attention. So, I asked Margot and Wildcat to wake me earlier than the morning bell the next day.

My petite, redheaded sibling was crammed into the room I shared with seven other girls, as she was about our age. There hadn't been space at RSI for all of my siblings, so we made do. Even if her cot was set at a right angle to ours and I ended up tripping over its legs in the dark.

Because of Wildcat's pinch before dawn, I was waiting next to the secretary station at the front of the school before Miss Barrios walked in. If she was surprised to see me standing there with a yawning Chance perched on my shoulder, she didn't show it.

"Good morning, Miss Fox," I said.

"Ah." Her lips twisted with amusement. "You're going to call me that too, hmm? Good morning, Miss Mouse. Eager for syllabus day?"

I shook my head while offering her a folded piece of parchment with a copy of the translated letter, signed with my personal symbol of a mouse and a stalk of heather. I'd jotted down the important parts in my journal, including the extra credit challenges. "I need to talk to you about Jackie," I said.

"About her partner?"

"I…yes." Not to be thrown off, I said, "You know those menfolk got handsy with her at The Last Stop."

She placed her bag down on the counter and rummaged through it. I watched her, waiting for some acknowledgment. A couple minutes ticked by, and I shifted my weight restlessly.

Eventually, I added, "She's not ready for a partner anyway. She needs an education more than to figure out what RSI is really about."

She looked at me out of the corner of her eye. I only spotted it because of the twinkle of wizard-blue magic which occasionally sparkled in her brown irises. "I don't disagree. However, it was a decision made by the headmaster. It is a test—"

"She doesn't need to be tested yet," I tried to interrupt, my tone pitching higher in frustration.

"—for you," Miss Barrios finished anyway. I gritted my teeth so I wouldn't simply repeat what she'd said. That habit drove my friends crazy. "I'm glad you advocated for her, but if we allow you to remove this obstacle, she will not be strong enough to handle the next one without your help. But you used your words to affect change, and that's what we want to see from you. It's easy to fade into the background and wait to see how events fall into place."

I nodded slowly, brow knotted.

"But you want some things for Jackie, yes? You want her to be comfortable, but more importantly, you want her to stay at RSI and take what it offers. For that to happen, she has to work with a male peer. We've selected one who may be just as afraid of her as she is of him. The assignment will not change." Her word had an air of finality. "So, what will you do to help your sister grow instead?"

Musty devils. I hadn't expected her to turn this around on me so thoroughly. Everything that could be a test at this school, was. "I'll have to think about that," I answered carefully.

"Good. There's time. Just don't forget to help her. Your plate is about to be quite full with other things." She withdrew a letter from her bag and offered it to me. My eyelid twitched when she suggested I should open it after filling my belly with some breakfast. It was as clear a dismissal as any.

I DIDN'T OPEN the letter Miss Barrios handed me until right before I was supposed to go to her class. In my defense, syllabus day was more involved than it sounded. Most of the instructors spent ten minutes giving an overview of what we'd learn in their classes this year, and then, once I was good and overwhelmed at the scope of knowledge expected, we jumped straight into learning.

My first class was Innovation…not the best start. Gone were the arithmetic workbooks; this year, I had to work on the group projects. At least I shared this class with my crew, except for Margot. Fariq would be my ticket to passing.

After that was Lithosian with Miss Liang, who didn't speak a single word of Altarian for the duration of class time. She was dressed as professionally as ever, with a shield-shaped pin bearing the RSI crest affixed above her shirt pocket. It was a recent addition, and she reached up to touch it occasionally, as if reassuring herself it was still there.

One person was conspicuously absent. Though he was raised speaking Lithosian, Fariq had been in this class with me last year. Miss Liang had called it social learning—he helped teach me his language, and I did the same for him and Altarian. Except now he was taking a class with a private tutor during this block.

I rely on him too much, I thought from my seat in the back of the room, next to a fiercely scowling Carmen. That was her focusing face.

Miss Liang spoke slowly and clearly, accompanying questions and instructions with hand gestures to match. My head was aching from concentration once class was dismissed, and I went to Self-Defense relieved to spend an hour doing something with my body rather than my brain.

"Well, this is one class I won't need tutoring in," I said to Carmen.

"We're not allowed to use Tosh Zorena," she reminded me.

Oh. Well, that explained why her mood was worsening even with the promise of some physical exertion. We checked in with the female Coach Stryker—there were two, a married couple, and they went by the same name. Judging by what I knew about RSI, neither of them was actually named Stryker. At this point, I wouldn't be surprised if they weren't married.

We went to the girls' bath to change into a lightweight version of the RSI uniform and got straight to work, no class overview required. After the warmup, the coaches announced we had a choice between free weights or partner work. I received a meaningful glance from Carmen and went to work on my upper body strength.

My arms were noodlelike when I took my schedule up to Coach Stryker, the male one, to ask where my Agility class was supposed to be held. The location was listed as "Tower A," which turned out to be the most inconvenient location to head to after attending Self-Defense in the gym.

RSI was built in a rectangle, with four pointed towers at each corner. The two at the back of the school were used for the library and the theater with its two-story seating. At the front of RSI, Tower A was the tower were Aldridge Hall, the main hall, met Irving Hall, the boys' hall.

Coach Stryker advised me to head through the Square, the grassy, open-air center of the school, as the fastest path. Then he suggested I run so I wouldn't be *too* late.

I was out in the sun, belly grumbling from the smells of lunch and the sight of students eating around the Square, when I realized I'd never opened the letter Miss Barrios had given me and was about to see her for two classes back-to-back. I tore into the envelope and nearly dropped the note within.

Heather,

You've been assigned as an apprentice to the Tailor Guild. We think this will be a good match for your skills. You'll be reporting to Orretta's Stitchery starting this weekend.

Headmaster Arthur Radcliffe

There was an address listed, along with a name for my point of contact. It wasn't like there was a Thief Guild they could assign me to. But tailoring? It was downright strange to say that was something I'd shown I could be skilled at.

I pondered the unusual choice as I came back inside Aldridge Hall and slowed my pace. My eyelid was twitching by the time I reached the junction where halls met. The seam of the door into Tower A was difficult to spot until it opened and Miss Barrios beckoned from the threshold. "Sorry I'm late," I burst out.

"Not at all. It's a far walk. Besides, you're not the last person." She gestured for me to head into the room. It was probably the smallest classroom in this school, with low ceilings and a handful of desks. Clusters of kids stood around, chatting.

"Hey, another new kid," said a young man. He was a little on the short side, but no one in here was built tall and broad for a fight.

Beautiful Sybella was next to him, her thick mahogany-colored hair up in a high tail. She barely glanced my way, as always, her acknowledgment seeming to skid right off me.

"Oh. That's Heather," she sighed. We were roommates but in different teams. She must've just been promoted to the intermediate level.

"Hello, Heather. I'm Ned. Welcome to the best class of the day," the young man said, spreading his arms as grandly as he could with the limited space we had. "I'm part of the team Knife's Edge. You may have heard of us."

Ned paused, making a show of waiting for about half a moment. "That's right. We've just made it to advanced after three years. I hear your applause, thank you." He bowed to my usual silence.

"Congrats. You'll have to tell me about it," I said. Wow, it'd taken his team three years to move up. I wanted to know why it'd taken so long so Five & Chance didn't make the same mistakes. "But my team just got to intermediate and we're in the same class?"

"That's because there are no levels here. Once you're in Agility, you're in Agility. There are easy and hard days, but once you climb enough walls, you've climbed them all. Am I right?"

"Not necessarily," I ventured.

Miss Barrios came in with a couple more students, bringing the group up to a dozen. "Causing trouble already, Ned?" she teased.

"Yes, ma'am," he answered in a similar tone.

She cleared her throat. "Well, let me get my two clorets in before you scare off the new blood. Welcome, everyone. If you're here, you've been assigned to my track, cleverly known as the Barrios track since I am the main and only instructor for it. While you're in this tower, you're among close friends. But what you learn here stays with you alone, to hone your skills. Your teammates are hearing similar things today in their first tier-two classes. Do you understand?"

I nodded. A few students murmured their assent.

"If it isn't immediately obvious, you've been selected for the stealth track. You are the thief in the night—unseen, unheard. Your work is that of a ghost, to make items disappear or move when no one is looking," Miss Barrios continued. A spark of excitement lit in my belly. Finally, a class I was going to be good at! "The stealth track is one of the smaller ones, as you can see. We are helpful to have in a spy team but not a requirement for all missions. What I will teach you will still make you an asset. Are you ready?"

This time, I joined the general response of the group, exclaiming "Yes!"

Agility and Craft were combined classes and lent extra time because they absorbed the half-bell lunchtime we'd otherwise have between them. Miss Barrios told us that some days, we'd get lunch, and others, we'd need to go hungry. I didn't care. I was on the *stealth* track and about to learn how to improve my skills from Foxglove herself.

We didn't go up into the tower today, but Ned promised there was an obstacle course and rock wall that magically shifted and adjusted to give us a fresh experience every day. I was going to be expected to master climbing, jumping, rappelling, and other feats, and I couldn't wait.

Craft was a class about counterintelligence. The older kids would receive missions from the Spymaster, if they were lucky. Otherwise, it was theory and scenarios, basically advanced book work.

Miss Barrios returned to the secretary's station when class time was over, trading places with an unfamiliar and bored-looking woman. I made my way upstairs to Language class and saw a smiling Miss Liang at the door to the assigned classroom. The strict Endolian woman rarely looked so happy.

Once she introduced what Language class was—a chance for us to learn the language of spy craft, both spoken and nonverbal—it occurred to me that I'd once eavesdropped on her complaining about having to teach beginner classes last year. *"I'm here to teach espionage, not basic language skills."*

I was excited to finally learn some espionage from her, but that didn't stop me from dragging when I reached my last class, Theater. My belly felt hollow without lunch, and I *really* didn't want to end my day with the "for fun" class that was mandatory for all students. The theater was the best-known feature of RSI, hosting frequent plays for the common folk of Kaiamear to come see. Last year, I'd gotten out of appearing in front of a crowd by volunteering with the backstage crew and painting backdrops.

That was not an option anymore, apparently. Miss Stone

announced I'd be in a leading role in one of the five plays this theater class would put on over the course of the school year. And no, I couldn't trade off with someone else.

CHAPTER 5

STITCHERY

I BROUGHT up this year's challenges with my team the next day, whispering under the cover of the general chatter of a full classroom. We were sitting around a table in Language class, waiting for Miss Liang to finish diagraming something on the chalkboard. I wasn't paying much attention, my back to the board.

"Where'd you get these?" Carmen asked. She'd stolen my journal to read the three challenges to herself.

"It was in the welcome letter," I said.

"It was? Guess I should've translated it like you said." With a shrug, she passed the journal back.

Well, she was already failing one of her classes. By the end of the month, most of us would join her in having poor marks at something. After comparing schedules, it seemed we'd been removed from our weakest classes but retained in those second-weakest. It's why I didn't have to report to Alchemy class anymore to mix the wrong musty chemicals together and discover dangerous reactions firsthand. I was thankful for that.

Though our tier-two classes all had different names and we were extra careful not to share the track we'd been assigned, we were all learning Craft, just in different rooms with groups of students who specialized in the same thing we did.

"Anyway," I said, looking around at my friends hopefully. "These challenges are going to get us noticed. What is number two referring to?"

There were mostly blank stares around the table, but Margot tilted her head as she read the challenges again. This lucky young woman was on a half-day schedule, only attending classes after lunch. She tutored noble children in the morning, as her position with her employment agency was essentially her apprenticeship.

She still had on a perfect face of cosmetics, despite having changed into the RSI uniform so she wouldn't stick out with her pastels in a sea of black. She pursed her painted lips thoughtfully. "Keys to the city are symbolic gifts. They are incredibly large and not items that strike me as easy to steal."

"Have you seen one before?" Vance asked.

"Certainly. There's a small ceremony where the lord mayor or a councilman presents the key to visiting dignitaries or those with a particular kind of celebrity. Sometimes, a citizen earns one for doing a deed of great value for the community. They've got a particular style…"

Margot picked up a quill and sketched a key shape underneath my list of extra credit challenges. The bit on the end resembled a pair of buck teeth, not something that would open any door if used like an actual key. Its bow was designed in a fancy shape that resembled a king's crown, with words "Key to the City" written across its stem.

"Imagine this, but two feet long. That's a key to the city," she said.

Two feet long? Musty devils. I sighed, already picturing the nightmare this heist would be. "So, we're supposed to steal one of these big keys from—"

"Attention, class," announced Miss Liang, bringing us all to silence in an instant.

I lifted and scooted my chair, craning my head around to look at her and what she'd placed on the board. My eyes widened in surprise at what I saw. "Today, we begin with communication hiding in plain sight. Part of being a spy is quickly picking up on cues and signals others miss. Case in point, drifter signs," Miss Liang said.

I already knew all the symbols she'd written in chalk along the board. She continued talking, but my mind was years in the past, walking toward Haladay Park on a sunny day with my small hand folded in Thylacine's. "Let's play a game, Heather," he'd suggested.

I'd agreed with enthusiasm. We played plenty of games on fun days like this. In retrospect, a lot of what Thylacine suggested was based on identifying patterns. How many people on the street were wearing blue? How many peace-keepers could I spot?

But that day, we started seeing how many signs I could spot on the buildings we passed. At first, I was bad at it and stomped my feet in frustration when he found the little symbols in places I'd overlooked. They were small and tricky, but eventually, I was trained to look at the sides of buildings, the stairs leading up to them, and the cobbles nearby to spot them.

Drifters, street kids, thieves, and…spies, I guess, had a system of shapes and common symbols. Thylacine had taught them to me over time. A set of hands meant the people in that building would help if you showed up there hurt. An X to avoid, an X circled to avoid at all costs, a baton for a peace-keeper residence, and so on.

"Does the food sign mean they'll feed us right now?" I'd asked later into this game. We passed a tavern with a check-mark symbol prominently displayed.

"It's not that easy. Look right next to it," he'd said. "Multiple signs next to one another are a complete message. This one's saying 'Will serve you a meal, but you have to work off the debt.' Means they'd make you scrub pots after you eat, or something like it."

I'd once been hungry enough in my Mouse years to go inside that tavern to see if they'd really feed me. They had, but during the two hours I'd been a barmaid to pay for it, the touching and pinching of the patrons had made me think the food hadn't been worth the work.

A sharp elbow met my side, and I practically jumped out of my seat. Most of the class turned to look at Carmen and me. "We're taking a quiz," she said in an undertone.

Miss Liang was erasing the drifter signs but leaving up the meanings. She was mid-explanation about us taking a memory quiz. Attention to detail was a key tool in a spy's repertoire, after all.

"What's *repertoire* mean?" I asked, an automatic habit at this point.

"Someone's range of talents, darling," Margot answered.

I nodded; that made sense. I was soon tapping the edge of a blank sheet of parchment, wondering if I should show off on something like this. On one hand, RSI already knew where I'd come from, so it wasn't like I had anything to hide.

On the other hand…well, it was Thylacine's knowledge. He'd taught me the drifter signs so I had some protection even if he wasn't there, or died; which he had, fighting Lithosians at the southern border.

What should I do? Sometimes his voice would come back in my head with advice. That's what maybe-fathers did, right? They gave advice?

As the minutes ticked by and my peers put their quills down, I reasoned Thylacine would tell me that I had a fresh start. It was time I showed Miss Liang and my other instructors who I was.

Miss Liang graded this assignment quickly and rapped

her knuckles on my parchment after resting it face down next to my open journal. "Good job," she said.

She'd given me full marks, a rare achievement in her classes. I gave silent thanks to Thylacine.

COME SATURDAY MORNING, I was awake, bathed, and dressed in my RSI uniform before the morning bells rang out. The sun had barely risen, and I scrubbed at my bleary eyes as I walked to my apprenticeship at Orretta's Stitchery for the first time.

When I'd jostled Chance in his little pouch this morning, he'd whispered, "No no. Too early." He was still asleep, just how I wanted to be. I already missed having the weekend to sleep extra, and I'd feel the lack of study hours if this apprenticeship took up all my weekend time.

I'd threaded Chance's pouch onto my old belt, as it was smaller and less conspicuous. The lack of a kit around my waist made me feel unprepared, but I'd foregone my cloak since we were still in the hottest days of summer. The only other thing I'd placed on my belt today was a pouch with the four clorets I'd stolen from Davit. I could buy a feast for lunch with that kind of money.

Orretta's Stitchery was toward the end of the main market street, where businesses and reputable establishments slouched together in some of Kaiamear's oldest, least main-tained structures. Miss Barrios had briefly told me I was starting with a light workload. Two days a week was enough to dip my toes in the trade and learn the basics.

Miss Barrios hadn't seemed to care when I mentioned I was no good at mending. "I know you can handle it, Miss Mouse," she'd said.

As I stood in front of the faded brick face of the squat building and eyed the crooked sign that read "Orretta's

Stitchery" in excessively looping script, my eyelid twitched with nerves.

I took a deep breath and approached the door. If I was not chosen to become a spy, this apprenticeship would shape my entire future. It would become my *job*, an honest livelihood to rely on, complete with guild membership and all the benefits that came with it. I needed to put my full attention on learning the craft and doing my best.

A set of bells rang out when I went inside and looked around. I startled at the sight of a mannequin posed next to the entryway, its oval, featureless head turned in my direction. Some jokester had carved its arms so the elbows were at right angles, meaning the paddles that made up its hands were raised and posed in an attack position.

The warrior mannequin wore a black dress that was scandalously short, with a part up the side that displayed a wooden thigh. It was made of some pretty material, though, that gave its corners a soft sheen in the morning light.

"Careful, lass. It's enchanted."

There were a few racks of ready-made clothing set a few feet back from the door. From behind one of them stepped a woman who raised an unimpressed brow when I jumped again. Maybe I'd earned that look by default, as her gaze skimmed me up and down, taking in the distinctive RSI uniform.

She was stout and red-cheeked, her forehead and upper lip bearing a sheen of sweat. Her dark hair was piled up atop her head haphazardly, at odds with the high-quality clothing she wore. The buttons artfully placed on her dress glimmered, and the material was an evenly dyed green.

I met her gaze for a moment and swallowed. The angle of her brows and the set of her squinting eyes confirmed she had a well of predator energy and an immediate dislike of me. "You must be the new apprentice. Heard we only get you two days a week?" she barked.

"Yes, ma'am. Are you Aria Reni?" I asked, naming the point of contact the headmaster had listed with this assignment.

"That's right. Well, come on, then. Tell me your name," she said, beckoning me further into the building.

We passed a desk, with a lockbox for money underneath it, set in front of a pair of curtained-off fitting rooms at the cramped end of the shop. Across from the fitting rooms was a crate and a long mirror, with a kit of pins, thread, and measuring ribbons resting open and at the ready.

"Heather," I answered.

She grabbed a ring with a handful of keys off the desk and glanced over her shoulder. "Heather what?"

"Um… Mouse."

The ringing of keys as she chased the right one on the keyring didn't quite cover her scoff. She unlocked a door set into the back wall, revealing the rest of the shop. My first thought was that it was a windowless box—but the whole shop was without windows, in keeping with most of the businesses on this side of the city.

The back of Orretta's Stitchery was so cramped as to be overflowing with half-completed projects, bolts of cloth, and a worktable half-covered in stacks of letters and other paperwork. I immediately felt uncomfortable and started to sweat from the heat back here when we were both in the room.

She rounded on me. "All right, Mouse. A few ground rules. First, you will refer to me as Mistress Reni. I am a fully invested member of the Tailor Guild, and you will treat me thusly." She counted off on her thick fingers. The room felt like it was heating further, and beads of sweat made their way down my neck.

"Yes, ma'am," I breathed.

"Second, if you last long enough to meet Mistress Orretta, you will treat her with the same level of respect. You RSI kids always come in here with such attitude, and we're both tired of disciplining when we're supposed to be teaching." Her slanted eyebrows lowered to a hateful expression. "Third, if I catch you trying to make off with any product or money, your apprenticeship is over."

"Understood, ma'am." I gulped a nervous swallow. It sounded like the uniform alone had heaped me into the same pile as her past apprentices. And judging by her rules, those kids hadn't made a good impression at all.

Her stance relaxed a bit. "Good. You look young, yet. Put in hard work, and I'll send a good word to your school so you can be forgiven for whatever sent you to RSI in the first place."

Mistress Reni waited for a few expectant moments, as if I would tell her my crime. Considering it was stealing, well, I doubted she'd ever trust me in her shop, so I kept my gob shut.

"Quiet one, hmm. Guess your surname's fitting," she commented. "Any questions or concerns before we get started?"

"What's the mannequin do?" I blurted. "You said it's enchanted."

She brushed the question off with another scoff. "Wait for someone to steal from the shop and find out."

I imagined it coming to life and throat-chopping a would-be thief. *Ouch.*

"Do you have any experience? Have you made or repaired your own clothes?" she asked.

"No, ma'am. In my old family, I cut hair. My siblings handled the clothes."

She crossed her arms and tapped the tile underfoot. Judging by her impatient face, I imagined she was wishing RSI had sent literally any other kid. My eyelid twitched as I waited for a few heartbeats for her to speak.

When she did, it was another bark. "Why'd they have you cutting hair?"

"Why...I could cut it straight," I said, my voice getting smaller. I wanted to shrink in on myself under her inspection.

With a grunt, she pointed toward a corner of the cramped room. "Good. Being able to cut straight is a requirement. Have a seat, and we'll start with the basics."

CHAPTER 6
EYE SPY

FATIGUE WAS AN OLD FRIEND, but I'd never met it on a full stomach until I'd spent another week on this schedule of nonstop school and work. The heavy-limbed, fuzzy-headed exhaustion reminded me of long days pulling the Lost Child con with adults from Springfield's gang. During that time, I'd often returned to my pallet feeling emptied of everything I could give.

Logically, I understood this level of tiredness was another way RSI was testing and conditioning me. I had to learn how to dig deeper and push my limits. Not every mission was going to be done under ideal circumstances. Sometimes a crew member or I would be tired, sick, or injured.

Speaking of my crew, I missed them. There were no team-based activities or challenges in the first fortnight, so we only saw each other at meals and during classes. By evening, they looked as wiped out as I felt, so dinner was usually spent in companionable silence.

I spent one evening a week with Fariq at language club and three more evenings with Carmen either learning more Tosh Zorena or holding the punch mitts so she could practice more advanced moves. The rest of the time, I studied until my eyes blurred and a headache set in.

Some of that was my fault. When I had an idea to improve myself, I'd picked up a book from the library that seemed interesting and sat cross-legged in one of the study nooks, reading it aloud to an audience of two.

I'd chosen a book of fairy stories, things I knew because they'd come up here and there. My older siblings in the gang would recite what they remembered to get the younger ones to stop gabbing and go to sleep. During special events, street performers would put on wigs, heavy skirts, and fake crowns to earn a little coin from passersby. These tales were a part of life.

But I'd never *read* them. And I was far too embarrassed to say the words out loud to anyone but Chance and Patches. Chance, bless that mouse, would scamper around impatiently during the most exciting bits, throwing out guesses for what would happen next. Patches, the librarian's calico feligryph, would *mrrow* from where she'd curled up in my lap.

"Sorry sorry," he'd squeak and climb on top of her to sit and listen.

Patches was quite old for a cat, but because of her Link to Miss Wilkes, she'd live as long as the librarian did. She had an air of encouragement, slowly blinking up at me when my gaze would slide off a tough word to find her face instead. Since I took off her enchanted collar every time we were alone, she was in her true form, the size of a wildcat with broad paws and a pair of feathery calico wings. Plus fluff. Lots of plump fluff.

"I have to figure this out," I told her, more speaking to myself than anything. "I can't embarrass myself anymore."

If I wanted to be a spy, I had to get better at reading. The skill affected most of my classes and even my apprenticeship.

The next time I was called on to read lines in Theater, I needed confidence.

When I had to read in Lithosian, it would be a world of help to understand the prompt and translation in Altarian printed in the textbook.

I had to write cyphers and decode quicker. And most urgently of all, I needed to read tailoring orders better so Mistress Reni wouldn't have another reason to yell at me for causing her to mess up a client's preferred sleeve length. She'd said things about my competency that still echoed in my head, and the woman barely knew me to make such assertions.

"I'm not incompetent," I'd muttered when I grew too tired to pronounce "superb" correctly. Patches had nuzzled my hand and put pressure on the book with a paw, encouraging me to close it. Her purr was reassuring.

I didn't mention anything about these reading sessions to my crew, not sure I was improving anyway. Fariq still had me read aloud instructions and texts in Innovation class and language club, and I felt like I did as middling as ever. Gods help me when I saw Mistress Reni again this weekend.

I was still dwelling on her rebuke when Miss Barrios passed by my table on a Tuesday morning. Though I hadn't noticed her do it, she'd slid a small envelope under my bowl with an oval lump at one corner.

Brightening, I forgot my woes and snatched it up. I turned to Vance, who sat next to me with an alchemy book open in one hand. He had a hint of dark circles under his eyes and chewed his porridge without relish. When he raised a brow, I whispered, "Looks what I got."

Unlike most everyone else, Vance didn't jump to correct me when I got excited and a hint of my old life showed itself. He just turned his book upside down on its pages and gestured for me to open the envelope. We leaned in to read the note after I plucked out the Eye of Acuity and hid it in my palm.

Miss Mouse,

I've learned a couple of things about this artifact since you trusted me with it. First, it is activated by a simple rhyme followed by naming the person or place you would like it to show you.

Second, as with many tools of power, this one has a mind of its own. It may continue to show you the same person or place for days after you make a request and refuse to budge off that scene. It also seems to understand intentions and will not show you something if it thinks you're not meant to see it.

In my experiments, it didn't work for me when I asked it to show me someone I'd never met or a place I'd never been to.

While it may be quite useful, even invaluable, I can see why it would frustrate the likes of the pair who stole it from you. Use it wisely, and remember, Manny expects you to keep it safe.

It was signed with a small doodle of a fox and a PS with the needed phrase.

"Nothing is beyond my reach, with this Eye I unleash," I muttered.

When the Eye activated, I nearly dropped it in surprise. The oval glowed with specks of light, refracting a light blue loop. It looked eerily like an eye gazing back at me expectantly.

But I had to decide what I wanted it to look at first. "The power to watch..." I continued quietly. "Manny."

The magical eye closed into a line of blue before fading completely. I held it up to my face and looked into it, but it was inert, so I placed it down with a disappointed huff.

"Lame," Vance said, taking it up. More confidently, he whispered what he wanted from it. "Nothing is beyond my reach, with this Eye I unleash the power to watch Madam Morashi."

A glow rose from the Eye. The blue light played across his skin, winking out for him as well. Across the table, Carmen and Fariq were watching us experiment. She was still eating while he'd finished his breakfast and folded his hands politely on the table. "Perhaps you are asking it for too much," he suggested.

"Here, you try." Vance tossed the Eye to him.

"Careful," I hissed.

Carmen smirked and asked, "Isn't that thing worth a fortune?"

Fariq caught it, saving the gemstone from getting acquainted with the wall. "What is phrase for this?" he asked.

"*The* phrase," Carmen corrected.

I passed the note across the table, and Fariq asked the Eye to show him Margot. The magic seemed to wink out on him as well, but he handed me the pendant with a smile. I held it up to my eye, closing the other by reflex.

Instead of being at RSI, I was suddenly in a room with Margot and a girl. They were seated on a piano bench, and Margot was playing a musical scale over the keys while naming the notes. I was a fly on the wall, or a speck of dust, watching from Margot's right side.

"Try adjusting the angle," Fariq suggested. I startled and blinked, present in the cafeteria again. The instant transitions were jarring. Across the table, Fariq was tilting his hand back and forth.

I still held the Eye, but instead of an opal, its face was a tiny moving portrait of Margot playing piano with the girl she was tutoring. I was speechless with wonder, mouth parted. If this tool of power didn't have a mind of its own, I could use it to spy on anyone or anything. It was *exactly* the kind of thing Morashi Venom thought it was. She had already killed several people to get her claws on it, but I had a true understanding of why now that it was activated in my palm.

When I looked into it again, I tilted it and felt a wave of vertigo when the room around Margot panned as swiftly as my fingers moved. I flinched away from it, dizzy. "That's enough of that."

I passed the enchanted pendant on to make its way

around the table, with Vance and Carmen taking some time with it.

We only got up when a teacher warned us we were going to be late to class. At her curious glance down at the Eye, I realized we'd been the opposite of stealthy by trying out the magic like it was a toy.

I slipped it into Chance's pouch, vowing to keep it there until we had more privacy.

"MARGOT NAP NOW," Chance reported three days later. I was in Agility, which meant he rode on my shoulder while I jogged up the set of spiraling stairs that led to the top of Tower A.

Chance had taken the duty of helping me guard the Eye seriously since it was either in his pouch or my pocket, the two places he frequented most. Since the Eye was stuck, for lack of a better term, on Margot, this meant he regularly updated me on what she was doing. Margot was not too comfortable about it, as she didn't know she was being spied on until I told her and had her look into the Eye. She saw herself and said, "Oh, but my hair looks terrible today. It's this dreadful humidity."

"Sounds nice," I grunted out about her current nap. My calves burned as I reached the top of the tower and spared the view out of the window a quick glance. To stop would mean at least two of my classmates would pile into me, and I did not want to trip down the staircase. We used it to warm up most days and passed four circular floors besides the class-room at the bottom.

It was just wide enough for two people as long as we had clever enough footwork not to shoulder-check one another on our way up or down. There were no railings. Collisions had already happened a few times, and I'd earned a twisted ankle tossing myself onto the third floor last week to avoid falling on someone else. Sparks of pain still jolted through my foot on the way down the stairs from that mishap.

Miss Barrios called us to the second-story room at the end of the warmup. Part of the wall up the tower was dedicated to a set of rocks jutting out of the bricks made for climbing. With all of us off the stairs, she raised her wand and activated a spell set into the bricks. Sections of the spiraling staircase slid back from the wall, creating rectangles of space that someone could wiggle through. The rocks moved and set themselves into a new pattern.

I rubbed my palms on my thighs, swallowing my nerves. The climbing wall was a treat to the older kids, who timed their journeys to the top. There were specialized gloves for gripping the rocks and a harness to prevent anyone from a multi-story fall. Since only one person could climb at a time, some of us milled around while the first kid started climbing. Others took to the stairs, calling out encouragements.

I gravitated toward Ned. He was friendly enough and able to carry on a conversation with just my expression. Apparently, I didn't control my face very well. He cast Chance a curious glance and said, "Hey, Heather. Why do you have a pet mouse anyway?"

I shrugged. Chance was usually disinterested in my classes, except for Agility and Craft. He sat attentively on my shoulder during that time, wanting to learn these particular skills. "He's cute," I said.

"She talks to it," one of the other older kids added, her tone scornful.

I felt my shoulders start to hunch, and Sybella scoffed. "You've never talked to your pets?" she asked.

"I used to with my dog," Ned said, nudging the older girl. "What other pet is she going to have here? I'd bring my dog if I could, but he's way too big."

"I guess," she said, changing the subject quickly. I flashed Sybella a grateful look, which she ignored, as always. "My cousin knows a gryphon rider cadet. She says that he and his friends have to take their gryphons to every class. And there's only one staircase up and down the fortress. Can you imagine how packed class changes must be?"

"Insane," Ned said in agreement.

I half listened to their conversation. As interested as I was in learning everything about gryphon riders, Miss Barrios had caught my eye and raised three fingers and then a thumbs-up for encouragement. I was third in line, then, behind two of the older kids who would take a while to climb. My track record wasn't great by comparison.

When it was my turn, Chance jumped onto the rocks ahead of me, staying one up from where my fingertips landed. I was halfway up the floor when he thought it was safe enough to talk. "Tomorrow weekend, yes yes?"

I nodded, arms shaking as I reached for the next handhold and shifted my weight upward.

"We have fun?" he asked hopefully, peering down at me over the edge of the rock I was reaching for. "Sleep long? Take nap too? You too tired."

"Can't," I huffed out.

Much as I didn't want to, my third weekend working for Mistress Reni was looming. After she'd tired of teaching me the basics, she'd had me help her with fulfilling the shop's gigantic backlog of orders. That's when I'd misread one, gotten yelled at, and been sent back to RSI early with the threat to fire me if I messed up again. Who knew what would happen tomorrow?

I kept climbing, hand over hand, lost in my own thoughts until Ned shouted, "One more, Heather!"

The afternoon sunshine slanted shade over the rocks up ahead, smaller ones to make it more possible to fit the gap of stone where the stairs had parted for the climbing wall. It was the furthest I'd ever gotten, and Chance chattered happily from where he was now hitching a ride atop my head as I hoisted myself into the shaded box.

I couldn't logically explain what happened next. Rock surrounded me on most sides, and my mind jumped back in time to another box of stone. My jail cell. I froze with my head and shoulders in the gap, eye twitching from the sudden panic thrumming through me.

The feeling over my skin like the many skittering legs of the bugs that'd occupied the cell with me that night. The walls were closing in, squeezing the air out of my lungs with a pitiful wheeze. I shook so badly that my grip slipped, and I fell until the harness pulled taut, bouncing my body a handful of knuckle lengths off the ground. Chance clung to my hair so hard I felt his tiny claws digging into my scalp.

Shaken, I pawed at the hooks holding the harness around my torso. "You have to put your feet on the ground first," Miss Barrios said, tone gentling when she got a look at my face. She pushed my hands away and took care of freeing me from the straps. "Ned, will you stand in for me a moment?"

He came forward, and I saw the way he tried to look at me, though I'd ducked my head to hide the trails of wetness on my face. I tried to get a hold of myself, breathing in soft hiccups. *It was just one night. Less than a night.*

Miss Barrios guided me down the stairs to the cramped classroom. Only then did I break into full sobs and gasping breaths. "Heather, look at me. You're going to follow my lead, okay?" she said. She guided me through calmer, steadier breaths that filled my chest.

You're at RSI now. No one's putting you in another jail cell. My thoughts weren't doing a good job of calming me down. All my classmates on the stealth track had just seen me have a panic attack. The embarrassment swiftly rose, so I was crying *and* mortified.

"Tell me what's going on. It helps to talk about it," she invited.

Usually I wouldn't share my innermost thoughts, but she'd caught me in a vulnerable time. It all came flooding out. "I just...I saw the jail cell I was in. You know, Yule night," I said between labored breaths. "It was like the stone was closing in around me. And then I fell, and everyone saw it. I can't go back there. I'm so embarrassed."

She nodded slowly, wearing a look of understanding. For a moment, her hand hovered toward my shoulder, but she curled her fingers away and said, "Why don't you go get some lunch for you and Chance? Take a little break and come back. We'll be learning Craft when you return."

CHAPTER 7

UNCOMMON FEARS

I HOPED the other stealth track kids forgot about my fall after the weekend. I'd just been wishing for a day off, but the next day, I woke with the morning bells and dressed for my apprenticeship without a word of complaint. It'd be nice to have something to worry about other than that my true peers would mock me for panicking and crying on the climbing wall. They hadn't yet, but I'd purposefully returned to Craft class late enough that few words were exchanged at all.

Chance was extra cuddly, though, and awake as I walked to Orretta's Stitchery. I held and pet him for comfort. "Maybe Mistress Reni will be in a good mood," I suggested.

Margot said it was a good thing to put positive ideas out in the world. "The gods bless those who pray and those with nothing to hide," she'd once told me.

Maybe that's how it worked for noblewomen, but Mistress Reni was already red-faced and sweating when I entered the shop. "You're late, girl," she snapped.

I froze, wondering if I'd just gotten myself fired.

"Don't just stand there," she added irritably, turning and heading into the back room. She listed everything on the agenda today. A fitting at eleventh bell, a big order to fulfill by Monday, and a mountain of paperwork to sort. As she listed the latter, it seemed she was looking forward to it the least. She eyed me and scoffed. "Since you're no good at reading, I'll have you practicing the basics 'til the fitting."

Ouch. I suspected I knew what her animal was if she kept making barbed comments like that. With a flinch, I rustled around for a few objects and sat in a corner to show her I wasn't so incompetent that I'd forgotten how to thread a needle.

Mistress Reni had helped me understand that tailoring was a mix of several skills into one job title. The first thing I needed to do was learn to sew, and that meant I practiced stitching straight on the same abused strip of cloth while she bustled about the shop and pretended I wasn't there.

Until she needed something. Then her shout of "Mouse!" would echo to the back room, and I would tentatively peek out to see what she wanted.

Usually, this was accompanied by her gesturing for me to go over to someone who'd wandered in to browse. I wasn't all that much help, but I realized she also wanted me to keep an eye on folk if there was more than one guest or client around at a time.

She'd only summoned me twice so far, leaving me with my crooked stitches and Chance in the back. He explored and sniffed around, staying close to things he could hide behind, just in case Mistress Reni came back here. He brought me little trinkets, mostly shiny buttons or small, painted pearls. I was so nervous about the mannequin by the door that I didn't keep any of them.

Eleventh bell came, along with the murmur of female voices from the shop. Mistress Reni sounded a lot less irritable with customers in front of her, and I stabbed the cloth I held with more force than necessary, piercing through it to poke into my palm.

"Mouse!" Mistress Reni called sharply. I jolted, poking myself again, and tossed aside the musty needle with a glare.

I poked my head out of the back room just in time to hear a girl cry out in alarm and a woman gasp. The fitting was for the girl, who stood on the crate in front of the long mirror and danced on the tips of her toes, skirt lifted as she looked around for a mouse.

"Yes, Mistress Reni?" I asked.

The tailor shot me a look, her eyes bulging and angry despite her tone being relatively polite in front of a group of clients. "I need your help with fittings. Bring a form and a quill to take measurements."

My cheeks heated. I'd thought she'd told me about the fitting to get her mind around everything that needed done today. Though she hadn't said she'd need my help…it made sense that she'd expect it. I should've thought of that.

That fish-eyed look she gave me, though, solidified that she was a piranek in my mind. They were tiny fish with knife teeth and scales that reflected the colors of lakebeds. Considered minor ambush predators, they rested at the bottom of a body of water, waiting for something to swim by—then they'd strike for one quick bite, dart away, and settle somewhere else to wait for the next opportunity.

Mistress Reni had that kind of predator energy. She wanted to take a bite of me—and already had a couple times —but something about her seemed like she looked forward to it. Maybe even welcomed a chance to yell.

I did my best not to present her with many opportunities. I stood just out of the way as she wielded the measuring ribbons and pins, quill poised over a blank form.

This family had come in with a set of ready-made clothing they wanted tailored to fit the girl perfectly. Mistress Reni pinned down the excess fabric and told me what to write. Mostly, the tunics were being reduced in size and shortened by a few knuckle lengths…I mean, a couple of inches.

The whole process seemed standard. I just envied the girl a bit. This kind of work was never done for me or my siblings growing up because it was simply too costly, even from a shop like Orretta's Stitchery. Clothes that fit properly were lucky finds amongst the older kids' castoffs.

Once that group paid their deposit and Mistress Reni secured it in the lockbox, she turned to me. "Back to your stitches, girl. Don't bother me until they're perfect," she said.

"Yes, ma'am."

I retreated to the back room to keep practicing and sighed once I was alone. I pictured spending years at this as Mistress Reni's apprentice. If I failed at proving myself at RSI, I could be here a long time. I'd maybe make the tradeswoman rank in the Tailor Guild by the time I graduated RSI, but my understanding was that tradespeople usually stayed on as employees under the masters they trained under.

I would have to dodge the wrath of the piranek until I was skilled enough to open my own shop. And she seemed like the type who would hold on to information to make the process take as long as possible. It would be torturous.

"We *have* to advance," I whispered to Chance. Why should I spend a decade or longer becoming a master tailor? I wanted to be a spy. This job could be an excellent cover, but I didn't want to imagine a future where I had to work for Mistress Reni every day.

I looked down and assessed my work with a hum. I was improving, one row at a time. My stitches may have still been more crooked than Jackie's handwork, but my hands were growing steadier and more certain with the needle. Maybe I'd impress Mistress Reni soon and that would make our time together more bearable. It'd be nice if she'd stop looking at me with that lurking piranek stare, awaiting my next mistake.

Mistress Reni kept me late both nights to fetch items for her as she hurried to complete the big order due Monday morning. Folk could be retrieving their finished garments while I ate a light breakfast and sleepwalked through my first set of classes. I woke up more fully in Self-Defense, both from physical exertion and dread.

Agility was next. I was about to face my peers again and probably the climbing wall, too. I almost turned to Vance and asked him to make me look like someone else so I could hide in the lunchroom rather than see what awaited me in Tower A.

"Something the matter, pipsqueak?" Carmen asked in the middle of a practice spar. My eyelid had twitched one too many times.

"Wishing I could skip my next classes," I answered honestly.

She scoffed. "You, skip? Yeah right."

She furrowed her brow in concentration and executed a halfhearted strike at my padded torso using the techniques we learned in Self-Defense. Now that I had some functional knowledge of Tosh Zorena, I knew this style of fighting was more direct than the flowing, dance-like moves of Carmen's art. She made it no secret she disliked not being allowed to practice her style of fighting.

The jabs we were taught were meant to be used with real weapons, and we were encouraged to strike weak points like the eyes and groin in a fight. Such things had been discouraged at the gym in Zoreen. But it wasn't practical not to use everything to one's advantage in an actual fight. I saw why Carmen grumbled about Self-Defense, but I was seeing where both styles had their use.

I forgot what we were talking about, too busy trying to stay upright. Carmen might be the stronger one, but I was elusive and slipped out of her holds. She punched my shoulder for a job well done when Coach Stryker called for us to switch partners. I almost didn't flinch, expecting her rough praise.

I hadn't seen Carmen happy since we'd returned from Zoreen. A few days of missing her gym would be expected... but it'd been what, three weeks now? I'd barely noticed the time passing, just like I'd hardly looked up long enough to realize my first friend at RSI was feeling discontent.

I had a weird, churning feeling in my gut when I went to Tower A for class and really looked around. The other stealth track kids had already assembled into their groups, and Ned waved me over to his. I wedged between him and Sybella, listening instead of speaking as always.

No one mentioned my panic attack. I would've been relieved, but I was in a weird mood. What else had I missed while caught up in my own problems?

Miss Barrios didn't have us on the climbing wall today, which was a relief. Instead, with a flick of her wand toward a rune engraved in the wall on the first floor, she set up the obstacle course...a maze of wooden walls, hurdles, small crawl spaces, and more. All of this sprung up and adjusted itself out of piles of junk placed to the side of each floor. Just like with the climbing wall, the obstacles set themselves up in a random order.

We'd only used the obstacle course a handful of times so far. To add to the difficulty, there were extra small magelight "guards" that patrolled the stairs and floors at random. They projected a beam of light forward in a foot-long cone and sounded an alarm if that cone found a sneaking kid. It was the end of the course for those caught.

The more experienced kids purposefully said nothing about the course to the newbies like me. I'd always gotten caught by the magelight guards before seeing much of what I was up against. I didn't expect today to be much different, though I took a moment to scout for guards to observe their patrol patterns before I rushed in.

There wasn't much to see. The room was made smaller by the wooden walls, which blocked sight of what was ahead of the first hurdle. I jumped it and ended up in a small space with a magelight rotating ever so slowly. There was a gap between a wooden wall and the stone curve of the tower that I was supposed to go into.

I wedged myself into that space, facing the bricks. There wasn't a patrol here, so it was dark in this corner, and damp. The way forward would be to slide sideways across this wall, toward the stairs. I was supposed to catch my breath but couldn't find the air. The walls seemed to close in again, squeezing out anything but the panic clawing at my throat.

I deliberately stepped back and let the magelight's beam catch me. The obstacle course flattened as it blared out its alarm. When I turned to leave, I realized Miss Barrios was standing on the stairs, watching me with a concerned furrow between her brows. "Heather—" she began to say.

"I don't know what's gotten into me. I'll do better next time," I said shakily. No one who called themselves a sneak got spooked by small spaces.

She held her hands palms up. "I believe you. We all respond to traumas differently. Whatever's going on, we'll work through it together," she said.

"Thanks," I mumbled, grateful to go back down to the classroom to wait as my peers tried the obstacle course next. As I waited, I considered what was triggering these sudden panics. The only thing they had in common were tight spaces and stone walls. My mind seemed to take it from there, screaming that I was still trapped.

I petted Chance and reminded myself I was okay. I even had the Eye of Acuity, which I could turn in to leave RSI and be a free spirit.

By the time we finished Craft for the day, I was more like myself again. Quiet, cautious, and looking forward to Language class. It was quickly becoming my favorite. My whole crew attended it and got to sit together, and what we went over felt very familiar.

We'd spent a significant amount of time learning drifter signs, where to locate them, and how to use them while out on a mission. Miss Liang had promised we were moving on last week, and when I stepped in, I saw the word "Uncommon" written on the chalkboard.

"Yes," I hissed under my breath.

I'd read the three extra credit challenges until I could picture them behind my eyelids. The first one was to "use Uncommon to make contact with five people outside of RSI." Fariq was right. We just had to be patient to find out what that actually meant.

Speaking of Fariq, he was the first of my crew here. His face lit up when he saw me, and he slid out the chair next to him. "Heather, hello. Can I ask you for a favor?"

I sat and dug out my journal. "Yeah."

"You don't want to know what it is first?"

I blinked, realizing it must be a big one with how he was fidgeting with his fingers. "Well, what is it, then?" I asked.

"I've been learning the process of smelting for the next stage of my apprenticeship. It's very fascinating," he said, dropping his voice. "I was wondering if you'd let me borrow your desda powder."

Swallowing wrong, I started coughing. He pounded on my back and looked at me with concern.

"*Smelting* and *desda powder* are not two ideas that go together," I whispered.

"Actually, they might." He flipped open his journal, where he'd taken extensive notes on several processes that included molten hot metal. He'd circled "oxidative buildup," whatever that was, and "flux" multiple times in frantic loops, which suggested to me he'd had an idea on the spot as someone talked about these concepts.

"Unfortunately, it is an illegal substance, yes?" he whispered.

"Incredibly," I answered. "What, exactly, are you wanting to use it for?"

"I'll give you short answer. I want to experiment with it. In theory, it might bond to metal during a key part." His finger tapped the word flux in his journal. "My builder friends want to try it, but none of us have the powder. I remembered that you do."

"I have a tiny amount," I hedged.

"That will do. I don't want to poison any Tulari…but if this works, it may make their jobs harder. If even a few grains of the powder bond to the metal, it could have anti-magic properties," he said.

My eyes widened. It would be an incredible breakthrough if he could make it happen. And if he happened to owe me some tools coated with this anti-magic stuff since I lent him the powder, all the better. I fished Chance out of his pouch and held him close to my face. "Will you go get the desda powder for us?" I whispered.

The mouse yawned and scratched behind one ear with his back paw. Judging by the pause, he was thinking hard. "I forget where it is," he squeaked.

"The small pouch with the red powder in it," I insisted.

"Yes yes. I remember pouch but forget where I hide it." He hunkered down dramatically, like he thought I was going to yell at him.

Musty devils. I was glad we were having this conversation now and not when I needed the powder to disable mage spells or traps.

I stroked a couple of fingers down Chance's back. "It's okay, sweet mouse. Why don't you go look in your usual hidey holes and see if you can find it?" I suggested.

He perked back up and bobbed his entire body. "I do for

you!" He jumped off my palm, landing on my leg and scampering down my uniform from there. The last of my classmates were coming in, but he dodged and weaved around their feet with ease to disappear into the hall as Miss Liang closed the door.

"Thank you," Fariq said. I nodded, hoping Chance could find it and Fariq wouldn't use it all up. Now that all my siblings were here at RSI, I had no way of acquiring more without significant risk.

"What'd I miss?" Vance asked, having a seat.

Margot and Carmen had come in while Fariq and I were whispering but had struck up a separate conversation. "Just some lovely weather today, darling," Margot said primly.

He rolled his eyes. "I wouldn't know." The tone rolling off him was pure rozash acid. I inspected him and how he tugged at his copper bracelet. He was still tier zero, so he hadn't squealed yet about what he knew of Morashi Venom, or he was still being punished for leaving the school without permission.

It'd been several months by this point. Vance had to be ready to pull his own skin off from the wrist up for a chance at freedom.

"Fariq has a good idea," I blurted, just to change the subject. "He's got his builder friends in on it too. But if they're successful, I helped lots."

Carmen raised a brow, mouth open to pose a question, when Miss Liang cleared her throat and called our attention up front. "When a stranger comes up to you and says, 'I've lost my keys,' what do you say back to him?" she asked us all.

A few kids tossed out suggestions, though none of them were what Miss Liang seemed to want. "He looks down at your wrist and says, 'Perhaps you could help me retrace my steps.' As you go with him down the street and out of earshot of others, he tells you of a mission he needs help with. He has just spoken a bit of Uncommon to you and recognized you as a Crown agent from the marking on your bracelet."

On cue, we all looked at our bracelets. The tier-two etching of a pair of crossed keys sat prominently atop my wrist, and I nodded in understanding. "We are keys," I murmured.

"If someone approaches you to talk about keys and you've never met them before, they are probably asking for help. There are hundreds of word substitutions that work this way, and we call them, collectively"—she gestured at the chalkboard behind her—"Uncommon. A way to talk about classified information in front of others without them ever knowing. Think of them as metaphors."

A quiet noise came from the boy beside me. "Not metaphors," Fariq sighed.

I glanced over at him in surprise. Fariq complaining about something academic was a true rarity. Usually, I was the one groaning over a subject while he brimmed with excitement to deepen his understanding of it.

I'd already learned something like this in Jace's Menagerie, though we didn't call it Uncommon. It was possible that, for once, I would teach him something.

CHAPTER 8

L⊙⊙KING UP

Chance squeezed the tip of my nose in the dead of night. "I find powder for you!" he announced.

I think I mumbled something like, "Good mouse."

I woke again bleary-eyed with the desda powder pouch tucked up under my chin. There were no red blotches on the sheets to suggest any had escaped. Which was great, since there were only a few pinches left of the scarlet-red powder, probably not enough for Fariq's project.

If he needed more, I could source it for him. Thylacine and my older gang siblings had always discouraged me from going into the Shadowed Market deep in Kaiamear's slums, where alleyway tents and run-down buildings hosted several pop-up businesses rumored to offer most anything for the right price. But it wouldn't be hard to read the drifter signs for the next market day and go after Mistress Reni dismissed me for the evening.

The problem was, I owed Fariq for my belt. I'd promised myself to buy his gift honestly, but desda powder was expensive for a reason, made from crushed mushrooms grown in secret. Ordinary, magicless folk could handle the powder without a problem, but if a Tulari had skin contact or a taste of it, they would die nearly immediately. It rotted away spells and wards just as quickly and was the one substance available to non-mages that could counter magic effectively.

I'd need to replenish the powder for myself anyway, no matter how much of it Fariq ended up using. It was an invaluable tool for a thief used to identifying and deactivating magical traps on various jobs. So…that trip to the Shadowed Market would have to happen. The real deciding factor would be when and who I'd go with.

When I handed Fariq the pouch of powder under the table at breakfast, I read his face. Underneath the gratitude, the lines of fatigue and worry that etched his dark bronze skin matched what I saw in my expression each time I looked into the mirror.

My lips pinched into a frown. He had everything going for him. His Altarian got better every day, to the point he was rarely corrected on his grammar or pronunciation. No assignments with his name on them came back with failing marks. Though he was a self-named "geek," he'd gotten an apprenticeship that allowed him to grow the skills he enjoyed with like-minded friends.

He wasn't like me. I was still struggling to pass my hardest classes, Innovation and Lithosian, and disliked my apprenticeship more every time I walked into Orretta's Stitchery to find Mistress Reni already angry about something.

"What's wrong?" I blurted out.

He recoiled from the sudden increase in volume from my usual quiet tones. "Nothing is wrong. You've done me a great favor, thank you."

"Yes, you're welcome," I said, worried I'd misread him. "But you seemed stressed."

He shrugged and put the pouch into his pack to hide it.

"It's just Language class. Uncommon is…" His gaze darted to the kids at the table next to ours, all wearing copper bracelets. "Figurative language, it is hard for me. Learning a second tongue is tough enough before adding in hidden meanings and extra definitions."

"Oh." I'd noticed his dismay over metaphors yesterday, even. "I'll help you. It's not that hard."

The disbelieving look he gave me in return said that it would, in fact, be that hard. At least I'd asked and learned more about what was challenging him right now.

That weird feeling was back, rolling around in my belly. I needed to look up from my own problems and workload and see what else I'd missed.

When Jace trained me to be a thief, he took me on long walks through the market for people-watching. We were really there to observe what a good mark looked like, and I'd practiced so much that it became second nature. I'd picked up more from the experience than the telltale signs of wealthy folk mixing in with the less well off.

A Mouse needed finely honed skills to survive, to disappear at will, and come home with pockets full of stolen goods. Yet in RSI, I'd become too tired by my school-work schedule and stopped the habit of observing those around me.

I kicked myself for letting those skills dull. I had to do better.

So, I spoke a little and observed a lot. I got Vance to walk extra slow with me to Lithosian class and asked the question that'd been burning in the back of my throat. "We destroyed your contract. Why don't you just squeal?" I gestured to his copper bracelet.

"Don't I wish it was that easy, boss," he replied quietly. "You've never met M-Madam Morashi, and I hope you never do. Her m-magic…it…" He took a sharp breath.

It was strange to hear his usual confidence falter, but his

obvious fear woke a memory in me. We'd needed an all-key, and I'd suggested he should steal one from one of the Morashi mages. He'd made it clear that returning to his old gang was out of the question. *"I can tell you gang secrets now, but the others will know something's wrong if they see me again. Th-they would take me t-to her and...I'd receive the maximum c-consequence if I were taken to Madam Morashi."* He'd been tongue-numbingly afraid of her then, too.

"She would know you talked," I guessed.

We arrived at our classroom, and he ended the conversation with a drawn look and a whisper of, "She always knows."

Was there a worse devil out there than Madam Morashi?

Later, in Language class, I wedged myself between Fariq and Margot. The latter smothered a yawn. "Sleepy sleepy," I teased.

That was about all it took to get her to overshare. "Yes, I just had to take another nap. My newest assignment is killing me, darling. This family has four girls in different stages of life, yet they hired only *one* governess to take care of all of it on a half day schedule. None of them are getting the education they deserve, and I'm just *exhausted.*" She punctuated this by flicking open her favorite fan, pink and lacy, and fanning herself dramatically.

The Eye had stopped showing Margot a while ago and returned to its dormant state, but it'd showed me that, more days than not, she was catching a nap during lunchtime. I pulled a sympathetic face. "How much longer will this assignment be?"

"I'm not sure. It depends on what the children's parents want and can afford. The girls need consistency to flourish, but I've never wanted to quit and marry the first eligible suitor to come along more than right now. I'll produce my own dowry from our summer mission, if I must," she answered. She muffled a giggle behind her fan at the expression of alarm that took over my face and rounded my eyes. "Do you still think boys are gross, then?"

I opened my mouth to reply with an emphatic *yes* but noticed both Fariq and Vance looking over at us. "Most of them are," I said.

Margot didn't look convinced. "Hmph. Well, I was meaning to discuss this with the Spymaster anyway. I should still seek an advantageous marriage quietly."

My brows rose, and I exchanged a glance with Carmen, who had her pointy nose in a wrinkle over what we were hearing.

Margot didn't seem to notice, though. "Perhaps there is a gentleman spy looking to wed, who will help me spy on high society for the Crown. I should secure him before I become a spinster waiting for the rest of you to mature," she said.

It sounded like she'd been thinking about this for a while. I didn't jump in to point out that she was only two years older than me. My mind had skipped an inevitable fact for Margot…she was going to graduate from RSI sooner than the rest of my crew. If we were going to remain a crew, she'd have two years to wait for us, and that was a lot to ask of anyone, especially a noblewoman who'd come here furious about how her uncle's family had disgraced her and denied her debut.

I simply smiled back and said, "Maybe Manny can help with that."

I turned my attention back to Fariq and tried to help him understand as the class delved more into Uncommon. We made study cards of the vocabulary words Miss Liang provided for us to memorize.

I was dragging by the last class of the day, Theater. Work was well underway for the first production of the year, and Carmen had a minor speaking role, so she and I partnered up and went to the library for her to practice delivering her lines. She found a study nook, and I found Patches, snuggling the feligryph while Carmen read out of a spiral-bound press book with all the emotion of a wooden doll.

"Supposed to have some excitement, innit?" I suggested.

She answered with a shrug and tossed the play aside. I stifled a big sigh, realizing this was my moment to see how she was doing. I felt like I was prodding a kheneas knowing it was about to turn and kick me. "How is your apprenticeship going?" I asked.

Unlike the rest of us, she never spoke of hers. Even Vance had an apprenticeship, shut up at odd hours in the alchemy labs, making potions. But Carmen scowled and said, "I don't have one."

"I thought all intermediate kids did," I said.

"I told Miss Barrios not to give me one."

She didn't explain further, even when I leaned in expectantly. "What do you do with your weekend instead?" I asked.

Carmen's shrug was sharp. "I help my aunt. My three cousins overwhelm her sometimes."

I opened my mouth, poised to ask another question, but stopped. Carmen wasn't much of a talker on the best of days, but her curt replies were paired with a defensive hunch of her shoulders and a hint of memory shining in her eyes.

To the best of my knowledge, she and her aunt didn't have a great relationship, but there would be no uncle returning home to help with her cousins. So, Carmen had stepped up. Maybe she was prickly about it, but that was how she was about most everything.

She relaxed after a few moments and offered more information on her own. "When the youngest is a tot, maybe I'll start an apprenticeship for the coin. My choices were to become a junior peacekeeper or stay here and start instructing in Tosh Zorena. It wouldn't be so bad to be a teacher someday, I guess."

My brows rose. Her teaching her art to others was a

thorny subject, but to hear her come around on it… "I'm proud of you," I murmured. Patches made a soft trill, which I took for agreement.

And, of course, Carmen scoffed. "What for, pipsqueak?"

I didn't want to discourage her from the path she was on, so I said nothing. Sometimes Carmen took praise in a contrary way and quickly stopped what had earned it. Instead, I mimicked her usual energy with a shrug and gestured toward the play she'd tossed aside. "Your delivery needs work, though," I said.

Her lips relaxed from a full frown, as if she recognized the compliment-critique pairing she usually gave me.

Since the play I was cast in was scheduled to run sometime right before Yule, I could take it easier in Theater for now. But I listened to Carmen struggle to frame the right emotion in her lines and still wished to have her workload. She'd have three minor parts throughout the year; at least she could fade into the background some.

My time would come, and when it did, I would be front and center. Just the thought had my heart racing and my palms growing clammy.

I had a copy of *A Pinch of Nutmeg*. Miss Stone had let me borrow it early, as if knowing the lines on paper would help prepare me to say them, with emotion, in front of hundreds of people one day.

AFTER CLASS, I had some time to myself. I sat in a library nook, looking at the play I was supposed to be memorizing without reading it.

Jace used to say a crew is only as strong as its weakest member. After listening to my friends and their troubles, I realized we were all struggling. I hadn't even thought about the extra credit challenges and what it would take to get us to the advanced tier with my workload being what it was, and the others weren't focused on the team either.

Are we really in such a hurry to prove ourselves again?

But how will we become spies if we're overwhelmed by intermediate classes and requirements?

I reasoned that we needed a bit more time to sort out our struggles before we came together as a team worthy of a promotion to the advanced tier. But we would, and the Spymaster would be *so* impressed when we did.

That evening, I slid into a chair at Jackie's table. My sister ate with a gaggle of kids her age at one of the bigger tables. That included our siblings, Bear and Needlecoat, and her assigned partner, a nervous boy named Lloyd. Though I occasionally checked in with them, they didn't seem to talk to each other unless during a group project or for help on a tough assignment.

These ten- and eleven-year-olds still had their unmarked copper bracelets. There were probably some clever minds amongst them that'd figure things out faster than others. I'd tried hinting. Asking, "Notice anything weird about this school?" yielded a lot of confused looks amongst my crew of family. Jackie thought everything was strange: how RSI continued education past the end of fundamental school age; how we were fed three meals a day; how everything, including the uniforms, was free.

Still, I asked her tonight, "Hear anything interesting?"

The oath I'd sworn upon becoming a spy candidate was magically enforced. I physically could not tell Jackie she was at a spy school, not with spoken or written words. But I could encourage a bit of bad behavior.

Listening where I wasn't supposed to had gotten me here, after all.

"Some of the older kids learn how to hurt people bad,"

Jackie answered with a little shudder. "That's not what we're covering in Gym class."

Gym, right. Because it wouldn't be called Self-Defense for her yet. She must've heard something about the class the eighteen-year-olds were rumored to take right before they graduated: Lethal Measures.

"One of many quirks about RSI," I said. All I could do was hope she and the others put the pieces together eventually.

After I finished my meal, I went over to the table where my older siblings were gathered. The established spy teams kept to themselves by this age, so it was only my siblings that ringed this table. Ram was the center of attention, as always, and greeted me with enthusiasm. "If it isn't little Mouse!"

"Hey, Mouse," doe-eyed Lope—short for Antelope, for her tall, athletic figure—said from his side. I rarely saw Ram without Lope lately. They seemed to hold hands under the table a lot.

Dexis stood to grab a chair, wedging it in between her and Sidewinder, a young man named for… Actually, I think Jace just gave him that name because it was "neat."

"'Bout time you came 'round," Sidewinder said. He clanked his bracelet on the table, showing off that it was silver. We shared a brief, meaningful look.

Thank the gods one of my family members had figured it out. The copper color of a tier-zero bracelet was so distinctive to me now, since the moment most anyone swore the oath to the headmaster, they always picked a different metal or material. The bright shine of copper was a marker of confinement and a sign to watch one's words.

"Once I figure out the weird thing ya want me to notice, you're going to be the first to know, Mouse," Ram announced.

"Maybe you should tell Lope first," I suggested when her lips pressed into a smooth line. "Actually, tell—" I tried to say *everyone at this table*, but the oath's magic stopped the words from escaping. That was apparently interfering too much.

It didn't hurt, but it felt like an invisible hand had pressed its thumb to my windpipe until I stopped trying to talk. "The headmaster, I knows it," Ram finished my sentence for me.

That being said, he changed the subject, jumping around ideas like he usually did while the rest of my siblings kept up without a problem. I went back to my old role a little too easily, listening while they all paid me little mind.

They spoke of a couple of classes and apprenticeships. I turned to Sidewinder. "How'd you get to your apprenticeship…before…?" I asked.

"Miss Fox lets us out and back in, sometimes with a teacher escorting us," he answered. "I will say I have gotten a boost in hours now." He tapped his bracelet meaningfully.

I nodded. That made sense. Under the cover of the rest of the table's conversation, I asked, "Hey, could you tell me more about town shadow?"

Maybe I hadn't been as quiet as I thought I was, as the moment I said *town shadow*, everyone's eyes were on me. That was a term out of our version of Uncommon, for the Shadowed Market. "Why?" Dexis asked first.

I felt myself flush. "I was thinking about going," I said meekly.

"Have I missed something?" Ram asked, making a show of lifting his dinner tray and peering at its bottom side. "Ya know the rules. Girls gotta be fourteen, with one of the older boys with them. You're not going, Mouse. We'd tear up the shadows if you went missin'."

"I'm fourteen now," I reminded him. "And I'm out of cinnamon." In other words, desda powder.

"I gots some you could borrow," Sidewinder offered.

I bit my lip. "You don't understand. It's for a big cake."

He blinked in surprise, as did my other siblings. This was the part of Uncommon we hadn't learned in class yet, but word substitutions led to metaphors with no meaning past the conversation we were having. I meant *cake* like *mission,* and Ram was the first to say, "What kind of cake? Something you need help makin'?"

"Yes. Maybe with some prep work. I want to buy the cinnamon honest-like," I answered.

Ram snorted, a sentiment echoed amongst my siblings. "Right-o. Tell ya what. When they let me walk out of this school, I'll help you buy the cinnamon honest-like," he said. "'Til then, it's gonna be a bland cake, I'm afraid."

CHAPTER 9

EXPOSURE THERAPY

AT THE END of the week, I ate dinner quickly and gathered my things to hurry back to Tower A for a private session with Miss Barrios. A pair of young men followed me out, speaking loudly behind my back.

"Where do you think she's going?" Davit asked.

"Maybe she's trying to sneak into the boy's side to see her rat," Wyatt answered.

I felt a flare of irritation. The hall was empty of people, as most of the other kids were still eating dinner. These two had to have seen me leaving early and chosen to follow me. All the Davit's Day team were bullies, but Wyatt was my least favorite member. He was the one who would go the furthest out of his way to mess with Fariq or me to the limits of what wouldn't get him in trouble.

Wyatt would snatch a half-finished worksheet out from under my quill, trip me while I was holding a tray of food, or shoulder-check me into a wall in the busy hallway between class periods. Yet somehow, he was popular in RSI, which might directly correspond to his high marks and consistent leading roles in Theater.

Just ignore them. They want to see your reaction, I told myself in a voice that sounded a lot like Fariq's.

I stopped at the secretary's desk, hoping they'd pass me by. If Miss Barrios wasn't waiting for me in Tower A, she'd have the night off, which meant there was no one sitting behind the desk. There was a peacekeeper posted at the end of the hall by the door that led to Irving Hall and the boy's dorms. I recognized the pimply face of Brinsley, Vance's friend, under the distinctive crested helm.

"No secretary to cry to tonight, huh?" Wyatt sneered.

He seized my ponytail roughly, forcing me to look up at him.

"Ow! Let me go," I hissed.

Davit and Wyatt hadn't kept walking. Instead, they crowded me. My eye twitched, and I balled my fists when I saw the look they exchanged. Wyatt grinned, while Davit wore a frown that transformed into something…else.

I'd seen their expressions before. The gang men who'd liked to touch Menagerie girls would have the same flicker of intent cross their faces. Someone who had never been in this kind of situation would expect cornering, touching, threatening, and hitting were done for pleasure. But it was more than that. I'd figured out that it was also about power and control over an unwilling person.

Wyatt crowded me, so I turned and eased backward, the wooden edge of the secretary's table pressing to my lower back. He let my hair go when I was trapped between him and his friend. They both loomed over me, their expressions merciless.

"Let's just have a conversation," Wyatt said, his teeth still bared. My breath came shorter as I took in my options for how to escape from this situation.

Any second now, Brinsley would shout for them to get away from me. He had to have seen what was going on.

Yet all was quiet behind me as Wyatt leaned down and

lowered his voice. "That Lithosian boy does not belong here. Since you seem so dead set on defending him, neither do you."

"I've seen your team's name on the intermediate board," Davit added, emboldened when I seemed to freeze like a frightened mouse. "Just know, if you try to pose *any* threat to Davit's Day's position at the top, we will come after you."

Wyatt balled his fists, and I shifted my stance, expecting a blow. "I heard the first competition day is next week. Maybe we'll show you we mean business anyway," he said.

I took a deep breath, which shuddered in my chest. I'd let myself get put in this position by being too passive, too like Fariq, who didn't let anything like this bother him. As they were talking and threatening, I switched my inner voice to Carmen's. She wouldn't let herself be cornered. She also wouldn't let these boys have any power over her. And neither would I.

But Carmen would also have something snappy to say. The best I could do was, "I welcome it."

Don't hold back.

The last thing Wyatt expected me to do was take advantage of his stance, sweeping one of his ankles and shoving him at the same time. He fell hard, the wind knocked out of him. Davit was gaping when I turned on him next. He was a couple paces away and took a kick above his kneecap poorly, going down with a *thud*.

My eyes widened, shocked for a split second that had worked so well. For a moment, I hadn't seen Wyatt, but a blur, an impression of those who'd taken advantage of my size and meekness in the past. I had no remorse for grounding either of them.

But they were both groaning and starting to stand, so I took off running down the hall. Their pounding footsteps sounded right behind me once they recovered.

Brinsley was still standing at his post, grinning when I

went by and angled for Tower A. "I didn't see anything," he promised in an undertone.

I had the tower door slammed shut and locked behind me before there was an impact on the other side and the thumping of a fist on wood. I tuned out what their muffled voices said and turned to Miss Barrios, who sat in a chair with an open book in hand.

"Hi, Miss Fox. I'm ready," I said louder than usual.

Her surprised gaze narrowed over my shoulder, but she didn't comment. She put a bookmark in what she was reading and stood, beckoning for me to follow her.

The banging stopped pretty quickly as we left the door behind. I figured I could trust Brinsley to get the two hecklers to move on rather than wait just outside the door to ambush me.

If they'd seen it, Fariq would've been disappointed by my actions, while I pictured Carmen thrilled that I'd used Tosh Zorena in self-defense. Either way, I was guaranteed to need the art more often if Davit's Day used this as an excuse to use their fists outside the safety of RSI.

We kept walking up the circular stairs, toward the top of the pitch-black tower. She'd drawn her wand and set the tip to glowing, creating a sphere of sapphire light that I stayed inside. My palms were already clammy. Something about the darkness just out of reach and the stone closing in around us...it made some animal part of my brain want to bolt back downstairs and take my chances against Davit and Wyatt.

We got to the top floor, and she turned to me. "Do you know what exposure therapy is, Miss Mouse?" she asked.

"Not sure," I muttered.

"Some say the only way to conquer a fear is to face it," she explained. The crawly feeling that accompanied my recent panic attacks started creeping across my skin. She wasn't going to put out her wand's light, was she? She wouldn't do that to me...right?

Miss Barrios gestured to the circular room, with its stone walls and single, shut window. "I've rarely seen you afraid so intensely until we started training in this tower. It has seriously affected your performance in Agility class. Perhaps—"

"I can do better. Please don't take me out of the stealth track," I blurted, clasping my hands together.

"No one's leaving the stealth track," she said gently. "When you first came here, your file was empty except for a note to put your stealth skills to work. It's what a mouse was born to do. So, you must overcome your fear of being jailed."

I opened my mouth, then closed it. That was a nice, short way of putting it. I wasn't afraid of tight spaces—I'd been in plenty of those—but put my face to a stone wall, and I remembered being enclosed by them. My breath rasped too loudly, and the walls seemed to lean in as I thought about that one Yule night.

"It was…it was only one night," I said. The words were crushed from my lungs until I refocused my attention on her face and the bright tip of her wand. I took a deep, slow breath. "One night almost a year ago, at this point."

Her lips took on a skeptical slant. "Well, I remember the day after, and I would guess that was the scariest night of your life thus far."

My eyes watered. She was spot-on. I'd spent the night weighing two equally deadly choices: either squeal to the peacekeepers and face Springfield's wrath, or refuse to talk and receive the worst punishment the Gladbeck family could inflict on me for the Eye's disappearance. I wanted to tell her I'd faced certain death in the confines of that jail cell, but my tongue felt too swollen in my mouth.

"Aw, come here." Miss Barrios swept me into a hug. I didn't jerk away, as she might've expected, and ended up crying into her shoulder while she rubbed my back. Neither of us said anything, and I was going to keep it that way. Tears were weakness, something I kept bottled up, though it was nice to be held by someone I mostly trusted.

It was only after I'd recovered and sniffled while avoiding eye contact with her that she said, "Let's begin, then." With a flick of her wand, we plunged into darkness.

The walls leaned in again. As my eyes adjusted, they revealed hints of the stonework surrounding us, reminding me of where we were. Her hand found my shoulder, steering me to the window. "You play your role well, and you will never sit on the inside of a jail cell again." Starlight framed Miss Barrios's upturned face as we looked outside together. "And even if you did, it could not hold someone with the skills you'll learn here at RSI."

"Really?" I asked in a small voice. I turned my gaze up to the stars and the face of the moon, which peeked through a haze of clouds to limn the spires of the distant palace.

"That's right. And you won't be alone, with your carpenter mouse around to help."

"I left him with Margot tonight," I admitted. He'd been distressed when I'd told him that Miss Barrios wanted to help with my panic attacks, so I figured he'd be happier with her for the evening.

"Well, that's fine. He needs his own life too, however small," she said.

We chatted more about him and his recent antics while more stars winked into the night sky. I slowly relaxed, despite the stone room, despite the darkness. My logical mind pointed out the staircase and the window. This wasn't a jail cell. I wasn't in danger.

The moment I thought of danger, the air left my lungs, and I clammed up. Miss Barrios took that as her cue to light her wand and nudge me toward the stairs. "That's all for now, I think. Let's go enjoy our evenings," she said.

On the bottom floor, she pulled two things from her pocket to give me: an envelope and a key. I angled the key toward her wand's light and saw an A carved into its solid metal bow. "Access to the tower," I guessed.

She nodded. "Bring a lantern, your homework, and even Chance. But be careful with that. It's valuable."

I immediately slipped it next to the dormant Eye of Acuity in Chance's pouch.

"And the envelope is for your team," she added.

I pocketed it, sure it would be in a cypher that needed decoding. "Thank you, Miss Fox. I'll handle the exposure therapy myself. You won't be disappointed," I promised.

She lifted her hand, reaching for me. When I didn't flinch, she rested it on my shoulder. "As if you could disappoint me, Miss Mouse."

THE CODED message from Miss Barrios had been about the upcoming competition day. My crew was scheduled to have a briefing on it in the middle of the day Sunday—when we were all deep in our apprenticeships or other business. There was hardly a more inconvenient time.

I arrived at Orretta's Stitchery the day of and promptly told Mistress Reni about needing to attend a meeting at RSI. She scoffed, saying loudly, "Who pays you to come here and stitch crookedly? Not RSI!"

My shoulders rose at her tone. She paid me a guild standard rate for apprentices at the end of each weekend, sure. It was generous pay, but for only two days a week, it was just shy of two silver clorets. "It's not going to last more than a turning of the bells," I said.

Her already reddened face rapidly turned an ugly shade of purple. Her usual piranek expression accompanied it, and I braced myself for what she'd say, knowing I couldn't simply sweep her ankles out from under her to end the conversation like I had with Davit. She opened her mouth to take a bite out of me verbally. "No RSI kid has important meetings to go to. You're just lazy, trying to get out of honest work. Is tailoring too difficult for you, Mouse?" she asked with condescension.

I'd frozen again, so I had to force my mouth to move. "No, ma'am. I would be there and back before—"

"Please, I know you won't be back, 'cept to ask for your pay," she interrupted.

"You can keep—"

"I don't want to hear your excuses, kid," she interrupted again. Her voice rose to a full-lung yell at the end of her tirade. "You're not anything I haven't seen before. Soon you'll be here every other weekend, if that. The apprenticeship program is supposed to help kids like you better yourselves, make you all more *responsible*, prompt, and polite. Why does it *never work*? Why do you waste my *time*?"

I hunched further, just wanting for it to be over. Let her fire me already, if this was how she felt. She'd jumped to some conclusion that wasn't there... musty devils, I'd just asked to leave for a midday bell.

A terrible, shrill noise saved me from stumbling over some kind of reply. All the little hairs on my arms lifted, and Mistress Reni's wrathful gaze immediately shot to the door.

The rest of the hairs on the back of my neck stood straight too when something said, "Alert. Shoplifter alert." It spoke with magic in a tone that belonged to neither gender, formed on a hiss of air as a magical device activated.

I turned just in time to see the warrior mannequin move of its own accord, slamming a stranger in the shoulder with one of its paddle hands hard enough to break the wood with a sharp *crack*. I don't know who cursed more foully, Mistress Reni or the man who collapsed with a cry of pain.

"Not again," she muttered.

While she'd been yelling at me, the man had apparently snuck in here, snatched an armful of clothes off their hangers, and now lay on them while the mannequin rested a wooden paddle shaped like a foot on the small of his back. He didn't move. The mannequin kept releasing that eerie squeal and saying, "Alert. Shoplifter alert."

I looked up at Mistress Reni, my eyes as round as coins. "What now?" I asked in a small voice.

"Keep the shop open," she muttered. "I'll take care of this. Don't touch him or the mannequin."

She left with no more instructions, stepping around the downed shoplifter and leaving him there. He continued to lie on the ground for the better half of an hour, while I stood behind the counter with the lockbox, my fingers trembling under the wooden surface. The squealing eventually stopped, replaced by the man's troubled breathing as he lay immobile. The mannequin had to have some sort of paralysis spell on its foot to keep him contained for this long.

Chance peeked out of his pouch once the mannequin went quiet. "It safe now?" he squeaked.

"I don't know," I said, tucking him back into his little bed for now.

When Mistress Reni returned, it was with a pair of peacekeepers, who hauled the shoplifter away after greeting him by name. They sounded chummy.

"Any customers, Mouse?" she grunted on her way past me into the backroom.

"No, ma'am."

She rustled around back there for a couple minutes before emerging with a paddle hand identical to the one the mannequin had broken. "Damn mage said he enchanted these to be unbreakable. What a farce. The last one broke from its first use, too. I should've realized he was a charlatan." She waved around the carved wood on her way to the mannequin, which remained in its attack pose.

I stayed at the counter, not interested in getting anywhere near the thing. She barked something that sounded like "*alfissen*," and the mannequin lined up its feet, then slumped forward with a sigh of air.

"Deactivating," the magic said. I barely kept myself from gawping. That musty wooden monstrosity could be neutralized after all.

Mistress Reni replaced the broken paddle with the new one, grumbling all the while. She picked up the items the would-be shoplifter was trying to take and came back to the counter, heaping them in front of me. "Put these back," she ordered, and I rushed to do so while the mannequin was still deactivated.

While I hung the ready-made clothes and tried to tug out the wrinkles, she opened the lockbox and rustled around it, eventually uttering a satisfied noise. She beckoned to me when the clothes were rehung and slapped a silver cloret onto the counter between us. "Your pay," she said. "Take the rest of the day off and go to your 'meeting.' But you better be back next weekend."

Though the last thing I wanted to do was return here to face her and her creepy warrior mannequin, I put on an agreeable face and nodded rapidly.

CHAPTER 10

LITTLE WONDERS PET SHOP

I FLED Orretta's Stitchery before Mistress Reni could revive the mannequin. I was a few doors down from the shop before I slowed and offered my palm to Chance to place him on my shoulder. "What now?" I sighed.

"We eat good food now, feast for our survival. Yes yes," he said.

I twisted my lips. We'd just had breakfast in the RSI cafeteria, and it would be irresponsible to just go off and eat more… but that silver cloret was burning in my coin pouch. I felt the need to go spend a portion of it somewhere.

Half an hour later, I was at a table to one side of a busy inn, having plowed through most of a greasy serving of eggs and fried potatoes. Chance sat next to my plate, nibbling on a crunchy piece of potato. He knew to duck into my lap anytime someone came too close to our table, but on a busy morning like this, few of the staff had time to care that I had a small rodent dining with me.

"Oh, that was good," I said, clutching my belly. The cafeteria didn't serve fare like this usually. A Mouse could get used to the freedom of spending her wages around the city.

Until now, I'd done pretty good with saving the clorets, having Chance squirrel them away for me.

On second thought, maybe the clorets were better spent for food in my belly rather than getting lost when Chance forgot where he hid them.

"We have plenty of time before the meeting still," I said mostly to myself.

"More food?" Chance suggested. I had the feeling this mouse would eat until he was round, if given the chance. And honestly, so would I.

I thought aloud. "Hmm, we could go see the others at their apprenticeships. But I don't want to feel like the odd one out in a group as smart-like as Fariq and his new friends. Margot's assignment is with fancy noble kids, so they won't want to see the likes of us... Maybe we could visit Carmen. Her cousins were cute."

Chance cocked his head, rounded ears twitching. "Or we visit my family home, yes yes?"

He occasionally talked about living in a fairy house with his hilariously large family before we met. I pictured myself sitting close to it and getting swarmed by dozens of friendly mice. "Gods, yes. Where's your old home?" I asked.

Before he could say anything, I felt a touch of sadness, a hint of his emotions that was there and gone in an instant.

"I don't remember. Patches and nice boy bring me to you long time ago now."

My brows drew in confusion. "Nice boy?" I echoed.

He bobbed his entire body. "Nice boy bring treats, earn friendship with whole family, then bring Patches. She took me to you."

I asked a few questions about this "nice boy," but Chance seemed to have forgotten most of the details about him. He hid under my napkin when a barmaid came by to scoop up my plate, which I paid for. After I had my eight single cloret coins in change tucked away, Chance peeked up at me. "I remember he say he work at pet shop," he offered.

"Excuse me," I called to the barmaid, a little louder than usual. She came back to my table. "Is there a pet shop nearby?"

She gave me directions to the closest one, which had set up in a former inn. "We were just much higher quality and ran the last owners out of town. No bedbugs here, besides," she concluded. I slipped her an extra cloret coin and headed to it, hoping to find Chance's nice boy and no bedbugs.

The cobblestone street narrowed as I walked, a sign the shop was along one of the small tributaries at the very tail end of the main market street. The slums that hosted the Shadowed Market would be a stone's throw away, and I kept an eye out for any drifter signs suggesting when the next one would be.

I eventually spotted a chalk marking no bigger than my fist on the side of a building, with symbols for month and day —the next market would take place on a weekend, two weeks from now. Mistress Reni would have my head if I tried to attend it during daylight hours, if today's reaction was any indication.

Our destination was indeed an inn-shaped building, two-stories high with a distinctive pointed roof. It sat at a street corner, ready to host non-human guests for the night with a name like Little Wonders Pet Shop on a faded sign out front. I walked up an access ramp built of fresher wood than the rest of the building and entered a paradise.

I immediately went to the first kennel, where a curly-furred dog alternated between barking and whining at me. It wagged its tail as I kneeled down. "Who's a good doggy, huh? Look how cute you are," I cooed.

Someone cleared their throat, and Chance climbed from my shoulder, up my ponytail, to perch atop my head and balance on his back feet, presumably holding his front paws out to the stranger. "It's nice boy!" he exclaimed. Then he hesitated. "I think it nice boy. But humans all look the same, big and slow."

I looked up to see a lanky boy beaming at me. "Hello! Are you looking to adopt today?" he asked.

I cleared my throat and stood straight, a little embarrassed to be caught fawning over the first dog I'd seen. Where an inn's main room would've been was full of pets in cages and kennels along the walls and set up in neatly stacked rows. A few other people browsed the cages and spoke to a second young teen, while an older couple were in deep discussion in the back of the room with a man in a wheeled chair.

"No, I was just...looking for you, actually," I said, fidgeting with my fingers while Chance bobbed with excitement atop my head.

The boy's gaze drifted to my hairline, and his mouth dropped open. "Is that... Hey, little buddy. I see you found a friend."

"It *is* nice boy!" Chance chattered.

"I'm Thomas." He offered his hand for a shake. I introduced myself and Chance, taking his hand. "Is it just Chance? Most mice like him have very long names."

"No, it was..." I furrowed my brow, trying to remember how to pronounce his full name. "Chauncey Balenciaga the Seventh."

"Gods." Thomas shook his head and laughed happily. He had a friendly smile, though he also had a bad case of acne. He was fair-haired and had the kind of milky skin tone that only burned when exposed to sunshine. The patches of red and pink on his arms and knees suggested he went outside often, despite that.

"Can you take us to the fairy house where you found Chance's family? He's forgotten where it was." I clasped my hands.

"Oh, of course! But...I'm supposed to be working right

now. I'll ask my dad." He hooked his thumb toward the back of the room and edged in that direction. "C'mon, he's going to want to see Chance."

We waited to see the man in the wheeled chair, who turned out to be a Tulari. I'd met only a few mages in my life, but I thought there was something off about his healer-green mark. I couldn't put my finger on why, though.

Once he was done speaking to the older couple about their cat, he turned his chair toward us. I didn't miss the quick once-over he did, taking in my RSI uniform with a cautious expression, before noticing the mouse still perched on my head. He squinted.

"Remember when Patches came through looking for a special mouse, Dad?" Thomas asked.

"Ah, yes." A warm smile crossed the Tulari's face. At that moment, I saw a clear resemblance between him and Thomas. He introduced himself as Fletcher, the veterinarian who owned Little Wonders Pet Shop, and borrowed Chance to inspect him with magic. It was a free checkup, something Fletcher apparently did with every animal brought to him.

I had a late realization that they both knew what a little wonder was. It was even in the shop's name. "You know Patches?" I asked Thomas.

"Yeah! She's friends with my dad. His magic gives him the ability to talk to any animal." Thomas read the immediate and acute jealousy I felt when my face gave it away and nodded in agreement. "I wish I had it, too. But I do my best with the animals, despite not having magic."

I wet my lips. He spoke proper Altarian, so I doubted he'd understand Uncommon. Not that there was an established metaphor for what I was trying to ask, so I went with a clumsy, "But do you *know* Patches?"

He scratched his head, looking at me askance. For a moment, I figured he thought I was strange, hard of hearing, or both, then he answered, "I've taken her collar off a time or two. We can talk more freely once my dad gives me the go-ahead to take you to see Chance's family."

I figured that was wise, considering there were a few strangers within earshot. I watched Fletcher run his wand over Chance nose to tail-tip, the tool glowing with a green outline. He poked the mouse's shoulders and belly with it before nodding in satisfaction and scratching him behind the ears.

"He's a healthy young male nearing adulthood. Have you given any thought to his profession?" Fletcher asked as he handed me back my mouse.

"His profession?" I echoed.

Thomas jumped into the conversation quickly. "I can explain it to her, Dad. Chance wanted to go back and see his family but doesn't remember where the fairy house is. Do you mind if I take a break and show Heather where to go?"

Fletcher stroked his chin in consideration. "All right. When you get back, you give your sister a break through lunchtime."

Thomas beamed and nodded, turning and holding his arm out like he was about to take my hand. I eased away from him enough that he gave me a good-natured tap instead, and I clenched my teeth to hide my flinch. "C'mon, it's not too far," he said.

We passed by the girl who was working here too, and Thomas jumped to introduce us when she was between customers. "Shauna, this is Heather. She has a small beast," he said, pointing to Chance on my shoulder. She looked at him and made a small gasp. "And Heather, this is Shauna, my sister."

"Nice to meet you," I said.

"You too," she said to me once she'd twinkled her fingers at Chance. Shauna was also about my age, dark-skinned, with her hair pulled back in two knots. She wore a brown apron with the pockets weighed down by the outline of several things, and her worn pants were patched over at the knees with colorful fabric.

"You're leaving?" she asked Thomas with a hint of envy.

"Yeah, but you get lunch." He elbowed her playfully and walked backward, waving to her with both hands. She mirrored the gesture with a little pout.

Chance twinkled the digits on his paw back at her as I followed Thomas. "You're absolutely going to melt Margot if you do that to her," I whispered to him, and he perked up. "Just don't do it to strangers. They'll notice your thumb."

Thomas circled his hand so I would hurry and keep pace with him as we set down the street, back the way I'd come. "You must have questions, huh?"

"You know about little wonders," I blurted.

"Sure do. Though they call themselves 'small beasts,' which is what we say in front of most everyone who doesn't have a Link with one," he explained. "The second floor of the shop has special rooms for any little wonder who needs a place to stay to heal an injury or have babies in peace. It's a safe place for them."

"That's amazing," I said earnestly. How did I not know of this shop sooner? Patches should've told me about it, at the very least.

"Isn't it?" he asked with the same level of enthusiasm as I felt.

As we joined a road with more foot traffic, Thomas lowered his voice. "My dad has a small beast as well, but Shauna and I are waiting to meet our Linked partners. When they're not Linked yet, apparently the little wonders can sense the level of potential in people. Those with a small amount of potential stay without a beast, but the more they have, the bigger and grander their beast, up to gryphons and rozash and such."

"Oh…I must not have had much," I said, feeling a little

weird for a moment that I had such a small little wonder. Which was silly. I loved Chance.

He put his palms up and said quickly, "You have more than many people and a proper Link. And you're what, twelve? That's amazing. Chance is going to be around for the rest of your life."

"Fourteen," I corrected, feeling my cheeks heat.

"Right, well, I'm close to you. I turn fourteen in a couple months, as does Shauna. We were born a day apart." He stole an awkward glance at me. "Um, Shauna's adopted."

Yeah, I'd figured that out almost immediately. But I gave him the benefit of the doubt, considering he was probably like me...preferring animals to people. "I'm part of a big adopted family of all sorts of folk," I offered.

"That's neat." He flashed a thumbs-up. "I was going to talk to you about something else, though. What was it? Oh, professions! It's a carpenter mouse thing."

Chance perked his ears, listening intently.

"When they come of age, carpenter mice pick a human job and wear something to show their profession. It's usually nothing elaborate, as they can't make themselves detailed uniforms or anything. Wild mice just scavenge something and wear it. It's really cute," he explained, gesturing throughout. "Mostly, they're builders or gatherers of some kind, useful jobs to their families. When Chance reaches maturity, he will want to pick a job too, if he hasn't already."

"Have you?" I asked the mouse directly.

"No no," Chance answered, sounding confused. "I not remember this, but maybe I do same job as my dad, since I have same name as him."

"He's still thinking about it," I translated to Thomas.

He accepted that answer and chattered about the pet shop and its many visitors while we crossed the market towards a neighborhood. The building style looked familiar... We were close to where Carmen's aunt lived, only coming at the rows of buildings from the opposite side of RSI.

I listened intently to Thomas, still thinking he lived and worked in a paradise. He promised to let me visit the second floor as a trusted friend, considering I was already Linked to a little wonder. The real danger the animals were hiding from were those who would force Links on them or use them for their varied magics. All little wonders had something, from my carpenter mouse with his thumb and the spark of intelligence to use it, to the winged feligryphs hiding in plain sight around the city and beyond.

We eventually stopped at a patch of grass and trees that grew at the end of two rows of houses. Nestled between the trees were a set of tiny homes covered in cheerfully hued paint. Certain folk made and decorated these to attract fairies, but the tiny buildings were perfect homes for carpenter mice families.

Chance's pointed nose was a-twitch, his head swiveling around and soon bobbling with overwhelming excitement. "This is it! Home!" he squeaked. He barely let me put him down, jumping from my palm halfway to the ground to land, shake himself, and scamper the rest of the way into one of the fairy houses.

Thomas handed me a pouch. "We should sit. Trust me," he whispered behind a hand. I did so with him and looked in the pouch, which was full of seeds.

"You just have this?" I asked, echoing a question my crew had asked me many times.

"You never know when you need treats in the shop," he answered cheerfully. Well, I guess I was adding a couple more pouches to my utility belt, because I, too, wanted to be prepared to offer food to small friends.

The fairy home was quiet for a while before I heard squeaking. A *lot* of squeaking. Chance scampered out alone and investigated the new pouch I held, happily accepting a seed to nibble on. "Family want hear about adventures and you, yes yes. But they know nice boy bring treats. They say we have treats and talk. It take long time maybe. That okay?" He fixed me with his cutest face, complete with dark button eyes.

"More than okay. You need time with your family," I said.

He bobbed and scampered off, bringing back his family to spend time with us. Mice came flooding out of the fairy home...far more mice than I thought it could hold. I had the biggest smile as I distributed seeds and chatted with Thomas while Chance told stories. Chance's more curious family members climbed all over both of us, the boldest jostling to sit in my palm for pets.

Thomas watched it happen and eventually said, "You're a natural at this. Have you considered going into veterinary work? When your stay at the reform school is done, of course."

I glanced at my uniform and sighed. I wish they'd given me veterinary work as an option. Now that would be an apprenticeship I'd excel at.

CHAPTER 11

DRIFTING

I RELUCTANTLY BID Thomas and the Balenciaga carpenter mouse family goodbye to head to the briefing on the upcoming competition day. Chance radiated happiness from his place on my shoulder on the walk back to RSI and upstairs to the Aldridge Hall classrooms. He was abuzz with snippets of stories from the doings of his wild siblings, only quieting once we were inside the school.

My crew had been assigned a briefing in A203, Miss Liang's room. She was at the chalkboard, putting the finishing touches on the words "Signpost Competition" written in an elaborate, looping style. Miss Barrios was also there, fussing with a sheaf of parchment at the podium.

I scanned the room hopefully. Vance waved to me from the back of the room. There were two other clusters of rival intermediate teams, and I recognized Sybella's group first, SHINA. Named after each member's first initial, they were a girls-only team I saw all the time.

On the other side of them was Whisper, another team that'd been promoted to intermediate at the start of this school year. I'd admired their leader, Ross, for his cleverness in Innovation class and noted that Whisper seemed to have a mix of talents like Five & Chance did.

Everyone in this room was about the same age, and Sybella and Ross had their full teams in attendance. A blush stung my cheeks as I took a seat next to Vance. Maybe I was overreacting, but I thought it had to reflect poorly on me that half my team was absent...but they were busy. Fariq had thought he could get permission from his master builder to come, though clearly, he'd been told no. Carmen had flat-out refused to interrupt her weekend, while Margot had patted my shoulder and said, "I can't this time, darling. But I know you will keep me informed."

I took in the board again before glancing at Vance with a sigh. Signpost was Uncommon for drifter signs, and a certain someone wasn't allowed outside of RSI's four walls. "What's that look for?" he whispered.

"This competition is going to be in the city," I said.

"Well, of course. They all are." It took him a couple second before realization hit. "Miss Barrios made an exception last time."

My lips twisted doubtfully. That'd also been the day we'd set him loose. She wouldn't make the same mistake twice. "I'll ask her," I said anyway.

The briefing started as the city bells finished ringing in the hour. "Hello, Littles," Miss Barrios said, nodding to Vance and me at the back of the room.

"Good afternoon, apprentices," Miss Liang added more formally to the other two teams.

Miss Barrios adjusted her papers one more time and began reading directly from one with stilted formality while the other adult started sketching symbols on the board underneath the competition's name. "We're so glad you can be here with us at this hour. There are going to be times in your careers when the Crown needs you when it's inconvenient to your schedule. Especially for those of us who are not selected as full-fledged spies. Please put any quills or journals away. From here on out, briefings will increasingly resemble meetings with informants. Be present and attentive to get all the information you need to successfully carry out your mission."

I gulped a nervous swallow and sat straighter in my chair. Vance slowly put his journal away. "Try to memorize the symbols, and we'll write them down after this," I said to him in an undertone.

"All right, boss," he muttered.

"Our first competition day of the year represents a reset of team rankings. If you and your team do well, your reward is a higher placement on the ranking board," Miss Barrios explained once all signs of journals and ink vanished. I used my thumbnail to indent the symbols on the board into the skin of my inner arm while she talked.

"The higher your placement, the more likely your team will be invited to audition for one of the limited spots in the advanced cohort. Do well tomorrow, and you may earn the Spymaster's attention. Yes?" She gestured to Ross, who'd raised his hand.

"Will we be competing tomorrow with teams like Davit's Day, who have been intermediate level for a few years?" he asked.

"A good question. Yes," she said. My eyelid immediately twitched. "Since you all are new to the intermediate cohort, you will be given an hour head start. However, intermediate is where many teams sit for years, so it's a guarantee that those teams have an advantage even if we randomize the components of this challenge each time. All the better for your team to stand out if you do well!"

Miss Liang finished writing the symbols, ten in total, and stepped up next to the other adult. "Once this reset happens, rankings will update more regularly with the usual considerations: academics, team synergies, and mentor reports," she said.

"Now, for the competition…"

Together, they explained we would look for the ten drifter signs in the order they'd been written and told us the boundaries for how far from RSI we should roam in search of them. Multiple buildings would have the same sign.

With our grasps of Uncommon and our wits, we were to survive the day and bring back a token from each of the ten stops. The other hint they dropped was that the last location would be an inn with rooms for us to stay in—and if we failed to find it by sundown, we were to return to RSI to rest.

After a round of questions, we were dismissed, and I gestured urgently for Vance to come into the hall with me. We rounded a corner into Hawthorne Hall, and I presented him with my forearm and the symbols still indented into my skin. In some places I'd pressed too hard and would have symbol-shaped scabs, but it was a small price to pay once Vance had them copied down with ink and paper.

"Good thinking," he said.

"Thanks. I'm going to go talk to Miss Barrios now," I said, fidgeting with my fingers for a moment. "Do you want to wait here for a few minutes?"

He raised a brow. "Go talk about me, I guess. I doubt it'll make a difference whether or not I'm there."

I hated the traces of bitterness in his voice, knowing I'd feel the same way if I were stuck between RSI and Madam Morashi. I peeked back into A203, where neither adult had left. Miss Liang was erasing the symbols from the chalkboard, while Miss Barrios unerringly met my gaze the moment I looked at her.

"Yes, Heather?" she asked.

I eased into the room and shut the door, giving myself a little pep talk in my head as I inspected the ground. This was Miss Fox, the same person who'd given me a key to Tower A and been one of the few adults in my life to be kind without strings attached. Well, maybe that last part wasn't quite true… There were expectations at RSI, things I couldn't put my thumb on but *felt* myself being guided toward. Even though she was a part of it, she still seemed to genuinely care about me.

I looked up, noting Miss Liang's impatient glance and Miss Barrios still waiting calmly for me to find my words. "Will Vance be allowed to join Five & Chance for tomorrow's competition?" I asked.

The subtle shift of her expression answered before she even opened her mouth. "The last time he left RSI, he returned to Morashi Venom. We cannot risk him doing it again," she said.

"But—" I blurted. The exclamation lingered in the air, preceding facts I hadn't meant to say aloud. "He went back to help me save Jackie. We destroyed his contract with Madam Morashi together. He *can't* go back again."

She was unmoved, already shaking her head. "And yet he has produced no information since his return to help us apprehend his fellow gang members or the madam herself."

"I don't think he can," I said more quietly.

Shivering once from remembering his terror of Madam Morashi, I added, "He's afraid. You're punishing him for being scared."

Miss Liang cleared her throat. "It is not only a punishment," she said in her usual businesslike tone. "If Vance leaves RSI and his former gang apprehends him, they will eliminate him for being compromised."

Cold trickled down my back. "He's a formshifter," I argued with little fire.

"The same as a quarter of the Morashi mages, as far as we know. They will know how to identify him. And they will capture you and the rest of your team alongside him," Miss Liang said. Her dark, serious stare bored into my skull. "No child taken by the Morashi is seen again. You should ask him why."

Miss Barrios jolted. "There's no need for such a grim conversa—"

"You're coddling them, Sasha," the other adult argued. "If Five & Chance is going to keep Vance on their team, they should know exactly the evil he's seen. Because they are on the course to see it for themselves."

"Vance has knowledge that will help us. He is a spy candidate as much as the rest of his teammates, maybe the most important intermediate student we have! Once he talks, we will have the information to remove Madam Morashi at last!" Miss Barrios exclaimed.

"Listen to how obse—" Abruptly, Miss Liang cut herself off and turned to me. She sighed and scrubbed her face. "The answer is no, Heather. Vance remains here for the competition. Don't worry, you'll have more opportunities to improve your rank. Have fun tomorrow."

That was as clear a dismissal as any, and I left with my ears burning. Vance sat in the empty hallway where I'd left him, looking up with a brief flash of hope.

"They said no. You have to stay here for your own protection," I said. That optimistic spark guttered out just as quickly as it'd ignited. "And they want me to ask you about the kids that…"

I drifted off when he stood and shoved a torn piece of parchment at me. On it were the ten symbols we'd recorded.

"The kids that what? Disappear because of the Morashi?" He barked a laugh. "No, I don't want to talk about that. Not with anyone, not even you. Good luck, I guess."

He left me holding those symbols, storming off toward Irving Hall and, undoubtedly, the boy's dorm. There was a sinking feeling in my chest, like I'd swallowed a large stone and it threatened to get stuck midway down.

Chance, a silent observer still sitting on my shoulder, released an upset squeak. I nodded in agreement.

The implications of everything I'd overheard were still

settling on my shoulders. I felt alone, and not just because Vance had had an outburst and left. He was the only one of my crew to show up to the briefing. After all this, I doubted he would again. Add in the way the adults were talking, and we might lose Vance completely. He'd be shut in this school until the day he squealed, which might be never.

We needed him, no matter how dangerous it might be to be outside of RSI with him. He was still a loyal crew member, and without him…well, I saw what happened with most crews. You lose a member, and suddenly the group doesn't have the synergy it used to. Everyone else starts looking for a new place to be. I feared Five & Chance would be the same way and we'd drift apart.

There was no RSI for me without the friends I'd made, who'd put aside everything to help me when I needed it most. If we disbanded, there went my chance to become a spy. I didn't want to start over with a different crew. It wouldn't be the same if it wasn't Five & Chance advancing together.

I RAN FACE-FIRST INTO IVAN, one of Davit's quieter teammates. He had intentionally swerved in my way, and I was barely paying attention, too busy wondering if my crew was going to skip dinner since no one was at our table yet and the sun was nearly set. RSI's doors magically locked at sundown, even for those of us with the clearance to come and go from the school.

So, I looked up just in time to see we were going to collide and then bounced off of Ivan, staggered by our size difference. "Watch where you're going, rat lover," he muttered. With that insult, I didn't feel so bad that I'd reflexively reached into his coin purse and withdrawn more clorets than I'd expected.

I sat at my crew's table on my own and ate from my dinner tray without really tasting it. Suspecting a trick, I looked in my fist and counted seven single cloret coins. The last time Davit's Day had tricked me, the coins had been wood painted gold. It was more about the message—they knew I was a pickpocket and countered their typical trick of running into me by taking their money or slipping something less pleasant in their pockets.

But these coins all seemed normal. They were metal and stacked up in a neat tower, rather than having the imperfections of counterfeits.

"What are you doing?"

I startled and looked up. Fariq was sliding into the seat next to me with a meal, Vance on his heels. I beamed with an odd sense of relief. It wasn't like the crew was already disbanded or my dreams of us becoming advanced, and then spies, were dashed. We might've all been busy with our own things, but we still ate at the same table most nights.

Then I remembered he'd asked me a question. "Um, just counting my money," I said.

A tray dropped on my other side, preceding Carmen as she pulled the chair with more force than necessary and fell into it with an aggravated sigh. She noticed my attention on her and jerked her chin in greeting. I mirrored her without thinking.

The cloret on top of my coin tower fell with a clatter. I toppled the rest and spotted Margot sashaying her way over to us, chattering away with an unfamiliar girl before reaching our table. She fluttered her hand in farewell as her friend left and sank into the spot next to Carmen. "Do try not to frown so," she said to the scowling girl. "You'll get wrinkles in unfortunate places."

"Don't start with me right now," Carmen muttered back. She gave her mashed potatoes a moody stab with a fork.

My crew was quiet for a moment too long. I could just picture Margot continuing to chatter about wrinkles or Vance asking what kind of unfortunate places the wrinkles would go, but they didn't. No one seemed to be in a good mood.

I ducked my head and turned over each of Ivan's clorets to inspect for imperfections, the last test before they became mine to squirrel away. I still had no answer for what would keep my crew together. This year had already made us over-worked and weary, more on edge than ever.

"I'm sorry I missed the meeting today." Fariq spoke up first. "What do I need to know about it? Vance would not say."

"I'm not allowed to go," Vance said in a low tone, his hand making a fist around his own fork.

I turned over one of the last clorets again, uttering a "huh." Instead of answering his question, I offered it to Fariq and pocketed the rest. "Look, it's a misprint." I cracked a little smile. This was the kind of find I'd lived for as a Menagerie kid. Collectors paid more for misprints than the coins were originally worth.

Fariq took it and turned it over. One side had the likeness of King Cortes and a bold **1** surrounded by a raised circle. The other side had Altare's symbol of a gryphon rampant, but this one was stamped at the wrong angle, only noticeable when compared to the front.

He held it closer to his face after a moment. "It is… moving?"

"Huh?" I asked.

Turning his wrist, he showed me the symbol side, and it *was* moving, the whole gryphon rampant slowly swiveling half a knuckle length to one side and back. I scrubbed my eyes, but it was still in motion when I looked again.

"Let me see that," Vance said. He discreetly slipped his wand into his lap from its hiding place up his left sleeve.

Fariq passed it to him, and once he saw it, Vance put his wand back with a soft laugh. Resting the cloret in the center of his palm, he waved it back and forth. "It's a compass spell. Very simple magic. Where'd you get it?" he asked.

I felt a little cold drop roll down my spine as four pairs of curious eyes turned my way. "I acquired it," I hedged.

Vance raised an unimpressed brow. "Yes, from who?"

The little wheels in my mind were turning overtime. "Um, Ivan. I think he ran into me on purpose so I'd pick his pockets."

"Heather," Fariq said in a chastising tone.

"I know, I know. I've become too *predictable*," I scoffed. He had an expression that told me my predictability wasn't what he was disapproving of. "Compass spells are when two items point toward each other, right?"

Items enchanted with compass spells were amongst the most common magical knickknacks. I'd once had a woven bracelet with a single wooden bead that would point at its match, which I'd given to Jackie, just in case. She'd lost her matching bracelet shortly before the spell faded. It didn't last longer than a couple months.

Vance nodded. "He probably has an identical cloret that's pointing at this one. You can see the notch by the gryphon's leg right here." He indicated it with his fingernail, and then we passed it around.

There was a line that looked like normal wear and tear on a cloret next to the rearing gryphon rampant. It was almost like its birdlike front foot was pointing.

Musty devils, I'd been careful, and I'd still only noticed the compass spell with some luck. "Davit's Day wanted to track us tomorrow," I said mostly to myself. Dread grew like a living thing in the pit of my stomach as I imagined all the possibilities for why they would.

"And why does the likes of Davit's Day want to put a tracker on you?" Margot asked.

I took the enchanted coin and put it in my pocket for now, separate from my ordinary money. Swallowing thickly, I felt myself blush. "I started it."

I told them how Wyatt and Davit had followed me to my special session with Miss Barrios a couple of days ago and cornered me. "I used some Tosh Zorena to knock them over and ran. So, they must want to continue what I started with a more serious fight," I summarized after talking about the hair pulling and mentioning vaguely that they'd threatened me.

I didn't want to say "rat" in front of Fariq. The animal he represented may still elude me, but in the meantime, I didn't want him internalizing that insult instead.

"You can't just say 'some Tosh Zorena' and not give me details," Carmen demanded.

"Oh, sorry. It was very fast." I went back over the fight with her and named the moves I'd used. The sullen mood she'd brought to this table evaporated like mist in sunshine, replaced by, well, more traditional anger.

"I can see why you ran, but you should've shown those boys a real lesson first. If you'd used a scorpion tail strike instead to give Wyatt a black eye..." She sighed, nearly wistful at the lost opportunity. "Oh well. It will be five-on-two rather than two-on-one tomorrow, but I still like our odds."

"You're not *fighting* tomorrow," Vance scoffed. "Throw the stupid cloret down a sewage drain during your hour head start."

Both of Fariq's eyebrows raised. "So you were paying attention at the meeting. Also, I am in rare agreement with him. You should get rid of it."

"Hey, it's not weird that we agree on something—" Vance protested.

"I never turn down a fight—" Carmen said overtop him.

Margot cleared her throat primly. "If we could stop bickering for a moment, I have an idea." Everyone stopped talking and turned to listen to her. "Why don't we tie it to Chance?"

The mouse, who was nibbling on a morsel from my tray, looked up with a startled squeak.

Vance and I exchanged a glance. "Give 'em the runaround," I said.

He nodded in agreement. "The perfect decoy to mess with their heads."

Margot clapped briefly with delight. "And while they're distracted, we can go about the competition like nothing is amiss. Perhaps now it's a good time to explain what we'll be expected to do, darling."

CHAPTER 12

A TOKEN SLICE

"I KNOW it's last minute, but we could really use your help," I said to Patches early the next morning. I'd picked an out-of-the-way study nook on the second floor of the library to meet with the librarian's feligryph.

It'd turned into a briefing. Patches sprawled like a queen in her true form and listened to me talk about the competition and Davit's Day while Chance translated her trills and meows. He was a little offended I sought her out to protect him, but he was still a little mouse going off on his own in city streets full of feral cats and other predators.

In the end, Patches flushed her whiskers forward happily. "She says she help us. And she knows exactly what to do," Chance chattered.

I pet the cat in appreciation, and she took advantage, rolling so I scratched an itch on her neck that she couldn't reach. With her true form's size, her purr hit a deeper register that vibrated pleasantly through me.

She ended up draped over my lap as I pulled the Eye of Acuity out of Chance's pouch and whispered over it, "Nothing is beyond my reach, with this Eye I unleash the power to watch…Wyatt Freeman."

The glowing blue eye that refracted from the opal pendant watched me for several seconds. Had it sensed my indecision over which member of Davit's Day to track? The longer it stared, the more I expected it to reject my request and go dormant.

Eventually, the ring of magic expanded to the edges of the opal, and its surface became a tiny, moving version of Wyatt. I held it to my right eye, and the magic pulled me into the scene with him as an invisible observer, watching what he was doing over his right shoulder.

He was walking down a hall, a towel slung over one shoulder, and spoke to someone I couldn't see. "You know this is the easiest competition at RSI," he was saying.

"Yeah, but I don't want to lose our place at the top because you're embarrassed," Davit's voice replied.

I pulled myself out of the scene as easily as shutting my right eye. I had an idea about how this tool of power worked and tested it by holding it to my left eye instead. Now I was looking over Wyatt's left shoulder, seeing Davit next to him in sleep-rumpled clothes. In the process of transferring sides, I'd missed how Wyatt had replied, and Davit was speaking again. "You have to admit, it was impressive. Maybe having a kid her size lay us out is a sign that we should leave her and her team alone."

"What are you *talking* about?" Wyatt said with indignant fire. "If she's getting better at self-defense, then so is that Lithosian rat she spends all her time with. The school made a mistake letting in and training one of our enemies! And this… today, this is our chance to show them they don't have what it takes. They'll be begging Manny to let them leave RSI once we're done with them."

So that's his thought process. The most surprising part was the hesitation on Davit's face before he nodded in agreement.

"The longer the rat's here, the more of our skills he'll take back to Lithos," he said.

"Exactly." Wyatt nudged his side. "She's carrying the cloret as we speak. It shouldn't take too long to teach her team a lesson. We'll just do what we did last year for the competition."

Davit nodded in agreement. They were heading into the boys' bath, so I quickly pulled away from the Eye and stored it before I saw anything else. Chance and Patches both gave me curious looks. I had my thinking face on, lower lip caught between my teeth.

I pulled the spelled cloret out of my pocket and tucked it into the tiny harness Fariq had made last night in the innovation lab. It was made of discarded leather straps and slipped around Chance's body to place the coin against his belly. It was a snug fit but wasn't so tight that he couldn't wiggle out of it if it got snagged on something.

"We're on," I said.

My crew and I stood in a huddle close to the Whisper team, waiting for the city bells to chime so we could set off. Patches sat next to my ankle, chirping occasionally to Chance, who sat in the divot of fluff on her neck made by her collar. He chattered back to her, usually an out of context, "yes yes" or "Think once we confuse humans, we find good food?"

The chubby cat's returning meow sounded agreeable.

While we waited, Vance was probably getting started on his potion making for the day. He'd been in better spirits when I'd seen him in passing. It was hard to tell just from his smile and cheerful "good morning," but it seemed something about him had changed overnight.

But because he had to stay behind, we were at a disadvantage. I observed the other intermediate-level teams around us, counting mostly teams of five and six members. If they went for the same strategy I'd decided on, they could cover up to a third more ground than Five & Chance.

We were splitting up, going in the four cardinal directions for our hour head start before rendezvousing in front of a hattery a few blocks away that, according to Margot, was "impossible to miss." Fariq had copied the symbols we were looking for onto three new sheets of parchment so all of us could reference them.

I knew we could rely on him to see a pattern in the designs. Where I saw vague shapes, he noticed things half-outlined. The first symbol was either half an apple, according to him, or a C with a dot over it, which was still all I saw. Either way, I was going to check any fruit carts I passed for drifter signs.

I'd also brought along an empty canvas sack for carrying any tokens I found. I wasn't sure how the instructors would make sure we gathered things in order and figured they wouldn't be able to, so the rules were suggestions, as always.

It was a relief the competition was happening instead of our usual classes. At least most of my team was here and as engaged as I was in winning. I'd missed having my crew, with our different strengths, all focused on the same task. We could get a lot done when given a push.

There were teachers dotted in amongst the tide of uniformed kids that flowed out onto the street as soon as the city bells chimed. Nodding to my crew and mouthing "good luck," I struck out toward Kaiamear's docks in my assigned direction, north.

My fingers twitched toward Chance's pouch, where the Eye of Acuity would still show Wyatt. They would have to wait an hour before coming outside, but maybe they were talking about the competition since they'd done it before.

Or maybe they were just chatting about how best to beat us up. Glancing down to ask Chance to look for me, I saw

Patches had already carried him out of sight. I had to trust they knew what they were doing.

I picked a section of market streets I'd walked dozens of times. In the past, my attention was on the body language of strangers, looking for people worthwhile to try to pickpocket. Drifter signs changed often, sometimes daily. After so long, all the ones I spotted seemed unfamiliar.

I stopped in front of my favorite combination shop, both a bakery and a confectionary, nose pressed almost to the glass to watch a worker stretch taffy and another ice a cake and top it with rosettes of buttercream. The steps up to the door were marked with an X to avoid. In a way, I saw why. All the finished sweets were lined behind display cabinets except for the cakes, which waited to be sold by the slice on glass cake stands. It'd be impossible to snatch anything without being noticed by the staff. Who tried to steal from a place like this anyway?

I licked my lips. Well, maybe a sugar-hungry Mouse would. I would come back later, once the sight of all these sweets wasn't a…distraction…

The windowsill had texture, which my fingertips brushed as I turned away. It'd been painted white, but someone had come along and added a symbol to it a couple knuckle lengths across in a light gray. A triangle and a dot…the ninth symbol.

I gaped at it, hardly believing my luck. Well, I had a reason to go inside after all and did so while holding my breath so my next inhale would be full of the sugary sweetness inside. The woman finishing up her cake looked up, took in my uniform, and sighed audibly. "Can I 'elp ya?" She spoke like I was used to, not proper-like.

My gaze darted around, but I saw nothing that could easily be a token to take with me other than some food. It occurred to me belatedly that we didn't ask enough questions about what a token was, accepting at face value Miss Barrios saying, "You'll know what to do when you get there."

Well, an unamused worker was now staring as she waited for me to say something. My eyelid twitched, but I approached the counter across from her, carefully positioning my hands so my leather bracelet with its pair of crossed keys was visible. I switched to my old street tongue to match her. "Ya missin' a key, mum?"

She glanced down, and a hint of something tugged at the corners of her lips. "Methinks I'll be seein' lots o' lost keys soon. Little early, innit? Pie's still in the oven."

My brows drew together as I turned over her words. A slice of pie usually referred to one's cut after a job. She was probably saying that whatever token I needed to get wasn't ready yet.

"Can't a girl flash some silver early?" I asked.

She flapped her hand dismissively. "Bring somethin' more entertainin'."

That seemed to be all she wanted to say, as she reached for the bag of icing to finish with her cake. "Wait," I blurted. "How much for a slice of cake?"

"REALLY, darling? It's so early for cake," Margot said, marking the barest of protests before she ate the piece I brought her. The confectionary had squares of white cake, perfect for eating with your fingers, though she made it look dainty somehow.

We'd met at the hattery she'd suggested, which was indeed impossible to miss with its bowl hat-shaped roof, and then gathered under the awning of a nearby café. The city bells had rung the hour five minutes ago, which meant

Davit's Day and the other veteran intermediate teams were now roaming the streets.

While I'd found the fourth and ninth symbols, plus some cake for all of us, the rest of my friends had been a little less successful. "I found the first location," Carmen said, lining up four apples on the table.

"I found something, I think, but the person I spoke to wouldn't sell me anything," Margot pouted.

We turned to Fariq, who was inspecting the grain of the table closely. He flipped his hands, palm up, mumbling in embarrassment.

"Did you get any hints?" I asked Margot.

She rolled her eyes. "Only how hungry that particular person was."

I hummed, considering the pieces of this puzzle that we had. "At the fourth location, they didn't want my clorets. One lady told me her son was bored," I said, still puzzled by that. "And at the ninth, she said she wanted something more interesting than money."

Fariq smacked the table hard enough to startle the rest of us. "What if we are meant to take the tokens to each shop for a trade?" he said excitedly.

I brightened for a moment before remembering a snag to this plan. "Yesterday they said to bring back a token from each stop…"

"Follow my logic," he said, shaking his head. "We start with apples. At the next stop, we trade apples for…where did someone tell you they were hungry?" He directed the question at Margot.

She quirked her lips, hooking her thumb toward the hattery.

"You trade apple for hat. Then the next stop, the hat goes for something else, until we reach the second-to-last stop." He gestured toward me.

"A pie," I guessed.

"We take pie to the inn, showing that we completed each trade along the way," he said.

I exchanged a glance with Carmen, who shrugged carelessly. "Sounds about right to me," she said.

That sounded far too easy. "And," Fariq added while I mulled it over, "that prevents cheating. Because, Heather, you would skip all of this to just take the pie to the inn if you could."

"Hey, don't single the pipsqueak out for that. I would too," Carmen said.

"As would I. It is a competition, after all," Margot sniffed.

Speaking of which...I checked the Eye of Acuity under the table. The tiny version of Wyatt had an apple in hand, tossing it up in the air carelessly as he walked down a street. It wasn't long before he passed the fruit off to one of his teammates and stopped by a shopfront. With a glance to either side of him, he pulled a cloret out of his pocket and scrutinized it.

I put the Eye away and sat up straighter. We needed to get moving. "Let's test your theory and find the second stop," I suggested to Fariq.

"Great, but where? It has been an hour, and we found four of ten spots," he pointed out.

I stood, and my crew followed me. First, I checked the hattery. It had the symbol for our seventh stop. "So, we have one, four, seven, and nine," I said aloud, disliking that spread. "We're gonna have to hoof it and hope for good luck."

I gave Fariq an apologetic look before striking off in the direction he'd been assigned, fairly sure he'd missed a sign or two. While I scanned the sides and fronts of the buildings we passed, I had Carmen keep an eye out for any member of Davit's Day. If they ran into us, then it didn't matter that we had a decoy set up with Chance and Patches.

Hopefully, she would also spot other teams that were more successful than us as we snaked around several busy streets. I noticed a few drifter signs in the meantime and started pointing out the most obvious ones to Fariq, who breathed out in relief. "They are so much smaller than I expected," he whispered.

I nodded in understanding. "They get painted over a lot if they're really obvious. Look," I said, slowing to show him the side of a building, where the bricks were covered in patches of paint here and there. Some stubborn person had chalked the signs for "danger" and "attack dog" on a brick close to the ground, so small we had to stoop to see them.

I directed my finger toward the patches where these marks were painted over multiple times. "Sometimes these are the only sign you need. I would never go in this shop," I told him.

"C'mon, you two," Carmen whispered, gesturing for us to come over to her. "This is our second stop."

"Well, maybe just this once," I hedged. Fariq was still chuckling while we went inside. It was a little oddities shop, with the promised "attack dog" panting happily when we passed by the doggy bed right beside the door. He was plump and black, with a graying muzzle and a wagging tail when I offered my hands for a sniff and lick.

I stood back and watched Carmen talk to the shopkeeper. She showed her bracelet by balling her fist and flashing the back of it toward him. Then she asked, "Are you hungry? I bought too many apples this morning."

Well, not as subtle as I'd handle it, but he still brightened and traded an apple for what looked like a pile of metal. We left together, and she dropped it into my hands. "Guess Fariq was right," she said.

"He usually is," I agreed, smiling his way before turning over our new acquisition.

It was a tangle toy. I barely glanced up for an entire block, following the footsteps of my friends, as I tried to disentangle one of the oddly shaped bars from the mix of them. I'd have done it, too, if Carmen didn't snatch it back out of my grip.

Right, the competition. With one last glance at the tangle toy, which disappeared into Carmen's pocket, I kept my eyes moving for any drifter signs we might be interested in. This included plenty of backward looks, as if Wyatt and his friends would appear between one blink and the next.

And do what? My thoughts sounded like Carmen today, confident that we were in a busy market and relatively safe because of it.

After we found the third stop, the fourth was one I'd already found—on the opposite side of the city. When faced with the choice between wandering more to find a different shop marked with the fourth symbol or going to the guaranteed location, we picked the latter.

The tangle toy became a battered version of the board game Circles of Power. Then when we finally got to our next location, we traded the game for a live rabbit. I felt bad a living creature was being dragged into this competition, too. As I peered into the cage at its frightened red eyes, Margot said, "I have a hunch about where to take this little cutie."

She took us to an animal rescue on the edge of the boundaries we were supposed to stay in. And she was *right*. It was the next stop. They gave us a ticket for one free sandwich at a nearby pub. Though we scoured all four of the pub's walls for the next drifter sign, it wasn't the next stop, but we had lunch there anyway and held on to the ticket.

My feet were hurting from the unusual amount of walking that we were doing. But at least we'd stopped long enough for me to check the Eye again, just to see darkness. I ducked behind Margot's fan and held the Eye to my face.

"Why would they be down here?" Ivan's question echoed strangely. I heard the slosh of someone wading through at least ankle-deep water.

"Maybe they know we're looking for them and are trying to lose us. Focus," Davit hissed.

I blinked and put the Eye away quickly, though I grinned

like a loon. "They're trying to find us, but they're very lost," I reported to my crew.

"Some good news, at least." Margot snapped her fan closed and used it to point at a nearby table. The girls of the team SHINA were there, giggling about something and passing around a pointed hat that wouldn't look amiss atop a pirate's head. By the hat alone, they were two steps ahead of us.

"They must've found a different hattery closer to this place," I thought aloud.

"We could try asking them?" Fariq suggested.

Margot shook her head. "They have no reason to tell the truth."

He pressed his lips together, looking quite disappointed.

"So, I've been thinking," I said.

"Oh, dangerous," Carmen said with a touch of sarcasm.

I leveled a dirty look her way. "I've been thinking about the other extra credit challenges. Maybe the lord mayor has a key to the city in his office. We could plan a heist of City Hall over a weekend and check," I said to a crowd of disinterested faces.

Margot summed up what the others must've been thinking with a shake of her head. "I don't think that's a good idea, darling. City Hall isn't the kind of place to enter unannounced."

Carmen and Fariq made noises of agreement.

I felt myself wilt. "Do you have a better idea of how we're supposed to get that key, then? Or impress Manny?"

"I'm sure we will have an opportunity in time," Margot said breezily.

"We're not going to get to the advanced tier just waiting for something to come along," I protested.

Carmen scoffed. "Who cares?"

I couldn't hide the hurt that crossed my face when Fariq nodded in agreement with her. He thought that way too? "I do," I mumbled. "I thought… We have to qualify as a team. I can't do it alone."

Margot patted me on the shoulder. I took comfort in the gentle touch and just barely avoided crying in front of my friends. Musty devils, how embarrassing that would be. Nearly as bad as caring so much about something they didn't.

"I've heard it takes most teams years to be noticed," Margot whispered. "Don't we have enough to worry about without adding the extra stress of an advanced team's duties?"

I sighed and nodded reluctantly, but I wasn't about to let go of the goal so easily. Maybe I was failing as a leader and just hadn't convinced them. Or perhaps I just needed to be more patient.

"One step at a time. First things first, we win this competition." Margot exaggerated a cheerful tone and gave me a little shake until I nodded and returned to my meal.

We wolfed down the rest of our food and hit the streets again. I located a second hattery and was glad to see the seventh symbol painted on one of its lowest roofing tiles. There *were* multiple locations for the same stop, as promised.

As we searched for the sixth symbol, I wondered how RSI had convinced the shopkeepers to run this competition. Would they speak Uncommon to us and make these trades if convinced with enough clorets beforehand? Or were all these shops run by sleepers and informants, former RSI kids willing to help train the next generation?

The sun was noticeably lower in the sky when we finally traded our free sandwich ticket for an already prepared and bagged meal from a different pub. The girl who made the trade sounded like she'd done this too many times already. "*Another* ticket. Wow. I *love* free sandwiches," she said sarcastically.

With an attitude like that, I would've kept the ticket if I could.

We rushed to trade the meal for a hat, and while it wasn't a pirate hat, it had a brightly dyed green feather at the top. I used the inside of it to hide the Eye, as I checked it one last time to make sure Davit's Day wasn't tailing us. And it was still pitch-black where they were, so I figured that was a good enough sign not to eavesdrop on them further.

Our journey took us to a small local theater, where the hat became another ticket, this time to admit one person to their upcoming production. I lead my crew back to the sweets shop, where the worker who was decorating a cake this morning was just about to lock up for the evening.

"Oh! Guess ya figured it out after all," she said, letting us into the shop to trade our ticket for something in a white box. She told us not to open it and pointed down a side street before we went our separate ways.

My walk was more like a trudge, but I followed where she'd indicated and saw the point of an inn roof against the waning daylight, not too far away. I led my crew in that direction and heard Margot behind me. "I do hope they have salts. My feet absolutely need a soak after this competition."

"You stick your feet in salt?" Carmen asked her, beating me to it.

Margot scoffed lightly. "No, darling. You should soak your feet with me. It is truly blissful."

"If you say so," the other girl said skeptically.

They followed me into the inn, which bore the last symbol right above the door frame. There was a small receiving area, where a wooden sign sat on the counter between us and an empty nook. "No Vacancies" it read. The bar was in full swing at this time of the evening, with someone strumming a lute and singing to fill the air not already occupied by clanking mugs and the chatter of gathered folk.

Margot tapped my shoulder and pointed. A single man occupied the closest table to the door. She'd seen under a layer of hair, disheveled clothes, and grime fast—it was the Spymaster in disguise, Manny. He met my gaze and lifted a mug in salute, but his index and middle fingers made a nonverbal signal we'd just covered in Language class. "One approach" was the sign.

I turned to my friends. "You all wait here for a minute," I suggested.

They idled with various levels of grousing, but I approached the Spymaster alone and sat across from him. "How'd it go, young lady?" he asked.

"We made it. I brought you this, sir," I said, sliding the white box over to him.

He brightened and produced a fork out of nowhere. "This really is the best day of the year," he murmured, opening the box and flattening its sides to reveal a slice of apple pie. It was clearly the end of a pie, where it collapses into a delicious pile, with cinnamon-flecked filling oozing out of the sides.

I shook my head in a quick jerk. All this to bring the Spymaster a little piece of pie? We could've baked him five whole pies in the time it'd taken to acquire that slice.

He cut a big bite with his fork and popped it into his mouth. "Mmm, yes. Drusilla makes the best pies. You and your team have passed. Good work."

Having the Spymaster smile and nod at me made me feel a little tingly. As rare as it was to see him, his acknowledgment was a scarce currency. It felt like I was finally on the right track this year...that Five & Chance could still make it in his good graces and earn a spot as an advanced team, if only we came together for more moments like this.

"Also, we rented out all the rooms we could tonight, but it seems we are one short." Using his mug again to hide the motion, he signaled for me to reach under the table. Our palms touched, and he passed me a key. "Whoever doesn't sleep there can always use the stables."

"Thank you, sir." I already longed for my familiar cot in RSI and wished it was an option tonight.

He chortled suddenly. I followed where he was looking, and my palms grew clammy when I noticed Carmen's stiff posture and Fariq's defensive one. Then my eyes skipped to the bedraggled quintet of young men that made up Davit's Day filing into the inn, each looking like they'd completed a much different challenge than the one my team had faced.

Their uniforms were splattered with crumbly stains up to mid-calf. The familiar signs of fatigue showed in the hollows of their eyes and the slump of their shoulders. Ivan had what looked like a thick wad of cobwebs in his hair. And Wyatt in particular looked like he'd been dragged backward through some muck, with mud flecking his shirt and the exposed skin on his arms and face.

He met my gaze and clenched his teeth, his finger stabbing toward me. Though my eyelid twitched at the vitriolic promise in that one motion, all I did was point toward Manny. I held in my laughter at their state with effort.

Davit stepped forward, panting like he'd just finished running here. My nose wrinkled when he stood next to me and slid a box toward the Spymaster. He reeked of body odor and a type of mustiness I'd recognize from twenty paces away as coming from the sewers.

"We made it," he gasped out.

Manny glanced down at the box and hummed. When he opened it, there was a perfect slice of apple pie resting on a sheet of confectioner's paper inside.

"You bought this." His tone was neutral, but he closed the box and slid it aside in favor of taking another bite from the piece I'd brought him. Then he circled his fork to encompass Davit and his friends. "What, exactly, were you doing today to show up in this state?"

Davit's eyes widened, and he glanced at me. I smiled back as innocently as I could muster, shrugging at him.

Chance's little scratchy claws made their way up my pant

leg. He collapsed into my palm under the table, a soft and warm presence waiting eagerly to tell me something.

"Well, suffice to say, you need a bath," Manny scoffed, breaking the awkward silence. "Return to the school. I'll send word to have you let in."

With a duck of his head, Davit muttered, "Yes, sir," and trudged toward his team. They filed out the door, and Carmen lowered her raised arm from the attack stance she'd assumed while they stood there waiting.

"You see boys? We did good job, yes yes," Chance whispered. He offered his fist, and I bumped it gently with my own.

"Yes, clearly. But…what did you do?" I murmured back to him.

His jaws gaped in a big yawn. "Patches friend do it. You take coin off me now?" He rested his head on my thumb, giving me his best button-eyed look.

I took off his harness and glanced up. Manny watched me pocket the enchanted cloret with his brow raised. "I would spend that if I were you," he suggested.

CHAPTER 13

STRUGGLING TOGETHER

Fariq chose to go to the stable for the evening upon hearing there was only one room for the four of us. And after seeing two cots set up in the small space, I went out there too. I'd much rather sleep on hay than on a bare floor.

This inn had a big stable, at least, with two rows of stalls, most of which were already occupied by horses. It felt more like home than I realized it would. I'd spent more than one night sleeping in a hayloft, when various jobs took me further from home than expected. But I found Fariq in a stall, half-hidden behind a pile of hay. I knocked on the stall door to get his attention.

"It's me," I whispered.

He sat up, muffling a yawn. "Is everything all right?" he asked.

"Yeah."

I sat on the pile of hay heaped beside and above him. He nodded after a moment, relaxing and easing onto his back again, hands behind his head.

"Have you slept in a hayloft before? It's a lot more comfortable than most folk think," I suggested.

He shook his head slowly. "I don't like high places."

"Like, *really* don't like them? Because it would be a lot safer than just sleeping on the—"

"Heather," he interrupted. "Do you realize what the challenge was today?"

I shifted to lie on my back too, inspecting the wooden ceiling overhead. "If you're askin' something like that, you already know the answer."

"A metaphor. We turned apples into apple pie."

"In the most drawn-out way possible," I grumbled.

"That's not the metaphor," he sighed. "Compare it to the job RSI is teaching us to do. Information, rumors, gossip. They are the apples. And in the end…"

"We give Manny a slice of apple pie," I said, uttering a soft "huh" as I fluffed my hay into a better bed and then let myself sink further into it. It smelled pretty fresh, a woodsy note that mingled well with the scent of horse that filled the stable.

A few minutes passed in silence. Right as I was wondering if he'd fallen asleep, he said quietly, "I think it might be time I left RSI."

I sputtered in surprise and whipped to look at him. "What?" I blurted.

He didn't quite meet my gaze, dark brown eyes unfocused, but a frown tugged at his mouth. "I am not cut out for work like we did today. And I keep causing the team trouble."

Musty devils, he was serious. "You haven't caused us a lick of trouble," I protested.

"No, I have. All the attention you've received from Davit's Day started because you defended me when you didn't have to. Now they are pulling your hair, making you feel unsafe in the hallway, and trying to track you. I'm sorry," he said sincerely.

For a moment, he caught me off guard. But of course Fariq

would apologize when he didn't have to. He was far too nice for his own good.

"Don't be sorry. You did nothing wrong. I would start this grudge all over again without hesitation. You're my *friend*," I said. I wish he knew how much that meant to me. "We got them back. I still don't know what Chance and Patches did, but they had a *terrible* day, you can tell."

His lips pressed together, but they still wobbled with emotion. He sniffed and said, "They will only get worse because of it."

"Then we will too," I said firmly.

That seemed to be the right thing to say, as he breathed a quiet "Thanks, Heather." And then he lay there thinking. If the little gears in my mind were a set of mouse wheels, his had to be proper cogs turning a vast machinery of thoughts and ideas.

I waited to see if there was anything else in there that he wanted to talk about, hopeful he wouldn't continue reasoning his way out of staying at RSI. If he left the school, Five & Chance would crumple. His smarts and sound logic kept us together.

Eventually, he seemed to decide he wanted to talk. His tone was more casual, with that edge of sleepiness that could so easily give way to thoughtful sadness. "I did not come to RSI for what it really teaches. Miss Liang convinced me it was my only option for a proper education. Have I told you the story?" he asked.

I practically itched with curiosity. "No. All I remember is you were pretty new when I arrived."

When we'd first met, he'd spoken more slowly, measuring his Altarian to make sure each word was correctly chosen and formed. I'd always wondered how he'd truly gotten to RSI. The best answer he'd given me was that he'd asked to come and study with Miss Liang.

"There are villages along the border between Altare and

Lithos that claim little interest in either side," he began. I clasped my hands over my belly, feeling like this was just the beginning of a longer story he now had the words to tell.

"It was not the easiest area to live in. The desert brought its storms, and crops struggled to take root in its soils. My village, we always headed north to trade with Altarians for the food we needed. We practiced traditional Lithosian methods to make the tradeable goods that helped us survive. Our tongue was of the desert, but we were not of the desert. Our ancestors were. Do you understand what I mean?"

"Yeah. But it sounds like you all were Lithosian in most ways," I pointed out.

"Except for the one way that really matters," he said gravely. "We lived north of the border, which means we were Altarian. Unknown to us, we lived in an area I now know is called 'rozash alley,' the most fought-over land between both countries."

Even I knew what rozash alley was, the treacherous slice of land several miles into Altare, where Lithosian rozash riders frequently invaded, looking to destroy crops, land, and buildings since the start of the war. My stomach dropped with the heavy weight of dread at what he'd say next.

He scrubbed his face with a muffled sigh. "My father is a potter, and my mother is a weaver. I took after them both and learned from them quick. I'd attempt to diagram something just for fun and then try to make it with clay, or the other way around. It didn't turn out as well as it does now with the proper parts." He released a little self-conscious laugh. "My parents knew I had talent, but they did not want me to leave the village. Their way of life was…small. Not an inch to the north or south, and money, politics, language, none of it mattered. Only what I brought to the shop."

"But you wanted more?" I guessed.

"I did. I wanted to go to Altarian fundamental school and read more books and see the world they described. I just wanted more." His lips twitched downward, and he tried multiple times to keep speaking, grief heavy from the memory he tried to recount. "But we had to lose everything for it to happen. And when fate arrived, it was so fast. One day, we thought it was a forceful wind—sand goes into everything when carried on the wind—but it became stronger still with the screams of rozash. A flight of them must've seen the village and attacked, dropping fire, acid, and more sand over our heads. The sound...the *smell*. It was vile. My family was lucky to be inside, even though our home was hit by a sand blast. It collapsed on top of us. If we were outside, though, the sand would've...well, let's just say it is as unkind a death as burning in fire or acid.

"I blacked out from getting hit in the head and woke being crushed by a heavy weight. There were voices all around, people crying or yelling. A team of people were digging in the rubble"—he swiped under his nose, his eyes shining—"and it was an Altarian gryphon rider who lifted me out of the rubble. I was cut up bad and covered in debris and sand, but that man and his flight helped save me, my family, and the other survivors of our village. That was when I really decided that I was Altarian."

"Your parents are alive," I murmured.

"They are. They don't live in Kaiamear, nor do my sisters," he said. Well, that explained how he'd ended up on his own. It didn't sound like it bothered him very much to be apart from them. "We were taken to a center for treating people like us. Those who didn't fight yet were hurt because of the war. Miss Liang was there, translating and doing interviews with us individually. She made RSI seem like a kind dream...a place where I could learn Altarian and explore my skills as far as I could take them. I wanted it so bad, and my parents wanted to move south again and start over. It was the greatest fight of my life."

"You won that fight, clearly," I said.

"I did. I get to learn, like I always wanted. And it has been a privilege. In the meantime, I help my family rebuild by sending them my apprenticeship wages. But RSI has also become something I did not know I was agreeing to. I want to be a builder, not...not someone who makes apple pie."

I considered and yawned. My body felt like it weighed double and my eyelids, triple. "In every crew, each member has their role. It's the same thing as, uh, a team of us baking apple pie. I know we're not supposed to say, but I'm on the stealth track." I dropped the admission to a whisper, as if Manny would pop out of the walls to admonish me for sharing classified information. "My role is to be myself, a sneak."

"My track is logistics," he said.

"I don't know what that word means. Logistics," I repeated, trying to get my mouth around it.

"Like planning or coordinating."

"Ah, see?" I shifted onto my side. "Your role isn't to bake apple pie."

He had a fine line between his brows. "It is to...prepare for the baking?" he said, clearly becoming confused.

I waved my hand. "Forget the Uncommon for a minute. You didn't like what we did today, did you? That's not your role in the crew."

"It was today," he said, his mouth now set mulishly.

"But it won't *always* be your role. We're in school, where we have to learn the basics about every part of the job." I really hoped this helped him understand. "Someday you'll get everything you want. You just have to build things for the Crown too."

He tilted his head, inspecting me for a few moments. "If I graduate from RSI."

I met his gaze nervously. *Please don't leave RSI. We need you.*

"You've been talking about advancing a lot lately," he commented.

"It's the only way we become spies when we graduate," I murmured.

"Why is it so important?"

I held in a sigh. He was asking to understand. Fariq was a big picture kind of kid; he wanted to know where something was going and what steps it would take to get there. "Let's say Five & Chance left RSI. You could get a job like that." I snapped my fingers. "Margot would continue being herself and marry a nobleman. Carmen would return to her gym, and Vance could easily become an alchemist. But what will I do? Where will I go?" My eyes welled as I gave breath to the fear. "What skills do I have? Sticky fingers?"

"Don't talk about yourself like that," he admonished gently. "You're smart. You'll find something."

I frowned. "No, I'm not."

"Maybe not book smart. But street smart. You would be a good business owner. Or..." His expression grew thoughtful. "You would be a great spy. Better than me, for sure. I'll try harder for you, because you shouldn't be denied your dream because of me."

"Really?" I whispered.

He smiled and nodded. "Of course. You're my friend, too." I beamed, relieved. He considered for a moment, before adding, "Do you remember me asking for your desda powder for an experiment?"

"How could I forget?" I asked in a sleepy murmur.

"Well, it was a success. But it's taken on its own life."

I propped myself up on my elbows, shaking away cobwebs of fatigue for the moment. "What do you mean? Do you need more powder now?" I asked. I still needed to visit the Shadowed Market to see how much powder I could buy with the savings I had squirreled away.

"Maybe, if there's something you want me to make you. A group of senior inventors in the Builder Guild took over the experiment and the credit for it." He sounded disappointed, and I couldn't blame him. It was *his* idea. "It's big, Heather. Very big. They hypothesize that a large enough amount can give metal a magical resistant coating."

"Wasn't that what *you* thought it would do?" I asked.

"I didn't realize just how strong a coating it would be. We are talking metal that absorbs magic to make it harmless. Tulari have been the strongest people around." He tilted his head with a hum. "Until now."

"Gods," I breathed. "I'm going to get you more desda powder soon." Again, I imagined myself with a set of tools made from this metal. I wouldn't need the powder on jobs anymore. It wasn't just big; it was *huge*.

Mind abuzz, I left Fariq to rest for now. Before I could nod off right next to him, I made my way into the hayloft, just a shout away if he needed anything.

I TRIED to check every night for updated rankings. The room that held the ranking boards and the Wall of Achievement, covered in clorets engraved with a student or team's personal symbols, remained locked up. Since I suspected the door's lock was magically enforced, I didn't try to pick it, but I was sorely tempted.

Even once the rankings were calculated with the competition's results, the room wouldn't be open more than a couple hours every so often. After all, if someone wearing a tier-zero bracelet were to happen upon the room, they'd certainly have a few questions.

Eventually, I tried the knob one evening, and it turned. I entered the room with a thrill of excitement.

The space was like a shrine, each cloret nailed to the wall, floor, or ceiling representing a great deed. I'd added one coin here after completing the crown heist. I found it unerringly and ran my thumb over its engraving of a mouse and a stalk of heather for good luck. Its place on the wall was slowly being surrounded by newer, brighter coins. That just meant I needed to add more of my own.

Vance came into the room and found me inspecting the intermediate board, refreshed with new standings after the competition day. He deliberately scuffed his feet so I knew he was there and wouldn't startle. I was scanning the names pegged to the board and made a sound of dismay when I found Five & Chance at spot sixteen of twenty-seven. "I guess we did sneak in at the last minute," I muttered.

"That must mean all these kids didn't finish the challenge," Vance said, sweeping his hand to indicate the teams in seventeenth and down.

I nodded, distracted. "How are we going to get to advanced with a ranking like that? The Spymaster won't take a second look at us."

"Advanced?" Vance scoffed. "*Us*?"

"Yeah, *us*," I said with the same emphasis. "If we're going to be spies one day, sixteen out of twenty-seven isn't going to cut it."

His face was unreadable while he adjusted his jaw and considered. "Well, if anyone can get us there, it would be you, boss." I chose to ignore the skeptical twist to his tone. We would make it… We just had to try harder. I would push the team and convince them to focus, since now we had rankings to reference.

And Davit's Day was placed below us. It was a welcome shock not to see their team name in first place… They were down to spot stnty-one. Well, they had cheated and bought Manny a slice of apple pie since they'd known what he wanted. If they were truly as exceptional as they thought they were, they'd work hard to climb back up to the top. The best they'd do was second place behind my team. I would make sure of it.

I looked over at the advanced board, counting teams. There were twelve names listed when I could've sworn there used to be eleven.

Miss Barrios had said that advanced teams joined their cohort by audition. What did that entail? My friend Ned had gotten a spot after three years, and his team, Knife's Edge, was listed as the fifth one down. I made a mental note to ask him for more details on how it'd happened.

"Well, I'd better go study," I sighed. There was nothing I could do to improve our rank at this moment.

"Want some company?" Vance offered.

"Oh, I was going to go into Tower A..."

I explained I was going to sit in the highest place in RSI with a lantern and my flashcards. Instead of being dissuaded, Vance was determined to find out why I would do such a thing when I was obviously a big fan of the library and the librarian's feligryph.

With Chance around and the lantern burning as brightly as it would go, I'd worked up to spending a turning of the bells in the tower any time I studied in the evening. It was private, but my mind would still perceive that I was stuck in a stone enclosure and panic before long.

Hopefully, Vance would get bored and leave before he saw it happen. But I brainstormed a handful of excuses to leave early as I brought him up Tower A and spread out my stuff to study. He'd brought a portable alchemy setup that looked like a bucket full of powders and other ingredients, plus empty glass tubes and flasks of water.

Instead of studying with me, Chance sat at the edge of the bucket and observed Vance working. When the boy pulled out his wand and started drawing runes, I snuck more than one glance at what he was doing.

"I see why you like it up here, boss. Nice and quiet," he said.

I cleared my throat. "I don't. Like it in this room, I mean."

He hooked the glowing tip of his wand through a series of runes. It looked a little like threading a needle with the green writing he'd left midair, as it warped in the middle and trailed his wand with two even ribbons of magic. The wand went into a mixed-up tube of murky liquid, and he stirred the magic into it.

Only once he was satisfied with the potion and capped it did he ask, "What do you mean?"

I weighed sharing my fear with him. I could laugh it off and tell him not to worry about it, or maybe act like Ram and change the subject. But this was Vance; of all my crew, he seemed to understand me best. He'd see right through me if I wasn't honest.

"Miss Barrios calls it exposure therapy," I said, making up my mind. "I've been having panic attacks lately. Something about being in a room like this…a part of me thinks I've gone back to jail and that I'll be stuck between squealing and holding my tongue for the rest of a short life, so just being here—"

Vance tensed so stiffly that I stopped and eyed him with concern. He unclenched his jaw to say, "It helps you see what you're afraid of isn't so bad."

"Yeah. I'm trying not to be scared anymore. I can come in and out of this room as much as I want, to show I'm not a mouse in a cage," I explained.

He nodded once and went back to his potions. I thought that was the end of it and memorized a few more Lithosian words. There was a test tomorrow that I *had* to pass. I was failing that class with an overall grade a couple points below where it should be, but if I did well with the test, things would change. I was reciting a few difficult words under my breath when he asked, "Do you think it would work for me?"

I glanced over at him with a "Huh?"

Vance motioned to our surroundings with his wand. "Exposure therapy."

I put my flashcards down, my brows furrowing in thought. There was one thing that came to mind with him and fear. One person he was terrified of. "You could try it. You mean talking about Madam Morashi, right?"

His throat clicked audibly. "Right. There are things... I just... I can't. I *can't*. But if I want to leave this school and be a member of the crew, I have to figure it out."

"I'm not sure the adults will let you leave, even if you did squeal," I admitted. He hadn't been calm enough to hear everything Miss Liang had said about his tier-zero status last weekend, when the news that he would stay behind was fresh. But he listened intently now as I recounted the conversation about Morashi Venom identifying and eliminating him, and he blew out a sarcastic little laugh once I was done.

"Formshifters can't just wave their wand and identify other formshifters. I know how to keep myself safe," he said.

"Have you told anyone else that?"

He hesitated. So, no. If I had to guess, he hadn't grown to trust any of the adults at RSI. There was a chance he'd told me more about his former gang than he'd said to any of them. "Miss Barrios understands the old ways of magic. She shouldn't assume I'm helpless," he groused.

"I don't think that's the point. They want to protect you," I argued.

"They want *my information*, Heather."

"Why can't both be true?"

He snorted. "Do you actually believe we have any value to the people who work here?"

I opened my mouth to say yes immediately, then closed it. He raised a brow, making a beckoning gesture, and I sighed. "I think we have the potential to be valuable. You have information about your gang." I ticked off our crew by touching my fingertips. "Fariq has his smarts. Margot has her noble connections. Carmen has Tosh Zorena. And I..." I faltered.

"And you could steal a meal out from under the king's

fork with no one noticing if you wanted," Vance supplied. Chance squeaked from where he was sniffing his way through the bottles Vance had brought to the tower. "Sorry, and you're a mouse with thumbs, Chance. It's a good way of putting it, saying we all have potential. But actual *value*?"

"Something we have to prove we have," I said.

He rubbed at his eyebrow, where his Tulari mark would be if it wasn't hidden under a layer of magic. "I know you like her, but I'm not going out of my way to prove anything to Miss Barrios. If I'm going to talk…I need to practice. Will you listen if I try?" His green eyes shone with something like vulnerability.

I nodded. I couldn't say no when I knew how difficult it was for him to ask.

"Even though I'll struggle?"

"We can talk here. We'll struggle together."

"Even if…" He quirked his mouth. "What I have to say is really awful?"

"Then you won't face it alone," I promised.

CHAPTER 14
CURFEW

As far as my apprenticeship at Orretta's Stitchery was concerned, everything was back to normal. Despite having called my stitches uneven last weekend, Mistress Reni started having me work on the backlog of hemming and mending for actual clients. She even muttered something that could be considered praise for a weekend's work well done.

She released me late both days, and despite the curfew looming before RSI's doors locked, I still checked Little Wonders Pet Shop to see if I could steal some time inside. The drifter signs for the next Shadowed Market were placed more frequently along the walk from one shop to the next. It was happening next weekend.

The pet shop was closed both evenings. Chance and I still peeked in the window, and on Sunday, Thomas looked back at us. His face brightened, and he held up a finger before dashing out of sight.

"Think he let us inside?" Chance asked.

"I hope so," I said.

It took a few minutes, but Thomas unlocked and opened the door, leaning out with a big smile. "Heather! And Chance!

Have you eaten dinner yet? My dad says you can eat with us."

Chance perked up, looking at me imploringly.

Well, some of my older gang siblings might notice my absence, but I could find a nice toasty hayloft to rest in overnight before returning to RSI in the morning. "Sure. I mean, if it's okay," I said.

"C'mon, we're having veggie soup and bread." He ducked back into the shop, and I followed quickly before the door could close.

Thomas led me through the main room, where the animals were fed and bedded down for the evening. The other half of the first floor was modified for Fletcher's wheeled chair, with wider doorframes and a broad space for his workroom stocked with herbs, paddles, and swabs in little glass jars.

Savory smells wafted into the space, mixing in with the medicinal odors lingering in the workroom. There was a kitchen and table in the next room and one more doorway in the back that was curtained off. I assumed it led to Fletcher's room. Already seated at the table was Shauna, cutting a loaf of bread into mostly even pieces. She waved hello with the bread knife, and I waved back.

Fletcher was stirring the contents of a pot over a cooking fire. My practiced eye saw the rune on one of the chimney bricks, marking a minor spell which ensured all the heat and smoke from the fire was funneled upward rather than allowing for any of it to flood into the room.

"Hello, Heather. So glad you could join us," he said, smiling my way briefly before Thomas brought him a stack of bowls. He ladled a serving into each, which Thomas placed on the table.

"Thanks for the offer," I said, a little awkward. It wasn't like I'd been invited to dinner with another person's family before.

Fletcher said to his son, "Two small bowls as well."

Thomas rummaged in the cupboard for them while Shauna motioned for me to come sit next to her.

There was a small, pointy creature sitting on the table too, with a miniature place setting like it was part of the family. I inspected it and gasped. It looked like a hedgehog. I'd only seen pictures, but it was wildly cuter in person, with small, white-furred limbs and dark, round eyes. Its little nose twitched eagerly when Thomas set a saucer-sized bowl of soup in front of it.

"For Chance," Thomas said, passing me an even smaller saucer of soup. It was probably a good thing to limit his portion, despite how Chance squeaked a complaint.

Fletcher wheeled himself to the head of the table and said a quick prayer over the food, thanking Lord Orion for the bounty of another day's hard work. I kept my hand off my spoon, reminding myself to be a polite guest. That meant not wolfing down this meal the moment everyone else started eating.

"You may have noticed our other dinner companion," Fletcher said, pointing his spoon at the hedgehog. "That's my little wonder. His name is Edgimus."

"He's adorable," I enthused. Chance looked up at me with something akin to betrayal. "You are too, my sweet mouse," I whispered to him. He perked up and took a fistful of my bread slice to nibble on.

"He's a dreamhog," Thomas added. "Do you see how his spines are a little purple? One poke can send you straight to sleep."

"Wow. He's only the third kind of little wonder I've met, other than my mouse and Patches," I said.

"There are *lots*. Hopefully we can introduce you to some more," he said with a smile.

"I would love that," I said and meant it.

We chatted about a few types of rare little wonders the family had seen. Fletcher asked why I was in the area, and that led to me mentioning my apprenticeship and earning a sympathetic wince from the adult when I said I worked at Orretta's Stitchery on the weekend. "That's a fly or fall kind of apprenticeship, for certain," he commented.

I nodded in agreement. Most days, it felt like falling, but just a couple hours ago, Mistress Reni had attempted to say something nice about my work. This could be one of my better days as an apprentice.

"This is definitely a pet lover's house," he added almost apologetically when a cat came in and wound around my ankles, meowing. It darted away before I could pet it and ended up jumping into Fletcher's lap, where it stumbled, and he caught its momentum, helping it sit comfortably.

"If I had a house, it would be just like yours. Probably with all the animals out of their cages," I admitted.

He smiled fondly over at Thomas. "I'm so glad you all found a friend your age," he said before addressing me. "This is Tripod. One hazard of owning a pet shop is ending up adopting all the overlooked furry friends, and I couldn't stand seeing him in a cage any longer."

Tripod heard his name and meowed. His name was painfully literal, as there was a furry lump where one of his front legs should be. I immediately liked him. He was a scruffy tabby, the kind of critter my gang siblings would try to adopt and rehabilitate until Jace forced us to abandon the project.

"You must have a lot of pets, then," I said.

"Too many," Fletcher agreed.

"There's no such thing," Shauna put in. "I'll show you the others after dinner!"

I glanced at the adult to make sure this was okay, and he didn't seem to mind. "Just don't keep her here too late. You all have school tomorrow."

Shauna brightened and told me about the handful of pets they'd kept over the years. Some of.them were little wonders who'd moved in upstairs and simply chosen not to leave, fixtures the family fed and kept healthy, so they were basically pets. Once dinner was finished, we stacked up the plates and bowls, with Fletcher encouraging his kids to go upstairs. He called my name, so I hung back for a minute.

"Doesn't RSI have a curfew?" he asked.

"Yes," was all I said.

He narrowed his eyes. "Will you be in trouble for breaking the curfew?"

"Dunno, sir. This is the first time I've been out this late." Well, save for an extraordinary circumstance, but he didn't need to know that.

"Look," he sighed, scrubbing his face. "I know this is an unusual offer, but I really am happy you're here. Thomas and Shauna need to have more friends around. If you need a place to stay overnight, this shop was obviously an inn, and you can stay in one of the empty rooms upstairs. Just don't be surprised if you get unexpected company from our resident little wonders."

My eyes were practically shining. "Really?" I asked.

"Really," he answered, smiling at my enthusiasm. "And if you need someone to write to RSI saying you weren't getting into trouble, I will."

"Thank you," I effused before running off to find Thomas and Shauna.

The shop's upstairs was difficult to distinguish from an inn, with several rooms lining either side of a single hallway. The two kids had their names on the rooms that were theirs, toward the back of the hall, while some others were set aside for specific little wonder needs, like comfortable nests for maternity, play rooms for young animals, and spaces for illness recovery. There was a mostly empty room with a cot for visitors, where I'd sleep tonight.

As promised, they introduced me to a few of their adopted pets, plus the little wonders who hadn't fallen asleep yet. My favorite was a male bird named Wils. He was pretty big for a bird, with white and gray plumage and a flag of a crest atop his head that was a brilliant blue. "That couldn't be what they're called," I said when Shauna told me he was a crested alarm bird.

"I'm not joking. He's a crested alarm bird," she giggled. "If he screams, you'll hear it. Trust me."

Wils made a soft *rrrawk* noise and puffed out his chest feathers.

"Of course, Dad saw him for a throat injury, and I don't think he screams anymore," she added. Wils gave her a stink eye. It was a little uncanny to see a bird immediately understand something a person had said, but that bit of extra intelligence separated an animal from a little wonder.

Eventually, Fletcher called up the stairs for us to go to bed. I went to the visitor's room and hesitated at the door. "You would wake me up if there was trouble, right?" I whispered to Chance.

"Yes yes, always," he answered.

Against my instincts, I left the door ajar. There was a chance one of the cats or dogs they'd adopted would slip in, or maybe one of the more cuddly little wonders.

I woke to a harsh *rrrawk* in the darkest hour before sunrise and Wils perched at the foot of my cot, crest raised as he gave me a beady-eyed stare. The fluffy, medium-sized dog who'd joined me in the night lifted his head with a sleepy huff. He was a heavy weight across my feet, but I'd slept better with him there than I had in a long time.

"You're right," I croaked. "I should get back to RSI."

MY BRACELET HAD LET me into the building when I arrived with the first day bells ringing through the city. With the early wake-up from Wils, I got there right on time, a little before breakfast was served. I washed up quickly and slipped into a new uniform before sitting at my crew's usual table in the cafeteria.

"Hey, Mouse," Ram said before his heavy arm caught me around the neck. My older brother was probably the only person who could pin me to my chair without me immediately panicking. "You've got some explainin' to do."

I opened my mouth to tell him about my safe overnight stay in Little Wonders Pet Shop but closed it when he released me and turned his wrist. He was wearing a gold bracelet. That was the kind of flashy choice I expected him to make.

I tipped my head back. "You figured it out." I would've jumped up with joy if it weren't for the serious expression he'd leveled down at me. Oh. He wanted me to do some *explaining* explaining. My eyelid twitched as my smile turned shy.

Ram and I took the slow way to class. We were barely out of earshot when he started talking, and I wilted because he sounded angry. "I know you couldn't tell me, but still. I wish I'd known all the wonderful things ya promised RSI was also included the biggest possible drawback. I should've known it was too good to be true."

"What?" I practically whispered.

"The headmaster told me that, at my age, I could pay the Crown back for placing me in an apprenticeship by being an informant for the rest of my life." He dragged his hand down his face and blew out a sigh. "To work as closely with spies and *peacekeepers* as they need."

When he said "peacekeepers," it was with the usual scorn our family infused into the word. I immediately understood his anger, and it took a notch of tension off my shoulders.

"He wasn't saying you'll be a squealer," I said.

He scoffed. "Pretty sure that's exactly what he was saying."

"Ram, we's on the right side of the law now. That doesn't mean reporting cons and thieves"—folk like us, my tone implied—"but instead murderers and dangerous groups like Morashi Venom."

"They don't exist," he said nearly automatically.

"They do. I know a former gang member."

Just like that, a tangent distracted Ram. I was not forgiven, per se, but if he was truly angry about RSI's real purpose, he wouldn't have asked, "That why you need cinnamon?"

"No," I said, glancing around. I took his wrist and pulled him toward the nook in front of an unused classroom and dropped my voice to explain Fariq's experiment as quickly as possible.

Ram's eyebrows rose to his hairline and stayed there. He whistled once I mentioned I wanted desda powder-infused tools. "Town shadow comes together this weekend," I finished.

"I'll go for you. Do you want me to get as much as I can?" he asked.

"No. I mean, yes. I want to come with you," I said. He eyed me skeptically, and I jutted my chin out. "I'm fourteen."

"When did that happen?" he asked. I had a feeling he didn't want an answer. He'd always been a protective big brother, but now I was asking him to look at me more as a young adult who could handle herself. That transition had to be jarring. "All right. I can get you a good deal on the cinnamon and show you around. In return, your smart friend can make me a bar of this fancy metal."

Instead of saying okay, like I should've, a question tumbled out of my mouth. "What for?"

"To sell." He bounced his knuckles off my forehead. "You can't tell me about something that valuable and assume I won't want to flip it. Let me give you some older brother wisdom."

Ram and I resumed walking to our classes, and he

outlined the first rule for sellers. If there's not a lot of something, it's worth more clorets. The rarer and more sought after it was, the more expensive it would be. He'd find a buyer for this rare piece of metal and sell it, using the money to gain more desda powder and repeat the process. "I'll pay your friend in cinnamon, if he wants. Or clorets. Long as he's willing to make it, I'll fence it. Think of the money, Mouse."

We parted ways, and I did think about it as I went through the motions of my classes. Instead of taking notes, I stared at a blank page in my journal and overthought. He'd said "fence" as in selling illegal or stolen goods. Since desda powder itself was illegal, the metal treated with it would be too. Right?

Once the Tulari heard about this metal…they would want it outlawed. It was a direct challenge to their being and power, like the desda mushrooms themselves. I imagined Ram getting caught as one of the first people holding this metal, and *musty devils*, I sweated through several scenarios that led to him falling into the Morashi's hands because of it.

"Heather?"

Miss Barrios cut into my spiraling thoughts. We were climbing the rock wall today in Agility class, and another kid was already trying to reach the top. Instead of indicating that I was next, she was beckoning for me to come talk to her.

We stood a couple of paces away from the rock wall. I was ready to tell her I was going to do my best on the wall today when she asked, "Where were you last night?"

"Oh. I ate dinner at Little Wonders Pet Shop with some friends and ended up spending the night since it was after curfew," I answered.

"It would be wise to tell someone in advance next time. You're allowed out of the school to go to an apprenticeship and off on missions. Anything else might lead to you returning to a tier-zero bracelet," she said sternly.

I ducked my head, chastened. "Yes, ma'am. Would it be all right as an every once in a while kind of thing?"

"Yes. I know you aren't the type to abuse the system." Her eyes narrowed down at me like she wanted to take that statement back. I nodded in agreement. I would definitely search for ways to take advantage of this now that I had confirmation the magical lock system really recorded my comings and goings. "It's for your safety that we know where you are, is all."

"Understood," I said.

"By the way, congratulations on completing the first extra credit challenge this year," she said.

I gaped up at her before mentally running through the list of the three challenges. I'd read them enough that I had them memorized. Use Uncommon to make contact with five people outside of RSI. Steal a key to the city. And impress Manny.

Wait, had the first one really been that easy to achieve? We'd talked to many people in passing, getting what we needed with that bit of deflection that Uncommon offered. "The first one? It was hardly a challenge," I said.

She flashed a knowing smile. "By design, Miss Mouse. We don't disband teams that complete one challenge by the end of the year, if you recall. Most intermediate teams receive the first challenge by default and don't come close to the other two they're assigned. Those that figure out what the second one means or accomplish the third one are truly in line to be advanced."

My heart ached with yearning. That was *exactly* what I wanted. Advanced was just the next ladder rung up the climb toward becoming a spy. I opened my lips to pose a question, and she shook her head. "You're up next," she said, pointing to the waiting harness.

This time, I was too distracted by my thoughts to be afraid of the stone box where the rock wall and the second-story floor intersected. I glanced up to applause, as Ned, Sybella, and a few of my other stealth track friends had circled up the stairs to cheer. "Keep going!" Ned shouted.

Of course, that ended my attempt to climb up the rest of the wall, as I became too self-conscious of myself and especially my aching muscles. I fell and bounced in the harness when it caught my weight at the bottom. Despite the sudden fall, I was still proud of my progress.

CHAPTER 15

TOWN SHADOW

I spent a completely normal day with Mistress Reni, sewing as fast and as straight as I could with her demanding that I work faster. I didn't tell her I had somewhere else to be tomorrow or do anything at all to imply that she wouldn't see me, like asking for my wages for the day. The last thing I needed was for her to explode again and compare me to the past apprentices she'd gotten from RSI, because now I understood why their attendance became questionable.

They were training to be spies. There were other things to do. And they must've also wanted to avoid conflict with her.

I yawned deeply as I readied to visit the Shadowed Market. Ram wanted to visit as early as possible, since the sellers would have more stock and patience for his brand of aggressive haggling. I'd pushed back our departure time until it would be less suspicious to whoever was monitoring the times we left RSI.

But it was still earlier than my usual wake-up time when I glanced around the quiet girl's bath and decided it was safe. I reached into one of the pouches on my belt, moving little metal bits aside until I withdrew a tightly rolled piece of parchment.

My first and only official bank note, worth three hundred clorets. I would have to cash it in today to afford the desda powder I intended to buy honest-like. Chance had unearthed most of the clorets I'd asked him to squirrel away for me, but he'd lost two silver coins somewhere. That brought my loose money up to a respectable forty-seven clorets.

Maybe less respectable when counting the coins made me realize I'd spent over a third of my apprenticeship wages on food and a few small things that'd caught my eye. Mostly food, though. I vowed to be more careful with what was left.

I rolled up the bank note and secured it, giving my full change purse one last jingle before I headed to the front of the school. "We get breakfast treat?" Chance asked from his place on my shoulder.

I hesitated for about half a second. "The street crepes?" I asked. The mouse chattered with an eager nod. "Of course we are."

Ram was waiting by the secretary's desk, practically trembling with leashed energy. Sidewinder and Lope were with him, as was Wildcat. All of us were wearing street clothes rather than our uniforms.

"Let me see your bracelet," I said to Wildcat, surprised to see her.

"Ram told me what he was doing this weekend, and I asked to come along," she told me. Proudly, my redheaded sister displayed a leather strap identical to mine. When had she upgraded? We slept in the same cramped dorm room, and I should've noticed sooner. Still, I smiled and congratulated her.

Just a year ago, Wildcat was my biggest rival for sneak jobs in the gang. We were both built smaller, but while I was prey, with the tendency to be overlooked in a crowd or room, Wildcat had a predator's energy and grace. Folk noticed her for her looks and personality more than her hand reaching into their pockets.

Wildcat, Jackie, and I had shared the same pallet in the Menagerie. Once, we'd been as thick as folk assumed thieves were. But when I'd been separated from my gang last year, I'd assumed—falsely—that she was happy I was gone. Us both being sneaks had made us sisters in a different way, always competing and measuring our skills against one another and hoping to be the superior one. Seeing her here with our older siblings rekindled a nervous energy in my chest.

I just knew it was a matter of time before Wildcat joined the stealth track, and we would be sister-rivals once more. This time, we would compete for the Spymaster's attention, and she was just as likely to receive it as I was.

"All right, let's go," Ram said, interrupting my thoughts. He walked out of the school with the surety that we would all follow him. Which we did. It wasn't until we were several blocks away from the school that he spoke again. "Mouse, Wildcat, walk with me."

She and I bracketed him as he slowed to an easygoing stroll, jerking his chin up at the occasional passerby. Before coming to RSI, he'd made coin on street corners as a busker, and now he was an apprentice in the Entertainer Guild, so he probably knew several folk who waved or smiled his way.

"There're rules in town shadow," he said in a conversational tone, careful, as always, to avoid referring to the Shadowed Market by its actual name. "Watch your coin. Mind your pockets. Always buy food and drink honest-like. All the so-called games are scams to get your clorets. For this first visit, stay with me, Lope, or Sidewinder. And if anyone asks if you want a green gown, that doesn't mean what you think it does. You come tell me so I can punch 'em. Got it?"

"Yes," Wildcat confirmed, while I swallowed nervously.

"Mouse?" He glanced my way and sighed. "And I know it's cute, but put the pet mouse away."

Chance made an indignant snuffle. "For your own safety," I murmured, offering my hand.

"I want to see shadow place too," he squeaked.

"You can, from your pouch," I said.

He hesitated, and I felt a tickle of his reluctance to crawl into my palm and let me put him in the pouch. Yet he did so, and his pointed head emerged from the side of the flap to watch where we were going. When Ram went sailing past the street crepe maker without a second glance, his little nose twitched eagerly at the waft of sugary steam we passed through. Maybe we'd get one on our way back.

The morning market was busy, and I stuck close to Ram out of old habit. Vendors tended to shout toward him for attention on their wares rather than me. However, one voice stood out, high and urgent. A boy stood beside a stack of newspapers, flapping one in the breeze and shouting. He'd said "lady gryphon rider," and my head turned.

I flicked him a cloret on our way by, and he gave me a gap-toothed grin and a fresh copy of what turned out to be a copy of the *Voice of the People*. "The eldrafn race receives a new start," I read aloud from the top of it. That didn't seem related to the lady gryphon rider, Sivana Walker. The boy had probably said it to drum up impulse sales like mine.

"Well? Read it to me," Wildcat invited, offering her arm.

We locked elbows like we were half our ages and afraid of being separated in a crowd. She steered me away from obstacles while I read.

"To complete our coverage of the changes at the Gryphon Rider Academy and address recent rumors, there are indeed former eldrafn growing up with the youngling gryphons. Two, to be exact. It was my great privilege to sit down with Sivana Walker, one of these reborn birds, Revna, and her handler, Signe.

"These ladies were open about their theory that Revna and her kind were created as workings of the gods. They implied that it is the gods' will that the eldrafn who died in the Storm Front War begin a new race of flesh and blood birds. Revna takes the appearance of a falcon, though much larger than one, with signs in her feet and wingspan that she will be even bigger still. She was also mild-mannered and spoke Altarian during our interview.

"While we can only speculate what the final version of Revna will be as a blessed beast, it is clear that her magic relates to music. Revna sings in a voice that promises to be as pure as a minstrel's someday."

I continued reading happily, my imagination captured at the thought of an eldrafn being a living bird rather than a sentient storm. The reporter, Mira Galav, had barely described what Revna looked like, and that was the only disappointment in the entire article.

"Where'd you learn to read so good?" Wildcat asked after I finished it.

"All proper-like and everything," Sidewinder agreed.

I blinked in surprise. They seemed almost impressed, but that couldn't be right. "I been…" I coughed, blushed, and cleared my throat. "I've been practicing."

Sidewinder nodded. "Good on ya, Mouse."

We didn't have to walk much more before Ram said, "We're here."

There was no tangible shift in the air to reflect what I expected of the Shadowed Market. For as long as I'd been forbidden from going, I thought there would be men juggling flaming swords or shady folk hiding in every alley.

Instead, it was an extension of the market we'd passed through to arrive here, but with a backdrop of pockmarked tents and run-down homes. Some of the latter had their doors open and someone at the threshold to wave and beckon. Unlike the vendors selling honest goods, no one named their wares in their call outs. It was much quieter, with fewer other folk browsing around us.

I made eye contact with a man behind a table of what looked like dried herbs. Nothing that looked too special.

"Whatever you kids are looking for, I got," he called. That was a common refrain from several vendors as Ram led us down the street without pausing.

"My usual guy prefers alleyways," he explained. "Easier to duck into a hiding place if the peacekeepers raid town shadow."

"How often does that happen?" Wildcat asked nervously, beating me to the question.

"I seen it only a few times. It's not pretty for some of these folk," he commented.

He stopped at a vendor selling egg and sausage-filled wraps, just as easily changing the subject by buying and handing each of us one. I ate mine without complaint and passed Chance bits of the wrap to nibble on.

The Shadowed Market was the kind of place where one went when they had a specific need, but I slowed to eye tables at my pace rather than Ram's. He continued searching with Sidewinder, while Lope and Wildcat browsed with me.

Some vendors seemed, at first, like they could be placed anywhere along the main market street to sell their goods. Lope murmured what I was missing, and most times, it was because I had found someone trying to fence stolen goods. I also encountered normal-looking items that were hollowed out for the weapons placed inside them, and an abundance of illegal spell work.

Lope had to tell me the names of some runes so forbidden they didn't appear in typical reference books. Anything related to inflicting pain, persuading someone else's mind, or causing serious illnesses were considered hexes rather than enchantments. Most were placed on jewelry, which made already exorbitantly priced hexes completely out of buying range.

I wandered away from the tent of a Tulari vendor who'd hidden his hexes in the lining of clothing seams, feeling nauseous at how casual this cruel magic could be. A girl played a lute on the street corner and sang a jaunty tune, at odds with me coming to terms with why my family had prevented me from visiting the Shadowed Market. Little Heather might've tried on a hexed hat and come away with a bloody pox or worse.

I didn't miss how a handful of men watched us walk by with cold, weighing stares. Lope would close her arms around Wildcat and my shoulders, ushering us onward quickly with a stern look of warning for those observing us.

Still, one person began to follow us. I noticed him a couple times. He was staying behind other passersby, but I'd felt his stare from the way the little hairs on the back of my neck lifted. After we entered a building to browse, I turned to Lope and whispered in her ear.

She didn't seem too surprised by the news. "He's waiting for one of you to drift away from me. Stay close, and it won't be an issue," she said. I was puzzled that her plan was, apparently, to let him follow us.

Lope spoke to a man trying to sell painted plates and cups in the front room of this building, which turned out to be a house. She passed him a cloret while I eyed an upside-down cup with an unfamiliar symbol engraved in the underside. Did I even want to know what kind of hex that was?

"C'mon," Lope said, ushering Wildcat and me through the house and through a back entrance. We emerged into an alley and took a convoluted path that led us to another section of the Shadowed Market. Our tail would have a challenge trying to find us again.

For every scary moment, there was also the wonder of performers dotting each street with hats and buckets set out for stray coin. The juggler we passed wasn't handling flaming swords, but he had a dozen balls in the air at the same time. I could absolutely picture Ram taking his fiddle here to earn extra clorets.

We walked and browsed for half a bell before Ram and

Sidewinder caught up with us. "For your cake," Ram said, handing me a full pouch with a familiar sand-like texture inside.

I weighed it in my hand, eyebrows raising. "How much?" I asked.

"My guy owed me," he said, closing my fingers around it.

"Ram," I protested.

He mimicked me. "Mouse."

"How much? I was going to buy it honest-like."

"You wouldn't get a worthwhile amount honest-like." He shrugged. "Consider it an investment. Maybe get more from your friend that we can fence."

I closed my mouth before another protest could escape. Just as he'd told me to do earlier, I thought of the money. He may have just handed me a sack of gold for all we knew. All I had to do was give him a profit now that he'd invested in the desda powder-coated metal.

"Thanks, big bro," I murmured and secured the pouch on my belt.

"Time to go?" he suggested.

Lope reached out and took his hand. "It's not the full town shadow experience until they waste a few clorets on the games," she said.

Ram leaned over to kiss her on the cheek. "Waste," he echoed. "You know I hate it."

They looked into each other's eyes long enough that I exchanged a glance with Wildcat. "Them's in love," she said, sticking out her tongue. I echoed the gesture, and we giggled together.

"On second chance, let's let them see the games," Ram said, casting a playful glare in our direction.

The games, we learned, surrounded the couple block spaces where the Shadowed Market had set up. "There are guards to discourage any kids or folk who don't look like they belong in town shadow," Sidewinder explained since

Ram and Lope were determined to have a moment together and hung back a couple paces. "And the games are innocent enough. Just don't expect to do anything 'cept have a little fun and lose your clorets at them."

I viewed the games with the skepticism my older siblings had shown, looking for the scam at each stall and usually finding it without trouble. Three clorets to throw a ball at a wooden target reinforced at the base so it wouldn't fall? No, thank you.

"Try your luck! Pull a key and win!" a man exclaimed as I neared his setup. He had a basket resting on a table next to him and an assortment of boxes with decorative locks cluttering the street. They were painted like little buildings, forming a village square. It was cute, reminding me of fairy houses.

As my group passed him by, the man turned to Wildcat and me. "I see fresh faces," he said. "Just last month, a lucky girl just like you found a key to the city and won a hundred clorets. Maybe you'll be next?"

About halfway into his pitch, a shrill noise filled my ears, and I halted. "What did you say?" I asked.

"That's right, a hundred clorets. Each box has a key, and they are hidden in here." He gestured to his basket.

Sidewinder reached out toward me. "No, he's lying. You'll waste money. No one wins this game," he whispered.

I stood across from the man, who'd dressed in a suit and top hat despite the early autumn humidity that surrounded us. As quickly as I could, I scanned him from top to bottom for any sign of a key motif on his person. Nothing, just damp cloth.

"A key to the city," I repeated.

This was it. *This was it!* I could've burst with excitement.

"That's right. A very small key for a very small city." He flashed bright teeth and dug a tiny key out of his suit jacket's pocket. It was a less ornate version of the key Margot had drawn when we assumed the key we would need to acquire was two feet long. I squinted, seeing writing on the stem, but it was too small to make out. "How about it, young lady? Want to play?"

I nodded and reached into my coin purse. It was one cloret to play, he informed me and held the basket out to me. There was a cloth covering with a hole in the center. The basket was full of small paper eggs, and he instructed me to reach in without looking and pick one. "Crush it in your fist. Is there a key?" he asked, smiling as I reached in.

I lifted one egg free and squeezed it between my fingers. There wasn't a key inside, but something small and hard was there instead…a bright pink candy. That was not worth a whole cloret.

"I just want one of your keys. They're cute," I said. "How much?"

"Aw, that ruins the fun of the game! Would you like to try again?" he offered.

Well, I couldn't expect to finish the second extra credit challenge that easily. I flipped him another coin and reached in. This time, the egg had a blue candy within it. He told me it was tough luck and offered to take a third cloret off my hands for another chance. Narrowing my eyes slightly, I asked, "What's your name?"

"Ron Theovald," he answered, gesturing to the top of his tent. "Theovald's Keys" was painted on an overhanging flap. There was also a parrot perched on the tent, watching us. It was the same washed-out blue color as a winter sky, with a dark gray beak.

"Is that your bird?" I asked, distracted. With plumage like that, it was pretty and unusual.

He replied with the patience that told me he had to say this a lot. "If you're not going to play, I must ask you to step aside for the next challenger."

I reached for my belt and moved to give him another cloret, ignoring Ram's impatient call of, "Mouse!"

When I reached into the basket, the blue bird released a harsh *rrrr* noise. "Cheater!" it exclaimed. "Cheater!"

Eyes widening, I closed my hand around Chance and withdrew it without picking out an egg. The bird calmed down. It'd noticed me palming my mouse out of his pouch, I supposed. I'd hoped that Chance could sniff out the key hiding in all these dud eggs, but one stern look from Theovald had me backing up with an eyelid twitch.

I'd come back with my team. Together, we'd figure out how to get a key to the city from this man and prove we were worthy of the Spymaster's attention.

"Thanks, bye," I stated, scurrying away with my siblings. Cursing under his breath, Ram led us out of the Shadowed Market before word could spread that I'd tried to cheat at one of the games. Not that the unsavory folk there would even care.

CHAPTER 16

HUSHED UP

"NOTHING IS BEYOND MY REACH," I whispered.

The Eye of Acuity activated in my palm, the glowing loop of blue that looked so much like an eye fixing on my face. Its top half morphed into a slant or the fall of a magical eyelid to give it a distrustful stare.

I was alone with it in the classroom of Tower A, earning that glare with a request it'd already rejected dozens of times. This time, I spoke to it as respectfully as I could muster. "With this Eye I unleash the power to watch Ron Theovald. Please."

The magic immediately disappeared. I huffed a frustrated breath, ready to dash it against a wall to see if it would cooperate after some blunt force persuasion.

My palms sweated from my mental image of the opal cracking against the tower's stone wall. One fit of anger could break the tool of power, which was probably refusing me for a logical reason. I thought I'd been so clever, asking for that man's name. But the evidence was sitting in my palm, dormant. It hadn't been his real name.

I simmered in my disappointment. I'd been so close to figuring out the second extra credit challenge on the spot, and Miss Barrios had said it would set my crew apart and put us in line to be advanced. Now it felt like Ron Theovald was slipping between my fingers like water. What was I going to tell my crew when I didn't know who he really was and where to find him?

A knock on the classroom door interrupted my thoughts. Vance waved stiffly when I opened the door a crack. "Hey."

"Hi." I stepped aside for him to come in before closing and locking the door behind him. I grabbed the lantern I'd set on a desk and led the way up the spiraling staircase. This was our fourth evening in Tower A together, and he kept arriving later and later.

It'd been two weeks since I'd discovered Theovald's Keys. Life had entered a lull, where the most important thing I could do was wait.

Ram was filtering through his contacts around the city to figure out who Ron Theovald was. He thought I was acting strangely over a street grifter, even after I'd explained the challenge to him and our other siblings on our way back to RSI. Once he had a lead for me, I would tell my crew so we could finish the challenge and earn the recognition together.

Fariq was continuing to experiment with the desda powder he'd accepted, along with all the strings attached to it. I would get my tools, and Ram would have a bar of metal to trade in the Shadowed Market soon enough.

And Vance...he still hadn't squealed a peep to the spies waiting for his information. We were still working on our fears together. We settled on the tower's top floor and spread our stuff out. He had his potion kit, and today, I had my play. I was the one to break the quiet that'd settled in between us, reading my opening lines in a couple of different ways.

"So, your character's a baker," Vance said.

I nodded and lifted the press book so he could see *A Pinch of Nutmeg* inked on the front cover.

"Her name is Nutmeg," I supplied. "She's the oldest daughter of a pair of bakers. They named all their kids after spices. The play is about her being bad at baking, actually, and going away from home to find something else she's good at."

"Sounds like a good story."

I nodded in agreement. If it hadn't been for the anxious feeling coiled in my gut when I first read through the play, knowing I would one day perform as Nutmeg, I would have enjoyed it. "Miss Stone said when she picked *A Pinch of Nutmeg* for my class to perform, she knew I would be the perfect Nutmeg," I murmured.

He cocked an eyebrow. "You don't sound so sure about that, boss."

"The first two plays this year have two months to practice. But this one…" My belly quivered, and my eyelid twitched with nerves. "It's my class's contribution to the winter showcase."

Before we had a break to enjoy the holidays, nearly every RSI kid was involved with the winter showcase. It was a marathon of eight plays—one per Theater class—performed for the people of Kaiamear over two days right before Yule. Each was supposed to be holiday themed, but Miss Stone was pushing it with my class's play fitting the theme because of Nutmeg.

"I'll help you practice running through the whole thing if you can get another copy of the play. It won't be so bad if you're used to it," he suggested.

"Okay." Our gazes met as the distant city bells chimed the hour. He'd delayed long enough that the end of our time together was already looming.

With a sigh, Vance reached for the lantern. "Let's get this over with," he said. He shuttered it before I could protest, throwing our surroundings into darkness. My breath hitched. Before my eyes adjusted, I always had the sense that I was on my own in a pitch black room. A stone box with no escape…

"You're okay, boss. You're not alone," Vance said. His

warm fingers found mine, gently loosening my fist from where I had it clenched on the ground.

I took a deep breath. "Neither are you."

There was the outline of his wand, a gentle green glow. The sky was not fully dark either, giving Vance and our things a profile. Breathing in to fully inflate my lungs, I blew out a calmer breath. I could do this.

But could he? We'd tried three times prior. He'd told me a few rules for Morashi Venom and a bit about growing up in the gang but stumbled the moment the madam's influence was mentioned. And it was hard to talk about the gang while avoiding uttering the name of its leader.

His fingers trembled as he said, "My parents don't remember me. According to them, they never had a child named Vance."

I knew better than to interrupt when I heard the pain in his voice. His trauma was not mine to comment on.

"The...when we are taken, *she* is there to influence memories," he continued. "Mothers are made to believe their Tulari babies died in the night. But I was five... I still remember a couple things about my parents, even if they were forced to forget me. I saw the fight leave my mother's eyes. She became a staring doll while I was dragged away from her home. My father opened the door for the man who had to carry me when I wouldn't go quietly."

The corners of my eyes pinched, and I squeezed his hand in sympathy. My mother was cold and in the ground by the time I was four. Though her face was a kind blur in my mind, I couldn't imagine how awful it would be to witness her memories of me get erased so easily.

"I received new parents. Tulari who surrendered their baby to..." He swallowed with an audible click and held my hand like it was his anchor to here and now rather than the past that had to be filling his mind's eye. "Loyal Morashi mages marry each other as soon as they come of age. They celebrated each time they had a kid who developed the Tulari mark. That meant they get to raise it instead of…"

He cleared his throat, and I whispered, "You don't have to talk about it."

"How am I going to get out of this prison if I don't?" he sighed. "The madam…she is not natural. She will take babies born to Morashi couples who don't develop a Tulari mark and reward their loyalty with a stolen baby or child who is a mage. My new mother hated me. I could never replace the son she'd lost… In retrospect, I don't think she wanted a kid at all."

My breath threatened to freeze in my chest. "What does the madam do to the…" I couldn't even say it, as I was so filled with dread.

It'd been a mystery since we'd met and he'd proven that Madam Morashi and her gang of mages were real. Why did she have a use for dead children? What had she done to my missing siblings and the unblessed children of her gang?

Vance tipped his head back. His lips were moving in the dark as he struggled to expose something horrible. "She…s-s-she…" He trembled violently and crushed my fingers in his. "She eats them."

I gaped at him, wondering if for a moment I could've misheard.

"She eats *youth*," he clarified. His hold on me went limp, and he sagged. "She likes to call herself immortal. But she is a monster who only keeps the Morashi in line through the fear of being her next meal, among other threats."

I reached over and exposed the lantern's flame. Vance squinted at the sudden burst of light, his stark expression smoothing quickly to a practiced blank.

"I couldn't take the dark any longer," I fibbed. There was little doubt he'd miss the gleam of unshed tears in my eyes… welling there for my lost siblings that'd been murdered because of Jace and Springfield's cowardice. But I felt for him too, exposed to Madam Morashi's evil at five years old.

He met my gaze for a moment before looking at his wand, which he twirled between his fingers. "Thanks for listening. I shouldn't stay hushed up about all this," he said. "If...*when* I decide to speak to Miss Barrios, will you be there with me?"

"I wouldn't miss it," I promised.

SOMETHING in the air felt off through the next few days. At first, I thought it was just in my head as I came to terms with how some of my siblings had died when Jace and Springfield gave them to Morashi Venom. The longer I dwelled on it, the more angry I became and the more grateful I was that the rest of my siblings were safe in RSI.

No, something more serious had happened. The teachers whispered to each other behind sheaves of parchment, gossiping while the kids were supposed to be doing book or partner work. And the advanced teams simply disappeared... until the end of the week, when I could barely stand the sense of secrecy anymore. Miss Barrios wouldn't tell me what was going on, but Ned was back in class like he'd never left.

I waited until we gathered into our usual groups while the first kid of the day ran the obstacle course before asking Ned, "What's going on? Folk seem tense."

"Tense," he echoed with a mirthless laugh. "I bet we're all about to get a briefing on it in Craft, since you and the other new intermediates have your weekend apprenticeships. But I'll tell you early..." His voice dropped to a conspiratorial whisper, and I wasn't the only one leaning in. There was a keen gleam in Sybella's eyes. "I saw the paper myself. The *Kaiamear Gazette* just ran its presses for the last time with a lead article that claims Prince Isaac isn't dead."

I stared at him, uncomprehending. "He's dead?" I asked.

He did a double take. "What…*yes*! He's very dead," he hissed. "The Crown kept it quiet, but that's no excuse for a spy candidate not to know he was executed for starting the Storm Front War."

"I had no idea," I muttered, cheeks pinkening with embarrassment.

"Anyway, Manny's furious. He's got everyone not already dedicated to a mission looking into who the person is who's claiming to be Prince Isaac. Prepare to listen for any leads this weekend, is all I'm saying."

Ned was a hundred percent right. Miss Barrios sent all the advanced-level kids away and talked to those of us who remained, briefing us about the newspaper and even pulling out a copy. It was contraband now, and any additional copies were supposed to be fed into the fire.

"Someone is taking advantage of the king's compassion in not announcing Prince Isaac's fate to the public." As she spoke, she watched the newspaper as we passed it around for a quick scan. "Your task is to continue being the Crown's eyes and ears. Until further notice, if you overhear any information on this false prince or the rebellion he's trying to start under our noses, you are to write it down and report it directly to the Spymaster. Do you remember the spell on your bracelet that will magically send mail to his inbox?"

I wasn't the only one touching the small spell circle that was on my bracelet. "No locks," I chorused with a couple of other kids.

When she'd first told me about the spell, Miss Barrios shared she thought the full phrase was "No locks, only keys," which I thought rang more true than ever now that I knew the Crown viewed its spies as keys.

This was our chance to impress the Spymaster, as required for the third extra credit challenge. I doubted he'd have any time or interest in anything other than what would assist in apprehending this fake Prince Isaac.

I would listen for something helpful at Orretta's Stitchery. Mistress Reni had been in a foul mood with me after I'd missed a day without notice. Hopefully she wouldn't greet me with another sarcastic "Glad you showed up to work today" when I went in tomorrow morning.

CHAPTER 17

SALAMANDER

"Glad you showed up to work today," Mistress Reni said in a tart tone.

I shot her a resentful look. Musty devils, it'd been weeks since I'd visited the Shadowed Market with my siblings. The piranek just couldn't let it go.

"Bad attitude again, I see. Keep this up, and you won't have to suffer through an apprenticeship at all anymore." Before I could question what *that* meant, she listed off everything we'd need to get done over the weekend. My ears perked up at the sound of two fittings. I overheard the most conversations during them, usually women's bored gossip.

My excitement turned out to be misplaced. The folk whispering about revolution and resurrected princes weren't doing so in a place like Orretta's Stitchery. *Manny isn't expecting everyone to report in. That would be overwhelming,* I told myself on my way to Little Wonders Pet Shop for my weekly dinner with Thomas's family. I had dutifully informed Miss Barrios that I was going, as I did every Sunday, to avoid any chance of losing my access to the city.

They left the shop door open for me at this point, and I locked it behind me.

"Heather!" Thomas exclaimed. A few of the dogs barked.

I startled and looked around, but he was just beckoning to me enthusiastically from the main room. We went upstairs together, and Chance transferred from my shoulder to his with a squeak of "Nice boy!" as a hello.

I smiled in anticipation. Usually, a greeting like this meant there was a new little wonder in residence. I'd met a few creatures I would've never assumed existed and learned a lot from Thomas and Shauna, who had been rescuing and rehoming little wonders most of their lives.

He took me to one of the rooms set aside for gatherings of little wonders. There were toys, beds, and a perch for Wils, who raised his feathery crest and released a raspy caw when we came in. I murmured a hello to the alarm bird.

Thomas stooped and felt inside the crease of one of the pet beds. "Look at this," he said.

Standing, he uncurled his fingers, revealing a lizard hunkering down on his palm. Most of its hide was smoky gray, with a yellow stripe across its side and orange around its head and neck. "It's okay, mama. Heather's a friend. You can eat dinner with us if you show her your wings," he whispered.

She looked at us both with an overlarge red eye, unblinking. We'd gathered nearly shoulder to shoulder to watch what she did next. Though she was tensed to bolt, she apparently decided dinner was more important than hiding, as she gave her whole body a shake and unfurled wispy dragonfly-like wings from her back.

"Whoa," I said, awed, as she flapped them in a buzzing blur and hovered off Thomas's hand.

With a zip of speed, she flew away, but I felt her slight, surprisingly warm weight on my scalp when she landed on top of my head.

"She's a salamander," he explained. "They have a flap of skin where they hide their rolled-up wings when they don't need them, so they hide in plain sight. She's here because, well…a human stole her eggs."

The lizard released a sad chirp.

"I know, girl. We're going to find them," he said, gaze fixed above my hairline. "Heather, salamanders have a unique life cycle that starts in human hearths. Salamander eggs are little pebbles that are incubated in fire. Mother salamanders bathe in the fire too, so they stay hot even when the fire is extinguished, to make sure the eggs are comfortable. Neither the mother nor the eggs is supposed to leave until the babies hatch and steal an ember of fire. This warms them from within for the rest of their lives."

"So, someone reached into a fire and stole her eggs," I said in disbelief.

"Yeah."

"Hopefully they didn't hurt the—"

He interrupted me with a quick warning look. "That's all she knows about it." He started for the door, and I followed, cluing on quickly that he didn't want to have a negative tone around the salamander mother. She was probably there when the eggs were taken, too small to defend them.

"Do salamanders breathe fire?" I asked, also all too aware that she was burrowing into my hair as we went downstairs.

"Sort of. They retain heat. Smiths and glassblowers know about them and try to attract them to their forges because they're good luck," he explained. The salamander chirped close to my ear in a tone that sounded like agreement. "They're probably the best-known little wonder, and even then, most people don't believe they exist."

"You clearly exist," I murmured to the salamander, reaching up to touch her. She darted behind my ponytail to evade my fingertips. Meanwhile, Chance was scampering back and forth between Thomas's hands, half playing and half accepting pets.

When we reached the dinner table, Chance returned to me

and sat next to my plate, nose a-twitch for what Fletcher was cooking. The family avoided eating meat, I'd learned, so it smelled like roasted veggies and potatoes.

Shauna, Thomas, and I chattered away in the meantime. A bystander would have trouble getting a word in edgewise as my friends and I caught up on a week's worth of events. They talked about the shop and fundamental school while I shared what little I could about my classwork and apprenticeship.

Inevitably, we chatted about little wonders. Certain species were having early autumn babies, and I was excited to see some tiny feligryphs and illusion foxes since Shauna hinted that a few of the expectant mothers liked to stay here for the winter while their litters grew.

"Of course, they also want to avoid..." She drifted off and shook her head. "Let's just say the eggs aren't the only baby little wonders missing right now."

"There are more?" I asked.

Dread coiled in my belly when Thomas and Fletcher both turned to Shauna with meaningful looks. She looked at me and shrugged rather than answer.

The salamander crept out of my hair and snuck down my shoulder and arm one painstaking knuckle length at a time, eyeing us warily all the while. I pretended not to notice her while still feeling her warm hide each time it shifted against my skin.

Who would steal salamander eggs? I bit my lip as I considered.

Or any other baby little wonder? If anyone would know something was amiss, it was the trio sitting around this table with me. Yet they obviously didn't want to discuss it.

I went to help Fletcher serve dinner. Plates for humans, and little bowls for Chance, the salamander, and Edgimus, with the contents cut into smaller pieces for them. Fletcher said a prayer to Lord Orion, and we dug in.

After a weekend of nothing relating to the *Kaiamear Gazette* and the article that'd riled up the Crown's agents, and my attention focused on little wonder theft, I was shocked when Thomas turned to me and asked, "Did you guys in RSI hear anything about a newspaper article this week?"

"The older kids were talking about something going on," I said carefully.

"I bought a copy, but a peacekeeper snatched it out of my hand," Shauna grumbled.

Fletcher placed his fork down with a clatter and told me what I already knew about the article and its contents. Sometimes he spoke to me like a father, a particular brand of protective and cautious I'd rarely heard. I had to smooth my hackles each time and remind myself that he had good intentions. He knew I was an orphan and had clearly gotten used to adopting those he liked.

"If anyone approaches you about joining Prince Isaac's cause, agree to nothing and get away from them," he ordered. "The article was clearly written to be divisive. But more importantly, you cannot trust anyone who would spit in the Gatekeeper's face in such a way."

My ears perked up. "Who do you think benefitted from the article? And there are folk going around trying to recruit for a cause?" I asked.

Fletcher clearly hesitated. "The only people that could stand to benefit are Altare's enemies. Perhaps a Lithosian wrote it, hoping to set off a riot?"

I'd seen Ram and my other older siblings deflect difficult questions enough to realize Fletcher was avoiding some truth he knew. But I didn't press. He could revoke my invitation to eat with them every weekend, and that was not worth a bit of information.

"As for the recruiters, yes. They haven't come around here yet," he said.

"The maids and servants whisper they're visiting the wealthy first," Shauna said conspiratorially behind a hand.

"Gathering clorets for 'change.' Nasty business all the way around," Fletcher muttered.

Especially bad business for the Crown. It turned out that I had something to report to Manny after all. Maybe it wasn't enough to impress him, but hopefully it was adequate to help locate the false prince and his associates.

I WAITED to submit my report until after I talked to my crew during Language class the next day. Unfortunately, my crew hadn't discovered anything else worth adding to the report, so I simply signed *Five & Chance* under what I'd already written and began doodling little animals. A mouse with a stalk of heather next to a kheneas posed to kick. Then a chameleon with half of it shaded differently than the other half. And a fluffy dolly cat with a gemstone collar.

My quill tip tapped where the last animal would go. I snuck a guilty look over at Fariq, who was listening intently as Margot told a story about her day so far.

With my older siblings, Jace gave names that fit about as well as a cast-off sweater. Like Sidewinder, something tough for a boy, yet the man he was becoming was not venomous or serpentine. But Sidewinder liked it anyway and wore it like it fit him.

I'd give Fariq an animal that might come to represent him. Jackie was still becoming a Feligryph, after all, slowly blossoming at RSI even if she still wore an unmarked copper bracelet.

If he didn't like it, it wasn't like it mattered all that much. This was the last animal I assigned, the last friend to become an honorary member of the Menagerie before its street kid traditions became dust in the wind.

I drew a salamander with a little tongue of flame rolling

from its mouth. Miss Liang was calling the class to order, so I'd explain the decision to Fariq later.

I folded the report and touching it to the symbol on my bracelet. "No locks," I whispered. The parchment disappeared in a blink, fading out of my hand and into Manny's inbox.

I looked up to see Miss Liang had written "Information" on the board in fancily looping script. "Recent events have made it clear that we need to discuss this topic early," she said. "Information is your lifeblood. Gathering it, however, is a skill that you must be taught. Sifting through it, separating truth from lies and speculation from reality…that's another skill. Any information you've turned in about the false prince situation is likely about to be thrown out because you haven't learned or practiced these skills yet."

She glanced my way, her dark eyes reading the crestfallen expression on my face. Why even ask us to be the Crown's eyes and ears, just to discard what we figured out?

She was unapologetic. "It is the nature of spy work, especially when you're new to it. So, let us embark today on learning the basics, which you will hone with time, practice, and your Craft classes."

I sighed and took notes. She was right. Gathering information was a skill, and I'd spent last weekend hoping to eavesdrop on important information rather than actively gathering it.

In overview, Miss Liang touched on what tools each of our classes gave us for gathering information. Our specialties taught us to eavesdrop or intimidate. But Theater was crucial; with some acting, anyone could have charm when they needed it. Assuming a cover required those skills; without proper training, it was difficult to become someone else without making mistakes and getting caught lying.

Halfway into the lesson, I put my quill down and listened with uncommon focus as she talked about the difference between informants and information brokers. "Your average informant is a graduate from RSI who was not chosen for full-time spy work or a sleeper assignment. However, we also call bystanders to events who will talk to us informants as well. Anyone can be an informant under the right circumstances."

She wrote "informant" on the board and "anyone" underneath it. Next to those words, she wrote "broker" and then drew a cloret symbol.

"And then you have information brokers. These are people who are unaffiliated with the Crown and make a living selling intelligence to any interested parties. A talented broker will have a front of some kind, where you exchange clorets for their information under the guise of doing something else. You will want to meet and develop a working partnership with at least one trustworthy broker. They can be the difference between success and failure during dangerous missions."

"Musty devils," I whispered.

Vance glanced over and nudged me. "What's wrong?" he asked.

Eyes wide, I didn't make a sound, but my lips formed two words: Ron Theovald.

THE NEXT SHADOWED Market was this upcoming weekend. I didn't plan on going, but Ram did. Fariq had produced a bar of metal for Ram to sell, an easier task than shaping the tools I'd asked for.

It took a couple favors, but toward the end of the week, Sidewinder pressed two clorets into my palm. I tested to make sure the freshly applied compass spell on each was working, and I later drew Ram aside to give him one. "Will you spend this at Theovald's Keys?" I gave my headstrong older brother my best puppy dog eyes.

He wrinkled his nose. "This obsession is no good for you." Despite his best efforts, he hadn't found out any more information on the man. Ron Theovald, or whatever his name was, was as secretive as a full-fledged spy.

"I'm not..." I began to protest, then took a solid breath. "Ram."

"Mouse," he said, mimicking my scowl.

"He's an information broker, and I'm going to acquire something from him. Okay?"

Ram gaped for a moment, then flashed his teeth in a grin. "Sounds fun. Can I help?"

I gestured impatiently toward the cloret he held.

"*More* than spending one measly coin?"

"Every person has their role in the crew. You're helping me complete a job, and that's enough," I said.

He rolled his eyes and ruffled my hair. "I'll get used to my kid sister as a boss eventually, right?"

CHAPTER 18

AS TRAITORS DO

Margot looked up from the cloret in her palm to squint at me with suspicion. "Your plan has one glaring hole," she said. "What if this Ron fellow turns in his clorets to the nearest bank for safekeeping?"

I tilted my head with a hum, trying to think like an information broker when I'd only met one briefly. "He might. But you have to consider that he wants to keep a low profile."

"So, he hoards sacks of money in his home? No wonder you want to track him." She turned over the second spelled cloret, which was pointing toward Ram on the other side of the school. It was early morning, before Margot went to work, and we whispered in the hall. The only person who'd walked by at this hour was Wildcat, a cheerful morning person just like Margot. I envied that about them.

Sighing, I scrubbed a hand down my face. "I don't think he hoards his money, but I can't imagine his front makes all that much. Instead of visiting the bank every time he carts out his game, he could turn in all the clorets along with the wages from his legitimate job. If he has one."

It's what I would do if I were him.

"Honestly, darling. Isn't this going a little too far?" Margot pressed. "You're planning on breaking into a stranger's house."

I put up my palms. "We're only stealing a key, for the extra credit challenge."

She sucked on the inside of her cheek, flipping the cloret through her fingers as she considered. "Why is the challenge *this* important?" she asked.

"If we want to get noticed by the Spymaster and become advanced…"

I drifted off when she released a heavy sigh. "I feel like that's all I hear from you. Advanced, advanced, advanced. Are you not, just, absolutely buried under the responsibilities you already have?" She was going teary-eyed, a hitch to her tone. "Because I am. How am I supposed to balance a job, classwork, trying to find a suitable husband, *and* advanced tier responsibilities?"

My eyes stung, mirroring her. "I don't know. But don't you want to be a spy? We can't become spies unless we get Manny to notice us. And this is going to get us that."

She put on a wobbly smile, patting my shoulder. "I do want to be a spy. Clearly, not as much as you do."

"The thought of working at Orretta's Stitchery as an informant…" I shuddered.

"I know, darling. Work is dreadful, isn't it? But it is a fact of life." She glanced away. "Look, if I am holding the team back, I can go. You all can become advanced without me. I've always stuck out as the eldest. Bumbling around the spy work when you and Vance, especially, run laps around me in strategy and street knowledge."

A tear escaped the corner of my eye, tracking down my face. "Margot, no," I protested. "You can't just leave. It's just…it's a busy time. But we need you. It's not Five & Chance without you charming everyone we meet."

"You're too kind," she murmured. I waited with my eyelid twitching until she came to some decision in her head and nodded. "I would be foolish to up and leave the moment things get tough, wouldn't I?"

"I'll help you as much as I can," I promised. "Though I don't know nothing about, um, finding a husband."

She released a twinkling laugh. "Oh, come here." She held her arms out for a hug and waited for me to step closer before we held each other. Margot gave excellent hugs, almost as good as my brother, Bear. "Sorry to give you a scare. I'll figure something out…it's not like we'll be advanced tomorrow."

"Not tomorrow," I agreed. But hopefully soon.

She released me and pocketed the spelled cloret. "All right, let's give this a try. I'll pretend to catch ill this weekend and use my free time to track down where the other coin lands on Monday morning. But if it's in a bank, I will be cross with you. I get so little free time."

"Of course. Thanks, Margot."

"If this is successful, when should I find time in my schedule for the upcoming heist?" she asked in her ultra-polite noblewoman's tone.

"Next weekend. One day for the crew to recon and potentially another for the job," I said.

That gave me a week and a half to help Vance and think of what I'd say to Mistress Reni when I earned her ire for another day or two of missed work. But it would be worth it to cross off the second extra credit challenge.

We nodded to one another, and she turned to leave for the morning. "Oh, and Margot," I said, causing her to pause. "It's not a *heist*. It's a *spy operation*."

She arched a brow back at me, lips twitching. "Just like we're a *crew* instead of a *team*?"

I beamed. "Exactly."

VANCE and I continued to meet in Tower A when we had time. After he'd talked about Madam Morashi's eating habits, we'd veered toward safer topics to discuss in the dark of night with the lantern covered.

I ended up filling the space between us with tales of the Menagerie and my best jobs before RSI. It was easy to talk to him about it; he'd grown up running cons and stealing to survive as well. His "new parents" had brought him up in the Morashi way: survive with the gifts you were born with, or die. In a way, our circumstances weren't as different as they seemed.

In another way, they were quite different. While I had stories of my siblings and how they'd earned their names, Vance rarely mentioned other kids. Young Morashi mages were raised together and pitted against one another by the time they reached his age, but he was supposed to attend the Tulari Academy. The boy he'd once fancied was also his greatest rival, another formshifter who was probably at the Academy right now. I understood a key truth about Vance then and slipped it into my metaphorical pocket.

The evening after I distributed the spelled clorets, I'd laid out on my back, inspecting the dull gray shapes of the stone ceiling above our heads. Vance was resting somewhere to my left, with the shuttered lantern just within arm's reach of either of us.

"We're running a job soon," I said. "I want you to be there."

He was quiet for a breath, before I heard his metal bracelet striking the wooden floor.

"You've come so far. You've said her name and told me her most evil secret," I added with a shudder of revulsion.

"I haven't told you everything," he whispered.

"Could you talk to me about it with a couple of adults present?" I asked. My heart was a lump in my throat as silence stretched between us.

Maybe I was pushing him too hard, too fast. He could sit this next job out. There would always be another one to come.

"I have to make a confession first. One I don't think I could tell anyone else," he murmured. "Can I tell you something just between you and me? A secret for forever?"

"Forever. I'll shake on it," I agreed.

"No spit, though. That's gross."

I made a sound of agreement. We fumbled in the dark before he caught my arm, and we awkwardly shook with opposite hands. He didn't let my hand go, and I didn't mind it. It wasn't unusual for him to need the contact when he spoke of his time with the Morashi.

"You're not going to use magic so I can't squeal on you?" I asked.

"I don't think it's necessary. You wouldn't. I'm trusting you here," he said, sighing. "It's just...embarrassing. Despite how she took me from my parents, I used to love the madam. More than I'd ever loved the gods or my own mother, my real one. I think the only reason I stopped feeling anything positive for the madam is because I haven't seen her in so long."

"Love," I echoed. My skin pebbled as if a chill breeze had swept through the room.

"I was also so afraid of her. We all were." It sounded like he was getting lost in his memories again, rushing to say them before he was overwhelmed by fear again. "She can steal the life from anyone, even an adult, and leave them a husk. Her claws have poison in them, too. Anyone she injected with poison would scream and writhe on the ground in agony for only a few minutes before they died. I've seen her murder multiple people like this, even fellow mages. She made examples of them to keep us loyal.

"But there was just...something about her, something irresistible. When she smiled at me and said I was a credit to the Morashi, I just wanted to please her. She was there when I got my tattoo. I wanted it because she said it would unlock the depths of my powers. The moment the tattoo was inked and she left the room, I hated the damn thing. I can barely stand to look at my real self in the mirror."

"Your brand," I said.

"Yeah. They purposefully made it an ugly snake. When they put it in a place I would want to hide it...I mean, that was a choice too. It was calculated to mess with my head and shape my magic." He paused, his breath shaking in the dark. Was he crying? I gave his hand a comforting squeeze.

"I...I just can't believe I wanted it to happen," he said miserably. "Now I can barely cast normal healer spells. Half of my magic—of who I am—is tied up with the ability to change appearances and hide flaws. She *damaged* me, Heather."

"I'm sorry," I murmured. "It was wrong for her to force her will on you."

"Logically, I know that. She has magic no other mage does. I haven't even told you the half of it...but...she's just unnatural," he said. I felt him shudder. "Yet when I imagine returning to her and the gang, I'm excited."

"What?" I asked in alarm.

"Don't worry, it's just some spell of hers lingering. I would never go back," he promised fiercely enough that I believed he was sincere. "Besides, she would...s-she would kill me. I would be the next husk...or traitor mage twitching on the ground from her poison."

"She's not getting her claws on you again," I promised.

His grip on me tightened in the quiet moments that followed my declaration. Maybe he was wondering what a Mouse like me could do to help him, should he be discovered out on the street. My brand of trickery resembled child's play compared to what he'd shared of the Morashi's exploits.

"I'm not afraid of being captured and taken to her. They taught me formshifting too well," he whispered, nearly too quiet to catch. This was the secret he wanted to air out. The one I would never squeal. "But if I see her again…I just might forget to hate her. I wouldn't be able to help myself."

Musty devils, that was so heavy, I felt its weight settle in my chest. Poor Vance. He needed his crew to look out for him, to make doubly sure his former gang didn't catch him. "If you forget, I'll just have to be there to remind you. She deserves nothing from you. Especially not your life," I said.

What I wouldn't do to see his face right now. He sighed out, "Thanks, boss." And it seemed like the end of his confession. And logically, the end of our conversation tonight. I withdrew my fingers from his and reached for the lantern.

"You don't think less of me, do you?" The vulnerability in the question hurt.

I adjusted the lantern's shutter, letting him see my serious expression. "No. That would be like me blaming my sister for being skittish after all the abuse she suffered at The Last Stop." It struck me that I'd just defined his childhood in one word. "You were abused too. I think you're just realizing it."

His fingertips drifted to his neck, tracing the curved lines where his snake brand hid under a layer of magic. Those fingers curled into a fist. "I'm already a traitor, according to the Morashi. I'm ready to own it. I'll squeal almost everything I know to the Crown."

VANCE WENT to speak to Miss Barrios, and nothing happened right away. It was Friday afternoon when a pair of unfamiliar men walked into my Language class while Miss Liang was mid-lecture. They were definitely sirs, wearing pressed suits and glancing around the full room with hawkish stares that narrowed in on the table where my crew was sitting.

The men spoke to our teacher, who nodded once, pressing

her lips into a disapproving line. "Vance and Heather, pack your things. You're dismissed for the day," she said.

He and I exchanged a knowing glance. I felt the gazes of all my classmates as I put my journal away. Carmen nudged me, an eyebrow raised. "It's a good thing," I whispered.

Her nostrils flared. She'd want to know what, exactly, we were doing and why she wasn't called out of class too, but I could tell her later, when there weren't so many people in earshot. I left the room with Vance; one man took me one way, and the other took my friend in the opposite direction.

"Hello, Heather. Don't be alarmed. Your teammate has agreed to submit to questioning about his experience with a dangerous group," he said, brisk and businesslike.

"I'm aware, sir," I said.

He continued on as if I hadn't spoken. "What you are about to hear is the definition of top-secret information. Vance has stated that he will not talk unless you are in the room with him. It is unusual but not unheard of, and we have honored his stipulation. You will be placed under a magical oath not to repeat any information you learn in that room to people not employed by the Crown and Spymaster. Is that clear?"

If the oath was phrased that way...I'd learned plenty of information about the Morashi outside of the room they were about to place us in. My lips twisted, but I would've agreed to it regardless for my friend's sake. "Yes, sir."

"We will ask you to leave if you don't take this seriously. Don't distract Vance from telling us the whole truth. It would be wise for you not to speak at all unless your teammate needs your support."

This man definitely didn't know me; I was guaranteed to do that anyway. "Yes, sir," I repeated.

He had a few more rules for me, but it summed up into variations of "keep your gob shut," which I agreed to readily.

We went downstairs to the headmaster's office, where Miss Barrios waited outside with a book bound in black leather.

"Remember this?" she asked, tilting the yellowing pages in my direction.

My eyelid twitched as I nodded. It was the same book on which I'd sworn my original oath to keep RSI's secrets as an agent of the Crown. A registry of graduates that would one day have my name immortalized in ink.

Vance and the sir escorting him arrived a minute later. We filed in together, and the office was already occupied by three people behind the desk, seated close together with quills, ink, and journals at the ready. To my surprise, none of them were the Spymaster. Headmaster Radcliffe himself sat to the left, but the other two stern-faced adults were strangers.

Once the door was locked behind us, Miss Barrios turned to Vance. "Will you agree to take a dose of truth serum so there's no doubt you're sharing the whole truth with us?" she asked.

He tisked. "I've been dosed with vlorine serum fairly recently. It's standard for all Morashi mages."

She nodded, seeming unsurprised. A furrow must've marked the space between my brows, as Vance glanced at me and whispered, "The two serums have a reaction if they meet in a person's body. I would die if I drank truth serum."

I was fairly sure this had been covered in Alchemy last year, but I'd been pulled from taking that class for a reason. I'd been hopeless at remembering all the various ingredients and the way they interacted with each other. But it made a sick sort of sense that Madam Morashi would prefer her servants dead rather than forced to tell the truth.

The other adults watched as Miss Barrios had us swear different oaths on the registry of graduates. I swore not to share anything I learned in this room today with non-spies, and Vance swore to share what he knew without telling a willing falsehood.

There were five unoccupied chairs on the other side of the desk. Two were set up in front of the desk while the other three formed a semi-circle behind them. It was pretty obvious Vance and I were to sit boxed in by adults. The little hairs on my nape rose. Every adult in this room had predator energy, especially the people seated behind the desk.

No one introduced themselves before Headmaster Radcliffe started talking. "We're going to ask you to dig deep in your memories and tell us everything you can about Morashi Venom. Spare no details, even about things that you believe are common knowledge. This may take a while, and none of us want you to feel rushed. You will be excused from any class, club, or apprenticeship until we've exhausted every avenue of interest. This will take some time, but this information is a priority."

Hesitantly, I raised my hand.

"Yes, Heather?" he asked.

"I need to send word to my mentor to let her know I won't be in the shop if this takes up the weekend," I said.

"Already done," Miss Barrios said from behind me. "Don't worry about a thing, Littles. We're just having a conversation."

Vance gulped a nervous swallow. "I'm ready." His tone suggested he was ready to bolt, but he squared his shoulders and took the first questions in stride. The adults had him start from the beginning, when he was taken from his parents' home.

Quills moved all around us as Vance talked. When he hesitated, the scratching sound continued on without him for a few moments before stopping. He was more matter of fact with the details of his kidnapping than he'd been when he'd told me this story in Tower A. "The madam worked a spell on my parents, and they forgot who I was."

The woman sitting next to Headmaster Radcliffe lifted a

palm to stop him. "Sasha, tell me about memory erasure spells," she said.

"Healer Tulari can develop spells to target and weaken certain types of memories from their patients, ma'am. Usually, they're used to lessen trauma and stress by making difficult events seem like distant memories," Miss Barrios answered.

"Could a crafter-class healer make parents forget their five-year-old child?" the woman asked.

"An ordinary one? No. But this is Madam Morashi we're talking about," Miss Barrios said.

The woman gestured for Vance to continue talking. His hands had started shaking when the madam's name was mentioned. "I'm not questioning your memories. You can expect us to cross-reference spells with our expert to measure what our adversary is capable of," she said.

Slowly, his shoulders relaxed, and he picked up from where he'd left off. I took a moment to really look at the woman, who looked like an average middle-aged Altarian. Her tanned skin was freckled generously on her arms and face from the sun, and her dark brown hair was coiled atop her head in a perfect bun. The other adults called her Agent Steele.

Next to her was Agent Cairn, a tawny-skinned man sinking gracefully past his prime years. His face was relatively unlined, though the tight coils of hair on his scalp and beard were pure white. Like Agent Steele, he wore nondescript clothes. Unlike her, he asked no questions. Instead, he made sure Vance had a glass of water and offered the occasional words of encouragement when my friend would falter or reach for my hand.

This whole process wasn't an interrogation, but it was still something found in the hells. We took breaks for food and rest, and also for Vance to hide in the nearest teacher's office to break down. I may have agreed to swear to keep what I knew of Morashi Venom secret, but the real undisclosed fact was how often Vance wept bitter tears while I failed to truly console him.

"I'm a traitor," he whispered in fear.

He repeated the same things over and over, as if he didn't even hear himself anymore.

"I don't want to die."

"She'll use her poison on me."

"She'll find out. She always does."

Miss Barrios would come check on us, just to find us both crying and Chance scurrying back and forth across the carpet in distress. Something like regret touched her features each time. Still, she was the one to call us back to that room, session after session, day after day. The sounds of ordinary school life passed by the door as they spent five days poking and prodding Vance's memories for everything they could extract.

What he'd told me in the dark of night really had been scratching the surface. Vance confirmed a rumor that Madam Morashi could steal magic from other Tulari in the same way she took vitality—through something that looked like a kiss but was far more deadly. He recalled spells she'd used, running the gamut from healer to wizard to magic that defied Miss Barrios's knowledge or explanations.

He produced names and locations. Demonstrated his formshifting magic and, despite his obvious discomfort, showed his true face and brand to the adults. He revealed that his last name, Bradford, belonged to his spiteful Morashi parents. He'd always been Vance, but his true surname was lost. It was pretty clear after all this that Madam Morashi had reached into his memories the day he was taken, too, as he could recall nearly nothing of his first five years of life. Maybe somewhere in that process, she'd altered his mind so he'd fear her endlessly.

The sessions only stopped after those five days because

Vance couldn't produce anything else the adults deemed important enough to write down. He'd been rung like a dishrag and looked it, too. I felt the same way. It wasn't my memories or trauma to share, but I'd been on the emotional journey with him all the same.

Agent Steele gave us each a cloret for the Wall of Achievement before she left. One face on each was sanded to a blank, ready to be engraved with our personal symbols and immortalized on the wall. "You have done the Crown a great service. I know it wasn't easy, but know we appreciate your contribution toward us eliminating this dangerous group," she'd said.

Agent Cairn had waited until she left with the two suited men before reaching into his pocket. "Perhaps you will want this more," he said, pressing a coin pouch into our hands. Vance's was clearly heavier, but my eyes still widened at the glint of gold I caught inside of mine.

We thanked him sincerely before he left as well.

The last gift was for Vance, a new bracelet. He picked a slim leather band and we tapped our mostly identical bracelets together. His still had a tracking spell on it.

We'd been given the rest of the day off to recover and maybe catch up with our friends and classes. For the moment, we sat in the same teacher's office we'd used for breaks. Recovery felt like sitting in exhausted silence, shoulder to shoulder against the wall.

Eventually, he asked, "What's my animal?" He was rubbing the flat face of his achievement cloret.

I could hardly believe this hadn't come up before now. "A chameleon."

He chuckled. "I suppose that's fair. Though, they change color, and I change features."

"Close enough. I want you to have mine." I pressed my achievement cloret into his palm.

"What? Why?"

"I didn't do nothin'."

He looked over at me, mouth open in disbelief. I was getting used to his real face, as he hadn't covered it up with the perfectly crafted, symmetrical mask he'd customized for himself. His Tulari mark was placed over his left temple, an unusual spot that left him with no eyebrow on that side. All his features looked odd at first since they were different—gray eyes placed a little too close together, frizzy brown hair rather than straight and sun kissed, a softer jawline. But I enjoyed seeing the real him rather than a façade.

He was also shaking his head at me. "What?" I asked.

"You're something else, boss," he said, smiling to himself.

I tilted my head at him quizzically. "What?" I repeated.

He only smiled wider. "Know what? After our upcoming job, I want to do something."

"Okay," I said, drawing the word out.

"Something fun. No stone rooms, no talking about the past. I want to take you on a proper date," he declared.

Like a mouse, I froze. Heat infused me from crown to toes, and my eyes widened. Had he thought...those evenings in Tower A were...*no*. No, he definitely wouldn't...

"How does dinner sound?" he asked. He spoke while fidgeting with his fingers.

Chance poked his head out of his pouch. "Yes yes!"

"Just you and me," Vance was saying. He glanced down at the mouse giving him button eyes. "And Chance."

That look was turned on me next, and I melted for my hungry little wonder. "I thought you kissed boys," I murmured.

"Yeah?" He shrugged, trying to act casual, but the jerky movement and shaky tone betrayed a lot of nerves. "I, uh, I kiss girls too. So? I mean, I know you and Fariq...you guys are a thing, huh? I shouldn't have—"

"No," I blurted. He was the one stilling now. "I mean, no, he and I aren't." *Musty devils*, this was awkward. "Let's do it."

"Okay. Yeah. I know a place, and I'll pick a face," he said. It was a bad joke, yet after a heartbeat, both of us descended into a fit of tired laughter.

CHAPTER 19

SPY OPERATION

LIFE HAD MOVED on without Vance and me while we'd been stuck in a room for five days. I'd gotten updates from Margot at night, when we were released for rest, but I'd still lost my grip on the plan for stealing a key to the city.

My hunch about Theovald was right, at least. The spelled cloret had taken Margot straight to a house, and she'd hidden the cloret and a slip of paper with the address in…where was it again? I checked the lining of my pillow, where she said she'd stashed it. I'd rolled my eyes at the time at her using another obvious hiding place.

I checked my pillow and prodded its filling. Nothing. I'd been so tired I was as forgetful as Chance since I must've moved the items to a more secure location.

Upending my bag, I rifled through my things, to no avail. Then, I checked in the trunk at the foot of my cot, where Margot stored a portion of her overflow gowns and garments. Still nothing. I sucked on my cheek and gave up, going to class.

My first class, Innovation, was in the middle of a group project. Fariq could've probably finished it on his own, but he and Carmen had formed a group and called Vance and me over to complete the circle. We were building pendulums, it seemed, from the diagrams on the chalkboard. I only understood half of the notations, so I was thankful I could follow Fariq's work for this assignment.

We sat in a corner of the room with a half-complete pendulum. The class settled into its usual noise level. Most kids needed quiet for concentration and whispered in Innovation, which meant it didn't seem weird when Fariq leaned over and murmured, "Are we doing something this weekend?"

Before I could answer, Carmen cut in. "Unless my cousins can help, I can't. My aunt's picked up weekend work."

That was a shame; she never seemed to be available anymore. My lips quirked, but I nodded.

"To be fair, I think it is a task that only requires Heather," Fariq said. He passed a cloth envelope across the table, partially covered by his hand. "I made you these."

I brightened immediately. My lock picks! The envelope was stuffed full, and when I opened it in my lap, I saw that he'd placed new tools next to each of the old ones.

"I tried my best to make them match. Sorry it took so long." Fariq held himself anxiously as I pulled out one of the new picks and tilted it toward the sunlight streaming in from a window.

I'd kept my picks in the best condition I could. They were handed down from another stealthy Menagerie kid when he'd aged out and been promoted to a place in Springfield's gang. I was used to their quirks since they'd passed from one kid to the next long enough to be dirtied, bent, broken, and repaired over and over.

The new tool I inspected wasn't perfect, but Fariq had taken care to get the metal tip's angle and point correct. I could deal with an uncomfortable grip. Like the rest of the new picks, it had an odd reddish sheen that looked a little rusted, though the metal was smooth and shiny.

Also, given how rare this metal was, I was probably holding a fortune in specialized tools.

Fariq was still watching me stiffly, so I made sure to say "Thank you" before I checked over the rest of the new picks quickly. He'd probably redone these several times to get them made as well as they were.

"Has this new metal of yours touched a Tulari yet?" Vance asked. "Or a real spell?"

I tucked the picks into their usual place on my belt while Fariq nodded and said in an undertone, "There's been a lot of testing already. What we've found is there's a maximum amount of powder that can be used before it's burned away rather than integrated. The result is a coating that is not as strong as the undiluted powder, but it weakens strong spells and destroys weak ones within ten seconds of exposure. And yes, we had a volunteer mage touch it. He received an awful burn, but he didn't die."

Vance hummed with discomfort. Fariq's gaze came back to mine, and he sighed. "While you were gone, your brother gave me more powder. A lot more. He sold the bar I made for him at a place he called 'town shadow.'"

"Okay." I had the feeling there was something he didn't want to say. "For how much?"

"He wouldn't tell me. But with how excited he was, it was a lot. I'm going to continue this business we've started since he's funding my personal experiments. All this to say, I cannot help this weekend either. Sorry. I want to, but I should work." He spread his palms apologetically. "And like you have said, my role on the team is to make useful things."

"And you have. These will help a lot," I said, patting the picks at my hip.

Vance gave me a meaningful lift of his brows. With his newfound freedom, the only way he'd miss the upcoming job would be if I canceled it.

Guilt squirmed in my gut about the lost address, and I

pulled a Ram, changing the subject to the matter of the pendulum project. Soon we were parting ways for our different class schedules, and I set to catching up with what I'd missed.

Miss Barrios called me aside out of earshot of the other kids during Agility, leaving Ned in charge for a moment. I'd been one of the first kids on the rock wall today and gotten to my personal best, nearly scaling to the fourth floor before my muscles hit their limit.

"How are you holding up, Miss Mouse?" she asked.

Oh, now she wanted to be chummy? She hadn't had a lot of sympathy for Vance or me during his questioning, and while it made sense with all those important folk around, it still chafed. I set my mouth at a moody angle and muttered, "Fine."

She cleared her throat. "I have interesting news for you."

The combination of "interesting news" and the flash of anger on her face suggested some intrigue.

"While we were otherwise indisposed, a letter arrived from Aria Reni on behalf of Orretta's Stitchery," she continued. Any interest I had iced over immediately into dread. She didn't have the letter in hand, so clearly there was something written within that she didn't want me to see. "You've been fired."

A couple of seconds passed before her words sunk in and my eyelid twitched. "What? But...you wrote to her, right?" Gods, I'd just started picking up the skills Mistress Reni wanted me to perfect. I needed an apprenticeship and later a legitimate job as my front, no matter how I felt about the one I'd been assigned. I couldn't be *fired*.

"I did. Listen, this was through no fault of your own. She was quite angry with RSI for assigning her another apprentice already. I don't doubt she used this as an opportunity to take it out on you and be rid of an apprentice. Because of the circumstances, we'll find you another apprenticeship." She reached for me, then hesitated as I eased away, shoulders lifting.

"With everything going on, it will take some time. But I'll be sure to help steer the headmaster toward picking an assignment where you'll thrive," she said.

I made a noncommittal hum. At that moment, it felt like there wouldn't be an assignment where I thrived. I hadn't liked the apprenticeship or the mistress, but my eyes stung from the rejection, nonetheless. I didn't know anyone else who'd been fired from their apprenticeship.

"Look on the bright side. You now have the luxury of time where your peers do not. Think of what advantage you could make for your team with a few spare hours."

I sniffed and swiped at my eyes, looking up at her. She was certainly right about that. "Has a new intermediate team ever impressed Manny?" I asked.

She showed her usual warm smile. "I remember a beginner team impressing him last year. Are you already planning something for the third challenge?"

There was a brief glint in her eyes, but that wasn't unusual with her magic. She wasn't implying Five & Chance was that team, was she? The crown heist had given him a good laugh and dozens of new spy candidates, but also their mouths to feed. Perhaps that was impressive. "No, ma'am. Not yet. I haven't even seen him lately."

Miss Barrios inclined her head. "The false royalty situation is personal, you know. Someone is impersonating his late nephew. I doubt he will be a janitor again until it's resolved. The challenge should be changed to impressing the headmaster, and honestly, that would be just as difficult."

I nodded in agreement and let that be the end of our talk. I had no idea how to impress either Manny or the headmaster, but maybe something would come to me in my extra weekend hours to come. Or not.

Later, I slid into my usual spot in Language class, between

Margot and Fariq today. I looked over at her and steeled my nerve to tell her the news. "Hello, darling. I have been so worried for you," she said first. "And Vance, of course, though I hear he's the reason you disappeared for the better part of five days."

"It was necessary," Vance said as he was sitting down too.

My eyelid twitched. I had to tell her, or I would burst. "I lost the address," I blurted.

Her eyelids fluttered for half a second of surprise. "Oh, that's quite all right. I wrote it down here." She flipped in her journal until she reached a page halfway in. My jaw dropped when her perfectly shaped fingernail tapped it. "Who takes a day off work for a task, just to write the results on one piece of paper?"

"I'd probably do that." I sighed, nearly slumping with relief. "Margot, you're amazing." We would have our second extra credit challenge completed in no time, even if only Vance and I made it happen.

She giggled, eyes creasing at the corners. "Oh, I know it. Well? What's the plan for this weekend? I relish the idea of a *spy operation*." She winked. "Just tell me what to do...boss."

Margot, Vance, and I established Tower A as our base of operations this weekend. We stayed on the top floor so we could talk openly.

Vance was the one who left in the early morning and took a walk across Kaiamear to the better-to-do section of the city, where Theovald lived. He'd dropped off Chance and returned smelling of the city and smiling wider than he had in quite some time.

I held the Eye of Acuity and its tiny moving image. We didn't know Theovald's real name. And though I suspected his pretty parrot was a little wonder, we didn't know its name either.

So, the Eye showed me Chauncey Balenciaga the Seventh and enlarged the world around him so the mouse filled up half the frame. I didn't hold the tool of power to my eye because I was going to get whiplash just watching the constant vigilance of his head twitching back and forth since the view followed over his shoulder.

Chance had climbed to a safe vantage point on the house across from Theovald's, and my gaze narrowed in on the porch swing. Color popped underneath it from a pile of blocky sensory toys made for small children and babies. *Kids*, I thought, heaving a sigh.

Theovald's house was completely ordinary, built with faded red brick and featuring a porch swing and an array of hanging planters out front. A burgeoning garden hugged the structure on all visible sides.

"He has a family we need to account for," I told Margot and Vance, who both nodded, unsurprised. We all waited around for something else to happen.

Theovald left his house with the ringing of the city bells. It was really him, not that I doubted my cloret trick would lead us to the wrong house. He fussed with a tie at his throat and the fit of the suit over his shoulders.

I grasped the Eye and held it to my face, watching what happened next over Chance's shoulder. He'd perked up and stood on his back paws, squeaking, "Heather want know about this, yes yes."

The man waved goodbye to a woman behind him, who looked to be about his age. She had a baby on her hip, who watched Theovald leave with big blue eyes. That was a turn of good luck… They were a young family. Children old enough to identify strangers were walking alarms.

Squaring his shoulders and taking a grounding breath, Theovald pulled a wheeled cart behind him, loaded up with his painted city of lockbox props. His parrot flew over in a blue blur to perch on his shoulder.

I would've pulled myself out of the scene, but Chance was still talking to himself in a quiet chatter. "I do good job at being spy. Not look away once."

What a sweet mouse. I needed to reward him with some treats once this job was done.

"Maybe I tell Heather I want my profession be spy? She know I good and sweet mouse, help lots." His jaws gaped with a yawn, and he dropped to all four paws, circling up into a ball on his perch. "She watch and see. I do good job..."

I jerked my attention free of the Eye, knowing Chance would be asleep shortly. And he wanted to be a spy too; that was adorable. I hoped he told me that's what he wanted soon.

"Okay, here's the situation," I said, telling my friends everything I'd seen.

Vance nodded thoughtfully, while Margot asked, "How long do you think he'll be away from the house?"

"Who's to say," Vance said.

"Most of the day, presumably," I said at the same time.

Both of them turned to me and waited. They wanted the plan, but I was still turning over variables and asking myself, *Could it really be that simple?*

WE WAITED UNTIL THE AFTERNOON, watching the house off and on through the Eye to be sure Theovald hadn't returned. Chance was growing restless, pacing back and forth on the ledge he'd found.

Margot went up to Theovald's house alone and knocked on the door. While Theovald's wife came to the door, Vance and I snuck around the side.

Though my plan had room for two people, Vance had

insisted on coming along. He'd given me a vial of a potion as precious as it was rare—invisibility. We'd gotten the ingredients for minor invisibility potions before, but now he could steal the occasional potion and tonic from his work for the Alchemist Guild.

Our chaos option today was to take the potions and run. They made us invisible for fifteen seconds, just long enough to escape a house if necessary. But I'd picked just past midday for us to execute the plan for a reason.

Midnight wasn't an option because of our curfew, but also because I suspected Theovald had an office he kept unlocked while his family was home. They wouldn't need to activate any home defense spells while his wife and kids were present. I still used my new set of red lock picks on the back door, just in case.

I'd picked this time suspecting that the kids would be napping. In the Menagerie, nap time was glorious. I'd loved it for the rest when I was small and for the peace when I was a little bigger. And so, even now, a part of me looked forward to exactly this time of day, even if it'd been ages since I'd last had a leisurely midday nap.

As long as Margot kept Theovald's wife occupied with whatever they were discussing at the door, we could be in and out with the key in no time. I slowly unlatched the back door once I'd unlocked it, sliding it open a sliver to see if we'd be within sight of the wife. I stiffened up.

"What's wrong?" Vance hissed.

I turned and put a finger to my lips, then pointed. The house wasn't set up like I expected. We'd have to sneak through a room riddled with discarded toys. Two kids slept here in separate corners, the baby I'd seen earlier and a small tot.

Vance met my eye and shrugged. We tiptoed through the room, carefully avoiding stepping on anything, and then I cracked the inside door and peeked into the hallway.

Margot's voice filtered toward us, a bright chatter, and Theovald's wife responded in kind. At least one thing was going well—Margot could coax anyone into a chat with her.

There was only one other room in the house, with the rest of the space used for an open front area. From this vantage, I saw hints of a dining table, couch, and hearth. The other room had to be where Theovald and his wife slept—so there was no office. If they had keys lying around, they would be in there.

I crept low to the ground to the master bedroom. The door was ajar, so I slipped in and held it wider for Vance before setting it at the angle it'd been at. Margot and the wife were still giggling away, so I took that as a sign we hadn't been noticed. Who knew how much longer Margot could hold her attention, though.

I whispered for Vance to check the closet while I rifled through the bureau. They had nicely carved wooden furniture, a matching set that consisted of a bed frame with a large headboard, a bureau, and a trunk at the foot of the bed. To complete the room, there was an upholstered rocking chair and a crib under the far wall's window.

My thief's senses triggered as I briefly eyed a couple of paintings on the walls and other decorations around the room that cluttered the space. This was a family that had money.

There was no time for hesitation on a job, so I pushed out the niggling feeling that there might not be a key discarded somewhere in all of this and started counting how much time had passed. If we couldn't find it in here in five minutes, we could try a more direct approach with Theovald later. Any more time than that, and we risked being caught.

The bureau's wood was not oiled. I had to lift and slide carefully to check drawers full of clothes without making much noise. We were one minute, seventeen seconds in when a furry shape leaped onto my knee, startling me. "You do next part without me?" Chance asked, looking up with his round, expressive eyes.

"Sorry. We're just looking for the key now," I said as quietly as I could.

"I help?"

"Sure." I thought little of it as he scampered off and started timing us in my head again, adding twenty seconds to the total time since I'd briefly lost count.

There was nothing of interest in the bureau. Vance put his hands up in a shrug, not finding anything in the closet. That left the trunk at the foot of their bed. I opened it, and my heart sank—it was completely empty. Maybe this was where the props for Theovald's game were stored.

I met Vance's eye, tilting my head toward the door. He pressed his lips in a stubborn line and pointed at the box I'd left untouched atop the bureau. I shook my head rapidly. It was an intricate box, probably for jewelry, but I'd already spied the distinctive tumbler on the bottom that suggested it was a music box.

He opened it anyway.

A beautiful melody plinked from the bottom of the box, which he slammed shut with more force than necessary. We both cringed as the laughter drifting from the front of the house faded to silence. Vance's eyes widened, and he gave me a sheepish look, but I was already closing the trunk and rushing over to him. I grabbed the music box and put it back in its place.

"Closet, now," I whispered, pushing him until he was wedged in with the couple's clothes and arranging them so it wasn't obvious there was a person there. Then I joined him, pushed the clothes around again, and pulled my invisibility potion off my belt. He took his out too and removed the cork without the distinctive *pop* potions usually made. He was doing the same for mine when Theovald's wife entered the room, and we hastily downed our potions together.

I counted down from fifteen with my heart in my throat. I

watched her from the gaps between her husband's hanging shirts.

It took her five seconds to stop in front of the trunk, hands on hips. She looked around, brow wrinkled in confusion. She didn't seem to be in any hurry to figure out where the noise came from. We hadn't left behind enough evidence that two strangers were in here with her.

It took twelve seconds before she crossed to the bureau and the music box tinkled away merrily. Something metallic rustled, and she muttered under her breath.

Please go. Nothing to see here. Go now.

The potion wore out, and my now visible gaze met Vance's with fear. She was still standing there, and if she turned her head, she'd see two pairs of legs in her closet. Vance mouthed, "What do we do?"

I made a fist with my free hand, the nonverbal signal to stop or freeze. He seemed to have trouble with this. Musty devils, I was never letting Vance be a sneak with me on any other job.

"Oh, hello little guy," Theovald's wife said, her voice dropping to a coo. She left the music box open and singing, her outline stooping toward the ground. "Did you get lost? This isn't a house for a mouse."

Chance squeaked back at her, too far away for me to make out the words.

Vance began to breathe a sigh of relief. I bugged my eyes wide, trying to communicate the urgency of the moment. "Hold. Still." I mouthed as exaggerated as possible.

"Let's get you out of here," she was saying, standing up again and heading out of the room.

"Follow my lead," I said under my breath, slithering out from behind the wall of clothes. I arranged it one last time when Vance freed himself and glanced at the open music box for one fleeting half-second.

It'd opened to several tiers of boxes that would nestle

together when the lid was lowered. They surrounded a spinning figure as music continued to tinkle from the box.

I stopped dead in my tracks. We had maybe two heartbeats before Theovald's wife set Chance outside and said goodbye to Margot, if she hadn't already. But the bottom of the box was lined with recognizable key shapes, and my hand darted out. I grabbed a couple, stuffed them into my pocket, then took Vance by the arm and went out of the room low to the ground.

The woman was just waving to Margot as our friend turned her back to walk away from the house. I grabbed the knob to the kids' room and rushed inside, Vance on my heels. With a practiced twist, I closed the door soundlessly behind us.

Finally, we breathed a pent-up sigh of relief together.

"Mama?"

This was a nightmare. It had to be. The tot was half-awake and shrugging off his blanket. It would only take him a couple more moments to realize we were strangers and scream.

Vance didn't hesitate. He crossed the room toward the tot and drew his wand, drawing a single rune with a practiced sweep. "Shh," he said, touching the wand's tip to the boy's forehead just as realization was crossing his little face. Sleep clouded his eyes immediately, and he slumped.

He tucked the kid back in and glanced at me and the hesitance I wore openly as I wondered if he'd just used Morashi magic on a tot. "That was a sleep spell. He'll be out for ten more minutes, maybe," he whispered.

The tension bled out of my shoulders as I nodded and gestured him toward the back door. By the time Theovald's wife peeked in to check on her kids, it was locked and we were creeping through her garden with her none the wiser.

CHAPTER 20

A FLASH UNDERWATER

I BLEW on the ink to speed its drying along. The note read:

Spymaster,

We have secured a key to the city for the second intermediate extra credit challenge.

Aren't you impressed we figured it out first?

Underneath, I'd signed Five & Chance, plus a line of our animal symbols. The question had been all Margot, who thought it wouldn't hurt to ask.

We'd gathered back up in Tower A to talk about the finished job and make sure we got our due credit for stealing a key to the city. It was our chance to debrief on what went well and how we could improve for the next job.

Vance had brushed off any criticism of his performance with, "Hey, we got the key, right?" He had an unrepentant shrug for me when I mentioned he wouldn't be a sneak again unless it was necessary.

Chance, now round around the middle from the street crepe I'd bought him as a reward, sat next to me on the floor, holding a key. I'd grabbed two, and they were identical, with "Key to the City" engraved in tiny print across the stem.

"Are you sure the spell will send the key, too?" Margot asked.

She and I both looked at Vance, who shrugged. "Probably not. It's meant for letters," he said.

"Well, it's worth a try," I said.

I tried to take the key from Chance's paws, and he clung to it with a protesting squeak. "No no! My key."

Blinking in surprise, I let the key go. I thought he was holding it for me, but he clutched it to his chest. "You want to keep it?" I asked him.

He bobbed an affirmative. "I do good at spy job. I have key. Now I'm a spy too." It wobbled between his paws as he turned it by its stem. "That okay, right? I make profession and help crew more."

Aww, goodness. I pet down his back and said, "Of course you can be a spy. But we've got to get you some clothes so you look the part."

He perked up, dropped the key, and darted around in excited circles. "Yes yes! I figure it out. I have profession now. Mom and Dad and uncles and aunts and siblings and cousins and nephews and nieces all going to be so proud!"

Margot muffled a giggle. "Look at him go," she said.

Chance halted his dash under my hand so I'd keep petting him. "We go tell my family soon?" he asked, clasping his front paws together.

"How does tomorrow sound?" I asked, which earned an enthusiastic "yes yes!"

Since one of the keys to the city was now spoken for, I took the other out of my pocket and placed it in an envelope with the note I'd written. Then I touched it to the magic symbol on my bracelet and sent it off with a murmur of "No locks." The parchment disappeared, and I waited for the sound of metal striking the floor.

And yet, nothing hit the ground. "Huh. It worked," I said. That was some knowledge to keep in my back pocket. Maybe

I could send Manny's inbox nearly anything, as long as it fit in a big enough envelope.

Margot clapped briefly. "Well, this has been delightful as usual, but I have a whole evening and tomorrow off and now to myself. I think I will be off, darlings."

Vance and I said our goodbyes, and Chance waved. As soon as she started descending the staircase, he turned to me. "Do you, um…"

"We go to dinner?" Chance said in the awkward pause as Vance tried to muster what to say.

"Do you want to go to dinner now?" Vance asked in a rush.

I flashed a shy smile. My first thought was that I should take a moment to freshen up, but one of us would probably explode with nerves if I took too long, so I said, "Okay."

It was a little early for dinner, but this way, we'd be back in time for our curfew. The last thing I wanted to do was to keep Vance out past curfew, considering how new his freedom was. He led the way out of RSI and down the street. He slowed his steps to match my shorter stride.

Chance made his way to my left shoulder so he could look up at Vance. He started suggesting various foods that we'd tried around the city…back when I had an apprenticeship and could try something new every week. We'd stuck to inns and shops close to Orretta's Stitchery, which was in the opposite direction of where we were heading. The streets sloped upward, and the palace on its high hill loomed over the surrounding buildings.

"What's he saying?" Vance asked, looking over at the squeaking mouse with a bemused expression.

I giggled. "He's guessing what we're having for dinner."

"Well, whatever your guesses are, they're wrong. We're going somewhere special," he said. He reached over and gently touched Chance on the nose.

I was pretty sure the mouse looked up at him with as much curiosity as I was feeling.

"And you're going to like it." After a moment, he added with less confidence, "I hope."

"I probably will," I said. The fluttery sensation in my belly promised I wouldn't be eating all that much anyway. What was wrong with me? It was just dinner with Vance. I knew Vance, had heard his struggles and past in probably too much detail.

And he knew me. In the dark of night in Tower A, I hadn't found it hard to talk to Vance at all. I'd told him things I'd hardly shared with another person.

Like how my favorite revenge reverse-pickpocket creature was a stinging centipede. It had too many legs and a painful pinch for the adults in Springfield's gang that deserved misfortune for messing with me or one of my siblings.

Or how I'd been the keeper of the gang's battered copy of *Animals of the World* to make sure everyone had a fitting name once they turned ten. To that, he'd asked, "Are you sure I'm a chameleon?"

"Positive," I'd answered. "Unless you want to be a fish." He hadn't wanted to be any kind of sea life, not that I could blame him. Chameleons were cuter.

The ease that'd been between us when we'd chatted in Tower A had a barrier in the light of day. We walked together quietly, stealing the occasional glance at one another. If we weren't two of a kind, I would assume I was doing this wrong. At least I could say that we both were.

It was quite the walk to get to where Vance wanted to take me. My nose picked up the scent of brine before we stopped in front of our destination.

"Huh. You were right," I said, eyeing the sign out front. I'd never have guessed we were going to an oyster bar. Chance sniffed the air, and I had the feeling he was a little dubious based on the smell coming off the river.

"I thought you might want to try something new." Vance had a boyish smile. He'd lit up the moment he'd surprised me. "My treat, of course."

"Are you sure?" I asked shyly.

He jingled his coin purse. It sounded full. "I don't believe in the bank, so I still have a little something."

I nodded at that. I'd already had Chance squirrel away the individual coins from the pouch Agent Cairn had given me. There was a likelihood I'd never see those clorets again, but I hadn't had time to run it to the bank, so now they were in some forgotten corner of RSI.

We headed inside and were sat at a table by a window. I'd tucked Chance away into his pouch since folk wanted a mouse-free experience when eating at a place like this. I gawked a bit. The furnishings were new, the table freshly shined and clean. The walls were different hues of blue, painted with shells, bubbles, and various kinds of sea life.

My favorite part of the establishment were the lamps, magelights held in place by the tentacle arms of hanging glass octopi. One was suspended over our table, though the light was off with sunlight still streaming through the windows.

The menu was an intimidating thing, with seafood cooked in most any way I could imagine and a few more. With Chance squeaking suggestions from my hip, I ordered the catch of the day baked in herbs. Once Vance ordered, the menus were taken and replaced with a basket of buttered rolls.

With sunlight playing over half of his face, I realized something. I didn't like his carefully formed fake face all that much, knowing it was a lie. It was too perfect, unlike the Vance I knew. I looked at him and imagined gray eyes instead of green, brown hair, and a Tulari mark over his brow.

Surprisingly, it helped. I plucked a roll and tore off a bit to feed to Chance under the table, asking, "Do you think we're going to be advanced after today?"

He shook his head. "Is anyone at our school impressed when we do what they've suggested?"

My lips quirked. I supposed he had a point there.

"I know it's important to you. Look, I hate to say it, but I think we're being held back by one of our teammates." He popped a piece of bread in his mouth and chewed, leaving me concerned about who he was going to name.

At the same time...I knew exactly which friend he was referring to. He waited until I sighed and said, "Carmen."

He put his palms up. "I know I'm one to talk. It just seems that any time we need to do something as a team, she puts on a bad attitude or disappears. And she literally uses you as a punching bag. I hate that."

"We're practicing," I said, defensive for her, though he wasn't fully wrong from an outsider's perspective. Since I still refused to hit her with any force, our evening Tosh Zorena practice looked like she was the aggressor. I wore the punch mitts and kick pads while she performed flowing fighting moves until she was tired and sore.

What he didn't realize was that she was teaching me, too. I could move with her and counter most anything she could throw at me at this point. "*She's* practicing," I added. "She's pushing herself to earn the title of Master of Tosh Zorena."

"What is she really learning, though, without practicing with someone who can teach her?" he asked. "No offense meant."

I shrugged, because I couldn't really answer that. "She's already a master because of the headband she inherited from her father," I said.

"You just said she's trying to earn the title," he pointed out.

I needed to think on that one and did so with a scrunched brow while nibbling on my bread. I thought of Carmen and the simmering frustration I glimpsed in her each time we practiced.

Vance waited and sipped from his glass of sweet tea. He did know me, because he said nothing until I finally did. "Clearly, she doesn't think she had earned the title. And I've been to her gym. No one around here can teach her the last secrets of her art that she doesn't already know," I said. Then I clutched the sides of my head. "Gods, I haven't even asked how she's been doing or if we can help her. She has to still be hurting from losing her father."

"Maybe. See if she's about to leave to take care of the rest of her family." By the lighthearted way he said this, I suspected he wouldn't be too upset if she left. That made sense—they were the two predators on our team, more likely to butt heads trying to get their way.

But Carmen was crew and my friend, and that *meant* something. She might be prickly, but she'd been there when I'd needed her most. The least I could do was return the favor.

"You think, once she comes around, we will…you know? Get to where I've been trying to take the team?" I asked.

He snapped his fingers and pointed at me. "You finished that stupid signpost challenge when she participated while I couldn't. You get her to try, and it won't be like we're limping along as Four and Chance."

I kept my thoughts on that to myself but knew: at some points this school year, it'd been Two or Three and Chance, sometimes just Me and Chance. RSI wanted to see how we did as a team with some external pressure applied, and we'd crumpled and were still recovering.

"I'll talk to her," I said, encompassing all my ideas and self-reflection in that one statement.

Our food arrived, and I took a deep breath of fragrant fish. It flaked apart for my fork and melted buttery smooth on my tongue. My eyes closed with the simple pleasure of that moment, before Vance had me try an oyster. He'd gotten a dozen of them placed on ice and resting in half their shells.

It was cold, slippery, and a little sweet. But I liked the unique taste. Chance poked his head out from under the tablecloth to give me pleading eyes, so I gave him a taste of my fish. I didn't think he could handle an oyster.

Since Vance shared, so did I. He savored a bite of fish. "You know, my dad took me fishing once," he said. He closed his eyes, and a furrow appeared between his brows. "We spent the better part of a day in a boat he'd rented."

I was hesitant to break his concentration. He must've been speaking about his real dad. "Did you catch anything?" I asked in a low voice.

"We got a few nibbles and a sunburn. But it was fun just to spend time with him. He talked to me about life…not that…" His eyelids flicked up. "Not that I knew much about that at the time or even remember what he said. It's all as elusive as the flash of scales underwater."

I tilted my head. "Maybe it will come back to you," I said.

"I'm hoping so." He frowned for a moment. "Anyway, that was delicious."

"This place was a great choice. Thank you for taking me here," I said. As he was opening his mouth to reply, I pointed at the octopus lamp. "Though I want one of these now."

"We could steal it."

For a prolonged moment, we both inspected it. He rubbed his jaw, and I eyed the way it'd been suspended on a hook from a loop of glass atop the sculpture's head. It'd be easy to lift if it didn't weigh as much as a small child, but impossible to smuggle out of the restaurant without someone noticing.

"But then we couldn't eat here again," I said.

He nodded in agreement. "Not worth it."

We laughed together and finished our meal. The conversation turned away from RSI, and I was glad for a short break from it. Despite the quiet start to our date, we finished it chatting until the angle of sunlight slanted, suggesting that we needed to return to the school before the doors locked for the night.

We did so holding hands. When it came time to say good-night and head for our separate halls, though, I chickened out of the expected hug or whatever and avoided eye contact. Vance squeezed my hand and said good night without sounding bothered.

See? I thought. *He knows me.*

CHAPTER 21

COUSINS

As THE CITY bells rang with the morning hour, Carmen woke with an exaggerated groan. I heard it since I'd been lazing in my cot and letting the morning fog roll out from behind my eyes one blink at a time. Most of our roommates had left to start their day already.

"You's okay?" I whispered.

"Yeah," she grumbled, leveraging herself up. "My aunt's going to be late to work if I don't hurry."

I followed her out of the room and down the hall toward the girls' bath. "Mind if I go with you?" I asked.

She startled slightly, glancing over her shoulder. "I guess."

She was only splashing some water on her face and arranging her hair, which was just long enough to run a comb through except for her longer fringe of bangs. I did the same, noting that I needed to cut my hair soon, which meant she was long overdue for one. In true Carmen style, she didn't want something so universal as her hair being used against her in a fight. Even though she hadn't been in an actual fight since this summer, as far as I knew.

Once refreshed, we changed into fresh uniforms and went to the cafeteria for breakfast in a bag. A sleepy Chance popped his head out of his pouch, just to disappear again when he realized I wasn't picking up anything special.

We were out of the school and heading toward her aunt's neighborhood when Carmen released an unrestrained yawn and stretched her long limbs over her head. "Don't you have an apprenticeship to go to?" she asked.

A little blush touched my cheeks. "I got fired," I said quietly. Maybe I should've mentioned it earlier, but it was still embarrassing.

"Heh. Really?" She looked over at me, eyes darting top to bottom. "What'd you do? Did a customer get disrespectful and you just had to…one-two?" Her fists darted out, shadow-boxing an invisible opponent.

"No—"

"Because that's how I'd get fired if I had an apprentice-ship," she said.

"I just didn't show up last weekend and was fired, even though Miss Barrios sent the shop a note."

"Oh, because of Vance." She frowned, smoothing out the bag holding her breakfast that'd been crumpled in one fist. "Why do you sound upset about it, pipsqueak?"

"I didn't do nothin' wrong. Mistress Reni even knew why I had to miss work…kind of," I grumbled.

"Did you tell her that?" she asked.

"No."

"When she fired you," Carmen said with more emphasis.

"She sent a letter to RSI," I said.

She threw up her free hand. "So, you didn't go over there and have her tell you to your face that you're fired? You didn't talk to her about the situation?"

My sheepish face really told her everything she needed to know. "I'll go talk to her, then," she said.

I did my best Chance impression, palms coming up. "No no. Wait. I don't even want… We don't have to have a confrontation."

"Ugh. Sometimes you have to fight for your own interests. No one else is going to do it for you." Her brows came down for her usual scowl. "Wish it'd happened to me."

Gods help the mistress or master she was assigned to when she finally picked up an apprenticeship.

After a few minutes of walking, she said, "Look, I'm just minding my little cousins. You've met them, right? It's going to be really boring."

"We could go do something fun," I suggested.

"Like what? We've played every board game and done everything you can do with a deck of cards about fifteen times over. I've read to them, we've done some gardening…" Her bangs flapped when she blew out a frustrated breath.

I gawked at her for a moment. *That's right. She doesn't have siblings.*

"I've got some ideas, then," I said.

We were nearly to our destination already. Carmen's aunt lived about half a bell's walking distance from RSI and never came to the school for a visit. The homes along this street were small, cramped things built too close together, with gardens that grew into one another.

I barely recognized the woman waiting for us as Carmen's aunt. The last time I'd seen her, she'd been disheveled and crying, but now she looked competent in a slate-colored dress and a bag over her shoulder. She kept the front door to her house ajar and held a sleeping baby. The look she exchanged with Carmen wasn't exactly friendly, but her tone was gentle as she offered the baby to her. "I need to be going."

"Yeah. Bye, Auntie," Carmen said gruffly. She accepted and held the baby like a fragile vase, cradled from the underside at a safe distance away from her torso.

"This one of your friends?" she asked, raising a brow my way.

"Yeah, that's Heather."

"We've met," I murmured.

A flash of recognition lit in her eyes, and she extended a hand to shake. "Gloria Montes. You two keep my boys out of trouble, okay?"

"Yes, ma'am," I answered, shaking her hand briefly.

Gloria left, and Carmen gestured for us to head into the house. I took another look at how she was holding the baby and held my hands out for him. She passed him over without hesitation, and I cooed, "Oh, you've gotten so much bigger."

"Still not a tot," Carmen sighed. "Might say something like 'mama' if you ask real nice."

We went to the kitchen, where the other two kids were already up and fed. Carmen still slipped part of her meal to them and made introductions. Their names all started with the same letter, so I took extra notice to memorize them. There was Augusto, the eldest at six years of age; Alvaro, who proudly displayed three fingers when I asked how old he was; and Alejandro, who was nearing his first birthday.

"I like to be called Gus," Augusto told me. Well, that made it a little easier.

"Okay. Well, do you want to go do something fun today?" I asked with a smile.

Gus eyed me skeptically, while Alvaro immediately exclaimed, "Yeah!"

I took them to my old favorite place, Haladay Park. As I suspected, on a nice weekend day, the open field by the picnic area was teeming with kids, parents, and dogs. I instructed the boys to stay where we could see them and set them loose, while Carmen and I sat on a bench with our backs to a picnic table. I sat cross-legged, more comfortable that way. She was a little slack-jawed as she looked around.

"My older siblings would take me here all the time. They'll run off all their excess energy and be napping just past lunchtime," I told her.

"Hmm, smart," she said.

Baby Alejandro stirred and started to cry. Carmen

fumbled him out of his covered wagon and tried to shush him. The attention she got from a few of the other parents sitting around us intensified when she didn't immediately figure out what he needed.

I promised to keep an eye on her older cousins before pointing out the little hut atop a hill used for privacy. She shouldered a bag of supplies and left with the baby, disappearing for long enough that I wondered if I should try to look for her. Gus and Alvaro were having a great time, fitting into a game where they tossed a ball to other kids.

Carmen returned, placing a now-burbling Alejandro back into his wagon gently before thumping onto the bench next to me. She blew out a stressed breath, looking frazzled. "I hate kids," she whispered.

That was really no surprise. "Your aunt can't find someone to mind them for the weekend?" I asked.

Her lips quirked. "That costs clorets."

"How many?"

"For two kids and a baby? Too many," she sighed. "She promised to make something work when Alejandro's a tot."

She sounded skeptical, and I couldn't fully blame her. Her aunt had to be something for them during the week, since Carmen had class and the boys weren't of age for fundamental school yet.

"I gots some spare money," I ventured.

Carmen rolled her eyes. "For the hundredth time, *gots* isn't a word."

I stuck my tongue out at her. "Anyway, maybe your aunt wouldn't be able to pay, but I wouldn't mind it so you could get a break."

"You'd do that for me?" she asked more quietly.

"Of course. I miss seeing you." *And caring for kids has made you extra angry,* I added on mentally, since that would just make her put up her defenses again.

"You see me every day," she said, putting them up anyway.

"I mean, we don't always get to talk or practice Tosh Zorena," I said.

She nodded in agreement. We sat and watched kids play for a while in companionable silence. If I wasn't wearing the RSI uniform, I'd join them. We were both getting the occasional disapproving look just by being here as troubled youths.

Carmen was the one to speak up, not looking at me as she asked, "Can I tell you something?"

"Of course."

"I wish I had an apprenticeship. I want to learn something new." Her gaze was pointed up at the puffy clouds slowly scrolling across the sky.

"It was kind of fun," I said. "Uh. When I did well."

"You just weren't in the right place. You need a pile of work, silence, and your mouse, and you'd do great," she said with a chuckle.

As I'd been playing with Chance by chasing him with my fingertips across my lap, I couldn't disagree. "That does sound nice," I agreed.

"I just...I don't know. Coach Stryker told me I need to diversify, and I've really been thinking about it. She's right." Her shoulders drooped as she spoke. "You said you miss me, and I wondered how you could because we practice my art together. But"—she made a pained face—"there's more to life than Tosh Zorena. I...guess. It's not a personality or a job, and I can't make it my way of life like I once thought I could."

I reached over and tentatively touched her arm in sympathy. She didn't flinch away, just finally looked at me with unshed tears pooling in her eyes.

I didn't know what Coach Stryker meant by *diversify*, but from Carmen's words, I had a good idea. Her dedication did make her hard to talk to sometimes. I was just lucky enough that she'd shared this part of herself with me by making me her first trainee.

Maybe that's why I felt comfortable to say what I did. "It's okay, Carmen," I told her. "You can still honor your family's legacy with Tosh Zorena and do something else."

She closed her eyes, and two tears streaked down her cheeks. "He...my father...he promised he'd teach me when he came back," she said in a low voice. "He was going to help me earn my mastery with the family secrets. Moves no one alive knows now. And I just...life would be different if he or my uncle returned from the war. My cousins would have a man to look up to instead of just me."

That had to be a devastating blow, with how much she'd put into learning the art. "I'm sorry," I said.

"I've broken the creed multiple times. You know I've misused what I know on those weaker than myself," she continued. "I've shown off for reasons that didn't include discipline and self-defense. I don't deserve to be called a master, yet here we are."

"Here we are," I echoed. I elbowed her side. "Also, so? Nobody's around that will tell the gym. You're Master Montes, and no one can take that away from you. And you can be something else if you want."

She sniffed and swiped impatiently at her nose, looking at me with a bit of disbelief.

"There are dozens of guilds you could join. Want to do something with your hands? Apprentice to a smith or a woodworker." That's where I could see her thriving. "Just don't join the Tailor Guild. I don't think you'd like stitchery." I could see her bending needles in frustration after getting poked one too many times. And those tiny tools were shockingly expensive, I'd learned.

Carmen smiled. Just a bit, but it was a start. "Thanks, pipsqueak," she said.

"Anytime," I said.

We stayed out until any part of me exposed to the sun warmed with the promise of a sunburn. On the way back, I bought all of us a smoked sausage from a street vendor. I savored mine, letting myself remember and miss Thylacine, just for a moment. We'd spent so many days like this when I was younger, but now I was the teen holding a small hand as I helped Carmen guide her cousins back toward their home. Life had moved on without him, just like it was doing for my friend and her family.

"Hey, do you guys want to see some fairy houses?" I asked, remembering that Chance's family didn't live all that far from them.

They enthusiastically agreed, and Carmen gave me a look. "How do you do that?" she asked.

"What?"

"Get them all excited."

I just smiled and shrugged. "I have a big family. I just remember what the little kids used to love. Besides…I promised Chance we'd visit his family." I dropped my voice to keep this between us, not sure how the boys would react to so many mice. She probably had a better idea.

Chance bobbled with excitement on my shoulder. "Family going to be so proud of me, yes yes!"

"How big is his family?" she asked.

"That's a great question," I said evasively. "I think they're still making more."

"So, they're just like any other mice. Just a little smarter," she said, raising an eyebrow. "I think the boys can handle it."

I nodded in agreement. She tried to narrow down how big, exactly, Chance's family was, and her eyebrows inched ever higher as I started exaggerating the flood of mice that would greet us.

Once we were back in the boys' neighborhood, I took them to the stand of trees where I remembered the Balenciaga family lived. Chance trembled with excitement, practically vibrating by the time I spotted the tiny painted houses folk set aside for fairies.

I lowered him to the ground first, while Carmen's two older cousins circled the houses. "Don't do that," Carmen had to tell Gus when he tried to pick one up. He was only about twice as big as it was.

She glanced at me and circled her hand, as if asking, "Where are they?"

Chance poked his head out of the second story of the house, through what was decorated to be a window. His pointed head swiveled left to right, and I immediately knew something was wrong. His distress only became more apparent when he jumped out of the house and went into the next one. He went into each fairy house before scampering back over to my feet.

I'd only promised the boys fairy houses, so they didn't realize something was amiss. I lifted Chance in my palm, and he squeaked, "They're gone! All of them!"

CHAPTER 22

GONE MISSING

Carmen's eyes narrowed when I told her I needed to go somewhere. She cast a reluctant gaze at her cousins. "They'll nap once you get them home," I said in an undertone.

"Something's wrong," she stated, and I nodded. "I wish I could go with you."

While I wished she could too, she had to take care of her family. I promised I would update her tonight and rushed off with Chance to visit Little Wonders Pet Shop. He'd curled into a distressed ball in my palm.

I navigated the midday crowd. Though distracted, I still noticed a set of slim fingers trying to sneak into my coin purse and swatted them away, giving the urchin a look of warning.

I sighed through my nose, knowing I'd have dozens of street kids finding me for a repeat of this...but I gave the urchin a silver cloret. He displayed gaps in his teeth as he gasped and bobbed toward me. "Thank ye, mum."

I put a finger to my lips and winked, indicating with a jerk of my chin that he disappear. He did so with the kind of haste I recognized all too well.

Shaking my head, I said to Chance. "If anyone can find your family, it's Thomas."

He lifted his head. "We go see nice boy?"

"Unless you have any ideas about where your family went."

"No no. We have fairy house. No reason to leave. Strange everyone gone. Another carpenter mouse family should move in but didn't. Empty house very bad sign, yes yes." He clutched his front paws in concern.

"Did you smell anything that didn't belong?" I wracked my memory for the poisons I'd learned in Alchemy class last year. "Something sweet, maybe?"

"No food smells."

"Any sign of a struggle?" I mused.

He snuffled thoughtfully. "Maybe. Claw marks happen in house all the time from fun. Hard to say if new marks from fun or not."

There had to be something. A family the size of Chance's couldn't just disappear with no traces. "No unusual smells at all?" I pressed.

"Um. No." His little nose twitched as he hesitated. "I not have words to explain."

Our communication wasn't the only problem. There was a sign on the door of the pet shop, stating that it was closed until further notice.

"Musty devils," I muttered.

I knocked anyway, and when no one came to answer, I unleased Chance. He fit himself under the threshold without needing any instruction. After what took maybe five minutes, the door unlocked, and Shauna's face peered out.

"Where've you been?" Shauna whispered. She beckoned for me to come in and handed me back my mouse.

"I still good spy. I find her," he chattered.

I pet down his back, focused on the expression on Shauna's face. She was clearly upset with me, but we'd only missed one weekend while Vance was being questioned. How much could change in that time?

Fletcher was leaning over to clean the inside of a kennel. "Ah, hello, Heather." Even his usual cheerful tone was dampened. The sinking feeling in my belly was only getting worse, accompanied by sweaty palms and a twitch in my eyelid that wouldn't stop. I might've combusted if they didn't tell me what was wrong soon.

Shauna turned her face away from me, her lips moving soundlessly as she asked Fletcher something and gestured. He looked at me from top to bottom with a frown, taking in the RSI uniform with a critical eye. When his blue eyes met mine, the determined set of his lips suggested he'd come to some kind of decision. "We need all the help we can get," he sighed.

He turned his wheeled chair and indicated I come with him. We sat at his kitchen table while Shauna stayed in the main room and picked up a rag to clean the rest of the open kennel.

Chance scampered across the table and stood on his hind legs before the veterinarian. The story of his family's disappearance tumbled out of him at double his usual fast-paced speech. Despite that, Fletcher nodded along and eventually drew a hand down his face. "I'm sorry this happened to you, Chance. You've come to the right place. We know where they probably are."

The mouse perked up. "We go now and help them find home again, yes yes?"

"I'm afraid it's not that simple," Fletcher said. "You're going to find this hard to believe… There is a group out there. A gang, some would say, made up entirely of mages, so secretive that many think they don't exist."

Every little hair on my body stood on end. "Morashi Venom?" I blurted.

His brows rose. "You've heard of them."

I froze for a moment at his disapproving tone. To him, there was no reason I should know about them, and I wasn't about to tell him I knew a former member. So, I cut straight to the honesty I could give. "Madam Morashi terrorized my old gang and killed a few of my siblings. I have definitely heard of *her*." My hands balled into fists on the table.

Fletcher took another long look at me, his gaze lingering on the taut white skin stretched across my knuckles. "That saves me some breath, trying to convince you she's real," he said far too calmly. "Recently, the Morashi have begun hosting annual auctions in and around Kaiamear. What they offer interests mages of all walks of life—that's how I first heard of them. Something's changed this year. They are probably looking to expand their list of buyers, as they have aggressively trapped little wonders of all kinds and taken them to an unknown location."

I gaped at him in horror. "You think they gathered up Chance's family to sell them?"

"Exactly. I couldn't be sure at first, when we had salamander and birds' eggs disappearing. Since we last saw you, the number of little wonders coming here asking if we've seen their babies, siblings, friends, parents…it's too many. Amongst them are witnesses saying the thieves are universally Tulari," he said.

"We have to do something," I murmured. My mind whirled through all the possible options. I'd talk to Vance; maybe he would know where the missing little wonders were taken.

"We *are* doing something. And this is where you can help us." He reached over to pat the back of my hand. "The pet shop is acting as a sanctuary for all the little wonders who can make it here. Our second floor is packed with small friends. If you or Chance come across any little wonders in the city, tell them to come here. The Morashi cannot reach them here."

For a moment, I had a flash of skepticism. It wouldn't

exactly be difficult to break into the pet shop. It had no magic defenses and, with the bones of an inn, had more windows than an average two-story building. Hells, *little wonder* was even in the name.

But there was wisdom in spreading a warning and giving the animals a place to go that was safer than their nests when the Morashi had proven they knew where to look for them. I nodded back and said, "I'll help."

"Me too!" Chance squeaked.

"Good. Thomas is out with Edgimus and Wils right now, doing just that. Perhaps he can take you around the city later to point out a few species you don't know about. He's a master at it." He chuckled fondly. "And you could also let Patches know. She's an older girl now, but she's probably still got a paw on feligryph gossip."

"Patches have many scary friends, yes yes!"

I glanced over at Chance curiously, wondering if he was talking about the creature that'd chased Davit's Day through the sewers. He still wouldn't tell me any details other than that it was Patches's friend.

"What about the group of little wonders the Morashi have already caught?" I asked.

Fletcher grimaced. "We're still developing a plan for rescuing them, if we even can. You have to understand. If Madam Morashi is involved..." He flashed his palms helplessly.

"You don't mean...you would just have them be sold?" I asked in disbelief.

His tone sharpened. "It's too dangerous to consider unless we have significant help, and I will hear no arguments to the contrary. You know what it's like, don't you? Considering she attacked your gang." His eyes narrowed on me in speculation. "Is that related to how you landed in RSI?"

I fidgeted under his scrutiny. "I don't want to talk about

it." That was a little quick and blunt toward my friends' father, so I added, "Sir."

"So, yes." He nodded in understanding. "If you ever want to talk about it—"

"I don't," I repeated.

"—I will be here." He gestured to his wheeled chair.

I wondered if I could trust Fletcher with such a story. It was bad enough that I'd let slip that I used to be in a gang. Any reasonable father would probably bar his kids from spending time with me after learning something like that. I dreaded the moment he kicked me out of the pet shop. He wouldn't yet, not with an ongoing·crisis I could help with.

Little did he know, I was going to help a lot more than just gathering little wonders here and there across Kaiamear. He'd handed me information that would impress the Spymaster. There was no way Manny wouldn't launch an immediate spy operation to diffuse this upcoming auction.

"I need to go for now," I said, rising from the table and scooping up Chance. "But I'll be back before you know it."

"Heather," he said, stopping me after a few paces. "Don't talk to the peacekeepers about this."

I couldn't help a little scoff. "I would never."

I SPOKE TO CARMEN FIRST, encouraging her to come back to RSI for dinner. She noticed how scared I sounded and had me sit on her aunt's couch. The boys were still napping, so they wouldn't overhear us if we were quiet.

Carmen dropped onto the couch next to me. "I take it you found out where the mice went?" she coaxed.

"Kind of. It's big. Really, really big," I told her.

"Gods, you still sound terrified, pipsqueak. Tell me what's going on," she demanded.

I clasped my shaking fingers and told her everything I'd just learned. Once I had, she lay back on the couch, sinking deep into the embrace of the fabric. "No," was all she said.

"No, what?" I asked.

"I know what you're thinking. You're going to get the team together, and we're going to save all the little wonders. I just want to say preemptively, *no*. It was one thing tricking that pair of idiots who stole the Eye from you to save your sister." She chopped at the air, scowling. "It's entirely different to face the Morashi directly."

"We're not," I protested immediately. "We're telling Manny for the third challenge. A warning about a Morashi auction has to impress him. He'll know what to do from there to save all the little wonders."

Carmen raised an unimpressed eyebrow. "And?"

"And as an intermediate team that's already finished all three challenges, we'll be a part of the saving," I added. I hated how doubtful she seemed as she sucked on the inside of her cheek.

She gusted out a sigh. "No one's seen Manny in weeks."

"I'll talk to the headmaster, then," I said, not to be deterred. "And Miss Barrios and any other teacher who will listen. We can't just let the auction happen. Not just because of the animals." I lifted my shoulders and called on my inner Ram. "Think of the money, Carmen. Think of how much Madam Morashi stands to make by selling rare creatures to fancy nobles with more clorets than sense."

"Mmm. Go with that angle." She jerked her chin toward me. "If you want anyone to care, lead with the money, not the animals."

My face surely reflected my scandalized reaction.

"Just trust me, pipsqueak. You know who you should really talk to before you go to the headmaster?"

"Vance," I said.

"Margot," she said at the same time. We exchanged a

glance. "Fine. Talk to the whole team before you do anything else."

I promised her I would.

AND I WOULD'VE KEPT that promise, too, had I not nearly walked into Headmaster Radcliffe upon returning to RSI alone. Dinner was still hours away, which meant Fariq and Margot were still working.

The headmaster was just coming out of his office. I heard the door slam as I was turning my feet toward Hawthorne Hall and the waiting softness of my cot. I had every intention of lying down long enough for my heart to calm before I got my crew involved in what I'd learned.

"Good afternoon, Miss Mouse." He stopped in the hall, standing with legs spread. It was the kind of pose where a predator like him expected prey like me to stop and talk to him.

I reluctantly lifted my face to meet his gaze. "Good afternoon, sir," I said.

He tilted his head, putting on a friendly smile. "Everything okay?"

I could tell from his expression that it took him almost no time at all to realize that everything was not, in fact, okay. My overall demeanor and the downcast mouse hanging off my shoulder gave me away before I could even open my mouth.

"Do you want to talk in my office?" he suggested.

"Are you taking over the third challenge for the Spymaster?" I blurted.

He chuckled. "You're going to have to remind me which challenge that is."

"To impress the Spymaster," I prompted.

His expression shifted, a clear glimmer of interest in his

eyes. "I didn't realize your team was assigned that one so early. From intermediate on, we tailor the challenges more."

Oh. I hadn't known that, but it was something I'd over-think later.

"As you know, the Spymaster is a busy man. If it's something worth his attention, I will write to him for you," he offered.

That was good enough for me. I mentally apologized to my crew and stepped into his office, taking a moment to look into the curio cabinet where the fake version of Stone's Crown rested. If I could steal this, I could convince Headmaster Radcliffe I had learned something the Spymaster would want to know immediately.

I sat across from him as he took a quill and parchment and took notes on what I had to say. Taking Carmen's advice, I stressed the Morashi were running a money-making endeavor by auctioning magical creatures.

Ultimately, after I shared everything, he looked down at what he'd written and asked, "Is this all?"

My heart skipped a beat. "Y-yes?" I stammered.

His eyes shifted as he scanned the page before he folded the paper neatly. "Well, I will send the message along for you. The Spymaster will see it soon."

CHAPTER 23

SHAINA

Over dinner, I retold my findings a third time to my whole crew. The one thing I didn't say was that the headmaster and Manny now knew what I did. Before this conversation, I thought disclosing what I knew early was a mistake, because Vance would have more to add to it. But he paled to a violently ill shade and excused himself as soon as I revealed the Morashi were hosting an auction.

Besides, it was clear everyone had a different opinion on how to proceed.

"If we stay quiet and gather more information, we can supply the Spymaster with the when and the where, not just that it's happening. That way, he can make a complete plan to stop the event," Margot reasoned.

Carmen still wanted nothing to do with it. "It's too dangerous for a group of kids, even kids like *us*, to take care of it."

Though not entirely surprising, Fariq mostly agreed with Carmen. "We report what we know, and that's all. The peace-keepers should handle it," he said.

Vance didn't return to the table, leaving his meal practi-cally untouched. I threw it out for him and guessed he was out of any potential job involving the Morashi until further notice. It was too soon after the trauma of his questioning. But without him, we were still a fractured team.

I went to bed while worrying into my bottom lip with my teeth. My worries weighed down my gut, which churned no matter how I laid out while trying to get comfortable.

There's no way I can save the little wonders alone.

But I was going to see it done. Those lives had more value than another lining of clorets in Madam Morashi's coin purse.

I HAD A FITFUL SLEEP, so when paper crushed against my chest after I moved my arm, my eyes peeled open immediately to see what it was. It was before sunrise, so I took a candle into the hall and inspected an envelope dangling from my wrist.

A corner of the paper was still attached to the spell rune on my bracelet. I had to give it a hearty tug to free it, bending the missive out of shape. Frowning between the letter and my bracelet, I tried to remember if any of the adults had mentioned this rune could send me correspondence.

I opened the letter before sighing and going to retrieve my journal and something to write with. The Spymaster had returned the key to the city I'd sent to him and coded his message. Either the cypher was a difficult one, or my tired mind kept making mistakes, but I ruined a few pages in my journal with scribbles and ink blots trying to decode what he'd written. I slowly woke up in full and made a passable translation.

Miss Mouse,

Congratulations on completing the key to the city challenge. However, you still need the physical key, don't you? You are also mistaken about completing it first. The team SHAINA showed their key a couple days before Five & Chance.

I am not impressed with your half-baked effort to report on an event the Crown is already well aware of. We are facing a serious rising threat to the stability of Altare, while animals are auctioned all the time. Pursue leads to the identity of the false prince and his accomplices and leave anything and everything to do with this auction alone. That is an order.

Instead of any kind of name, Manny had inked in an intricate gryphon rampant at the bottom of the message. I stared at it while my candle melted down to a stub. Miss Barrios had taken to signing notes addressed to me with a fox, taking after the old Menagerie tradition of drawing our animal namesakes rather than any further identification. She was welcome to do so, as our mentor and Big Sister.

But the incredibly busy Spymaster had taken the time to draw a gryphon rampant and sign this…cruel message…with a symbol to represent himself. Why would he bother? He didn't give a lick about the Morashi's auction or the little wonders disappearing across Kaiamear.

"Half-baked," I seethed aloud. That one stung because it was true; I still didn't know when or where the auction would take place, while it was old news to Manny. I thought he'd take my report and run with it. Foolishly, I figured he would care about the Morashi's doings and the little wonders. I'd assumed I would have help in saving Chance's family when there was no hope of that.

My gaze skimmed the last line once more and my eyelid twitched. *That is an order.* I checked my decoding one more time, hoping to change the finality of his words. But there was no mistaking it for anything other than what it was.

The only thing that puzzled me was the extra letter in SHINA's acronym. Had they added another member? Who did I know whose name started with A, who was looking to join an intermediate team?

Also, why'd he return the key? I definitely didn't need it anymore.

A creak sounded nearby. I looked up as Wildcat left our shared room with a towel and a fresh uniform over her arm. She smiled, ever a perky morning person, before getting a good look at the state I was in. I imagined it was quite the sight—rumpled hair, dark hollows under my eyes, and the tense way I sat with a letter held between my fists. Not to mention the way I was gritting my teeth and trembling with restrained emotion.

Her eyes widened. "You's ok—"

"Aleena," I said.

She startled and glanced around. "What is it?" she asked, dropping her voice.

I hadn't called her by her real name for the better part of four years. While she thought there was some urgency, I was busy staring at her bracelet.

Wildcat and a few of my siblings were given the freedom to leave RSI much faster than I had. I hadn't questioned it before; I'd just been glad to have her company in the Shadowed Market...where she'd overhead me talking to our older siblings about Theovald and the key to the city challenge.

Musty devils. There was a universal truth shared between thieves and spies. It was easier to steal an object or information from someone who'd already gone through the hard work of getting it. I had a strong hunch that was what'd happened to me.

I blew out my candle and stood, advancing toward her. "Did you squeal on me, Aleena?" I asked in a low, accusatory tone.

She backed away from me. Just one step, but it was enough. "It's not like that, Mouse. I just..."

"You joined Sybella's team," I said. For a moment, my anger gave way to confusion. "An intermediate team?"

"Miss Liang allowed it, long as I'm passing my classes,"

she said. Her shoulders sagged. "How'd ya figure it out so fast?"

"Your team name changed," I gritted out.

She scuffed a foot, looking anywhere but at me. "Sybella invited me to join her team if I could acquire an advantage for her. So, I told her about Theovald's Keys. She already stole an address from your pillow."

Well, that explained why I couldn't find Margot's note. But I could hardly believe what I was hearing. "You could've joined my team!"

"You's all didn't ask." She sounded hurt.

I pinched the bridge of my nose. Maybe I didn't ask, but that was because I didn't know. RSI encouraged teams to stay in the five- and six-members range. No one had mentioned a beginner-level kid could join an intermediate team. Or that two kids in the stealth track could join the same team, because undoubtedly, Wildcat was going to be taking Agility and Craft with Sybella and me when her schedule changed.

"I...I assumed," I said weakly. "It's not too late. You could still join Five & Chance."

The sad returning smile she gave me was as clear as a shout. It *was* too late. "I need to have a different boss than the sneak that would always get picked before me," she said.

I opened my mouth, but only a small gasp sounded. That felt like a blow straight to the kidneys, aimed to drop me to the ground in agony. She was never intending to join my team, and if SHAINA hadn't picked her up, another team would've. We were bound for this moment, and I hadn't even seen it coming.

The door opened behind her, and Wildcat scooted to the side, revealing a bleary-eyed Sybella. She closed the door soundlessly and gestured for us to come with her. "Thought I should toss my two clorets into this chat," she said.

While Wildcat gave her a grateful look, I knew my face gave away that I was grudging at best, resentful at worst. But

I had some words for Sybella I was grateful I didn't need to contain until the classes we shared at midday.

I crossed my arms, tucking the Spymaster's letter and my journal between them, before following both girls down the hall. "By all means," I said.

Sybella nudged Wildcat toward the girls' bath. My sister turned, trying to catch my eye, but I kept my face turned away. "Go," I muttered. I was too aware of how tired and irritated I was, which would lead to me saying things I'd later regret.

Wildcat left to take her bath, while Sybella led me toward the library. "This is your preferred spot, I think," she said, heading up to the second floor and the last nook. She drew the curtain and gestured for me to go inside.

"Stop looking at me like that," she sighed once she drew the curtain behind her and sat across from me. I liked this study space for its cushions and size—big enough to have meetings with my team. That Sybella knew that meant I was predictable, and she'd cared enough to notice it. "If the odds were the other way around, you would have done the same thing. Admit it."

"I don't see how that's relevant," I said defensively.

She sighed and adjusted the pile of her mahogany hair over her shoulder. Even sleep-rumpled and without makeup, she was a pretty girl with graceful limbs and long, deft fingers. She reminded me of a more confident Wildcat, a well-fed feline ready to hunt for the sport of it. If she could teach some of that poise to my sister, I could admit she would be a better team leader for her than I would ever be.

"Can you listen to me for a few minutes? With an open mind," she asked.

I pressed my lips together and eyed her distrustfully. But I still nodded. Sybella was difficult for me to read, yet my instincts told me to hear her out before I sought space to plan my revenge.

She suppressed a yawn. "I was going to tell you today about the challenge and Aleena. I should've figured you'd learned about it before I could explain. Look…I've been listening to you and your team for a while. You may think you've been careful, but in places you think are safe"—she gestured to encompass the nook we were in—"you are entirely too unsubtle."

My brows raised. "You've been spying on me," I stated.

"Royal. *Spy*. Institute. Don't think for a moment that I'm the only one," she said, rolling her eyes. "When you first got here, I thought the system would eat you up. You were one of Springfield's pets, after all."

"Pets," I echoed. Only certain groups referred to the Menagerie kids with that label, and I began looking at her in a new light. "Were you—"

"I'll tell you about me if you agree to my offer," she interrupted. I closed my mouth and waited, nursing a queasy feeling in my belly. "I know about the Eye of Acuity and that you carry it on your person. You've used it enough in our room when you think I'm not looking. Not to mention having complete conversations with your mouse. Clever thinking, by the way, making him the sixth member of your team. No one would expect it."

My throat felt dry suddenly. I needed to be so much more careful than I had been. Clearly, the walls had eyes and ears, even in my dorm room. "Do you know what he is?" I asked.

"You've called him a little wonder. I've put together enough to understand he can complete tasks for you." She shrugged casually. "Look, I know you well enough to realize you're going to fix every mistake you've been making now that you're aware of them. Last year, I watched you transform from a twitchy girl afraid of your shadow into the leader of *the* top-ranked beginner team. I wanted to know exactly how you worked, because in the end, I will lead SHAINA to the spot right above yours when we are all advanced."

I shook my head slowly. If she thought she was going to outdo Five & Chance, then we would have a true rivalry. One I would ensure my crew won.

"Now that both of our teams are complete, I recognize we are still years away from final rankings. I want to make you a deal, Mouse. Let's work together." She was completely serious. I inspected her for any sign of falsehood as she made her offer. "Tie your team's fate to mine. We float or sink together with double the resources and twice the talent. Why should we attempt to weaken each other's teams when it will only mean other groups will take the top opportunities away from us?"

"You want to be..." I searched for the right word.

"Allies. Confidantes. Sister teams," she supplied.

It was smart. A better idea than us leaving this library nook enemies, despite the blows to my pride. I didn't want to have a team I couldn't trust sleeping in the same room that I did. Yet, I asked, "Why Five & Chance? Are you allied with any other team?"

"I feel like I could trust you and some of your friends. We have a lot we can offer each other. I have no other alliances. I'm in the business of winning, not carrying dead weight to success," she scoffed. "Besides, you just learned something big. I can tell by..." She gestured toward me. "I mean, I can just tell."

I could've told her the Spymaster had already ordered me not to pursue it further, but I didn't want to discourage her from this alliance. "If you agree, we are crew. That means loyalty until the bitter end," I said, extending my hand.

She shook on it. "Then we are crew, and you never betray crew," she said with familiarity.

"You're a street kid, too," I noted.

Pressing her lips together in a fine line, she nodded. "I was saved a year before you got here. Are you familiar with the Third Street Jokers?"

Ah, musty devils. That was the name of a rival gang to Springfield's. Their turf bordered ours, but they had deeper pockets with multiple clubs and pleasure houses funneling money to their leader, a man who hid his identity behind a painted mask and a gaudy jester's hat. He was known, rather unoriginally, as the Jester.

"We were told to stay well away from them," I said, thinking back on how often they'd harried Menagerie kids. I'd gotten more than one beating from losing stolen valuables by having a Joker steal them from me. "But they occasionally tried to run interference on our jobs. Or we'd plan a job, just to see Jokers already on site."

A strange expression crossed her face. "Do you remember stealing a vase from the Altarian Heritage Museum?" she asked.

I immediately knew what she was talking about. I'd been twelve, lent to a small crew that included Cartier and Rozma, plus a couple of other large adults. We'd gotten word of the arrival of an antique gold-rimmed vase at the same time a pack of Jokers had, obviously, as they were in the process of stealing it when we arrived.

While the adults brawled outside, viciously enough to attract the attention of the museum guards, I had snuck inside and found the vase at the same time the Jokers' sneak had. It'd been big, nearly coming to my knees, with huge wing-shaped handles. She'd grabbed one handle while I'd taken hold of the other, the two of us tug-of-warring the priceless artifact between us.

"Please, I need it," the other sneak had begged. She'd had her face and hair covered by a dark scarf...

But there was only one reason Sybella would bring this up. "That was you, with the Jokers," I said. I felt the sting of guilt for how little I'd cared for the other kid's begging. "At the time, I'd thought the vase's sale would be the only thing that'd get my siblings through the winter. I couldn't let you have it."

"It was only fate that my handle broke first. I would've taken it from you and handed it to the Jester without a second thought had things been different. Instead, he beat me bloody for losing it to one of Springfield's pets," she said, eyes downcast. "You didn't wear anything over your face. I recognized you immediately when you came here."

"Is that why—"

"Yes. Whatever you ask, the answer is yes," she interrupted. "I didn't want to think rationally about it...but I came to realize that you were as much a victim as I was. The men in our life are meant to protect us, not send us into museums after dark to steal what shouldn't be taken."

I thought of Jace and his wealthy man's house as I murmured, "That's right."

"For what it's worth, I forgive you and look forward to our partnership." She eased to her feet, and I did the same. "Shall we meet this evening, both of our teams, to discuss how we will complete the third challenge together?"

I considered for a few moments. I would need some time to go over what'd just happened here and everything she'd told me. "Give me a couple days. There's something I need to do first," I said.

CHAPTER 24

ANY LEAD

THE REST of the day proceeded as normal, but I was mute, trapped in my head with all of my thoughts for company.

I'd assumed a lot of things and was lucky Wildcat had caused me to trip over them, because I would fix them to gain a proper spy's secretiveness. I'd thought I was unimportant enough that no one at our spy school would take notice of my doings. If Sybella was listening in on my crew and me, who else was?

The thought that I was being watched was suffocating. A mouse wasn't meant to be seen or heard, and that was my preferred existence as well… unless the teachers, headmaster, or Manny wanted to see how well Five & Chance was doing.

I invited my old friend paranoia to keep me company as I eyed the kids who sat at the tables around the one my crew habitually took. Were they listening at meals? Were they watching us in the halls or in our classes? I didn't dare take out the Eye of Acuity where it could be spotted.

I avoided talking about the auction with my friends by staying quiet and shaking my head occasionally. "Remember when she had a moment like this last year? She's brewing some big plan," Margot said for me during Language class. They left me be.

Instead of making a plan, I was weighing the implications of the Spymaster's order. *Leave anything and everything to do with this auction alone*, was his exact wording.

I'd never been great at following rules, orders, or instructions, but my usual response to something I didn't like was to hide from it. Until recently, most of my problems went away if I avoided them long enough.

I could obey Manny and let Chance's family get sold, alongside all the other little wonders that'd been captured. From what Fletcher said, it sounded like the Morashi had already gathered dozens, maybe even a hundred intelligent animals. While I knew that, I had no idea where to gather leads on what Manny really cared about: the false prince.

If I were to defy the Spymaster's order, I would risk being removed from RSI. Manny wouldn't want spies that couldn't follow a simple directive.

But...what if I could stop the auction without involving Manny and his resources? If I didn't cause him trouble, surely he would be impressed I ruined the Morashi's event without involving any Crown officials. No peacekeepers. No spies. Just Five & Chance, SHAINA, Fletcher's family...

And all of my siblings. All of them that could leave RSI, at least.

I would need to thread the eyehole of a tiny needle to pull it off. That was what really occupied my mind as I went about the motions of going to class. Because I had no intention of doing as I was ordered. However, I suspected Manny already knew that. I had to proceed carefully.

In Theater, we were released to practice our lines, and I darted into the library, making kissy noises to summon a certain plump feligryph. She came running up to me with her tail up and wound around my legs as I led her to a study nook—a different one than where I'd talked to Sybella this morning.

I opened my journal and tore out a piece of paper. After jotting down a message on it, I rolled it up into a tight scroll and placed it in Chance's paw. Bringing him up to my lips, I whispered what to do in a voice too quiet for anything but his little ears to hear.

He bobbed in agreement and scampered up to Patches when I placed him on the floor. "We go outside, yes yes? I have something to tell you," he squeaked to her.

"I NEED you to do something for me," I said to Vance over dinner. It was the first thing I'd said to my friends all day and earned a small startle.

He looked over the table at me, a surprisingly sheepish expression on his face. "Yeah? Well, I need you to know I'm sorry for charging off yesterday. It was just surprising that you mentioned the—"

"It's fine," I interrupted abruptly. He recoiled, brows lowering. "Sorry. I just want to talk where we've been meeting."

"Okay?" He extended the word out.

"Great." I flashed a brief smile and went back to my food. Everyone else at the table exchanged glances, but I wasn't about to talk about the threads of my newest plan in earshot of anyone I didn't trust.

I set aside a pile of veggies for Chance, hoping he would return soon. It was a risk to send him outside RSI without me. Patches would protect him for part of the journey, but I figured she would be at Little Wonders Pet Shop upon learning about the auction from Chance. I hoped she could help Fletcher as much as he thought she could.

The group in the cafeteria dwindled while I waited, absently stirring the dregs of my food to make it look like I was still eating. Margot, Fariq, and Carmen got up to go about their evenings too, while Vance leaned back in his chair, eyes closed. I was about to call it quits when I felt the familiar scratching of Chance's claws as he scaled my pants leg.

He flopped in my lap and extended out the rolled note. "I do good spy job for you, yes yes," he said.

"Good mouse," I said, bumping fists with him before setting him before the veggies I'd saved. He started nibbling while I unrolled the note.

On one side, my message: "I need information. Where and when will Theovald's Keys appear next?" And on the back, a scratched-out reply. I smiled and tucked the note away.

"Man very confused," Chance said. "But I stand on his foot until he reply."

I muffled a giggle. "You did such a good job."

I got up when Chance had a full belly and told Vance to give me half a bell to do something before we met up in Tower A. He nodded, looking at me with a raised brow. Maybe he was overflowing with concern, or curiosity, or both.

But first, I visited the theater's prop room and retrieved a coil of rope. I stuffed it in my book bag, warping it way out of shape with the bulk of how much rope I needed. Only then did I return to the front of the school and unlock the door to Tower A, letting Vance in a few minutes later.

I had the big coil of rope half undone, one end of it tied around my waist. He eyed me and frowned. "What the hells are you up to?"

I lifted the rest of the rope onto my shoulder and started for the staircase. "When I first got to RSI, I looked everywhere for a way to escape," I said.

"How'd that go for you?" From the scuff of his footsteps, he was following me.

"All the spies here had already made the exits Mouse-proof. I was trapped," I sighed.

"It's the bracelet."

"Yeah. They thought of everything. We only got freedom on their terms, and now it's monitored." I eyed my bracelet in the dim light of the falling evening. Though I'd grown used to it over time, it still made me uncomfortable that it didn't come off. And if it could send me messages from the Spymaster, there had to be more it could do that I wasn't aware of.

"Don't I know it," Vance grumbled. "But that doesn't tell me what you're planning."

I shrugged, though the rope was heavy enough to limit the movement. "I think I've found a hole in RSI's security, but I need your help with getting in and out."

At the top floor, I stopped before the window and looked down. Vance did the same, then glanced my direction. "At least give me a hint as to what's brewing in that mind of yours first," he said.

I lowered the rope to the ground and then followed suit, sitting heavily. We had time, as we'd need to wait until after dark before I escaped with no witnesses. "All right. Just between you and me," I said.

"And Chance," he added, since the mouse peeked out of his pouch, paws clasped in concern.

"And Chance. I already reported the auction to the Spymaster, and he ordered me not to do anything else." For most of my crew, that would be the end of things. But I could trust Vance to have a defiant streak similar to my own. "So, I want to bust the auction without his help. If we do it right, he'll be mighty impressed."

He whistled low. "That's real risky, boss."

"Right. Which is why I need more information before doing anything else. So, I'm going to go get it." I hooked my thumb toward the window. "I want it to look like I'm following the order, but I can't avoid skipping a day of classes. I figure if me leaving and returning isn't recorded, the teachers will assume I'm sulking in my room. And I left a note for Margot and Carmen to tell folk that was what I was doing."

Vance tilted his head. "You haven't even heard what I have to say about the auction."

I felt a little chagrinned, since I'd assumed something yet again. "I thought you wouldn't want to talk about it. Do you know when and where it'll be?"

"Don't get me wrong. I *don't* want to talk about it," he sighed. "But I will, for you. I don't know when, but I have a good guess as to where it'll be. If I'm right, we could run a job on the location and steal back the animals before the event."

He told me an address of an abandoned and run-down warehouse by the river. The perfect place to stash little wonders. His voice grew thready with fear as he spoke. "Promise me you won't go there alone. J-Just remember they're there. The m-madam could be there at a-any time."

"I won't," I said, trying to put him at ease. "I won't send Chance alone, either. They might have magic that tells them when a little wonder is around."

The mouse squeaked in outrage. "I can do it. I good spy!" I shook my head and ran my fingers down his back. There was no way I was taking a chance with his safety.

Vance nodded, squeezing his eyes closed while he worked on steadying his breathing. "Okay. We can talk about all the other stuff I remember from the other auctions later. I did setup work for them, so I saw a lot. This will be the third auction the...the madam has done. The second was larger than the first, so..."

"This one will be even bigger still," I murmured. That's what happened when an organization got away with something illegal with no repercussions. They only returned worse than ever when it suited them.

We lapsed into companionable silence as night fell. Vance

got up to light a lantern, putting it between us to hold back the shadows. He didn't question how long we would wait, just eased his hand over to mine slowly, as if I'd startle away when his fingers covered mine.

When the evening bells chimed softly, I sighed and stirred. "It's time."

I explained what I needed him to do before I slowly eased the window open and leaned out over the several-story drop. Wind gently ruffled the end of my ponytail. If I kicked off the side of the tower at the right moment, he could lower me outside of RSI's fence. Otherwise, my feet would land on the school's lawn, and the fence had a standard enchantment that made the wood too slippery to climb over.

It would be nearly impossible to escape through any of the lower windows with the height of the fence, but that didn't stop Vance from gulping as he looked down too and asked, "You sure about this?"

I nodded and handed him the rope. He held it steady for me when I placed my feet on the sill and turned, stepping down to plant the soles of my boots against the stone of the tower. Vance inched me downward until I tugged the rope twice and pushed off the tower with all my strength.

The world whirled around me as Vance lowered me the rest of the way to the ground as fast as he could. I spun midair until I jerked to an abrupt halt on the street side of the fence, my feet dangling inches from the ground. Heart thumping in my ears, I straightened my legs and stood, quickly untying the rope from around my waist. Vance reeled it back up.

I trembled with excitement and nerves. It'd worked! As soon as I waved to Vance and set off down the street, it sank in how alone I was. I kept to the shadows and made myself a small, hunched figure as I walked downtown. A few drunkards called out, others too busy with a bottle in hand and an arm around a friend, carousing off-tune outside of the taverns I passed.

Eventually, I made it to my destination and knocked insistently at the door, below the sign indicating that the pet shop was closed. Thomas answered, already dressed for bed and looking a little sleep rumpled. He saw me, and his eyes widened. "Heather?"

"Hi, Thomas. Can I spend the night?" I asked.

He didn't call to Fletcher as he nodded and stepped aside. "Hope you don't mind sleeping with a bunch of little wonders. There aren't any more empty rooms," he said.

I didn't think I could emphasize how much that wasn't a problem, as long as none of them tried to eat Chance.

The room I usually borrowed at Little Wonders Pet Shop had a family of illusion foxes who crowded the foot of the bed, a heavily pregnant pig-like truffle hunter set up in a nest to one corner, and a flock of mismatched birds that roosted on the bedposts and curtains. We minded each other through the night, and I woke up to one of the foxes cuddled between my arm and chest. I'd suppressed a squeal of delight at seeing its sleeping face first thing in the morning.

Through Chance, I learned that the biggest fox was missing her kit, and the rest of her family had taken shelter here to avoid joining the baby on an auction block. To describe the mother fox as *big* was not quite accurate when none of them exceeded the size of the fancy purse dogs noble-women carted around. They had white-brown fur, gigantic ears, and the cutest faces, but they communicated with Chance with yips and screeches that set my teeth on edge.

In the night, a warm presence had burrowed into my hair.

I carried the salamander to breakfast on my shoulder; she chatted with my mouse, and he translated for me. Her name was Flicker, and she recognized me. She wasn't quite the same shy salamander anymore, as she let me handle and pet her with a couple fingers down her soft scaled back.

"I have a friend you should meet. He works with metal sometimes," I told her.

She chirped hesitantly. "She still not trust most humans," Chance said.

"You'd like him," I promised.

As soon as I reached the family's dining table, her dragon-fly-like wings rolled out, and she darted straight for the tower of pancakes set up in the center.

"Ah-ah," Fletcher said, using a newspaper to gently swat her away. "We've talked about this, Flicker. You have to eat food suitable for salamanders, not our table scraps."

She circled around to land next to the extra plate set up beside Shauna's place. Tilting her head up, she fixed me with pleading red eyes. "Thomas! Breakfast!" Fletcher shouted.

Shauna was coming back to the table with a small pitcher of syrup. She covered the spout when a glowing blue butterfly fluttered closer, and she spoke to it in a low voice. It came for a landing on her arm and rested there, its wings opening and closing slowly. Sitting next to me, she beamed. "We're overrun," she said happily.

"Absolutely overrun," Fletcher bemoaned. "Don't let any more little wonders onto the table. They all want more food than we can give them."

I couldn't imagine how many clorets they were putting toward food every day. With the business closed, it had to be increasingly difficult to make it work.

"Are you opening for business again soon?" I asked.

"Not when folk can see all the little wonders we're trying to hide," Shauna said.

Fletcher sighed. "We have to soon." When his daughter shot him a surprised look, he circled his hand. "We'll think of something. It's only temporary, after all."

"Sorry for imposing. I just needed a place to stay for the night," I said to Fletcher, who simply smiled.

"I'd rather you sleep here, where you're safe. You're always welcome," he said. My chest felt warm, and I took his invitation as the gift it was. The pet shop was like a home for me already.

Thomas rushed to his seat, and we tucked into the pancakes. Despite promising not to feed the little wonders, I still snuck Flicker onto my lap and gave her bits of pancake. Chance and Fletcher's dreamhog were given small bowls of oats, and my mouse scarfed them down happily.

I chatted with my friends for a while before getting up and doing a few chores around the pet shop as a thank you for the food. Fletcher remained at the table, reading the newspaper, while we cleaned up and then fed the adoptable animals and the pack of little wonders on the second floor. There weren't any feligryphs amongst the group, not even Patches, who Thomas mentioned seeing yesterday.

When the city bells rang in the tenth hour, I bid my friends farewell and started walking. Theovald was going to be close to Temple Row today, posting up his game in the Sunlight Plaza. This would mark the closest I'd gotten to one of the gods' temples since I was little more than a dirty-faced urchin.

It took me a couple of hours to get to Sunlight Plaza, dodging crowds, carts, and horse-drawn carriages in the throng of the hopping market street. I always used the market roads when I could. They were safest, even if they were unbearably crowded.

Sunlight Plaza was a circular space with paved paths crisscrossing patches of earth with manicured trees, shrubs, and flowers. If seen from above, it apparently all formed the symbol of Lord Orion, the same spell circle that appeared on the faces of his Tulari.

A fountain made of a gold-plated version the god himself, swallowed up by billowing robes and balanced on a platform that looked like a carved cloud, marked the center. Water rained from the cloud to make a pleasant burble that lingered in my ears as I searched the paths for Theovald's Keys. Several performers jockeyed for the attention of well-dressed ladies and their kids.

I found him set up behind one of the temples, the silver and white one for Lady Nilara. He had a crowd today, several little kids waiting with clorets clutched in their hands and one adult woman minding them all. Since they seemed like a group, I hung back, well aware of what I looked like in my rumpled RSI uniform this close to the houses of the gods and the palace.

Theovald wore a suit with purple-hued fabric and a fancy top hat today. I watched him bend down and speak gently to each kid, getting giggles and smiles from them, even though no one pulled a key from his basket. His soft blue parrot watched from its perch on a nearby tree. When I finally approached him, the bird took wing to land on his wrist. "Rrrr! It's the cheater," it squawked.

"And the mouse," Theovald said quietly, eyeing Chance from his place on my shoulder. He took me in for a moment before putting back on his showman's smile. "Here to play honestly this time, young lady?"

He offered the basket and bent down, his ear closer to my mouth. "Have you heard about an auction?" I whispered while handing him a cloret and reaching into the basket.

"There are plenty of auctions happening in and around Kaiamear. Could you be more specific?" he asked slyly as I crushed the egg I pulled. There was a bright green candy inside, which I gave to Chance to nibble on.

Sighing, I handed him another cloret. While we were engaged in the motions of his game, anyone waiting behind us wouldn't think there was anything suspicious going on. It was a darn good front. "The Morashi one," I murmured.

"They don't exist," he answered.

This time, I slipped him a silver cloret piece rather than a copper one and pointedly slipped my gaze toward his parrot. "Little wonders are in danger."

The bird fluffed its feathers and tilted its beak toward Theovald. He patted the back of its head gently and considered with a twist of his mouth. "Fine. I *have* heard of their auction. What, exactly, do you want to know about it?"

I took a single egg and pocketed the candy inside of it. He shook the basket at me. Clearly, I was paying by the sentence here. His time was becoming rather expensive. Slipping him another cloret, I said, "When and where it will be."

"Ah, thinking so small. Don't you want an invitation to the event?"

"Yes." That might be a lot more useful, considering it would have a location written on it. I didn't pay him another cloret, waiting.

"All right, two gold pieces, and it's yours."

I spluttered. Two hundred clorets—that was madness. Considering I'd given most of my earnings to Carmen, he was going for a good chunk of my savings. To buy myself a moment to think, I paid another cloret and took my time fishing around for an egg.

He offered me a way out before I said anything. "Perhaps you have information of your own to trade. I saw you with a young man before. I believe you called him…Ram?"

"My brother," I said.

Theovald had a gleam of intrigue in his eyes. "Ah, excellent. I've had clients wondering where he's getting his red metal ingots from. Perhaps you'd care to shed some light on the matter?"

I bit my lip, wondering how many Fariq had made and Ram sold to bring this kind of attention. "I don't know where they come from," I fibbed. "But I know what they's made of. I can tell you that to trade for the invitation?"

"By all means, yes. I'm awfully curious," he said.

I told him about the process while fishing out yet another egg. This part, I didn't understand so well, but at least it kept Fariq's name out of an information broker's mouth. All I really knew was that desda powder was added in the process of making steel to give the metal a magic-resistant coating. Plus, it was still being tested.

He nodded, satisfied. "A fascinating idea, and incredible illegal. Well, as a first-time client, I want to give you a bonus. Consider it advice for your brother. He's attracted a lot of attention in short order. He may want to count his clorets from a safe place for a while and let someone else fence the next set of ingots until there are more on the market," he said in a tone of warning.

I gulped a swallow. Considering their rarity and value, Ram could get himself killed over them, and that's what Theovald was too polite to do more than imply.

"And as for the invitation, come back and see me on Saturday. I'll be in the Moondancer Square, just a few blocks from here. Take this to show that I owe you and bring it back on Saturday." He took my hand to shake it, pressing something key-shaped into my palm.

He'd given me my third tiny key to the city. I thought about several things at once. First, that I would have to delay meeting with Sybella until this weekend, when I had the invitation in hand.

Second, that I would need to see Ram as soon as I could in person, because he was far too headstrong to take a warning if I only wrote it down and had Chance deliver it.

And third, to smile and say, "Thank you." I let that be the end of our conversation and left the plaza many clorets poorer. I started snickering when I was sure I was out of earshot. Manny had returned the key I'd give him, assuming I'd bought information rather than taking the key directly.

Musty devils, I guess I didn't need to break into Theovald's house after all. Oops.

CHAPTER 25

THREADING THE NEEDLE

Vance and Carmen hoisted me back into RSI the evening after I spoke to Theovald. My feet didn't touch the lawn or fence, and no adult asked where I'd been once I returned to my classes like I'd never left.

I considered myself patient, even though I felt the weight of stress and worry pressing down on me from sunup to sundown. Waiting for the weekend to come was excruciating, even though I kept busy. There was plenty to do to prepare while not looking like I was preparing at all.

I talked an awful lot about the false prince while not talking about the false prince at all. I'd learned just enough about the spy version of Uncommon to be dangerous, blending it with my street-kid lingo to whisper it in the ears of my eldest siblings first. Ram—who took Theovald's warning with a scoff—plus Lope, Sidewinder, Dexis, and more… They all knew I was looking for information on the "false prince," AKA the Morashi's auction, and why. And considering we were still a group named after what kind of animal that represented us most, everyone agreed to help quietly.

We talked about the false prince's associates…the rest of

the Morashi mages. And, of course, their accomplices, non-mages either attending or serving at the event.

I expanded my reach through my siblings, who had internships they were excelling at and friends they'd gathered who were willing to gossip. By Friday, we knew what I'd originally gone to Theovald to figure out: when and where the auction would be, plus the names of the catering, entertaining, and personal security companies servicing the event.

Jackie unexpectedly came to sit with me and my circle of brothers and sisters at dinner on Friday. I was mulling over what to do with the information we had. It was clear we had to act before the auction actually occurred; as great as it was to know who would take Morashi money, I didn't think it would apply to the job.

"Hey, Heather," Jackie said.

"Yes, sweetling?" I asked, distracted by my thoughts.

"Are we at a spy school?"

Dexis, who'd been sipping from a glass of water, spluttered and coughed. Sidewinder pounded on her back while I turned to my sister in surprise. I wanted to say "You figured it out," but my oath bound my tongue. She hadn't made her own oath yet.

Instead, I asked, "What makes you say that?"

Jackie scrunched up her little nose. "Everyone's been acting so weird lately. And you've been talking about the false prince, while that's not what you—"

Ram reached over and covered her mouth. "Shhh." He yelped a moment later when she bit him.

"When you tell the headmaster and talk to him..." I fought the feeling that an invisible hand was trying to close around my windpipe. Each word was a careful navigation of what I could and could not say to someone who wasn't a spy candidate yet. "Don't talk about us, okay?"

"Why?" the ten-year-old asked immediately.

Judging by the pinched-faced looks of everyone around

the table, I wasn't the only one struggling to form an explanation. "Trust me," I ventured.

Her confused face softened. She did trust me, even when I was clearly acting strange. "I'll talk about a different group, then."

"Use Davit's Day. Make them seem dumb," I suggested out of pure spite.

"Okay," she said agreeably, getting up to do just that. I nodded in approval and watched her walk toward where the headmaster and a couple of teachers stood at the back of the cafeteria.

I turned back to my siblings and sighed. I continued speaking in a quiet, conspiratorial tone. "As I was saying, we have time." Nearly a month, with the auction occurring on a Wednesday. "We'll bring the false prince to justice and impress the Spymaster." At least, I hoped so, for the last part.

CARMEN INSISTED on going to see Theovald with me that weekend. This also meant that I helped her get her cousins to a minder to watch them for the day. She stretched her long limbs and had a bounce to her step as we walked to Moon-dancer Square.

Amidst the anonymity of a crowd, I told her the rough sketch of what I was planning. Though she insisted on hearing it, she scowled and asked the occasional needling question. Carmen was great for finding holes in even the best plans. She was always at least a little skeptical and gave me another angle to consider from.

"Just stealing back what's already been stolen won't put a stop to anything. They'll find more animals to sell or go after the ones we took back," she pointed out. "And where will they go anyway?"

"I know a place. An abandoned house in a good neighbor-hood," I said.

"All right. What if they put tracking spells on the animals, though?"

I bit my lip. Though Chance hid pouches of desda powder for me, he never came in direct contact with it. I was worried that he, as a magical creature, would find it as toxic as Tulari did.

"I'm going to ask Fariq to make something special for that," I said. If he could mass-produce strips of desda-infused metal, which he had named red steel, we could use them to weaken or destroy the traps and enchantments we could expect to see from the Morashi.

"As for the group stealing more animals…there's no stopping them. We're still a bunch of kids with no other support," I sighed. "But we can save more than they'll be able to sell. Chance will have his family back."

The mouse squeaked agreement from my hair. He clung to the space above my ponytail today.

"That's like tripping an opponent without pinning them. You're not going to win the match that way. They're just going to be angry when they get back up," she said.

"If you have a better idea, I'm all ears," I said waspishly.

She glanced down at me, startled. "Just saying, that's all."

She was uncharacteristically quiet the rest of the way to Moondancer Square. The area was smaller than Sunlight Plaza, with a clear theme for the worshipers of Lady Nilara. The path was studded with a massive mosaic that formed an eight-pointed compass with all the faces of the moon circling it. A community garden shaped like a crescent moon was situated to the left of the square.

Since it was a more open space, I spotted Theovald in a suit and top hat next to his city of painted boxes quickly. He stood on his own, ignored for a pair of performers a few yards to his right. A fiddler played and danced for a group of kids and teens while a juggler kept time with the pace of her music. Carmen had to nudge me, as I watched in fascination too.

She stayed in my shadow as I approached Theovald. "Hello again. Fine weather today," he said.

I glanced up. There was more blue than cloud above us. "Yeah." I shifted on my feet, feeling awkward. Theovald was a blank slate to me, a man with a family at home but no name, just like he didn't know mine. That was probably how it would remain, for both of our sakes. My gaze naturally drifted off him in discomfort, finding his bird perched on the covered basket where he kept the paper eggs. "What kind of bird is that?" I asked.

He held his arm out and clicked his tongue. The parrot flew to his wrist, and he rubbed the soft feathers under its beak with a gentle finger. It closed its beady eyes and leaned in happily. "One about as rare as you assumed her to be," he said.

Well, that was delightfully vague. When I'd asked if they'd ever seen a little wonder that was a blue parrot, Thomas and Fletcher were stumped. Considering they were smart birds anyway, Fletcher had thought she wasn't a little wonder at all. I guess he was wrong.

"And I assume this is your friend?" he asked, gesturing toward Carmen.

"Here to make sure you don't try any funny business," she answered.

"Oh no, young lady. I offer a completely legitimate service. Let me prove it. Do you still have what I gave you the last time we talked?" he asked me.

I nodded, tilting my hand to show him I'd palmed the key.

"A free first round for you," he said, picking up the basket of eggs and rattling it toward me. As he bent down and I reached inside, he whispered for me to pretend that I'd pulled a key. "Open the short box with the sun in the top right corner."

I crushed the egg I pulled in the same hand where I held the key. I put on my Theater skills and showed Carmen, exclaiming, "A key! I finally got a key!"

She pulled out the extent of her Theater skills too and did her best to fix her usual scowl. "That's...great," she said without enthusiasm.

A gaggle of kids abandoned the fiddler and juggler, turning their excited faces toward me to see which box I'd open. I wondered how often they saw someone open one, considering Theovald's front. I inspected each of the boxes before finding the one he'd mentioned. The lock was a flimsy thing, easily busted or picked if I were so inclined.

Instead, I used the key to open it and peered inside. "Ah, a good choice! She's won three hundred clorets and a special something in that envelope. A little birdy told me it's for a free meal," Theovald announced, as I scooped out a pile of silver coins into a pouch and picked up a square envelope, which I secured under my belt immediately.

I waved to the kids and then to Theovald, who tipped his hat at me with a showman's smile. The kids clamored to try his game now that they'd seen someone "win" something.

I led Carmen halfway across the city before we stopped at an eatery with a patio. "Did he really give you that much money?" she asked.

I tore into the envelope and scoffed. "No. Most of them are too light, probably painted wood."

"Most?"

"I think he gave me back a silver I paid him," I admitted. I assumed he felt I'd overpaid rather than him doing something extra out of kindness.

The envelope held a blank strip of parchment and a letter.

To My New Client:

There is a level of secrecy maintained for an event like the one you've asked me about. The piece of parchment included in this letter is written in a mage's version of invisible ink. It is an identical copy of an original invitation. Say the password "cabexios" over it, and you'll be able to read it.

If you intend to attend this event, you will need to produce this exact invitation. It will be checked by a mage who might attempt to murder you if you provide a forgery. Best of luck with whatever you'll do with it.

It wasn't signed with a name, not even Theovald. My eyelid twitched. No forgeries. Got it. I passed the note to Carmen and picked up the invitation. "Cabexios," I said, though I definitely didn't say it right. I'd never seen that word in my life.

"Ca-bex-ee-ous," Carmen said slowly.

I repeated it back and said it under my breath a few more times to memorize it as ink bled into the invitation, revealing a fancy design. It had a hand-inked border and bold calligraphy.

You are cordially invited to a one-of-a-kind event. Are you a Tulari in need of unique reagents? Or perhaps you have dreamt of owning a living myth? Creatures big and small will be sold at auction price.

Creatures for sale: 71

As I read it, the 1 blurred and changed into a 2. I blinked in surprise. Magic, indeed.

It listed the date I expected to see, with an address that corresponded with the warehouse Vance had told me about. Centered at the bottom of the invitation was a symbol of a dagger with a snake winding around it, fangs bared.

"Great, we just have the one," Carmen muttered. She folded the letter and put it aside, holding her hand out for the invitation.

I gave it to her. Though I'd said the password already, she glared at it until she said the password too, before her gaze darted over the parchment. "We can do a lot with one invitation," I murmured. "But only if we need it."

IT TOOK a lot more talking than I was used to, but I won over a few key people during the month we had to prepare for extracting the little wonders before this auction. I had hope that we would thread the needle: infiltrate the warehouse with the right people, at the right moment, unseen. A perfectly executed job.

I spoke to Sybella next, one-on-one, as we ambled aimlessly down a road. She'd insisted that we link arms and keep our voices high and giggly, like we were a pair of friends out spending time in the sunshine.

"The Morashi don't exist, though," she giggled halfway into my explanation.

"They do, though," I said. Eventually, I showed her the invitation with what could only be the symbol of Madam Morashi at the bottom—a dagger and a snake.

"My team's in," she said. "But we need numbers. This is a one-trip kind of job."

When I agreed, she told me she'd check in with a few of her contacts in the city to see who could help discretely. I agreed with only a bit of hesitation. The bigger this job got, the less confident I was that it could be done right under the Morashi's noses. If we truly needed this many hands to help us, we would need an enormous distraction to get the Morashi's eyes off us while we stole the animals in one fast strike.

My crew was in too, despite lingering reservations. With them, I was honest about the Spymaster's message and the reason I was trying to go ahead with this. I couldn't call myself Chance's friend if I didn't save his family; plus, we were using mostly non-spy resources to finish the job. Fariq was the most reluctant to agree but saw he was outnumbered four-to-one once I was done talking. He went with the group after expressing a worry that we'd only get punished for this "scheme."

Afterward, I met separately with Vance and Fariq in Tower A. Vance only supplied information, too scared of Madam Morashi to consider going to the auction location personally. He shared relevant information he could remember of past auctions, and Fariq questioned him endlessly about the cages we could expect to see the little wonders in and how sturdy they were.

"We need a tool that can both open cages and neutralize magic," Fariq mused. He checked over the notes he'd taken in his journal before nodding slowly. "I know what to do. And I also have an experiment to show you sometime, Heather."

"Sounds good," I said, curious as to what it could be. It had to have something to do with red steel.

He didn't end up showing me the experiment right away, and I ended up forgetting about it. I needed to find Jace's old house, when I'd only visited it once, months ago.

The next weekend, I paid a visit to an inn I only vaguely recognized by daylight. But when I sat down at one of the tables, I let my memories fill in the gaps. Margot made a face as she tried to eat the porridge at that seat. Miss Barrios sat there…Fariq, there…and at the head of the table, the Spymaster himself.

Nodding to myself, I stood up and left, ignoring any looks I received from the patrons and barkeep. I just needed to retrace the steps I'd taken with Manny from here. While I did, the ghost of our conversation haunted me.

There was a fork in the road. I took the left-handed one. *"I like it when RSI kids don't come in with blind loyalty. It means you think critically,"* he'd said as he'd steered me in this direction the first time.

Down this road, I'd debriefed him on the crown heist. We'd passed by that home...and this home...all of these houses, with their plain decorative lawns. I hadn't realized where he was leading me at the time. It'd seemed like we were ambling blindly in a nicer part of the city.

We'd talked about Miss Barrios's real name, an identity that was lost with a fake death. I'd learned her name, Ana Salavieja, in the process of saving Jackie. Miss Barrios had wanted her name recorded on the Morashi device that'd shackled Jackie to The Last Stop. I ran my tongue over my teeth as I lingered on that thought, even while I picked the proper side street and continued walking at a casual pace.

"It's amazing how well you can hide in plain sight," the Spymaster had said when he stopped...here. I turned on my heels, facing a rich man's house. Jace's former home, before his arrest and the seizure of all his items. A proper ending to befall the man that took advantage of my siblings and me and others like us for decades.

It was in this spot that Manny made me choose to stay in RSI. *"We cannot fix every problem, Miss Mouse. We don't save many orphans, but we do stop wars and make the worst criminals disappear in the dark of night. Do you understand?"*

"I understand," I murmured in the present.

But I did, more so than ever. There weren't enough spies or resources to save everyone or solve every problem. The Spymaster, for all that he knew and controlled, was still just one man. I tried to picture how he would react to my plan, but I barely knew him. He was just like Theovald: someone with a fake name and a private family, who I had only had a couple of genuine conversations with past his cover.

I made my way into the house. There was no one on the street to see me pull out my lock picks and unlock the door. I toured several empty rooms stripped of everything but the barest essentials on the first and second floors.

I paused in the breakfast nook. Manny and I had sat at

that window, where he'd revealed so much my head had spun. He'd made me realize how small I truly was, a speck of information the spy network had already catalogued front and back. They'd connected the Menagerie to Jace, to this house, to Springfield's gang…to me and my siblings and everything we'd ever stolen and fenced.

What were the chances, truly, that Manny didn't know what I was up to?

Was he letting me have my plan? Or was punishment coming for defying his direct order?

I knew who I needed to talk to next.

THE INVITATION to the auction passed hands multiple times. It stayed with Fletcher's family the most, growing soft with how often it was handled. When I went to retrieve it, I had to say my hellos at Little Wonders Pet Shop. It was open for business again, with Fletcher and one sibling on the first floor. The siblings traded out duty on the second floor, keeping the little wonders secreted there and as entertained as possible.

I went upstairs to get the invitation from Thomas's room and ended up spending an hour chatting with Shauna and tossing a myriad of toys down the hall. With Patches's help, there was now a flock, or a clowder, or a cluster, or just…a bunch of feligryphs that were newly moved in. As was typical of cats, when they were awake, they were incredibly bored without a chance to play or hunt.

The maternity room had feligryph kittens too, as it was the season. That room was full, considering there was a litter of illusion foxes and the truffle hunter had also had her piglets. It was a similar situation down the hall as more and more little wonders hid from Morashi Venom here. I wanted to share the news of Jace's empty house so badly, but it wasn't the right time.

"Oh, it's changed, by the way," Shauna said once I finally retrieved the invitation.

I looked at it warily. The number of little wonders for sale was up to 138, but that wasn't the biggest change. Red ink formed a new line on the right side of the invitation, left in less than pristine penmanship.

An exceptionally rare triple-headed rozash!

My brows rose in surprise. "Rozash can have three heads?" I asked.

Shauna shrugged, wearing a troubled frown. "Apparently."

"Well, I'll bring this back soon," I said, holding the invitation up. We said goodbye with a quick hug, and then I went back to RSI.

Sometimes Miss Barrios would work on the weekends, but I didn't catch her until the next week began. I whispered in her ear during Agility that I wanted to tell her something, and her response was, "About the auction? Finally. I was thinking you'd forgotten about me."

CHAPTER 26

HONORARY EMPLOYEE

THAT EVENING, when I had a private conversation in Tower A, it was with Miss Barrios. She set up a magelight on the bottom floor, illuminating the desk she sat atop. I paced the room with restless energy.

"How much do you already know?" I asked. I'd wondered for hours after she casually mentioned what I'd been working on for weeks at this point.

"I know enough," she answered. "After last year, I was hoping you trusted me enough to bring me into your plans earlier than this."

She didn't seem angry, just disappointed.

I hesitated, teeth sinking into my lower lip. "I couldn't risk you telling me to stop." She might be the only adult who could convince me to consider the danger of what I was planning.

Miss Barrios raised a skeptical brow. "Like I would do that. Morashi Venom deserves worse than having their auction inventory disappear." There was an undertone of fire hidden in her words, a flash of hate on her face and the clench of her fists.

Yes, she is going to help us. I'd guessed right.

"The Spymaster is unlikely to select your plan for that reason, however," she continued. "Plus SHAINA's trust in people associated with the Third Street Jokers. But we still have some time to refine what you have before he makes his final selection."

I stopped pacing, jaw hanging. "What do you mean?" I whispered.

She smiled at my reaction, taking it in for a moment before she had pity on me. "You're approaching the threshold to advanced. Congratulations. It's just as you wanted, a chance to be seen by the Spymaster."

I stared at her, still dumbfounded. "He's selecting a plan," I said. She nodded, waiting as it sank it. "I'm not the only one making a plan for the upcoming auction?"

"Five & Chance, plus SHAINA, is being considered alongside five advanced teams right now," she confirmed. My lashes fluttered as I tried to wrap my mind around this. "This is common the higher you rise in RSI. Look at it this way… To get out of the beginner tier, your team proved you have the basics down. You acted like a team of spies with an easy challenge, stealing the fake Stone's Crown. Everything else you did with it afterward was just a bonus."

"Right," I said.

"The transition from intermediate to advanced happens when a team shows its unique character and skills. The Spymaster wants his teams to provide their own spin on achieving the same goal: the completion of a mission. To add to that, an advanced team is one that comes up with a workable plan without needing to be told what to do. Critical thinking," she explained.

"But…" I clutched my head and closed my eyes, focusing on my breathing for a moment. She was acting like this revelation was no big deal, but I was seeing a pattern. I'd tripped over the promotion to the intermediate tier, and it felt like I was stumbling and falling into a hole with no warning this time. "The Spymaster ordered me not to do anything with the auction."

She laughed, and I cracked my eyes open to glare. "Have you ever told a teenager not to do something? Especially with something they care about," she said, still chuckling. "It was a test. Everything at RSI is a test. You should know that by now. Had you heeded his words, Manny would overlook you and keep you at intermediate level until the next opportunity arose."

"Without telling me I could've…what…" I stammered.

"That's right. However, let me tell you what happens next. Once your plan is complete, you submit it. We call it bidding. Manny then will review all bids for the Morashi's auction. If he picks yours, you will be tasked with leading it…with our help and supervision, of course. That will be your audition for the advanced tier."

"*That's* the audition?" I sputtered. So, there was still a chance to fail even after my plan was picked by the Spymaster over five more submitted by older, more experienced teams.

Miss Barrios confirmed as I sat next to her and tried to calm myself. This explained a lot. Why did most teams never make it to advanced? They waited for orders. They were obedient. There was nothing wrong with that, but clearly the Spymaster wanted something different.

Something Uncommon, I thought with a hint of amusement.

"Let me tell you what I have planned." I was surprised to face her with heady relief lightening my chest, knowing I wasn't actually defying the Spymaster. We were all on the same side. It was a *test* all along.

"By all means."

"And I have a request," I added, feeling bolder than ever.

Her smile was amused. "All right."

Miss Barrios listened to me well past sundown, making

sweeping edits to my plan to cut out what she knew wouldn't work. She was a little dubious about my crew's chances of being selected by the Spymaster, but I had more hope than ever. One out of six was better odds than the "no" I thought I was up against.

THE NEXT AFTERNOON, after my classes were over, I reported to Little Wonders Pet Shop with two buckets full of RSI's kitchen castoffs. Fletcher raised a brow when I showed him the scraps of perfectly good food that hadn't been eaten by the students yesterday. "I have permission to come here after class every day and be an extra set of hands," I told him.

Fletcher didn't seem as excited about this as I was. He frowned as he said, "We still have a week or more of..." He gestured overhead. "I can't have you laboring for free for however long. It's not right."

I put on my most polite act. "That's okay, Mister..." Gods, what was his surname? "Um, Fletcher. Consider it labor for all the times you've let me sleep here. Speaking of which..."

His eyes narrowed slightly at my bumbling topic change.

"If there's any space at all, I could sleep over? Better to walk back to RSI in the morning rather than late at night." I put on a winning smile. Chance balanced on his back paws on my shoulder and clasped his front paws.

Fletcher hesitated before lowering his shoulders in defeat. "Shauna," he called. "Get Heather one of your spare aprons."

She looked over at us from where she was pouring dry food into a cat's bowl, her face lighting up.

"Thank you for the extra food, by the way. You can take it up and help Thomas upstairs," Fletcher said to me. "We're going to appreciate having you as an honorary employee."

I WAS a little surprised at just how much cleaning my honorary employment included. Sure, I saw the front side of keeping this many mouths fed, but I just kind of overlooked the back end. I spent hours a day shoveling, bagging, and disposing of the pet shop's waste.

Miss Barrios had told me we shouldn't relocate the little wonders until the auction had ended. I'd seen the wisdom. If any of the Morashi caught wind of this many animals being moved to an empty house in a nice neighborhood, it would be disastrous. So, I took my turn helping tend to the menagerie stuck upstairs.

Many of the temporary residents were irritable—they weren't pets, yet the close quarters living with a few humans and the intermixing of natural predator and prey animals had tensions stretched to their breaking point. I helped shuffle room assignments, putting the tiny prey creatures like carpenter mice, salamanders, and what looked like voles together to keep them separate from the feligryphs and other carnivores.

In spare moments, I stitched together new toys out of fabric scraps and strings. There weren't enough toys to go around, so these were a hit, especially when I suspended a vaguely bird-shaped toy from the ceiling in one room.

Time passed quickly with plenty of work to occupy it. My crew and Sybella's team had assembled to write and submit our plan to the Spymaster. All we could do was wait and see what plan the Spymaster chose and if we would have a role in it.

"Have you heard the news?" Fletcher asked me over dinner one evening, breaking through my worries over whether my plan would be picked and what I'd do if it wasn't. Smiling, he slid a newspaper across the table.

The top headline read "HALL OF HEROES TO UNVEIL NEW STATUE OF LADY GRYPHON RIDER" with a slightly smaller line beneath it, mentioning the event was open to the public.

"Do you want to go? I could mind the shop for an evening," Fletcher offered.

Both Thomas and Shauna turned to me, looking giddy. "I would love to," I said, to cheers from them. "But the second floor..."

Fletcher waved off my concerns. He was going to close the shop on the Saturday of the event and deputize Edgimus and a few of the other little wonders to help him upstairs. He could talk to all the animals with his magic, after all, and wasn't worried about keeping order.

I read the article and nibbled on my bottom lip thoughtfully. The auction was taking place less than a week after the unveiling. What if I...no. I'd be one of hundreds of people coming to an event like this. There was no way I'd get a moment to talk to Sivana herself. But I couldn't help daydreaming about meeting the first lady gryphon rider.

DID I say that time passed quickly? I lied. As the days passed and there was no sight of Manny, nor word from him, I wore tracts in my dorm room while talking to Margot, Carmen, and the whole of SHAINA since their team was all girls.

"Our plan is foolproof. There's no way he's picking a different one," Sybella said calmly from her perch on her cot.

"You'd think we'd know one way or another by now," Carmen grumbled.

The other girls exchanged glances and shrugs. Wildcat intercepted me mid-pace and hugged me. I hugged her back. After making an alliance with her team, I'd gotten over myself. She was doing well as a member of SHAINA, with her new teammates tutoring her through anything she didn't know in her beginner classes. That kind of support was what I wanted for my sister.

"It's going to be okay. You're just going to wear yourself out," she whispered.

"He might not pick our plan," I murmured back.

"Then you'll have another chance to become an advanced spy candidate a different time."

I shook my head slowly. "It's not that." At her playful glance, I put my palms up. "I just don't trust another team to care as much as I do, is all."

If only passion equaled success. The days trickled into hours, and I failed at keeping my mind off the upcoming job. No matter which plan Manny picked, I could only hope to have a role to play.

Nothing changed until the day before the unveiling. I was sitting in the prey animal room upstairs. Against the rules of the prey room, a gloomy feligryph was curled up in my lap, and she was not Patches, who barely stopped moving during this crisis. She was a small, sweet mother named Smoky who'd only recently given birth. Her kittens had been snatched while she was out hunting, a common story amongst the other little wonders here.

I checked the auction invitation out of habit and nearly fell off the bench where I was perched. One moment, Smoky was self-soothing and kneading her paws against my thighs; the next she was a blur shooting across the room. The smaller little wonders around her scattered, but she was shooting me a wide-eyed look of betrayal, her blue-gray coat and feathers standing on end.

"Sorry, so sorry," I said, while holding the invitation in front of my face.

The tally of little wonders had been erased somehow. The red ink on the side of the invitation now read:

Over one hundred small creatures from your wildest imaginings!

An exceptionally rare triple-headed rozash!

Young gryphons* just waiting to Link with you!

***Number to be determined.**

"Thomas! Shauna!" I shouted, racing out of the room.

Shauna raced up the stairs while Thomas poked his head out of a different room. "What? What is it?" he asked.

I thrust the invitation at him, and he read over the changes, paling sheet white. He passed it to Shauna and mouthed, "Gryphons?"

Shauna looked up a few moments later, exclaiming, "Gryphons!"

My two friends went straight to the same headspace as I occupied: panic. Where had the Morashi gotten gryphons from? Link-worthy young gryphons, no less. It was one thing to steal little wonders, but gryphons and even the three-headed rozash were going to grow up into mighty beasts.

Fletcher called our names from below, and we exchanged a glance. "Maybe he'll know what to do," I said. All three of us traipsed downstairs together, though Thomas peeled off to help a patron as Shauna and I waited for Fletcher to read the invitation.

Humming, Fletcher gestured for us to follow and wheeled into the private half of the shop to talk to us. "The Crown is about to come down on this event with the fury of all three hells," he said, cracking a grimace in an attempt to smile. "It's our lucky break, in a way."

Shauna nodded, while I breathed a "Huh?" Well, neither of them realized the Crown was already involved.

"All gryphons are property of the Crown and the Altarian military," Fletcher explained to me. "Though it doesn't specify how many…there's only one place where the Morashi could gather a significant number of young gryphons that aren't already Linked."

"The Gryphon Rider Academy," Shauna supplied, following his logic without trouble.

"Wait, why there?" I asked.

He shook his head. "I'm sure Thomas has the articles clipped—the *Voice of the People* ran a special on changes at the Gryphon Rider Academy. Sivana Walker talked in depth about how the gryphons will choose their riders this year. The adult beasts insisted their young be allowed to age to a point where they can think critically about who they want to make a permanent Link with."

I needed to read newspapers more often. Fletcher made it his daily habit to browse the latest news, which was delivered on the pet shop's doorstep every morning. "So, this created a vulnerability," I remarked, though my thoughts were spinning much faster than my tongue.

Were the Morashi intent on putting their own on gryphon back and sending them to infiltrate the Gryphon Rider Academy? Or perhaps they were hoping to sell the beasts at the highest possible price to the wealthy who wanted to see their son or daughter have the prestige of being a gryphon rider. Either way, Morashi Venom benefited.

Did the lady gryphon rider know where the young gryphons had gone? I sincerely doubted it.

But...she should know about it. I saw an opportunity pass right before my eyes. My plan for the auction had had one hole we hadn't been able to patch: the nature of the distraction that would get mage eyes off us while we snatched the stolen animals. The document we'd submitted to Manny said "explosion or other," which Sybella thought was enough, but I hadn't.

"I need to go talk to someone," I said. Fletcher and Shauna had continued talking while I'd retreated into my thoughts. They glanced up, startled, before Fletcher motioned for me to leave.

"Do I know Sivana Walker?" Margot echoed before hiding her giggles behind her lacy fan.

That was about the reaction I'd expected, but it was worth asking. "I figured the message would have more impact if it came from someone she knows," I said.

With a sparkle of intrigue in her eyes, she closed her journal and stowed it away. I'd caught her studying under a window in the library. The dinner bell would ring throughout RSI at any moment. Every moment that passed reduced the chance I'd get a message in the post today.

Besides, the lady gryphon rider would be in Kaiamear tomorrow for her statue's unveiling. The easiest way to bend her ear would be to catch her at the event. But, again, I would be one of hundreds of people attending. If Margot knew her, that would increase the chance we could get a moment of her time.

"*What* message, darling?" Margot asked.

I beckoned for her to lean in and whispered in her ear. She held her fan like a screen and nodded, gasping and humming in reaction to everything.

"You want her to what, swoop in?" She made a swooping gesture with her free hand.

"No. What could be more distracting than Sivana Walker showing up with a few gryphons, peacekeepers, and Crown agents? The Spymaster will be impressed for sure if we can bring her in," I whispered. It seemed reasonable to me, at least. The Morashi would sweat heavily, and we would save little wonders and baby gryphons alike.

Margot stood, brushing out the wrinkles in her skirts. "In that case, I have an idea. But we will have to hurry."

First, she had me change into the dress she'd decided on lending me for the statue unveiling. I had to be more "presentable" than wearing my RSI uniform. I'd already temporarily altered the waist and shoulders of this dress to tighten the fabric. Even though this was an old dress Margot had outgrown, she'd still filled it differently than I did. It was also a pastel pink, a color I didn't think I looked good in.

She stuffed my feet into a pair of flat dress shoes before we left RSI and she hailed a carriage. Only once we were rolling to the destination she'd told the coachman—Temple Row— did she explain her idea.

"While I don't know Sivana, I know of her sister. She's an acolyte in the Temple of Nilara," she said while fanning herself casually in the stuffiness of the carriage. "If you let me do the talking, darling, I think I could convince her to pass along a note."

"Brilliant," I said.

By the pleased creases around Margot's eyes, she was definitely thinking, *I know*.

"I don't have anything to write a note," I added. We'd left our supplies back at the school, and my waist felt way too light without my belt. Chance was lost somewhere in the billows of my skirt, hopefully not ruining the material with his little claws.

Her gaze darted from me to the bare carriage floor. "Oh. Well, there's a reflection room where you can use the temple's stationary. I'll find Clarissa Walker while you do that. Try to make it quick, would you?"

"Okay." I hoped my face didn't betray my nerves at the thought of going inside the Temple of Nilara. That touched on a part of my life I didn't want to explain to anyone, least of all prim Margot.

The carriage dropped us off at Temple Row, and Margot tipped the driver extra to stay here and wait to take us back to RSI. "We have to be back before sundown, darling. Curfews are the worst," she chattered.

She gave a fluttery laugh at whatever the coachman said

in reply and waved in farewell, coming over to hook her arm in mine and steer me to Lady Nilara's temple. There was a short line on the steps leading up to the two-story structure. It was as pristine as an ancient building could be, its white marble face and silver-plated sculptures freshly scrubbed.

"Um. Where is this reflection room?" I asked Margot in an undertone.

She glanced over at me in surprise. "Don't tell me this is your first time here."

I shrugged, letting her believe what she would. It was only a brief wait until we were allowed in the temple and a gray-robed girl was greeting us with a cheery "Mother's blessings upon you!"

Margot tapped my arm and pointed to a room off the front foyer. It looked to be about the size of a closet, but I dutifully separated from her to head that way. "Excuse me," she said behind me. "I'm looking to speak to Clarissa Walker. I'm afraid it's terribly urgent."

I entered the reflection room and took a shaky breath. It was about as tiny a space as I expected—and worse, the walls were stone. One person was already here, a woman seated in a pose of meditation with a quill and inkwell set in front of her crossed legs.

You're not trapped here. Look, there's another person.

I took another, slower breath to ground myself. With Vance's help, I'd gotten a good hold on my irrational fear of stone rooms, but I wanted to get this over with all the same. A table took up a good third of the reflection room. It had a stack of quills in various tattered states, piles of parchment squares, envelopes, a few pots of ink, and two prayer boxes, one marked "Anonymous."

I wetted a quill and stared at the parchment I'd snatched off the top of a pile. In my rush to get to this moment, I hadn't put enough thought into what this note would actually say. It had to be short and compelling, saying just enough to get Sivana's attention.

Hi, Sivana, I scribbled. So far, so good. I couldn't tell her anything about myself that would convince her to go along with this. Still, I wrote, *I'm a big fan.*

Looking down at that single line, I considered balling up the parchment and starting again. Did I want her to cringe and stop reading then and there? Well, there was no use wasting good parchment. I wrote out the rest of what I wanted to say first.

My friends and I know where your baby gryphons are and want to help you get them back. Go visit the Little Wonders Pet Shop in Kaiamear. Tell them Five & Chance sent you.

I read it back while drawing my personal symbol of a mouse on a stalk of heather out of pure muscle memory. Well, it wasn't a terrible first try. Even if she arrived while I wasn't there, the family could tell her what was going on.

There was a knock on the door. Margot opened it and slipped her arm up to the elbow inside, making a grabbing motion.

"Give me a second," I whispered. She kept her hand extended but held her fingers straight. I finished inking the rest of the crew's animals without the usual extra details and stuffed the note in an envelope, fitting it into Margot's hand.

I caught the door before it closed behind Margot's arm and peered out into the foyer. She was deep in conversation with another gray-robed girl, who accepted the note with a tight nod. When I saw her face, I suppressed a gasp and stepped back, hiding in this little room.

No one in the Menagerie prohibited religious worship, but it'd never felt like a good fit for me. Part of that was the first and only visit I'd paid to this temple. There was no way to sugarcoat it: I was a dirty urchin seeking comfort that day. Jackie was a difficult tot to mind, and I'd just wanted my mother. So, I visited the Mother's temple.

Clarissa Walker looked exactly like a younger version of the woman who'd been standing in the front foyer that day. She'd bent in her pristine white robes to be more at eye level with me, her lips pressed into a disapproving pucker when she'd learned I was there alone. Then she'd taken me to a section of the temple set aside for minding children and bathed me, clothes and all.

She gave me a biscuit and a pat on the head afterward. In retrospect, she was trying to care for me. I'd been so accustomed to the mustiness of the Menagerie house that I hadn't realized I'd smelled… It was one of the first times I realized the scent lingered behind me like a foul-smelling ghost. But it'd been so mortifying that I'd never come back. What if that lady grabbed me for another scrubbing?

I sniffed myself subtly, a habit I thought I'd broken. Though I smelled fine, I remembered the stink of the Menagerie house like it was still present. That wasn't a scent one forgot.

Eventually, Margot opened the door and peered in. "Let us be off," she said, reaching for me. I let her twine arms with me and tug me toward the exit. Only when we were in motion did she whisper, "What's the matter, darling?"

I breathed a little easier when we were descending the steps away from the temple, heading for the carriage still waiting for us. "Just worried about what's coming, you know?" I fibbed.

"Of course. You worry enough for all of us combined. It's going to be fine." She grasped my arm and gave it a little shake. "Even if this didn't work and we're not picked, it's not the end of the world to stay where we are. We will advance one day, no matter what happens. I'm still along for the journey."

"Well, I'm glad you are," I said honestly. "You bring a lot to the crew."

"You flatter me," she giggled, though the happy creases around her eyes added, *I know.*

CHAPTER 27

UNVEILED

The next day, I was in Shauna's room, getting ready for the unveiling of Sivana Walker's statue. She laced up the back of my borrowed dress and plopped me before a mirror to do something with my face and hair. We chattered and giggled while she braided my hair and played with different styles. With little wonders occupying pretty much every space on the second floor, we had an attentive audience.

Chance perched on the vanity, handing up hairpins and ties one at a time. He had far too much help, with several of his new carpenter mice friends passing them along from the box Shauna kept them in. The butterfly with glowing wings was back, fluttering around my head to see what we were doing and avoiding the buzzing dragonfly wings of a trio of salamanders hovering nearby.

I'd recently cut my hair to shoulder length, so Shauna had to redo what she was trying a few times before she gave an approving nod. "What do you think?" she asked.

She'd given me a braid down one side of my crown, ending with a small, wispy bun. With a touch of cosmetics around my mouth and eyes…I looked different. Cute, maybe. Someone meant to be seen, not a sneak trying to be a wallflower. "I really like it," I said. Rising, I gestured toward the seat. "Your turn."

Shauna had donned a dress, too. It was made of stiff fabric with a bold orange color transitioning to red at the bottom hem, complimenting her skin tone nicely. She hesitated and said, "Have you worked with my hair like mine before?"

"I have a lot of practice," I promised her. "When I was a little younger, I used to cut and style most of my siblings' hair, no matter the texture. My little brother, Bear, loves having his hair braided in rows. He still won't go to RSI's barbers, preferring that I take care of it."

"How do you have so many siblings?" she asked curiously.

I'd talked about them enough at this point without mentioning the Menagerie or gang by name. At first, I was worried she, Thomas, or Fletcher would judge me for where I came from. Then it'd become a habit.

Well, they'd accepted me into their home often enough that I thought I could trust her. I told her about the Menagerie and Springfield's gang while my fingers fell into a familiar pattern of twisting and braiding. I took her hair down from its pigtails and braided small sections down her scalp before tying off the ends but left some of her hair to fluff out. Once I was done, I planned on gathering each end to leave a poof at the base of her neck.

Her mouth fell open the more I talked. It was freeing to be honest about the nature of my servitude to Jace and the exchange of stolen goods and completed jobs for the bare minimum he offered me and the crowded house of kids I'd lived with.

"Let's just say we all left that situation. One of us ended up in RSI and...well, it's so much nicer there, so we all went," I concluded.

There were tears brimming in Shauna's eyes. "My gods,

Heather. I wondered why someone as nice as you ended up in RSI. I had no idea…"

I hugged her around her shoulders, hoping she wouldn't cry. Not for someone like me, who absolutely deserved to be in RSI. She sniffed and held on to my arms. "It's a good thing, I promise," I said. "Don't believe all the rumors. The school helps put troubled kids on a better path, without all the torture you may have heard about."

"Can I tell you a secret?" she murmured.

Multiple little wonders perked up around the room, from Chance and the other mice turning their faces toward her, to Flicker, who'd landed on one of her braids like a decoration, plus Smoky the feligryph, reclining on Shauna's bed, pausing mid-lick of her paw to look up at us.

"Please do," I said, muffling a giggle at our nosy audience.

"My dad has written to RSI a couple of times, trying to get you released. We never would've guessed you, uh, wanted to be there," she said.

I blinked in surprise while the animals went back to what they were doing with their equivalents of shrugs. "He has?" I asked.

"Yeah! He wanted to surprise you with your freedom as a gift, but there's been no reply from the school so far. I guess that explains it."

"I'll tell him…" I bit my lip. Telling Shauna about the Menagerie was one thing, but Fletcher? He meant well. I just needed more time before I trusted any adult that much. "I'll tell him something."

I finished with her hair and was touching up the makeup she'd already applied when there were an obnoxious series of knocks at the door. "Dad says it's time to go," Thomas announced on the other side of the threshold.

"One minute," I called back, still trying to put little wings on the corners of Shauna's eyes. Margot made this look so easy, but they kept being uneven when I tried them.

Thomas had to knock again before I was satisfied with the job I'd done. I opened the door, and his mouth dropped open at the sight of me. His eyes drifted downward. "Heather?"

"Yeah?" I asked.

His eyes snapped back to mine. A tinge of red drifted up his cheeks to the top of his ears. "C'mon, it's time to go. There's a carriage here for us," he said.

There was? I didn't think Fletcher would spend money on a carriage when things were so tight around the pet shop, but obviously, I was wrong. He waved to us in farewell on our way out the front door. "Have fun," he called.

A coachman held the door for us, offering a boost to Shauna and me. Already seated inside was Margot in a gown of pale peach, fanning herself and petting a smug-looking Patches curled up on her lap. Across from her was Carmen, and it took every bit of my self-control not to laugh.

Carmen was quite unwillingly in a dress as well. Her expression was stormy, and all her limbs were crossed, but she'd at some point sat still for a flattering face of cosmetics. It had to be Margot's magic at work again, somehow convincing the tall girl into this.

I plopped onto the bench next to Carmen, while the siblings fit in with Margot. "You look pretty," I whispered.

"Don't start," she whispered back.

Oh, I was just getting started. "I didn't know your lashes were so long. Do you know how many girls want lashes like yours?"

"No, pipsqueak, stop it," she protested.

"And look how strong and lean your arms are," I said, flexing my own. I had some toned muscle now, but it was nothing compared to the strength she'd cultivated with her regime of daily practice.

Carmen stopped scowling and uncurled from the corner

of the carriage to flex her arm next to mine. We both wore shortened sleeves, and she had on a pair of dark blue gloves to match the hue of her dress, but her flex was still far more impressive than mine.

"I guess," she said, but I'd gotten her. She didn't take up her defensive pose again.

I made introductions around the carriage at that point, old friends meeting new ones. "Fariq and Vance are with a few of your siblings in the other carriage," Margot told me before asking Thomas and Shauna a few polite questions about themselves. Patches purred away since she continued petting the feligryph. Now that the carriage was in motion, Margot had temporarily taken off her collar to rub her wings, too.

Evening was creeping in quickly. It was the time of year when the sun seemed to set more quickly than ever, but at least RSI had relaxed its curfew tonight because of so many students attending this event.

Any time the common folk were invited to the palace, it was sure to draw an enormous crowd. Other than the annual Yuletide feast, it was a rare occurrence when the palace gates were open to the public. The carriage slowed as it entered a line up the steep cobbles leading up to those gates. Countless folks flowed past the carriage window, kept a safe distance away by other figures placed at regular intervals with authoritative stances, tones, and whistles they blew occasionally. Peacekeepers.

"It'd be faster to walk," Carmen commented.

"Don't be silly, darling. We're not getting inside the Hall of Heroes anytime soon. You might as well relax," Margot said.

"Isn't that the whole point of this?" the tall girl grumbled.

Margot circled her half-closed fan. "Of a sort. Perhaps you haven't been to an event like this before. It may be 'open to the public,' but the only people in the hall when the king and Sivana give their speeches are going to be a handful of servants and the top crust of society. Afterward, we're going to be lined up to walk through the Hall of Heroes to view the new statue. Then we'll be allowed to mingle for a while in a hallway with finger food and beverages. There will also be a dinner, of course, but I suggest we make a strategic exit after we see the statue to beat the crowd home."

"Do you think we'll see Sivana?" I asked.

At the same time, Thomas asked, "Will there will be gryphons?"

"It will take a miracle to get close to her, if we see her," Margot said to me. "As for gryphons...likely not. It's too dangerous to have such a large, sensitive animal in a big crowd."

Thomas wilted with disappointment at that news. "I just want to meet one in person. A gryphon rider came in while I was out of the pet shop. Shauna met him and his gryphon."

This was news to me. I glanced over at her curiously.

"Yeah, it wasn't a very long visit or anything. He was there with his lady, and they looked at the dogs." She was being entirely too vague, I thought. "His gryphon was as tall as I am and like a walking cloud of white fur. I just wanted to pet her, you know? She got down and pressed the tip of her beak into one of the kennels and whistled at the puppy inside, who was definitely scared enough to try hiding. The rider told me not to get any closer because she was shy of strangers. They left shortly afterward without the dog."

"Wish I coulda been there," I murmured. Though I doubted I'd try to pet a gryphon as tall as Shauna—which was actually kind of short in gryphon terms, from what little I knew of them—no matter how fluffy she was. But I would've definitely admired her from a safe distance.

We eventually were offloaded at the palace gates, joining the crowd being funneled in a straight path past the beautifully manicured gardens into the palace itself. We processed through the grand foyer with its ancient tapestries and drapes of white and gold fabric bearing the gryphon rampant of

Altare. The movement of the crowd drew us down a path to the great hall, where dinner was served to massive groups in events like this.

Most of the long tables were full, people sitting shoulder to shoulder and eating the small foods the Crown offered. The baskets were well distributed, bearing a light snack at most. Chance and I were both nibbling on buttered bread rolls when a team of palace servants hushed everyone and directed our attention to a tall magical device set up in the center of the room. It was an odd creation, with a long, narrow base and several protrusions stretching from it in every direction. It looked almost like a bouquet of metal flowers with bell-like ends.

I stopped thinking it was weird when a man's voice came from each bell, magnified to echo in the vaulted ceiling of the great hall. "Good evening, people of Altare." It was the king, who had to be in the Hall of Heroes as he spoke. He welcomed several additional people by name, including the lady of honor, and promised dinner and refreshments for everyone once the unveiling was complete.

As the king spoke about this "momentous occasion," I scanned the crowd for any sign of my siblings or crew. The problem with taking separate carriages, or walking, as I assumed most of my family had done, was that everyone had arrived at a different time. He was mostly done with his speech when there was a tap on my shoulder.

Vance stood behind me, while Fariq was fitting onto the bench between Carmen and Margot. "Found you," Vance whispered.

I was feeling a little squashed when he wiggled into what little space remained between me and Thomas. It was tight enough that he had to fit in sideways and put an arm around me.

"You look nice," I murmured. He'd put on a button-down

shirt and a dark vest overtop it that matched his uniform pants.

"Theater room," he answered. "Someone told me they've got a lot of clothes and costumes back there to borrow."

Hmm. I'd been the one to tell him that.

He propped his chin on his fist and just looked at me for a bit. It looked like he was thinking about to saying something when the king announced, "And now a few words from our newest Hero of Altare, Sivana the Wild!"

Cheers and whistles erupted around us, loud enough that I imagined she heard them all the way from the other side of the palace. I sat straighter, beaming with excitement, while Margot clapped close by.

By the time the crowd was shushed, there was a demure *tap tap* on the magical device linked to the one in the great hall. Then, a woman was speaking. She expelled a breath, like the beginnings of a hello, before starting again. "Hello, everyone. It's a great honor to be here with you tonight."

Sivana launched into a list of people she wanted to thank, and as I listened, I frowned. She sounded off. Not necessarily nervous, but her delivery was very formal and stilted. I wouldn't be surprised if she were reading off a prepared speech. Maybe that's all it was and I was scrutinizing her too hard.

"It is humbling to stand here with the likenesses of heroes past and know my face will be immortalized amongst them. I only did as any true Altarian would in serving my country with duty and honor. As did my gryphon, Arimus. We are beyond honored to share this moment with you all and see our statue for the first time tonight. How marvelous it is that it was completed so quickly."

A few phantom chuckles rose from the magical device, belonging to the crowd listening to the speech live. They were echoed in the great hall as more folk joined them.

"Without further ado...shall we?" she asked someone we

couldn't see. There was a shuffle of noise, then gasps and applause for the unveiled statue. Again, a few people in the great hall started clapping, which was joined by more and more folk until there was applause all around me.

Once the noise died down, the line to the Hall of Heroes was started, and we all jockeyed to be as close to the front as possible. My friends and I ended up somewhere in the middle of the pack, shuffling along at a relatively quick pace, considering. The line snaked around public halls and a few viewing rooms full of art or, in one instance, a single insanely valuable weapon.

Vance, who kept a hold on my hand so we wouldn't be separated, murmured in my ear, "I know you could steal it if you wanted."

I muffled a giggle, startled into blushing. He was truly fluffing up my skills. We only glimpsed the Sword of Altare in its impenetrable glass case, a hint of light gleaming off the gold of its pommel. If that wasn't enough of a deterrent, several armed guards and a Tulari wizard holding an intricately decorated staff stood in the room with the display, eyes on the crowd rather than the magical weapon.

"You hear it's cursed?" I whispered back.

He scoffed. "That's a tale for fishwives. It's just that no one but the royal family know how to use its enchantment."

I gave him a skeptical glance. There were whispers of times past, when the most valuable sword in Altare hadn't been so well guarded. Anyone who took it met with a gruesome fate exactly three days later, their bodies found mutilated next to the pristine sword. The case was for our protection, not its.

"Likely story," I remarked.

We inched forward, ever closer to the Hall of Heroes. I hadn't been inside this part of the palace before, but I'd heard most kids saw it multiple times during fundamental school. It was one of many things I wished I'd experienced, rather than having a nontraditional education. But if I had visited the palace for a trip to this hall, Jace would've coached me on ditching my class to find rich pockets to pick or valuables to smuggle out in a book bag. It was probably for the best I beheld the Hall of Heroes for the first time when I had no reason to steal anything.

A pair of guards controlled the line, letting in a handful of folk each time a group exited. While we waited, a few palace servants circled, bearing platters of sparkling drinks in little fluted glasses and tiny plates of small bites. I snagged one of the latter before we were allowed entry, eating a tiny triangular sandwich that had tomato and cucumber smeared with a spicy oil. Chance, who I kept hidden in a dainty handheld clutch, happily nibbled on the cucumber I snuck to him.

The flow of the crowd slowed when we were in the Hall of Heroes, with more folk milling around certain statues in clumps of gossip. I kept eating to keep from gawking. There were rows of larger-than-life statues, each belonging to a hero of old with a plaque detailing their great deeds.

Vance stayed with me as I stopped before the occasional statue of a man or woman, taking it all in. People flowed around us, either more servants or folk who wanted to see the newest statue and then leave.

I didn't note the faces of those around us until we approached Sivana's statue. This was the busiest space in the hall. There were still many people around who were dressed like the top crust of society or the military. But, as expected, Sivana herself was long gone, as were any gryphon riders who'd accompanied her. I eyed a few well-dressed Tulari suspiciously as I slipped by them, unnoticed.

I craned my neck up to behold the newest statue, Sivana the Wild and her gryphon Arimus rendered in marble. Though it's accepted that statues have merely a passing resemblance to the person they're supposed to emulate, it was a high-quality attempt. She had a young, pretty face and flowing waves of hair held back from her face by a pair of riding goggles. She was posed to hold a sword in front of her body, with a shield bearing Altare's gryphon rampant overtop her other arm.

Coming around her stone back was a life-sized gryphon, looming overhead with a snarl and one taloned foot extended mid-rake. Arimus's had carved stone feathers over his bird face and folded wings, tufted triangular ears, and a thick coat of fur over the rest of his body. I reached out to touch the curve of his beak.

"No touching the display, miss," said a familiar voice.

I froze and looked over my shoulder, thinking I must be mistaken. But that was Manny standing behind me, wearing the same palace livery as the rest of the servants and bearing a platter of drinks on his fingertips. I turned around and forced myself not to gape. He'd slicked back his dark hair and tamed his beard until it was just a ring around his mouth.

"Oh, sorry," I said, while my fingers twisted at my side. I signed, "What's the plan?" and looked at him hopefully.

He signed back, "Come with me," while he spoke. "It is a lovely tribute, isn't it?"

He stepped away from the statue, giving other people room to see it too and continue their circuit of the hall. I followed him to where he took up a post against a wall. "Really nice. It seems fast that it's already made," I said.

"Certain minds felt we needed a distraction," he remarked. He fixed me with a look that was pure calculation. "Tell me what you need, miss."

Meanwhile, he signed "two questions" by his hip, followed by "move on."

"You have quite the selection. How do you pick just one?" I definitely meant the plans submitted to him for the auction, but to anyone in earshot, I was talking about the drinks he held. I reached for his platter, taking down a bubbling pink one.

He smoothly removed it from my hand and placed it back where it'd been perched. "You seem much too young for that, miss," he remarked. My face fell. Did that mean he hadn't picked my crew's plan? "But I don't pick just one if there are multiple quality offerings. Try this."

He offered me a different drink, holding it cradled carefully within the nonverbal sign that I'd learned meant "standby" or "patience" depending on the context.

I took a sip of the bubbly fruit juice. "That's good," I said. "What role does this one have?" While twirling the little flute, I pointed it at my chest.

"An important one, I would say," he answered.

I cracked a smile and said a little thanks, forcing my feet to move away from him. It'd look weird if I stood around conversing with a servant for a long time, but I wanted to ask him at least ten more questions rather than just two.

But I had a bounce to my step as I left the Hall of Heroes. Excitement zinged in my veins after seeing the Spymaster in person and hearing that I had an important role to play with the upcoming auction. With everything at stake with Chance's family and the missing little wonders, that was the only answer I'd accept.

There was no doubt Manny already knew that, too.

CHAPTER 28

PREDATORS

WE TOOK Margot's advice and piled into a carriage before most folk were done eating dinner. That didn't mean I hadn't scraped several plates of finger foods clean and drained a few flutes of juice along the way. I'd found my siblings after talking to the Spymaster and spent some time with my arm around Jackie, admiring the expensive art on display in the public palace hall we'd all crammed into.

It was the dark of night when we dropped off Thomas and Shauna, waving farewell as the carriage continued on to deposit us in front of RSI. One of the older teachers was holding the door, letting us in for the evening.

I collapsed face-first on my cot and slept well into the next day but woke with wide eyes and hurried out again after a bath and a change of clothes back into my uniform. I left the dress Margot lent me out, intending to undo the stitches that'd temporarily altered it to fit my body better.

Little Wonders Pet Shop was open every day of the week, and I slid in with an apology on my tongue for being late. It was already busy, so Shauna tossed me an apron, and I got to work. I cycled from the first floor to the second, cleaning and chatting during lulls between customers.

"How was the unveiling?" Fletcher asked.

I beamed. "Great. The statue itself was neat. They carved Sivana and Arimus together."

He nodded, and I assumed he'd heard about all of this down to the detail already from his kids. But the mention of her name reminded me… "I need to tell you something," I added.

"Oh?" He seemed a little concerned by the sudden shift of conversation.

"I wrote a note to Sivana, asking her to come to the pet shop. If we want to stop…what's coming," I said carefully, monitoring a customer who was circulating the room, coming within earshot of us. "I think she might do it."

Fletcher's face fell. "The invitation changed again," he said.

My heart sank with dread. "What now?"

He motioned for me to lean in, whispering in my ear, "It specifies that there are nineteen young gryphons for sale. If they were really stolen out from under her nose, the Crown will absolutely get involved. But I doubt she will come around here even if she receives your note in time. I appreciate the heads-up, though."

I murmured something in agreement and got back to work. All I could do was keep my hands busy until the Spymaster announced the plan—mine, I was sure, or part of it at least. With only a few days until the event, I wondered what else he was directing beforehand. It made no sense that something this large relied so much on teams of kids that attended RSI.

ON MONDAY, Fariq was the first of my team to be called out of class. We were in Innovation, just getting settled after breakfast, when a kid still wearing an unmarked copper bracelet came in and whispered to the instructor. "Fariq, headmaster's office. Now," the man announced.

My friend's complexion was too dark for a blush, but he was clearly flustered as he stood from his desk with bewildered sluggishness. Heads turned across the room and watched him leave.

There was only one explanation for this that made sense. "It's the job. Finally," I murmured to the rest of my crew.

Fariq didn't return to class, so there was no way of knowing what'd happened next. But then Vance was called to the headmaster's office at the end of Innovation. He left with a whispered promise to tell me what was going on, then he, too, didn't return.

In my next class, Lithosian, members of Sybella's team left one at a time. Nessa, then Harper and a girl I was less familiar with. Sybella looked over at me from where she sat a few desks away and signed "it's go time." I nodded in agreement.

By the time I was in Craft and there was a knock at the door, I tensed up, thinking it had to be for me. Ned and a few of the other advanced folk on the stealth track were missing today. It reduced an already small class to nearly no one.

Miss Barrios listened to what the kid at the door had to say and turned to the rest of the class. "Sybella, you've been called to the headmaster's office," she said.

Oh, come on! I shot a jealous look over at her as she jumped to her feet and twinkled her fingers in farewell.

"You're probably next," she whispered on her way by.

She was right. The same kid came back towards the end of Craft, and I was already gathering up my things when Miss Barrios turned and met my eye. She chuckled when I scurried out the door, making the brief trip to the headmaster's office and knocking.

"Come in," called the headmaster.

I entered and took in the room with a blink of surprise. Seats had been placed in a circle in front of the headmaster's desk, most of them occupied. There was a small table in the center of this arrangement, heaped with an assortment of items. "Hello again," said Agent Cairn, flashing a friendly smile.

"Hi," I murmured.

Next to the older gentleman was an unfamiliar woman with rounded spectacles perched on her pert nose. She had a lap desk with sheaves of parchment in two neat stacks, plus a quill in hand and another in reserve next to an uncapped inkwell.

And beside her sat the Spymaster, his hands laced over his stomach. He wore overalls, back to his cover as one of RSI's janitors. "Miss Mouse, have a seat," he said, gesturing to the empty one that completed this circle, bracketed between him and the headmaster.

My eyelid twitched as I did as he suggested. This assembly of important spies meant only one thing: I was about to find out how I would save Chance's family. The mouse poked his head out of his pouch, and I transferred him to my shoulder. The notetaker flinched at the sight of him.

"That's a little wonder," Agent Cairn whispered behind his hand to her.

Chance squeaked and waved at her. She swallowed audibly before her quill went scratching down a clean piece of parchment.

"I believe some congratulations are in order," Manny began. "We always say spots for advanced-tier teams are limited, but there is never a restriction on talent. In a few short days, we are likely to have fourteen advanced teams."

All the moisture evaporated from my mouth. *He picked my plan.* But I wasn't celebrating yet, nor was any other adult turning in their seat to give me kudos. There was a job to complete first—the audition.

"Five & Chance, plus SHAINA, has put forth a winning bid, with a few…creative adjustments," Manny continued. "Miss Mouse, this means you and Miss Creedmoor are directing your peers. Considering the nature of the mission, that will be a third of our friendly faces. Crown agents will handle the rest."

Only a third? Musty devils, he has *been busy.* My face pulled up in a stressed smile. *This is what you wanted. It's time to show him how competent you are. How much like a* spy *you are.*

"Okay. I'm ready." That came out less like the confident assertion than I wanted to make, but I clenched my hands in my lap to hide how I was shaking.

"Not yet, you're not. Let's review everything from the top…" The Spymaster gestured to the table, and Agent Cairn picked up a slim length of metal. It passed across the circle into my hands. "First up, your teammate Fariq's invention."

Fariq had labored over several versions of this tool before we'd agreed upon this one. Small enough to hide, it was a crowbar on one end and a lock breaker on the other, with a small disc of red steel on its underside. He'd made dozens of these things in what little spare time he had, enough to equip a group with the means to free little wonders—and young gryphons—from their cages.

The men asked me several questions about it. What was it for? Why had I wanted this design in particular? It was really just the start of an hours-long session where we reviewed every aspect of the job. They told me what I'd be expected to coordinate and what fell to Sybella instead. And it was a lot, as one could expect of an audition. But the Morashi were about to suffer a huge setback, and I relished my role in it.

I WAS GIVEN time off class to prepare. I promptly left RSI yet was later than usual for my honorary employment at Little Wonders Pet Shop. It was a chillier than usual autumn day, so I kept my cloak on. Shauna was on the first floor this afternoon, wearing her jacket under her apron.

"It's been pretty slow today," she told me as I got to work cleaning kennels and cages. To my relief, she'd already done a lot of it already. Keeping the animals' spaces clean felt like a never-ending job without some kind of help.

I glanced over at my friend, wishing I could tell her the good news. Manny was going to have a senior spy handle talking to Fletcher to "hire" him to help us. Accommodations were being made to move the family to Jace's house the night of the auction. Fletcher would know how to respond to any medical emergencies present in the animals; Shauna and Thomas were considered helpers. The undertaking of reuniting families would be best handled by those who knew about little wonders and how to handle them.

This itchy feeling of knowing information and not being able to share it... When and if I became a full-fledged spy, it would become common. I couldn't offer her a kernel of hope that we would come out of this okay, and that felt selfish.

I ended up saying nothing, and Shauna drifted away to help Fletcher with something. When I was mostly done cleaning each cage, he caught my eye and motioned for me to head upstairs. I nodded and did so, going into the prey room and closing the door.

Stripping off my apron, I sat on the bench in the back and leaned my head back against the wall. I took more than my fair share of breaks in this room. It was peaceful, despite the number of the smallest little wonders and how they swarmed me when I was doling out treats or attention.

Smoky preferred it too, as the feligryph was already here before I sat down. She paced back and forth over my lap, not quite purring, but soaking in the affection of my fingers drifting through her fur or over her wings. Flicker and a couple other salamanders landed on my sleeve, their big red eyes clearly asking for treats.

Which I had, of course. I'd snuck away a pouch full of small berries that'd been to flavor this morning's oats and fastened it to my belt for just this moment. "Here you go," I murmured, distributing berries.

Chance got the first one, Flicker the second one, and then I became quite popular with the other mice, voles, and the single silver rabbit who'd appeared at the shop. He'd nearly been purchased for the beauty of his plush fur on his way past a customer as Thomas carried him toward the second floor.

Smoky circled up on my lap, huffing when any other animal tried to share the space, even Chance, who retreated to my shoulder to groom his belly fur. The silver rabbit ended up by my right hip, and the salamanders warmed any lingering chill from my hands. The only thing to interrupt this cozy moment was a muted voice, Fletcher calling to Thomas.

I stirred, murmuring, "Well, I guess that's a sign I should get back to work."

Something unsaid passed through the little wonders around me. Heads snapped up, facing the same direction. Smoky stirred and loosed a low growl, her fur fluffed out with sudden fear. The rabbit dove under the bench without hesitation. He hid himself within the folds of my apron, followed closely by several smaller little wonders.

When I bent over, murmuring, "What is it? What's wrong?" Smoky fit herself in the space between my back and the wall, pinning my cloak down.

I arranged the apron to hide the quivering little wonders taking shelter under it. More of the small creatures had climbed onto me for cover. The salamanders disappeared into the back of my hair, by the feeling of heat and pinpricks of pain on my scalp. More clung to my cloak, ignoring the warning hiss from Smoky. I sat very straight not to crush anyone by accident.

"What's going on?" I asked, looking around. There was no sight or sound of a single little wonder. Just evidence of them, with the little cushions and colorful toys we'd set out. "Chance?"

His tiny voice came from somewhere in my cloak. A big something was coming, *yes yes*. Clearly a big predator.

Voices approached the door, preceding Thomas opening it and announcing, "Hey, Heather, look who's here!"

My eyes widened to the size of dinner plates when he stepped aside. In walked two people and three gryphons, immediately crowding the small room with their presence. The smell hit me next, like sunshine and wind met leather and sweat, plenty of sweat and an earthy musk that had to be from the gryphons themselves.

My eyelid twitched hard. Was this real?

"Um, hi," I said, waving shyly to the pair of strangers. They both wore fur-lined leather getups and heavy cloaks. The man's gaze swept the room with a hint of scorn. A noble of some kind, I could only guess. And the woman…she had to be Sivana, with her pair of riding goggles sitting atop her crown of bright red hair.

CHAPTER 29

CHANGE OF PLAN

"This is Heather," Thomas said to them. "Heather, this is Sivana. Not that she needs an introduction here, huh?"

The redhead seemed thoughtful, a line appearing between her brows as she looked me up and down.

"And Acton," Thomas continued.

"Charmed," the nobleman said. He had an accent like Margot's, incredibly crisp in that single word.

"And the gryphons, of course. Arimus, Sunset, and Ironfeather."

The large beasts had settled in a pile of feathers, leather harnesses, and fur. I brightened as I looked them over. Real gryphons, close enough to admire. The gryphon that had to be Arimus had stretched himself out against the wall, his eyelids lowered. He wasn't so huge now that he'd lain flat. He made a soft murr sound from his golden beak as Sunset nuzzled his neck.

Sunset was the largest of the three, a brilliant red and maroon over most of her body, shading out to orange and yellow at the tips of her wings. Compared to the sun-kissed brown of Arimus and the dark gray of Ironfeather, she stood out. As if she sensed my stare, she looked up with canary-yellow eyes and fixed me with a predator's fierce gaze.

I glanced away, my heart pounding hard in my chest. The Hero of Altare and the nobleman that'd arrived with her were the less intimidating beings in this room, and at some point, Sivana had crossed her arms and gained a skeptical expression. She was…not what I expected. Not when I'd seen her likeness in marble, captured in a perfect moment.

This Sivana was disheveled, with exhausted half-moons under her eyes. Her freckled cheeks, nose, and forehead were reddened with the onset of a sunburn, her lips chapped and dry. Acton didn't appear to be faring much better. They were both fresh off a long ride on gryphon back, clearly.

"Which of you sent the note?" Sivana asked with a jerk of her chin.

"I did," I said. I held my fingers still in my lap.

It'd worked! Despite the skepticism from everyone, here she was, summoned by the note we'd passed off to her sister.

The Spymaster had been equally skeptical just hours ago when I mentioned it. "Let's assume—and hope—such a high-profile individual doesn't show up. We will have to find a place in the plan for her," he'd said.

Well, she was here. She needed that place in the plan, as did Acton and their three gryphons. "Um, did you ask for Five & Chance?" I asked, feeling how awkward things were growing between us. They had to think I was no authority figure, just an RSI kid who'd dared to reach out to them.

Chance scampered up to sit on my shoulder, lending his quiet support. He quivered from his perch, eyes fixed on the gryphons.

Sivana and Acton glanced at one another. She lifted a brow and said, "I didn't need to."

Oh, yeah. I was losing them fast. She sounded like she was ready to leave, and it could've been the uniform I wore, giving them no benefit of the doubt for me.

"Well, we weren't expecting you so quickly," I rushed to say. "But I meant what I wrote. I've wanted to help you get your baby gryphons back from the moment we heard they were stolen. There's a lot we have to talk about, but first…"

I drifted off as Thomas left, muttering something about chairs.

"You okay. You want this, yes yes?" Chance squeaked.

"I did," I whispered under my breath. If I could get my nerves under control, these two could be assets to the upcoming job. I saw exactly where an angry gryphon rider could shake up the Morashi.

Chance rubbed against my cheek. "Then you do good job. No need be scared."

I cracked a little smile for him, petting down his back gently. My bolstered nerves started to fray again when yet another rider and his gryphon came into the room as Thomas dragged in chairs one by one.

The gryphon rider was introduced as Noah, while the speckled white gryphon that piled on top of the others was Puzzlebox. I eyed her smaller size and the puffy white fur that covered her body. They had to be the pair Shauna had met. Noah was a big man, tall and strong, but sat at a lazy slant and immediately drew up a leg to make a figure-four on his knee.

When Thomas closed the door, the gryphons filled the space, spreading out around their riders' feet. A vague headache pinched either side of my temples from their presence. Gryphons were well-known as having psychic abilities, communicating mind-to-mind to each other and their Linked riders.

The pinching sensation intensified as the riders got settled, and Ironfeather stood, walking straight up to me. His big gray eyes were fixed on my shoulder as he inched closer and closer, making a soft croon as he leaned down to see Chance.

Sivana, who'd sat next to me, grabbed his beak and

pushed him away. He made a sound of denial as she said sternly, "Ironfeather, manners."

He was back a moment later. Musty devils, he was going to eat my mouse. As I was wondering which was faster—his lunging beak or my snatching hand, Chance hopped off my shoulder and onto his beak with a laugh-like chatter. Ironfeather tilted his beak, eyes crossing. He shifted his weight back and forth on his birdlike front talons, and Chance chattered, "Hi hi! I'm Chauncey Balenciaga the Seventh, but call me Chance."

I turned to Sivana, who watched them interact without concern, and blurted, "Do you know what a little wonder is?"

"Can't say I do," she replied.

This was how I got her to see me as more than just some kid, I thought. I held my hand out and called to Chance, who jumped without fear, knowing I would catch him. "Maybe we wrong about big beast. He nice," he chattered.

Putting on a smile for his sake, I held him out to Sivana. "Here, take a look at him. He's a carpenter mouse, one of the smallest little wonders. He's got thumbs!"

Brow furrowing again, she held her hand out next to mine and let Chance transfer to her palm. I bent, careful of the clingers-on I had that weren't quite ready to meet a gryphon, and retrieved a cat toy for Chance to hold. Sivana held him closer to her face with a hum of surprise.

"Is this a mutation?" Acton asked.

"No, he's a different species," I said quickly. I didn't want them to think there was something wrong with my mouse. "Little wonders are like him…similar to a kind of animal and usually able to blend in with them but still different and magical in their own way."

Sivana passed Chance to Acton while I spoke. The nobleman cringed and held him at arm's length.

Jumping in to help me, Thomas said, "If you saw the

hedgehog on my father's shoulder, he's a different kind of little wonder. There are dozens of different species, and they all have small magics. Like your gryphon is a blessed beast with a big power, telepathy, each little wonder has a small power. Carpenter mice have thumbs, dreamhogs like the one my father owns can put anyone to sleep, and so on."

Ironfeather edged closer to Acton. The man's head tilted to one side while the gryphon's turned in the other direction. Maybe they were communicating mentally, as the next moment, Acton placed my mouse back on the gryphon's beak. Tapping his front paws in a little dance, Ironfeather circled what little space was left in the room while Chance squeaked something I couldn't hear.

Sivana cracked her first almost smile since she'd gotten here, watching them. "Next thing you're going to tell me is that they can Link," she said.

"Well…yeah. Chance and I are Linked," I said. "Which means I can understand him."

Sivana's blue eyes unfocused for a moment. Now *that* had to mean she was talking to her gryphon, as her face shifted like she was having a silent conversation. She pinched the ridge of her nose with a sigh, shaking her head slightly. "All right, that's interesting and all, but what does it have to do with the stolen gryphon younglings?"

"Background information," I said, eyeing her and her quieter companions for a moment. She was definitely the one to convince of the three of them. I just hoped she would work with Manny and the spy network. They were all in the military… That means they did as they were instructed, right?

I searched for a way to even explain how big this upcoming auction would be for the rest of us. "Fletcher, Thomas, and Shauna run this operation, one of the only places a little wonder can come and be themselves."

"We provide medical attention and a safe space for births and elderly care," Thomas added.

I twisted and tried to extract Smoky from my shadow. She resisted when I tried to pull her free, growling a warning. Sivana noticed and made kissy noises, rubbing her fingers together.

"Really?" Acton muttered. He glanced toward Noah, who shrugged.

"That means any information about disappearances makes it here quickly," I explained, softening my voice to a coaxing tone. "Smoky, c'mon, little lady. We can trust them."

Cautiously, the feligryph emerged from behind me, crawling into my lap with her wings clamped tightly to her side. She gave the riders a distrustful look when they gasped in awe at her beautiful, unique appearance.

"How?" Sivana asked, eyes widened. "How have there been winged cats like her, and I didn't know it?"

"Little wonders are great at hiding in plain sight. This is Smoky, a small feligryph. I know one that's twice her size." I soothed her with gentle pets, trying to get her to relax and spread her wings more. "She came here for help after her litter was stolen."

"She's one of the most recent victims. Little wonders have been disappearing at random all across Kaiamear," Thomas said.

Sivana's face tightened with a deep frown. "And you think the stolen gryphon younglings are one more disappearance?" she asked.

Thomas reached into his pocket, withdrawing the battered invitation to the auction. "You're going to find this hard to believe."

"We've come a long way hoping to believe," Acton practically sneered. I narrowed my eyes at him while his focus was on what Thomas was doing. Maybe I could give him the benefit of the doubt that he was just stressed and concerned over the missing gryphons, but I hated his haughty air.

Thomas explained the invitation and how to use it to

make the ink visible. "Cabexios," Sivana said. When Acton glanced over her shoulder, she tilted the parchment.

She read it aloud when Noah cast a curious look their way. "You are cordially invited to a one-of-a-kind event. Are you a Tulari in need of unique reagents? Or perhaps you have dreamt of owning a living myth? Creatures big and small will be...sold at auction price."

Paling, she coughed and swallowed, her eyes roving over the sheet. A deep rumble sounded from the corner of the room. Arimus lifted his head, talons curling. Sunset cooed and nuzzled him again, clearly trying to distract him.

As her grip on the invitation became white with strain, Thomas jumped in to say, "If you would keep the invitation kind of nice. It's the only one we have."

She startled and handed it back to him, then turned to her friends. "It really is revenge," she said. Her fists balled at her sides, mirroring Ari's curled talons.

"You think it's..." Noah drifted off, his gaze going to Puzzlebox, who bumped his leg with a friendly chirp. Her wings quivered when he scratched between her ears and found a sweet spot she must've loved.

I took a deep breath. This was where I convinced them to work with us. We were on the same side.

"We have a plan," I said. Sivana's blue gaze pierced me, but she was listening and nodding along now. "And we can find a place for you within it if you all agree to a level of discretion. The auction is very soon, but it can still be canceled and relocated if, err, the Tulari in charge realize they're going to have more guests than the folk they invited. Which means you shouldn't try to run to the peacekeepers and overrun the place they're set up at. They'll be gone like..." I snapped my fingers.

After a long moment of scrutiny, Sivana said, "Fine. What do you suggest, then?"

I smiled, glad this seemed to be going well after all. "We

can do a lot with one invitation to the event. My crew and some friends will be infiltrating the auction already. With some creative use of the invitation, we can set up a disguise and a false identity for you to get inside for your role."

I hesitated, only seeing one place for her in the plan that'd already been created.

"The biggest thing is, we need an auction-ending distraction, a huge disaster for those running the thing. That's where you come in. How many angry gryphons can you bring to Kaiamear in the next couple days?" I asked hopefully.

Sivana's eyes unfocused again when Sunset looked up from Arimus. The crimson gryphon tilted her head.

"Enough to make the most epic distraction you've ever seen," Sivana said.

I grinned. *Perfect.* "Then we'll be in touch with more information soon," I said.

To her credit, she didn't question who "we" were, just lingered to ask a few more questions about little wonders. Acton smiled over at her, while Noah seemed to be nodding off in his chair.

The riders didn't stay much longer, which didn't surprise me since they were all exhausted. Noah held the door, and out shuffled the gryphons, with Sunset leading Arimus to the threshold with her tail draped over the back of his neck. Puzzlebox followed, bouncing behind them with a cheerful twitter.

"Time to go," Acton said to Ironfeather. The gray male sat on a cushion far too small for his bulk, eyes still crossed trying to look at Chance. They were chattering away like a pair of old friends.

Ironfeather tilted his head up at a stubborn angle. After a longer pause, Acton sighed. "Yes, say your goodbyes to the mouse."

After the big beast made a high chirp, Chance squeaked, "Okay, bye bye. We talk more later, yes yes?"

The gryphon made a murring noise and stood, prowling over to me. I still couldn't get up with several trembling bodies pressed to my back, but Ironfeather lowered his head and angled his beak so Chance dropped straight into my lap. Even with the mouse delivered, Ironfeather looked at me expectantly with a pair of intelligent bird eyes. The pinch at my temples was back, more intense than ever.

He bent further to nudge my arm. I glanced over at Acton, who waited with more patience than I gave him credit for. Hoping I wasn't completely misreading the gryphon's intentions, I reached out and ran my hand up the silky feathers from the base of his beak to his tufted, more catlike ears. I got a couple scratches behind one ear in before Ironfeather was satisfied, bumping my forearm with his beak before he trotted away.

My palm tingled from the contact as I waved a last farewell to the group and exchanged a dumbfounded look with Thomas when the door closed behind them. Dozens of pairs of small eyes peeked out of their hiding places now that the gryphons were gone.

"She got your note," he said.

"Consider the Morashi's auction as good as busted," I replied, both excited and scared of how much Sivana and her promised epic distraction would change the plan. "By the way, do you have some paper and a quill I can borrow?" I needed to send another message right away. Hopefully, Manny saw it just as quickly.

CHAPTER 30

THE SCRIPT

I woke the next morning with a note attached to my bracelet. It was signed with a gryphon rampant again.

Now is not the time for practical jokes. Come to the headmaster's office if you were serious.

I swallowed thickly at the tone I read into the brief message. Manny sure sounded meaner when his words were written without the context of his usual unflappable presence. But I was definitely not playing a practical joke on him, so I rushed out of the pet shop and back to school before the breakfast bell rang.

Knocking, I entered when the Spymaster's muffled voice called me inside. He sat alone in the circle of chairs from yesterday, thumbing through a stack of parchment marked with neat script. A mug of tea steamed in his other hand. I envied how calm he seemed. The auction was taking place tomorrow, and he could've been reading routine correspondence and bills rather than the details of the job to come.

"Good morning, sir," I said.

He tipped his mug toward me. "So it may be, Miss Mouse. Have a seat and tell me about your evening."

I took the chair across from him and told him everything

about my meeting with Sivana and her rider friends. He sipped his tea and listened with a thoughtful expression. "It really happened, sir. I wouldn't lie about this," I concluded.

"I never said you would," he said. I almost opened my mouth to point out that that was exactly what he'd written, but it wasn't my place to argue with the Spymaster. "As we speak, Miss Walker is having breakfast with my brother. He has been briefed that her appearance here is a surprise and a danger to the plan we've already set in motion."

"A danger?" I echoed.

"You meant well, inviting Sivana to Kaiamear to help us. Did you write to her hoping to impress me?"

He seemed so unamused by the idea that I began to sweat, my eyelid twitching. My reaction was answer enough, so he placed his mug aside to lean forward and look me in the eye. "Do you remember when I told you extra information about my past?"

"Yes, sir," I answered nervously.

"There was a reason for that. Please, relax," he said with a sigh. I tried to force the concern from my face and listened. "As a prince, I received grand gestures, sometimes daily. The best, most perfect offerings our fellow Altarians could produce. Sometimes even a life's work. I've worn exotic fabrics and perfumes and tasted foods grown so far to the east that it was a wonder they arrived here delicious and unspoiled. And what did I tell you I did with all that?"

I saw where he was going with this already. "You gave it up," I said.

"My father grew too blinded by the same indulgences to see the suffering of the common man, who starved while he had too much of the best life can offer handed to him. Gate-keeper rest his soul, but I did not want to repeat his mistakes, nor let my brother do the same. It has taken time, but I no longer require someone else's grandest gestures to be impressed with them. Especially from young spy candidates."

He gave me a meaningful look. "What I want to see from you is growth, Miss Mouse. I've found the most impressive thing a teenager can do is outdo the person they were yesterday. It may not sound like much, but consider how many days must pass between now and the moment you graduate."

"That's a lot of growth," I murmured.

"It is. And where will you go, now that you have invited a Hero of Altare to a mission? Hells, even after you stole this and collapsed the entire structure of the gang you used to belong to." He hitched a thumb over his shoulder, pointing to the gleaming replica of Stone's Crown.

"I...don't know," I admitted. It was a daunting thought, but I would figure it out with my crew.

"It would be unfair of me to set my expectations even higher for you." He spread his hands in a helpless gesture, like he couldn't control it. "Especially when you are the reason Vance Bradford finally disclosed his knowledge of Morashi Venom. Or when you, technically, were the first new intermediate student to talk to an information broker this year. Not to mention my personal favorite of your accomplishments this school year, when you helped two young men from the Davit's Day team to the floor single-handedly."

My brows rose. How had he even known about that last part?

"And you..." He shook his head. "*Stole* a key from the information broker's house."

"Yes? That's what the challenge said to do," I murmured.

He chuckled, genuinely amused. "I had the headmaster write *steal* rather than *acquire* a key to the city on one welcome letter. Yours. And you went above and beyond to do exactly what it said. I like how involved you are with your little heists."

My lips quirked. I didn't really like my efforts turned into "little heists" in his eyes.

"We could've stopped there, and I would've given you the extra credit this year for being impressed with you. You did it again, Miss Mouse. You've checked all three boxes. Your team will be promoted prematurely once more, and everyone's expectations of Five & Chance will adjust accordingly. Congratulations." He nodded toward me.

Though I guessed he had more to say, I still said, "Thank you, sir."

"But inviting Sivana Walker to the mission was a step too far. Never do something like this again without my go-ahead." His tone switched to censure in a blink. "She is not a spy, nor a proven discreet ally. Depending on what she does next, our mission objective *will* change completely. As incredible as her legacy will be as the first female gryphon rider, her military service is peppered with instances of extreme insubordination. She has also bruised my brother's ego more times than we can count."

He reached for his tea and took a long sip, muffing what sounded like a chuckle.

"However, if she does not go rogue with the might of Wild Flight behind her to bring the Morashi's auction down around their ears, she will certainly provide an incredible distraction. I will be speaking with her later today. I have devised a place for her in the plan and, if she agrees to it, will direct her to Five & Chance. Here is what you will do from there."

The Spymaster withdrew a sheet from his stack of papers and passed it to me. It was in his handwriting rather than the secretary's who'd been here yesterday.

"Make no mistake, you are to follow these directions exactly," he added while I was still busy scanning the page. "It's an order, Miss Mouse."

I looked up at him. There was the smallest crack in his

calm mask, a predator deadly and calculating staring back at me. "I mean it," he said with bared teeth.

Shaken, I ducked my head and murmured, "Yes, sir."

My heart sank. I saw these instructions for what they were—he was taking control so Sivana—and by extension, my crew—didn't wreck the mission. It was for the right reasons, but...this snipped away any notion that I was in charge of anything after submitting my original plan. It'd been pushed and pulled by the Spymaster and his team until it barely resembled what I'd thought up anyway.

Despite tomorrow being the day my crew ascended to the advanced tier, we were still just kids. Tools for the older spies to arrange as they liked.

"I understand, sir," I added. More than ever before, I did.

Then I ripped a page out of my journal and wrote a note to Sivana, word for word, what the instructions told me to jot down.

Hi, Sivana. We will get you ready for tomorrow. Come alone, and don't take a gryphon. We want to make you anonymous.

That written, I focused on the details of my crew's animals more than necessary, making the heather crisp around my mouse and the collar on Margot's dolly cat gleam with inked-in gems. It soothed the rough edges of my feelings. We were still talented, varied individuals expected to direct our peers, despite being given a script.

I folded the note and handed it to the Spymaster. He tucked it into the front pocket of his overalls, and his expression smoothed back into its calm blankness. "Tomorrow will be a good day for the Crown, Miss Mouse. We shall ensure it."

THERE WAS plenty to do in the time between my meeting with the Spymaster and the job tomorrow.

Ram and my older siblings joined a large group of advanced spy candidates, disappearing midday to orchestrate a culinary disaster that would put a catering company down several people to serve at tomorrow's event. They would present themselves as alternates to get "hired" temporarily.

It was odd to give Ned instructions when he'd always been the one to give me tips in our classes together. Before he left to join Ram, he patted my shoulder and said, "You're doing great. The whole school is going to be shocked, in the good way, when they see Five & Chance on the advanced board."

"SHAINA too," I reminded him.

He smirked. "Sure. Good luck with everything. Remember to try and have fun tomorrow."

Fun. Right. Like I wasn't already stressed. I had hints of Chance's fear for his family in the back of my mind. The little wonders prepared for the auction block weren't about to call tomorrow "fun." It wasn't my idea to wait until the day of the actual event to orchestrate the rescue, but that was what the Spymaster wanted.

In the evening hours, I went to Little Wonders Pet Shop, which had a sign on the door declaring that it was closed for the day. I knocked, and Thomas let me in promptly. "Hey, Heather. Guess what!" he exclaimed.

I forced a smile onto my stressed face. "What?" I asked, even though I already knew.

"The peacekeepers are going to take over the auction tomorrow. They're going to make arrests and free the little wonders. And we've been asked to help! We're going to relocate all the parents with missing children to the site where the captured animals are going to be taken." He was bright-eyed and earnest, and I was doing my best not to grimace. No one would tell the family they were working with spies, but *peacekeepers*? It felt like a low blow to put their name on the job.

"That's great news! What do you need me to do?" I asked, though I felt like I was exaggerating my joy too much.

He explained we were mostly waiting for the cover of night. Whomever the Spymaster had sent to talk to Fletcher had advised them well—to prevent folk from noticing them coming and going from Jace's empty house, the little wonders waiting to be reunited with their young and Fletcher himself would all enter the house after dark and wait there until tomorrow.

In the meantime, we loaded up wagons with medical supplies, food, and other necessities Fletcher would need overnight. The adult looked nearly as tense as I felt, as he wanted us to come back and sleep in the pet shop without him. When I said, "Don't worry, I've been out in the dark of night plenty. I'll keep us out of trouble," it didn't seem to convince him of anything.

Still, we wheeled out the wagons when it was dark. The larger little wonders walked with us, while the smaller and slower ones either found places in the wagons or on us. Edgimus and a couple of birds stayed with Fletcher, while I had Flicker and her salamander friends on one shoulder and Chance on the other. Thomas led the way to Jace's old house, as the agent had taken him here alone earlier.

I pretended not to know this was our destination and eyed the surrounding houses. The two on either side of Jace's were completely dark. Either the families inside had already gone to bed, or someone had paid them to have a tidy little vacation. Hopefully the latter.

Once Fletcher and the wagons were secured inside the house, Thomas, Shauna, and I returned to the pet shop safely and said our goodnights. I lay down but didn't catch a single wink of sleep, tossing and turning as my mind filled with everything that could go wrong tomorrow.

I MUFFLED MORE than a few yawns as I met up with my crew the morning of the auction. The Spymaster had sent a small note through my bracelet, confirming Sivana had agreed to cooperate with her part in the plan.

"There's no way it's really her," Carmen said, still in disbelief as we walked to the boutique the Crown had lent us for the day. My entire crew came along, all of us wearing street clothes and carrying bags full of items to conceal them from the curious eyes of any passersby. Since it was finally cloak weather again, I wore my utility belt fully loaded down with all the tools I owned.

"It is. I promise," I said for what felt like the tenth time. Seeing was believing for my skeptical friend, so I just had to wait for her to set eyes on Sivana to realize I was telling the truth.

Margot pitched in, "I, for one, cannot wait to meet her."

"They say not to meet your heroes for a reason," Vance said from behind us. He carried some of Fariq's inventions, the metal clanking with each step.

"Oh, hush. There's no place for such negativity," Margot scolded. She seemed to be in the highest spirits when we arrived at our location. The boutique's door was unlocked, and a quick scan of the building revealed we were alone. We went to drop our stuff off in the changing room in the back, which was big enough for a large crowd. There were three trifold mirrors with built-in small magelights and an assortment of cosmetic products scattered around them.

I briefed the crew on what we were doing. This was mostly a refresher for the sake of my nerves, but since we were alone, we could discuss the logistics of getting Sivana, Carmen, and me into the auction in three different ways. Vance seemed uncomfortable when I mentioned his magic…but the Spymaster wanted him to use his formshifting on Sivana, so there was no way around it. She was about to learn what he could do.

"We can trust her. We have to," I concluded. He gave an uneasy nod.

Margot left us to browse the prefabricated clothing, muttering something about the "perfect" outfit. Fariq started digging tools and items out of his bags.

"I may not have enough power to change her, Carmen, and you," Vance told me.

I considered before saying, "I probably won't need it. I'm the one sneaking in, after all."

He paled and shook his head. "I don't want you going in there without at least a bit of protection. If you… If the madam knows you and your face…" He took a ragged breath to center himself. "Where is the Eye of Acuity?"

I produced it from Chance's pouch, gleaming with iridescence from the magelights. I'd pulled my mouse out too and transferred him to my other palm, holding the Eye in my dominant hand.

"She cannot have that," he said, pointing to it.

I tilted it, scattering shards of color around us. He was right. If, in the worst-case scenario, I was caught by the Morashi, I would also deliver this tool of power to the woman who'd murdered for it. "Well, then you'll have to keep it safe for me." I caught his wrist and placed the magical pendant into his palm.

Vance wouldn't be going into the auction tonight. His job was to prep us with his magic and then head to Jace's former house to help when the stolen little wonders arrived. "Are you sure?" he asked, dropping his voice.

Honestly, no. I didn't want it leaving my person at all, but that was foolish. "Just don't use it stupidly," I said, crossing my arms.

He looked from it to me with a gleam in his eyes. "Nothing is beyond my reach…"

It activated in his palm with a flash of blue light.

"Don't do it," I said, realizing whose name he was about to use.

He smiled wider. "With this Eye I unleash—"

"*Vance*, no," I protested.

"—the power to watch Heather the Mouse."

The blue light seemed to wink out. He held it up to his face and tilted it. "Oh, it *is* weird to see yourself from this thing," he said.

I gaped at him. "It's going to watch me for at least a week! What if we need it for an important target?"

Pocketing it with a shrug, he said gently, "You *are* an important target. To me."

"Aww," Carmen interjected. "Now kiss or something."

"Please don't," Fariq added in.

I was already blushing, but their comments made it feel like my face was on fire. "What… We're not going to… You guys," I stammered, taking a step back.

That, of course, was the moment Margot's cheerful voice rang out, "She's here, everyone!" And in she walked with Sivana, completely changing the air in the room. We all turned to look at them.

Carmen's jaw dropped. "She's actually here," she said to herself in disbelief.

I told you, I thought.

CHAPTER 31

DISGUISING A HERO

Margot nudged the door shut behind her and Sivana. I forced my muscles to unfreeze and gave my head a shake, putting on the most pleasant face I could muster.

Sivana looked better rested, her stance confident, even though her expression was pinched with worry. Her gaze had a predator's sharpness as she took in my crew. Her bushy red hair was tamed in a braid, and she wasn't wearing her iconic riding goggles. Without her gryphons, she was significantly less intimidating.

"You remember Heather, then," Margot was saying, inclining her head my way.

I lifted my hand for a shy wave. "Hi."

Sivana glanced in my direction and nodded. Margot nudged her toward me and said, "She's all yours."

Musty devils. Okay. This is it.

I took a deep breath. "Hello. Welcome," I said more formally. "You got our message. Let me introduce you to the crew, and we can get to work."

She pursed her lips thoughtfully as I introduced her around the room. Her gaze drifted over each of us, assessing for the traits I shared, perhaps. "Margot is our outgoing friend. She can strike up a conversation with anyone," I said. And gods, did I envy her for that ability right about now.

Next was the boy who stood proudly next to his inventions. "This is Fariq, our genius," I said.

He put his hand out for a shake. "It's a pleasure to meet you in person."

Sivana smiled and shook his hand hard enough that he shook it with surprise afterward.

"Next is Vance, our Tulari," I said. He pinched his lips in displeasure. There was his biggest secret, out in the open. But the next moment, he forced a smile and shook her hand too.

Sivana eyed him, obviously not seeing his mage mark. "Really?" she asked. But the question sounded more like "ruh-really?" like she struggled to form the word.

"I suppose we're telling you all our secrets today," he replied.

A little line appeared between her brows. "If we're working together, I need to know what you can do."

"Yes, well, you'll find out," he grumbled.

"Anyway," I interjected quickly, gesturing to Carmen, who jerked her chin. "This is Carmen. She's a talented fighter."

Sivana's face lit up. "Oh? Weapon of choice?"

Carmen matched her energy immediately. "My body is the only weapon I need."

"My best friend's father taught me the same thing when he drilled me in hand-to-hand combat," the gryphon rider said.

I put my palms up, trying to signal to Carmen not to say what she was clearly itching to. She ignored me. "We should spar after all this," she suggested.

Sivana chuckled. "Perhaps later. One of us would walk away rather hurt from that encounter." She sounded like she was betting she would win, but I doubted she expected Carmen to pull out Tosh Zorena. Putting her hands on her hips, she addressed the room. "Well, it's a pleasure to meet you all. You must be the five of Five & Chance."

I blinked in surprise. "How did you—"

"Five people and a mouse named Chance," she pointed out with a shrug. "The crew I was told to trust because our interests align."

Sivana sat in front of one of the mirrors at Margot's urging. "That's right, darling. We're getting you into the Morashi's auction tonight."

While Vance and Margot eyed Sivana's reflection, I paced with a sigh. This was going to take a while, and there was little I was needed for. My tired mind immediately jumped to the job ahead.

"M-Morashi?" Sivana echoed in obvious surprise. My ears perked, both at her reaction and the hesitation in her speech again. I didn't realize she had some kind of stutter. It was kind of endearing, and she seemed to have it well under control.

"Morashi Venom. Heard of them?" Vance asked.

Patches chose that moment to jump onto the counter in front of Sivana and meow. The gryphon rider's mouth dropped open, and she admired the big feligryph while I whispered to Chance, "When did she get here?"

"She was here when we get here, yes yes," he squeaked.

Patches climbed into Sivana's lap, purring deeply from the woman's pets. "That's Patches. Looks like she likes you," I said. And the feligryph was a good judge of character, as far as I was concerned.

Sivana nodded and helped the cat get comfortable in her lap. "I can't say I know what Morashi Venom is. I know of a woman who claims to be a Madam Morashi, though," she said.

The air in the room changed. All of us were staring at her. It was rare for anyone to acknowledge the gang existed, let alone mention its leader without fear.

Margot was the one to break the silence. "Shall we share gossip, then? We do have some work to do to make you look like someone else."

"I'd like to hear what you intend to do first," Sivana said.

Margot gave me a meaningful look. I paced, searching for the way to tell Sivana she was part of a spy operation without the spy part. "We're one piece of a larger plan, one crew amongst many tonight. But because of you, we're the most important," I said carefully. Carmen stood and intercepted me, pushing me to stand behind Sivana's chair rather than continue wearing a rut in the floor.

I shifted uncomfortably under Sivana's reflected gaze. "Our success dictates everyone else's, basically. We're going with a simple enough strategy. One hand distracts while the other steals," I said.

"A smash and grab," Vance corrected.

"I thought we were just going straight for the chaos option," Carmen said.

Margot rolled her eyes toward the sky. "Can we keep it together in front of a guest?" she sighed.

Amusement creased Sivana's face. "No, please, go on," she invited.

"The first thing we're going to do is scope out the event," I said, repeating the highlights of the plan to her. "There's a viewing party that's happening throughout the day and ends right before the auction itself starts. Margot, Vance, and Carmen are going in, and if all goes well, Carmen will be staying and taking the place of a guard."

But Vance would not, in fact, go in. He'd wait outside to change my face and then head to the rendezvous point in Jace's old house with Fariq. There was no need to confuse the gryphon rider with all the little details, though.

Sivana raised a brow. "No offense, but isn't she noticeably younger than most guards?"

"Vance's magic will fix that," Carmen muttered.

I went back to summarizing the plan. "Once they return with their intel, we're sending you in dressed the same way as Margot. With a touch of Vance's magic, no one will look at you twice or realize two different people are using the same invitation. And then we wait for the right moment to unleash chaos."

My eyelid twitched. "You...did bring the gryphons, right?" She alone wouldn't be a big enough distraction.

"They're on their way," she said.

Phew. "That's the short version of your part in the plan."

"What about the peacekeepers?" she asked.

I frowned. "What about them?"

She eyed my reflection skeptically. "The Crown approved this plan? Without supplying peacekeepers to arrest those attending this auction?"

If only I could tell her how many people were involved in this plan. She seemed to think it was just us.

"They'll be waiting outside, darling. But since the Morashi are involved, we're not storming the event. There's too high a risk that someone, or something, innocent will be hurt," Margot said.

"Sometimes subtlety is the best option, and this is definitely one of those times," Vance said.

"There are other crews—" I said.

"About that," she interrupted, raising a hand. "The gryphons would like our allies to either wear something identifying or have a sort of gesture ready so they're not mistaken as the ones standing in between them and their babies."

We exchanged glances. This was a very last-minute request, but Manny could spread the word. It was important that no one innocent was hurt. I'd now been in the same room as a few gryphons, and I did *not* want to be on one's bad side.

"Palms up," Fariq suggested, flashing his. "It is universal for no harm."

I nodded in agreement. "We'll get the word out. Like I was saying, other crews are also infiltrating the event and posing as extra servants or guests. They'll be wearing pins of the Altarian flag. Anything more noticeable is bound to be spotted by the Morashi, and we can't have that."

"If that's what it takes, let's do it," Sivana said. Patches meowed and bunted her chest in approval. She released a quiet "oof."

Margot brightened with a broad smile. "Well, then! Time to get started. Pretend you've taken a day at the spa."

"Where we talk about gangs and misuse of magic?" Vance asked.

She picked up a brush and sniffed. "What do you think ladies discuss in their free time?" She let down the gryphon rider's hair from its braid.

I half paid attention to their conversation, heading to the back of the room with Fariq and Carmen to confer with them quietly.

"All right, look. You're technically not supposed to know any of this, okay?" Vance was saying. "Heather's trusting you with a lot of secrets already, so you can just add this as one more."

"Seems reasonable to me," she replied.

I turned to Fariq, whispering, "Are you going to give her any of your inventions?"

He nodded, gesturing to something to one side. "She's going into the thick of things. I think she needs my shield prototype. It's still being tested, but it can reflect magic," he murmured.

Sivana made a wordless shout, and we startled, looking over at her. She probed her nose while Vance said, "This is what I'm capable of. It's called formshifting."

She turned around in the chair to eye him suspiciously. "Are you in this gang as well?"

"I was. But I was shown the error of my ways." He tapped his bracelet, and she settled again uncertainly.

As he changed her appearance to be more and more like Margot, I turned back to Carmen to give her more instructions on what to do as a guard. But Sivana was talking, telling a story. I stopped mid-sentence, distracted. "—They called it the House of the Unstable. They were experimenting on battle beasts and a few unstable pyromancers. To steal their magic, I learned. Apparently, fire is the most difficult of Lord Orion's blessings to take from another."

Vance's jaw was tight as he drew runes with his wand, adjusting the more minute characteristics of her face. She was too browned by the sun to be a perfect copy of Margot, but he wouldn't change her skin tone unless he had to.

"Unfortunately for them, they picked the wrong pyromancer to experiment on. I tracked my friend Zizi to this place. In the process of liberating her, we were confronted by a woman projecting herself into the room where they kept Zizi. This was Madam Morashi. I couldn't tell you what she looked like...but she had eyes I couldn't look away from..." Sivana stroked her chin as she spoke, brow furrowed. "And long and sharp nails, just like claws. Despite it being a projection, I could almost feel them digging into my skin."

"Oh, yeah, that was definitely her," Vance confirmed with a shudder. "The thing is, she can look like nearly anyone. She's a master of formshifting, but no matter what she looks or sounds like, she can't hide those sharp nails or bright green eyes. Everyone with formshifting has at least one limitation. For me, it's voices."

"Oh?" she asked.

"Yeah. I can make you look like most anyone, but you'll always sound like yourself."

"We'll have to work out a way to sound similar," Margot interjected.

"Well, whatever guards are in place won't notice much

amiss past the accent, darling," she said with a spot-on noble-woman's accent.

Margot clapped for her trick. "You're a natural! I knew I liked you."

"That's all it took?" she asked, still using the noble accent.

"Heather liked you first, and I find that she's an excellent judge of character," she said. My face heated immediately.

They put the finishing touches on Sivana's disguise and made a show of leaving. With a sigh, Carmen shouldered past me to go with them. Margot's tan doppelganger watched them go with a thoughtful expression.

I stepped out of the room for a moment to write the Spymaster a quick note about the gesture we'd decided on to show the gryphons that we were friends. After I touched the note to my bracelet with a murmur to make it disappear into his inbox, I went back inside and pulled up a chair to sit with Fariq.

"What if Carmen gets discovered for having the wrong uniform on?" I asked him.

"Didn't the older, err, people we're working with notice they just wore black?" he asked. He was right, and we'd had her dress similar to what the advanced kids had spied.

It was just the tip of my worries for what could go wrong, but now that I'd asked and he'd replied, a whole flood of them bubbled up. I ran through every worry I had for the auction, and he and Chance reassured me it had, in fact, been thought of.

He and I both startled when Sivana interjected her opinion too. She angled her chair toward us and joined in where she could. As far as we all knew, the plan was airtight.

Eventually, I asked her, "What's it like to ride a gryphon?"

"I'll take you up in the air for a ride if this works out," she said. I hoped that was a serious offer, because I would take her up on it. Few people could say they'd taken a joyride on an actual gryphon!

"It will," I murmured, though I still fidgeted with my fingers nervously.

"It will," Fariq repeated, nudging me. Chance flashed a thumbs-up from a countertop nearby.

"See? Even the mouse agrees," Sivana said with a chuckle. She went quiet after that, her gaze unfocusing like she was talking to her gryphon again.

MARGOT AND VANCE returned after a couple of hours. While Margot took Sivana aside to give her an identical set of prefabricated clothing to what she'd been wearing, I whispered to Vance, "You're back?"

"I didn't forget about changing your face too," he said. "I made Carmen look like an adult. She's in, as far as I could tell from a distance."

I nodded, distracted. Sivana went into the room to change and emerged as Margot in disguise. Her body shape was more athletic than Margot's, but they were passably the same person if one didn't look too closely. "Good enough," I said. "I have something for you."

I'd stolen a dagger for her, actually. The gym had a stash of weapons in a locked side room...not that locks ever stopped me. It didn't feel right to send the first female gryphon rider into danger without a weapon on her person. She secured it against her calf with a nod of thanks.

All of us circled up around Margot and the rough sketch she'd made of what we were about to walk into, a warehouse attached to a three-story tower. "First floor had most of the little wonders. They are keeping the more valuable creatures in the tower," she explained, pointing to the second story. "All the gryphons are here, plus a rather exotic-looking rozash and a handful of the rarest little wonders. They intend to have the actual auction here." Her fingertip slid to the third floor of the tower.

"That's perfect for an aerial attack," Sivana noted. "Did you see the roof?"

"We were barely allowed onto the second floor, darling. But I will tell you the whole place is run-down. They've covered the flooring with carpets and sprayed plenty of perfume to mask the mold smell. It's still dreadfully musty in some places." She flapped her hand under her chin, probably missing her fan.

"I've forgotten to ask. Where is Thomas in all this?" Sivana asked, glancing at me.

I was a little surprised she remembered him. "He's at the rendezvous point to help with any medical emergencies," I said.

I motioned to the little purse Margot had given her to complete her outfit. It was already loaded with what she needed, including the address to Jace's former house hidden within its lining. She raised a brow after I showed it to her. "The locals won't notice the sudden influx of little wonders?" she asked.

"Let's just say it's more private than you think," I hedged. "Also, Fariq should tell you about this." I pulled out one of Fariq's tools from the bottom of the little bag, hidden under a handful of items, the battered auction invitation, and the silky cushion that should've been the purse's bottom.

Fariq took it from me and launched into an explanation. "You have a crowbar hook here for opening cages with leverage. And a lock breaker on the other end. But what really makes it special is this." He flipped it over and pointed to a small circle of red steel. "There is interest right now in materials that weaken or remove magic, both in traps and enchantments. This is a prototype that should do just that. Press the metal to something you think has magic, and it will do its job in ten seconds."

"Really?" she asked in surprise. She tried to hold it closer to inspect it, but he didn't let it go. He tapped his cheek meaningfully. "I can't touch it with Vance's magic on me?"

"It can't touch your face, at least," he said.

"How will I know when it works on something enchanted?" she asked.

"I made this intending for it to be used on any magical locks you find. They'll have tiny runes engraved on them. They'll flare with light when touched by the prototype. After ten seconds, if there's still light but it is dimmer, the spell was weakened. If the light is gone, no more spell," he explained.

"And you made this yourself? What is this metal?" she asked, pointing to the red steel.

Fariq gave her an apologetic smile, shrugging with both palms out. "I'm afraid I cannot tell you much more."

"Except if you're friends with a Tulari, don't touch them with it. It'll leave behind a burn," Vance said.

"A-ah-all right, then," she said. She placed the tool back into its hiding place in the purse.

"Wait here," Fariq said, going back into the changing room.

He emerged with one of his inventions in hand, plus a box and a ribbon to hide it in. It was a shield of red steel with a handle melted onto the back of it. He presented it to Sivana with a little bow. "It would be my honor to let you borrow this. It's a prototype too. I made it from spare parts, so it is small, but it is a shield. More combat-focused."

He threaded his fingers through the handle and swiped it through the air. "It erases runes as a mage writes them, disrupting spells."

"Sure to hurt if you punched them with it, too," Sivana commented.

"Punch? No. Very thin metal. You would warp it all out of

shape. I wanted to make it as big as possible so it can also intercept completed spells. It has a cone of effectiveness that's a little wider than it is." He placed the shield in the box and laid it down on the table.

I watched in fascination too when he showed the size of the cone by using both his hands to make a twisting motion over it. He said, "In theory, if you catch a spell at the tip of the cone, it will reflect back at your enemy. If it hits the sides, it will reflect at an angle, which could be dangerous with others around you. And any spell that hits the metal will be lessened or nullified."

My eyes widened. *This* was what Fariq had been working on at his apprenticeship? I needed to pay closer attention.

"In theory?" Sivana echoed.

He nodded. "In theory. None of us have fought a mage, but it seems likely you will tonight."

"Well, thank you. This is an incredible gift, and I'll let you know how it worked," she said. He smiled happily and packaged it like a present. After she did some adjusting, it fit in the clutch. "Also, I have a friend I think you should meet. She can get you into the Military School of Engineering when you're a little older. You seem like you would be a great fit."

Fariq's mouth rounded with shock. "I'm happy to be of assistance," he said, ducking his head.

With that said, we discussed some last details and assured Sivana we would change clothes and join the event behind her. It was about time she headed out to take her place there.

"If you can't find any of us, Carmen will be the one to give the signal. The hired guards are wearing all black tonight," Margot said.

"Otherwise, I will give you the signal," I said, showing her what it looked like. I spread my fingers and faced them toward each other across my chest.

Sivana nodded slowly. "When you do that, you want me

to call the gryphons in?" she asked. "When about in the proceedings will you give this signal?"

"Before anything is sold, hopefully," I said.

She gave an uncertain laugh. "Hopefully. A simple enough plan. Best of luck to us all, then."

"Good luck," I echoed, flashing her a smile. A lot was riding on her bringing in her gryphons to distract the Morashi, after all. Many small lives at stake tonight.

She left for the event, and the rest of us breathed out some tension now that she was gone. I went into the back room alone to change into a servant's suit. It was a dusty prop from the theater department, sized too small to receive regular use, which meant it was out of style compared to what the other servants at the event were wearing. With how late I was sneaking into the auction, it wouldn't matter much. I put an Altarian flag pin into the lapel and adjusted the outfit, which was tight around the shoulders and middle.

That done, I rejoined my friends. "All right, good work, everyone. You two should be off," I said, glancing over at Vance and Fariq. "And did you really mean you were going to sneak back into the auction?" This was directed at Margot. Now that Sivana had our only invitation to the event, there was no way she'd get back inside.

She smiled mischievously. "No, but there's a sizeable group of your siblings I'm going to join over on SHAINA's side of events. I would rather be a part of the movement to grab cages and run," she said.

Part of the trade-off in not using Sybella's street contacts was that we had to find numbers somewhere. But everyone in my family who'd figured out RSI's secret had agreed to the second half of the plan, to run into the event as chaos struck and the Morashi would be distracted. It was probably the best place for Margot now.

We waited a few minutes before heading to the door.

Margot went one way, Fariq the other, while Vance let the door close and turned to me, wand out.

"Oh, right," I murmured. I held still while he worked his magic over me. My face tingled all over by the time he was done, and the magic over his own face was fading, revealing the shape of the tattoo on his neck and the green color of his Tulari mark on his brow.

It didn't fade completely—he still had a tiny amount of magic left to maintain some of his chosen appearance. Still, I smiled, glad he'd saved this for me in case it helped.

"Thanks, Vance," I said.

"Good luck." The apple of his throat bobbed before he leaned down. He placed a kiss on my cheek, brief and light. If it were from anyone else, I would've flinched away. But I hadn't, even when I saw what he was going to do. I put that knowledge away for now, knowing I'd turn over this moment and relive it, wondering if it meant more than it probably did.

It took me a few seconds to realize I'd frozen and flushed, and he eyed me like he was sure he'd done something wrong. "Um, thanks," I said awkwardly.

He scratched the back of his head. "Yeah."

"I'll see you later, okay?"

"Okay."

This time, when we walked out of the boutique, it was him going one way and me the other.

CHAPTER 32

WHAT'S NECESSARY

THE TIGHT SUIT didn't come with a cloak, and I left my belt behind at the boutique since it would be conspicuous with this disguise. I'd secreted as many of my tools on my person as possible, hiding them like some folk hid weapons. When one of the tools was a bag of desda powder, it essentially was a weapon where mages were concerned.

I was going to approach the warehouse where the auction was being held from its least secure side, from the river. Trade vessels were too big to travel this far upstream, so any goods inbound to Kaiamear were loaded onto slender barges to reach their final destination in the warehouses or the heart of the city's market. As long as I could make it onto the right one, I'd be delivered right to the job.

The few bridges built over the canal had a standard height, however, and I eyed the drop to the dirty brown water below after picking the bridge closest to the warehouses. This wouldn't work. In broad daylight, someone would spot me if I jumped, and if that person's scream didn't alert the bargeman of the vessel I landed on, my cursing over a broken ankle would.

Time was ticking down as I considered my options. I ended up walking alongside the river until I found a choke-point where the water naturally bent. All I had to do was pace and wait—the right barge came along after I didn't jump into two bearing loads of fish. If I'd used those for transport, the Morashi wouldn't need to spot me. They'd smell me instead.

The third had a bored man at the front, steering the weight of several towers of crates slowly down the river. He stared off into the water as his boat drifted past where I waited. Keeping my tread as light as possible, I stepped over and down onto the back of his barge, tipping it to the left with the introduction of my weight. He breathed a sailor's curse and did something to right the vessel while I put a tower of crates at my back and waited.

Chance peeked out of the suit's collar. "We take swim today?" he asked.

"I hope not," I whispered. It depended on how big the leap would be between the barge and our destination and who had replaced the guards on that side of the building. All I knew was that there were a few adults who'd infiltrated the personal security company providing the muscle. Removing hostile eyes from the river was a priority.

Worst-case scenario so far, we jumped, missed dry land, and ruined the desda powder when the pouch was saturated with river water.

And if the guards turned out to be unfriendly, I would have to run. Carmen, who was already inside, would be the one to give the signal to Sivana for the distraction. *It'll be fine.*

But my eyelid still twitched. My primary objective now was to put a hole in the ward, sneak in, and then weaken spells and pop locks to make the process of grabbing the animals easier. Every little bit helped.

We passed under a bridge, the tower of crates not scraping the underside by a few inches. I peered around them to the bargeman, who was still going through the motions of his job. An idea struck me, inspired by his reaction when my weight had made his vessel dip.

When the warehouse district was in sight, I counted the ones we passed. The one I wanted was several in, sagging toward the river from its age. As we approached it and the rotted boards that remained of its dock, I went to the left corner of the barge and heaved my weight up and down to unsettle the boat's balance. My efforts were minimal, as the barge was weighed down more by its cargo than by me, but the bargeman still noticed, cursed, and overcorrected. The back of the boat fishtailed in the water.

When it was closest to the warehouse and I'd made eye contact with the guard standing in the shadow of its central tower, I took a running leap. My feet cleared the dock, which was sure to collapse from any pressure, and my boots landed in the mud. I lost my balance, arms pinwheeling as I started to fall back toward the river, but a pair of strong hands caught me and tugged me to dry land.

"That was close," Ned whispered. He eyed me uncertainly.

"Ned? I thought you were going to be inside," I whispered back.

"You sound like Heather," he said, sounding confused.

Oh, right. I wasn't wearing my own face right now, courtesy of Vance. "I am Heather, promise. Why are you out here?"

He frowned but didn't seem to question it from there. "Last-minute change of plan. Manny switched my team's roles with a team of adults when we learned how strong the ward they used is. We haven't found the wardstone yet, but we're pretty sure it's in the river." He took a moment to point out the three guards within our sight. All of them were his teammates, which meant we could talk without being discovered.

I glanced toward the lapping brown water. The Spymaster had mentioned the ward. It functioned as a bubble that blocked all sight and sound of what was going on inside of it unless one was able to find and smash the wardstone, which mages notoriously left in the hardest-to-access places they could think of. As counterproductive as it seemed, wardstones had to be outside of the radius of the ward. It was their one huge security flaw. The biggest, strongest wards had to be maintained by multiple stones set equal distances apart.

We had to take down the ward to effectively get in and out of the warehouse. Creating a hole in the ward was a start, as weak wards began to collapse on their own if they were damaged. But if this was a powerful one, with multiple stones, a single hole wouldn't be enough.

"Did you get tasked with going for a swim?" I asked.

He grimaced. "Yup. I'm supposed to try to make a hole in the ward from the outside first." He pointed upward, toward the solo windows marking the second and third floors of the tower. "One of your teammates is supposed to open the second-floor window."

"For me to sneak in. I was supposed to make the hole," I said, nodding.

"Right. You know that tool you gave me, with the red metal? She's going to apply it to one side, and I'm going to use it on the other. Then, I'm supposed to take that swim."

"Well, let's simplify the job a bit," I murmured, bending over to untie the pouch of desda powder I'd strapped to my calf under my now mud-spattered pants. I opened it to show him the red hue of the powder. "I'll make the hole in the ward and then drop this down to you for the wardstone."

"Is that desda powder? You just…have this?" he asked in disbelief.

I shrugged and tied it around my wrist, moving my gaze up toward the second story window. "I'm going up," I said.

"Good luck. I'll spot you."

Hopefully he wouldn't need to catch me. The climb seemed easy enough, but there was no rope or harness this time. I'd been practicing for this for months in Agility, though. My fingers and toes were accustomed to finding the barest handholds, which the tower had plenty of. Its stone was pitted with age and coated with layers of salt, dirt, and other things I didn't want to think about.

I inched my way up the tower, finding out the hard way that the deposits that'd hardened against the bricks still fell off. My foot slipped several times from dislodged clods of dirt. I could practically feel Ned's cringe on my back; he had to be watching my slow but steady progress when I found my footing again.

Every time I rushed when climbing the rock wall during class, I swiftly found myself falling. I didn't repeat that mistake now. *Slow and steady. One handhold at a time.*

Chance whispered praise to me from his place on my shoulder, mimicking the applause I'd get from my friends when I reached the next floor on the rock wall. I'd gotten close to the top before, my personal best at this point, so climbing this tower wasn't past my abilities. Eventually, my hand gripped the sill of the window, and I hoisted myself the rest of the way up and peered inside, seeing nothing but cobwebs and a thick layer of dirt on the inside of the tower.

That was the ward at work. I could be face-to-face with a Morashi mage on the other side of this window and never know it. Reaching into the pouch tied to my wrist, I flicked a pinch of desda powder toward the glass.

The crimson powder joined the rest of the dirt on the window. *Musty devils.* The wall of the ward was on the other side of the pane, which wasn't designed to be opened from the outside. I hung there, waiting, feeling the tension in my forearms now that I was no longer in motion.

I glanced down at Ned, which was a mistake. The drop was dizzying. I clenched my eyes closed and considered a prayer, not that the gods had ever listened or answered me before.

Please, I begged empty air.

My arms started to tremble. *Please, Carmen.* If I went down now, I didn't think I had the upper body strength to climb up a second time.

Just as I was considering making the trip down, there was a terrible shriek, and the window inched upward. I startled and scrambled for the desda powder, flicking it at the opening and watched the granules stick in midair. The ward became visible as it melted, sizzling like a sheet that'd caught fire, with the damage spreading and growing, small holes meeting to become larger ones right before my eyes.

This was accompanied by a blast of noise, the sound of many voices conversing at once. One particularly loud man was shouting, "What do you think you're doing?"

I saw movement headed for the other side of the window and ducked out of sight with a squeak of alarm. The pane slammed back downward.

Yet I could still hear him, muffled. "The guests will be coming this way any minute. Just what were you thinking?"

"I thought they might like some air, sir," Carmen answered.

I inched myself back up to see the ancient window hadn't taken this man's rough treatment well. A corner of it remained lifted. "You think these upper crust nobles *want* to smell the brine and mud outside?" he asked in disbelief. I could practically see Carmen's cringe from my vantage. "Look—I don't recognize your face. Are you new?"

"Yes, sir," she answered.

The hole in the ward was as wide as my shoulders— which I deemed good enough. I untied the desda powder from my wrist and let it drop to Ned, flashing a thumbs-up without looking down. Hopefully he could take it from here.

"You stand right here, peas for brains. Don't make me fire you mid-job," he ordered.

"Yes, sir," she said again, this time through gritted teeth. She balled her fists at her sides before inching to the right, blocking sight of the window with her presence.

I was still hanging on to the tower with effort. I took deep breaths, trying to think happy thoughts to distract from the pain in my arms.

A man's voice boomed out from the hole in the ward a couple minutes later. "Ladies and gentlemen, this concludes our viewing party. If all interested buyers would head toward the central tower, we will begin seating and the auction shortly."

I gritted my teeth. We were running out of time to take down the ward, which meant there would only be one entrance and exit to the event. This put everything at risk. Carmen shifted her weight on the other side of the window. She was worried…or expecting a fight.

I heard the clomp of shoes on wood and several voices passing by. "Move it along," Carmen said gruffly. "Let's go. Pick up your feet."

I braced my weight on the windowsill more to relieve the pressure in my arms. The voices faded to a murmur, followed by the shuffle of heavy feet. "Oh, do you think you guard this window now?" asked the same man as before in a sneering tone. "Head on up with the others."

Carmen didn't answer, except to whirl around and open the window as far as she could. Whatever the man was expecting, it wasn't for her to grab my elbows and haul me into the room. My chest and legs scraped painfully on the bricks and sill, but I lay out on the floor gratefully as Carmen fell into a fighting stance and made a blade with her hand, aiming it for the man's jaw.

There were a few shouts of surprise and motion around

us. "Little help, pipsqueak?" Carmen said, raising her other arm to fend off a second man.

A fight so close to the auction was definitely not part of the plan, but there was a string quartet playing music somewhere above us and no lull to the sound of conversation coming from that direction. I righted myself on the ground and lunged for the legs of a third man, who jogged over to help. He lost his balance and fell into the person who'd been bossing Carmen around. She grabbed him in a headlock when he lost his balance too and pitched to the side.

It took all of Carmen's strength and attention to keep her hold on that man, who thrashed and pulled on her arm as his face purpled. I stood and put myself between them and the two other guards. They loomed over me, noting my stature and smirking. The altercation was catching notice from more guards, drawing a crowd.

My arms felt like soggy noodles, but that didn't stop me from kicking out and nailing one of my opponents in the gut. He staggered back, hands coming up to cup his middle. Pain blasted the side of my face in the next moment, and my head whipped to the side, leaking a spray of spittle. It had to be a punch, and a follow-up strike landed square in my middle. It was like the guard had hit me with a leaden weight.

I fell back on the Tosh Zorena I knew well...how to take a hit. I tucked into a controlled fall, resisting the urge to whimper. If nothing was broken, I would have two huge bruises to show for this.

Something hot and wet sprayed the wood by my feet. I looked up in shock to see the guard who'd punched me clutch a wound drawn across his neck and fall, gasping wetly.

The adult who stood behind him, holding a bloodied blade, turned the point on another guard, stabbing the place where neck and shoulder met and twisting. She killed a third in the same time it took for Carmen to finally lay out the unconscious form of the man she'd been struggling with.

Carmen gave me a hand up, and we both gaped at the woman. She was dressed as a guard too, with an average face twisted with annoyance. Her dark garb hid any bloodstains. Behind us, there was a tussle and a pair of male guards helping a third to the ground as he struggled with his slit throat.

"You there, help drag the bodies out of sight," said the woman, pointing at Carmen and jerking her chin toward where her two teammates. To me, she demanded, "Why is the ward still up?"

The pain was waning, but I pressed my fingertips to my throbbing cheek. "We're still trying to find the wardstone. Uh, ma'am."

"Hmph." She bent and cleaned her blade on the clothes of one of her victims. "Quit poking at your face. You're just going to have one hells of a bruise tomorrow."

"Sorry. Sorry about..." I felt my gorge rise and tasted bile at the back of my throat. She'd murdered these men without a second thought.

"Look at me." She grabbed my shoulder, giving it a shake. I focused on her face with an awkward swallow. "They chose this fate and made their bed as enemies of the Crown. Get used to doing what's necessary if you want to graduate the institute with any prestige. Okay?"

"Okay," I said with effort, trying to focus on my breathing.

"Now that you've made a hole in the ward, what is your next objective?" she prompted.

I looked past her. There were several cages stacked in the middle of this room, each with a single beaked face looking out of it. They were watching us, I realized, standing still in their cages and staring. The collection of Sivana's missing gryphons were all trapped in cages with a rune engraved overtop the locks, and their little faces seemed…hopeful in a way I'd never seen on an animal before.

"I'm supposed to unlock cages, ma'am," I said.

"Then do that. I'll cover you," she said.

The other spies and Carmen were hiding the bodies behind the cages for now. They were closest to the stairs heading up toward the auction, while the woman spy and I stood right in front of the stairs leading to the first floor.

I fumbled for my sleeve, fingers brushing the tool I'd tied to my forearm with a length of twine. I willed my hands to steady for the job I had to do and settled in front of a cage at random. The young gryphon inside peeped at me, watching as I pressed the circle of red steel on the underside of the tool to the rune over the cage lock.

After ten seconds, the light inside of the rune faded. I flipped the tool around and used the lock breaker to destroy the lock. "I'm going to keep it closed for right now. Stay calm. You will be rescued," I said to the creature within. It flapped its wings and growled like a wildcat.

The rest of the gryphons were extending beaks and talons towards me, all wanting to be next. I murmured reassuring nonsense and worked as quickly as I could. My ears were perked for the sounds of the auction beginning above us. An announcer was trying to excite the crowd of wealthy folk.

I cursed some devils as I guessed someone could be coming here at any moment to retrieve a cage to put the gryphon within up to auction. I had about half of them open when I heard footsteps, but they were heading upward from the first floor.

A woman's authoritative voice accompanied the sound of boots on wood. I froze and ducked behind the cages, peering out to see the woman spy turn with her knife upraised. She jumped into motion, trying to bring the weapon down on the first person who stepped in front of her, a Tulari man with his wand in hand.

The spy hit him twice, once in the shoulder and again in the heart. His dead weight slumped to the ground just as the other mages behind him reacted. There was a woman dressed in an elaborate sapphire-blue robe and holding a wooden staff engraved with flowers right behind him. Within delicate curls of wood, the staff had several multicolored glass balls toward the top like apples budding off a tree.

She stepped to the side, and the men behind her rushed for the spy. One went low and grabbed her hips, pushing her to the ground. The other cast a spell, and stone shards dislodged from the walls, embedding in her arms and grazing the side of her head. For a moment, we made eye contact from where I'd frozen in my hiding place. "Run!" she shouted.

A dagger flew end over end toward the female Tulari, courtesy of one of the other spies. She noticed it and raised her staff, deflecting it with a single flick. It embedded in the floor point-down a few feet away from her. Green runes began to circle the beautiful staff she held, and she angled it toward the man who'd thrown the weapon. A coil of black, spiky vine sprang free of it, wrapping around his arm. He started to scream and pull at the thorns embedded in his flesh.

His partner had Carmen by the arm and was trying to drag her away and up the stairs to the third floor. She kicked and spat, fists balled as she tried to thrash out of his hold. "No!" she shouted. "Stop!" He covered her mouth and hauled her off her feet, carrying her no matter how she strained.

Trembling, I reminded my muscles to move, inching backward from the mages and toward the stairs to the third floor as well. "Well, well. Seems you're all alone," the woman with the staff said. It chimed as she swung it around, pointing it at the female spy.

There were sounds of scuffling and the spy spitting. "Kill me, then," she growled.

"Not until I can be assured that you're the end of this little…infiltration."

"I will tell you *nothing*, Morashi scum."

Somewhere above our heads, the announcer was calling out bidding amounts, and a strange feeling washed over me head to toe as I crept ever closer to the stairs. I made eye contact with the man who'd been hit by the vine spell. He was lying in a twisted pile of limbs, his eyes beginning to glaze over. "The…the ward…"

He slumped, limp. I bit down on my knuckle to not make a sound. *This can't be happening. This is all going wrong. No one was supposed to die.* "Someone has to give the signal," I mumbled, already feeling the numbness of shock settling in.

"You're not working alone," the Tulari woman was saying.

The spy that'd come to my rescue started to laugh, loud and discordantly. She laughed and laughed and then gasped, but I didn't look back as I lunged out from behind the cages and toward safety only a few yards away.

Something coiled around both my ankles and squeezed mercilessly. I fell face-first on the wooden steps, and Chance went flying, landing in a heap on a step several steps up from my head. Heart thudding in my chest, I choked out, "Save yourself."

A man seized my ankles and dragged me across the ground. My head hit several stairs, and dozens of stars coated my vision. He pulled me through the spatter of blood and past the blur of worried gryphon faces. I was dropped on the ground next to the female spy, who struggled to pry off the Tulari's hand. Her fingernails were dug deep into her neck.

"Make your peace now. My poison is always fatal," the mage said, sounding almost bored. Her bright green eyes flicked in my direction, brows raising. Horror twisted in my gut when I realized who she had to be.

I was lucky her mage lackey hadn't used a poison-laced vine to restrain my ankles. I tried to kick and shimmy it off of me, trying haplessly to inch myself away from these mages. The woman stood and slammed the butt of her staff into my shoulder, stopping my struggles by pinning my back flat to the ground.

"Just where do you think you're going, little *zibrak*? I deserve an explanation for what you're doing at my event," Madam Morashi purred.

CHAPTER 33

SKITTER SKITTER

MADAM MORASHI MET MY GAZE, working some kind of spell through her staff. Green markings appearing around it, winding through its glass orbs at dizzying speed. My mind grew hazy, and my eyelids slumped. Something like exhaustion weighed down every one of my muscles.

"We're compromised. Bring the girl," she said distantly.

The pair of male Tulari hefted me to my feet, and the vine fell away. They carried me between them, and I didn't fight. I had no energy to do so.

Screeeee! Something huge and furious screamed overhead. Madam Morashi cursed and bunched her skirts in two fists, hurrying down the stairs.

Thud. Thump. Scree! More and more creatures screamed and roared.

I swung like a ragdoll as the two men carrying me hurried after their madam. She took a sharp turn at the foot of the stairs and stood in front of a door set behind the base of the staircase. I vaguely heard a litany of orders she delivered to the men before they were gone, and I stood wobbling on my feet, moments from crashing to the ground in a boneless heap.

Madam Morashi snapped her fingers in front of my face and wrenched my head up so we made eye contact. I staring at those eyes, twin pools of green that shifted with dappled gleams, beautiful, depthless…until the world changed around me.

I was no longer in a warehouse at all, suddenly blinded by darkness. I could've been standing in a pitch-black tunnel. My breathing changed, roaring in my ears. That *smell*. Before my eyes adjusted, I knew where I was and what my fingers would find when I reached out.

A roughly hewn stone wall and the crawling legs of dozens of insects. I grabbed my wrist with a frightened shout, yet suddenly, the bugs were everywhere, crawling over my exposed skin and under my clothes. Lurching to the side, I hit another wall. It was closing in. Somehow, I knew all the surrounding walls were creeping forward.

I can't breathe!

I'm trapped!

"Interesting," the voice cut through the noise in my head. When I blinked, my eyes stung with a sudden infusion of reality. I hadn't moved an inch, despite what I'd thought. I had never looked away from Madam Morashi's gaze.

"A fear of being contained. Of jail cells…" She ghosted her fingertips over my arm. "And little skittering bugs."

Somewhere close to us, people were screaming. Gryphons roared in fury. Something smashed, and there was a heavy *thud* and the sound of metal screeching against metal.

Yet I couldn't focus on the chaos quickly descending toward the ground floor. Five sharp points dug into my cheeks and chin. The poisonous claws Vance warned me of were about to pierce my skin with the barest amount of extra pressure.

"Who are you, *zibrak*?"

I registered her harsh tone, yet her eyes…

There was a spell at work, whispering *"Do not resist"* woven with a thread of *"or else."*

My subconscious understood it perfectly, and I didn't resist. I said, "Heather."

Her fingers tightened, and the muscles around those enthralling eyes pulled with irritation. "And who are *they*?" She blinked, and just like that, the spell keeping me connected to her gaze broke. Her clawed fingers turned my head.

Breathing shallowly with how those pointed nails pressed into my flesh, I looked where she directed me to. There was Ram and Dexis and a small cluster of older kids in an advanced team. They were taking cages and passing them down a few hastily created lines of grabbing hands.

"Please don't hurt them," I said.

"Friends, hmm?" she said smoothly. She lifted her staff, and runes began to write themselves around it. With a flourish, she pointed it straight at Dexis.

"W-wait. Please. I...I know where the Eye of Acuity is," I blurted.

Madam Morashi's fingers loosened on my neck. My body still felt sluggish from whatever she'd done to me, but I still pulled away from her and aimed my elbow for her inner arm. She dropped the staff, and a beam of green and black magic twisted from its head, cutting through the ground.

The first well-dressed nobles were running past, and it was a miracle the magic only clipped a couple's legs. The woman of the couple had her heels disintegrated and her skin directly exposed to the spell blackened. She fell, dragging the man down with her. They disappeared under a stampede of more people as the bulk of the crowd swarmed the first floor.

"Oh, you will regret that," the madam said, latching on to my arm. Spell runes wrote themselves on my skin, sizzling like they were made of acid as they formed open wounds. My screams were lost in the sounds of the chaos around us. She tugged me one way, and I struggled and pulled with all my weight to free my arm of her hand and whatever foul spell she was working on me directly.

To make matters worse, an adult gryphon broke through the ceiling, landing amidst my friends and family. It was built like a female, all her feathers and fur standing on end as she roared loud enough to rattle my eardrums. Her head swiveled between the stampeding nobles and the kids backing away from her. They put their palms up.

I had a brief moment of relief before I...forgot. The tension and worries in my head fled as Madam Morashi finished her spell, a chain of runes that looped my forearm in intricate lines. My blood dripped from dozens of wounds, hitting the ground with a splish-splash after it saturated my sleeve.

"I don't have time for any more games," she stated. She retrieved her staff and pulled me out of the warehouse, through the door that'd gone unnoticed by the fleeing crowd. Cold hit my face, and my nose stung with the smell of brine.

In one practiced motion of her hand, she'd worked my jaw open, and her thumb pulled my lips apart. A small, suppressed part of me screamed, a shrill noise ringing in my ears that didn't escape despite my open mouth. Madam Morashi aligned our lips until they almost met in a foul kiss, and then she breathed in. Pain pricked down my throat and delved even deeper into my chest. It was like I'd swallowed a handful of tiny blades, and they cut all the way through me.

Swirls of bright green mist flowed from my mouth to hers. She inhaled for a few seconds before stopping, smacking her lips, and rolling what she'd taken around on her tongue. I tasted blood at the back of my mouth and swayed on unsteady legs while she swallowed with a sound of satisfaction.

"Youth come to blossom, still so sweet. I know you now, little mouse. Your essence tastes of hunger, fading innocence...and something I cannot quite decipher," she said thoughtfully. Another spell was writing itself around her staff, but this time, she reached up and let it wind around her hand. She used it to make a grabbing motion over my face and dislodged Vance's magic. It looked like a mask at first, before disintegrating into vapor that leaked around her fingers. She tasted that, too.

"I've been looking for you for a long time. How interesting it is that you've come to me, wearing the magic of a boy who rejected his calling. I hand-selected him to elevate as a member of my movement, yet he has chosen to ally with you instead…" She didn't look away from me, so I was still rooted to the spot. Still not resisting. "And he helped you infiltrate my auction."

Madam Morashi scoffed and bared her teeth in displeasure. "Heather the Mouse, do you know how many died so you could keep the Eye of Acuity from me?" It was a question she didn't want an answer to, as she didn't wait for a response. "No matter. It shall be mine now, and you will deliver it to me. Won't you?"

She was working another spell on me. I could tell the bands of runes were weaving around my body and making a net around my head. Any coherent thought was being packed away with a dense ball of magic, suffocating my will. It was worse than the first spell she'd cast, completely crushing me. Distantly, I heard my voice say, "Anything for you."

Her voice and movements were also distant. Producing a dagger that'd been strapped on her leg, she handed it to me. "You will find Vance and cut him with this. He will die in minutes…then you will take the Eye from him and deliver it to me. The spell will tell you where to go. Now, skitter skitter, little mouse. Or you know the consequences."

The madam would lock me in a stone box if I failed. I couldn't fail. I moved as if in a dream, with my eyes unfocused for anything but my new mission.

Vance had the Eye of Acuity. And I knew where Vance was. But…I didn't want to hurt him.

I don't want to do this. My feet moved me forward anyway. As little as I *wanted* to follow Madam Morashi's directions, the stinging of the spell etched in my forearm became white-hot pain every moment I considered not doing as I was told.

The only act of rebellion I could muster was taking a few wrong turns in downtown Kaiamear on the way to my destination, becoming temporarily turned around in an unfamiliar neighborhood. Eventually, I would kill him with the dagger I'd strapped to my side. It was written in my flesh. Then I would bring the Eye back to the madam. Nothing else mattered.

In the meantime, I continued to ache. It was not an exaggeration to say every inch and hair in or on my body hurt. My face and arms throbbed, my feet ached, but my head…that pounded. The madam's spell must've cleaved open my skull for how much it pained me. If I didn't find Vance soon, I just might succumb to the weakness pouring into my body with each step.

Do not resist.

I walked through variations of jail cells, strummed my fingers over confining metal bars only I could see. The spell promised that the next stone box would be real if I failed. I couldn't rest. I couldn't stop. Madam Morashi would lock me in a cell and feed me alive to a hoard of bugs to eat off my skin if I didn't bring her the Eye.

Many sharp, chitinous feet crawled over my skin. I could feel them, but I couldn't see them. I could barely see anything. Yet when I next placed my gaze on Vance or the Eye of Acuity, I knew I'd be able to see them perfectly. The madam wanted it, and I would deliver it.

Or I would die. I might…

Skitter skitter was a motion bugs made. It bothered me, deep down, that she'd attributed it to me, the Mouse.

Skitter skitter went the insects only I could feel. They didn't bite or sting yet. But I would feel that pain too if I failed.

I couldn't breathe…I was trapped…

Something sharper than insect claws latched on to my pants leg. I hardly noticed until there was a brush of fur when a small body slipped under my jacket and wedged itself through the tight fabric around my shoulder. My knees wobbled. I was so tired…I didn't have the energy to care.

Until a pair of sharp teeth cleaved one of the spell runes on my forearm. *Musty devils*, that hurt. A frisson of agony seized my arm as those teeth split another rune, then another.

The fog lifted…the darkness changed, becoming not so deep and all-consuming. I took a pained breath and nearly collapsed on the spot.

Someone placed a hand on my shoulder. Color, sounds, motion, and thought returned, and I blinked up to see Sivana's concerned face. "Hey. You okay?" she was asking.

I blinked a few more times. "Where…?" What was I doing? Why was I talking to Sivana under a streetlamp? When did it get dark? Why did everything hurt *so* much? All those questions packed in, and I was overwhelmed. "I must've…"

I should've asked if she was all right. The clothing we'd dressed her in was streaked with dark stains and rips; her hair was askew and caked in dirt.

I'd gotten here somehow, but the knowledge of it was fading like an old memory. All I knew anymore was that my body was lit up with agony from the inside out. It was a wonder I didn't pitch forward and pass out in Sivana's arms. But as I breathed steadily and recovered from whatever had happened, the pain receded enough for now. I just couldn't move one of my arms too much. It felt like I had several long scratches down the forearm.

"You're not Madam Morashi," I said, relieved at that at least.

Her brow furrowed in concern. "Far from it. What happened?"

"She looked into my eyes, and the next thing I know, I'm here…" And I was feeling more like I was *here*, present in my mind, with every passing moment. Fear chilled my skin, just a ghosting of insect limbs and iron bars.

What'd that musty mage do to me?

I looked past Sivana, spotting two gryphons behind her. No, three. There was a small gryphon in a cage next to Sunset's massive foot. "The plan! I think…it must've worked," I blurted. If she had a baby gryphon…she had to have set off the distraction. "I didn't quite get to the rendezvous spot, but you found me all the same."

After a short delay, she shrugged helplessly. She pressed a hand to her head, wavering on her feet for a moment. "A-ah-all I know is your plan helped save my gryphon's daughter. Do you have any tools to free her from this cage, though?" she asked.

I looked at the cage and laughed. If she'd known me better, she wouldn't have had to ask. "I always have tools."

I checked my sleeve, relieved Fariq's tool was back and secure against my left forearm. I kneeled in front of the cage and pressed the circle of red steel to the rune keeping the lock magically sealed. It flickered blue for a moment before fading completely. After that, it was a matter of prying off the lock and opening the door. The young gryphon inside was gone in a flash of red, diving to stand between Sunset's talons with a whine for attention.

Sunset bent and nosed what had to be her baby with a soft murr.

"Thank the gods for you," Sivana said, talking to me.

I blushed, flustered. "I just wanted to help."

We turned to watch the young gryphon bounce between Sunset and Arimus, who held himself at a stiff angle. He didn't bend his front legs when he leaned down toward the little one.

Tiny paws emerged from the bloodied cuff of my right arm. I offered my opposite palm to Chance, who immediately launched into a frenzied chatter. "Are you okay? I saw bad lady do something, yes yes, and I want help, but I small, so I went to get gryphon lady, but gryphon lady fly off after I give signal—"

"Chance, please. Take a breath," I encouraged. He spoke fast at the best of times, so when he was in a hurry, I couldn't make out what he was trying to say. He'd drawn himself up and wrung his front paws, concern practically radiating off him.

"I tell gryphons you need help, and they tell her. We come find you, yes yes." The mouse eyed me anxiously. "I bite bad marks on you too hard? I fix?"

"No, you did the right thing. I just need a healer now," I whispered under my breath. What bad marks? I didn't dare check what was hiding under my sleeve, even though I dreaded what I'd see. I wasn't about to make the larger-than-life Hero of Altare next to me worry for my sake. I was plenty worried about myself and the gap of time I'd forgotten between getting ensnared by Madam Morashi's gaze and now.

We'd be heading to Jace's old house soon, and there would be healers there. Arimus clearly needed to visit with a healer, the more I watched how he favored one of his legs. Sunset, too, as she had a large wound on her shoulder that I'd almost missed. The blood matting her fur was the same shade of dark red as her body.

Arimus was the first of the gryphon family to leave the happy reunion and limp our way. He tilted his head, and

Sivana mirrored the motion. She met him halfway and put a hand on his shoulder, guiding him until he loomed more than half a foot above me. "He wants to hug you," she said.

I gazed up at him, mouth rounding with awe. Petting Ironfeather had been one thing; he'd seemed sweet and young. This blind male was as much a Hero of Altare as his rider. He was a war veteran and an experienced battle mount who'd suffered the devastation of losing his sight and still managed to move on.

But if *he* hugged *me*, that was within the respectable boundaries of touching such a storied gryphon. "Oh, um, okay," I stammered out.

He lifted the leg I suspected was wounded, reaching forward tentatively as his talons brushed my side. They wrapped around my torso like a giant hand, applying gentle pressure to scoot me forward into his furry chest. I imagined his fur would be soft if it wasn't so matted with dirt at the moment.

I hugged him back, carefully wrapping my arms up and around his neck and broad shoulders. He tilted his head the way it seemed gryphons did when they were talking to their riders. But this time, he was trying to communicate with me. A pinching sensation grabbed my temples, and my abused mind seemed to give up any hope of resisting...

Oh. He wasn't saying anything with words, but I felt it. A feeling of his gratitude filled my chest, erasing my pain for a moment. Tears pricked the corners of my eyes at how pure and strong that emotion was. "You're, um, you're welcome," I whispered.

He murred and grasped a lock of my hair gently in his beak, giving it a tug, then released me and stumbled backward, dragging his weight to the side in a less than graceful moment. I wondered what'd hurt him...all of them, since I figured Sivana had to be hurt too but was doing a better job not showing it.

Arimus had made room for Sunset, who stood over me now. She was even taller and broader than him but just as aware of our differences. She leaned down and nuzzled my cheek with the flat curve of her beak. In that moment of contact, her gratitude was fierce and hot, colored by a flash of an even smaller version of the young gryphon in my mind's eye.

Had I just imagined it, or had she somehow said to me, *"Thank you for helping save my baby."* She went back to Arimus's side and clucked over him. He shook himself and clicked his beak at her, one of his wings flaring out while the other remained curled at his side.

Sivana had picked up the young gryphon and held her cradled upside down in the crook of her arm. It was a feat, as she was of a size that would put a large hunting dog to shame. I cleared my throat, knowing we had to get to safety and receive healing as soon as possible. "We should move to the rendezvous point. Everyone else should be waiting for us there," I said.

"How far is it from here?" Sivana asked.

"About a bell's walk away." It was a complete guess. I didn't know where we were, but I could figure it out when we got to some street signs.

Sivana frowned, staring off at nothing for several seconds. "Have you ever ridden a horse?" she asked out of nowhere.

"No?"

"It would be faster if you rode one of the gryphons. Sunset is offering if you guide us," she explained, gesturing to the massive maroon female. I almost didn't believe it until Sunset kneeled down and tossed her head toward the saddle tied on her back. Sivana still had to give me a boost, as I didn't trust my sore legs. My face split with a broad grin as Sunset stood and her muscles shifted below my legs. I was really riding a gryphon!

Sivana mounted Arimus in a practiced vault, still holding

the young gryphon, and we started walking. She flashed an apologetic smile and said that was all the beasts were up for after the day's excitement. I figured they were too hurt to fly and didn't question it further. I guided us in the right direction when we finally found a signpost. It wouldn't be much farther now.

"You be okay?" Chance asked again. He clung to Sunset's fur and watched me with continued concern.

"I will be," I assured him, even though I'd forgotten what Madam Morashi had done to put me in this state. Just the thought of her had chill bumps rising on my skin, and I shuddered. "Thank you, by the way. I think the only reason I'm okay is your quick thinking."

He perked up. "I good spy," he said proudly. One of Sunset's tufted ears angled backward.

"You're the best mouse I could've ever asked to Link with. I love you," I said earnestly, reaching over to pet him. Hopefully, the gryphon interpreted his comment as some carpenter mouse silliness.

"I love you too," he squeaked.

Sunset released a coo and glanced over her non-wounded shoulder at us briefly. Her big yellow eye blinked slowly.

She then turned her beak toward the sky as a big shape arrowed for a landing in front of us. "Sivana!" exclaimed a man in a distinct accent.

Oh, great. It was Acton, the snobbish nobleman.

Except he didn't seem all that stuck-up this evening as he leaned past Ironfeather's shoulder, looking over Sivana like he could see anything in the dark. "Are you all right? Where've you been?" he asked, voice softening with concern.

"I'll be okay. You've missed...quite a lot," she answered evasively.

He chuckled. "I would imagine so. Seems we always do, eh, Ironfeather?"

The gray gryphon twittered and nodded in agreement. He

turned and laid his leonine tail over Arimus's shoulders, leading the blind gryphon along. Acton turned in the saddle to face Sivana better. His gaze skimmed over me, too, and his brows rose for a moment of surprise, but he didn't have a snippy comment. I was grateful for that.

"What'd we miss?" Sivana asked him.

"A group of kids showed up out of nowhere once one of them disrupted the wards around the event," he began. "It was at the same time Wild Flight landed and started to carry on. They worked together to steal cages, passing them hand over hand to get them all removed quickly."

Five & Chance, plus SHAINA, was getting promoted to advanced for sure. As long as Carmen and I didn't get disciplined for the deadly fight that'd occurred after I'd put a hole in the ward. My lips turned down as I remembered… The lady spy who'd come to our rescue had to be dead. And her partner, he died right before my eyes.

Sivana and Acton were talking about a gryphon that'd died, too. *Musty devils*, how many casualties had there been to carry out the job?

We could've skipped putting a hole in the wards, for how little it'd helped. Then those guards would still be alive, and Madam Morashi would've probably walked right past Carmen without even noticing her. And Carmen—was she okay? My headache twinged, and I held my head with a soft groan.

I just barely remembered her fighting the last spy dressed as a guard as he dragged her away from Madam Morashi. His quick action may have just saved her life, because she was the type of friend who'd try to fight the mage who'd killed an experienced spy with one flick of her staff.

"Some of Wild Flight saw what we were doing and helped us move and relocate the cages. We retrieved them all, I believe," Acton narrated.

"Hear that? You should see your family soon," I whispered to Chance. I heard his teeth brushing together in an excited chatter.

"The same group of kids were the ones to break into the cages holding the younglings. Things calmed down quite a bit once the mothers were reunited with their babies," Acton said.

"And everyone is at the rendezvous point now?" Sivana asked.

"Everyone but us," he said dryly. "What happened with you all, then?"

Sivana lowered her voice, but I heard something about "friendly healers."

"There are several," Acton whispered back.

That was a relief. "We're here," I said, pointing to Jace's former house. The gryphons stopped, and the two riders dismounted. Though Sunset kneeled down, I eyed the drop and felt how numb my legs had gotten and hesitated.

Acton came over and offered me a hand down. I stumbled, nearly crumpling as the wounds in my arm pulled and awoke with agony, and he caught me. "Right, straight to the healers with you, too," he said, getting a good look at my face.

I flashed a grimace and nodded in agreement. The walk to the front door felt like a trek through a pitch-black tunnel, and a familiar feeling of a memory just out of reach iced over my skin. I blinked, and I was setting my knuckles on the wood, knocking in the proper sequence to get immediate entry.

I glimpsed the first couple of rooms. There were a lot of people and animals here, sleeping in puppy piles beneath blackout curtains.

"What is this place?" Sivana asked behind me.

"A safe house," I answered offhandedly. "Until someone buys it, at least."

She, Acton, and their gryphons went one way, and I made

for the other. I walked a few paces before stumbling. It was Vance who caught me.

Vance!

I reached for the dagger at my side, still compelled to use it even if I'd forgotten how it'd gotten there in the first place.

He had the green glow of his wand's tip pressed to my forehead before I could draw the weapon. My fingers went limp, and my eyelids shuttered.

"Heather." His voice echoed strangely. "Hold on just a little longer…"

Darkness claimed the space behind my eyes.

CHAPTER 34

RECOVERY

I HAD A LONG REST. Folk say they "slept like the dead" when it was a dreamless unconsciousness. That was implied as a pleasant experience.

Well, I slept like the dead in a worse way, as if I would never wake up. Which is silly, in retrospect, as my consciousness floated to the surface often enough to hear snippets of what was going on around me.

"I don't know the spell you're talking about," an unfamiliar woman said. "Let me just look—"

"No, if you don't know it, I'll find someone who does," Vance argued.

I didn't fall into a dreamless sleep for too long before the voices returned.

"Madam Morashi did this. You're certain." This time, it was Fletcher.

"I saw her," Vance said.

"You've been here," Fletcher pointed out. There was an uncertain pause. "Look, I can't. I…gave up the ability to work healing spells on people. But I know who can fix this. Give me your word that you won't tell a soul about what you're about to see."

Vance swore it in magic, I think.

"Thomas," Fletcher whispered afterward. "Go get Shauna. Tell her to bring her wand."

The darkness claimed me again. I was adrift, floating on a slow river as time trickled by. There was no pain anymore. Was I dead? Because I imagined the sun-washed lands to be… well, brighter and full of people. My mother would be there for sure, waiting with the big, comforting hug I'd needed so badly when her soul departed to the next life.

I wasn't in the hells, because then it would be a lot hotter and I'd be punished for my crimes. Laying in one spot, that wasn't a punishment.

Carmen joined me somehow. "Why have you been hiding her here?"

"I can't say," Vance replied.

"She needs to be back at RSI! The Spymaster has to hear what happened from her."

"She just needs to sleep. She needs time." He sounded upset and frightened. "Madam Morashi stole at least a year of her life, and there are going to be…adjustments."

Adjustments? The thought slipped away, but the voices didn't stop.

"…Wish you'd wake up and see it. We have a real-life gryphon here…" This was Thomas.

"Get well soon, darling. I don't think Vance will forgive himself any other way…" And Margot.

"…And received that promotion you wanted so badly." Finally, Fariq. "I wish you hadn't cared so much. This seems like the price you paid for us…"

WHEN I DID WAKE UP, it was with a great intake of breath and the energetic thumping of my heart kicking off to a gallop in my chest.

I knew that roof. I was in one of the guest rooms of Little Wonders Pet Shop, and the pressure of the sheets around my legs suggested I wasn't occupying this bed alone.

I shifted and winced. Yes, I was still alive, because the pain was back. But this time, it wasn't because my insides felt scraped raw or the aches of muscles were pushed to their limits. I just hadn't moved in long enough that I was stiff.

A furry face popped up over one of my eyes. "She awake, yes yes," Chance reported. I felt the claws of another mouse climbing onto my face, peering down next to him. "This my brother, Videl Balenciaga the Fifteenth!"

The little brown mouse squeaked and waved his paw. "Nice to meet you," I croaked from a dry throat.

There were no people around, but there sure were mice. I propped some pillows behind my head and met Leith Balenciaga the First, a pure white mouse and Chance's mother. There was also Chauncey Balenciaga the Sixth, a fully brown mouse and also his father, with that name. Every other mouse was a mix of their colors, with long names and even longer family lines I was in no state to remember. This room had to be absolutely swarming with Chance's family.

Speaking of which, Chance barely remembered where he hid my desda powder stash, but he remembered all his siblings' names? To be fair, we only got through a couple dozen of them before there was a grumpy meow from Smoky, who woke from her place by my legs. She had three tiny kittens snuggled to her belly, their teeny wings and paws trembling as they dreamed.

"Sorry sorry," Chance replied. "I finish showing you siblings later."

"Okay," I murmured. I slowly inched myself up to a sitting position, too tired and dizzy for such a simple task. Many concerned faces watched me, mostly from the carpenter mouse family, but also from a few other little wonders I'd befriended recently. The nightstand hosted Flicker and a few tiny salamanders resting under her unfurled wings. Their scales were translucent, showing an ember of fire in their chests.

Wils the crested alarm bird released a harsh croak when I noticed him perched on one of the bedposts. And the silver rabbit peeked his head out from under the bed shyly, nose twitching.

I wanted to reassure them, but I wasn't sure what exactly was wrong with me. My head was full of fog and fluff. Nothing really made sense. The last thing I remembered was walking into Jace's old house, and now I was here, and they were all worried…

The door creaked as it opened, and when I startled, so too did Wildcat as she walked in. "Oh! You're awake," she gasped. She was holding a small illusion fox in the crook of her arm.

"Wildcat, what's going on?" I asked.

She nearly hurt herself by doing a snappy turn and racing away, shouting that I was awake. I heard her running down the hall and sighed. She returned with a glass of water and pulled up a chair. The fox went on the chair while she leaned over me, helping me take measured sips rather than letting me gulp the whole thing at one time.

"How're ya feelin'?" she asked.

"Tired. Confused," I answered. The water was helping me feel more awake, but I didn't think I had the energy to leave this bed yet. "What happened?"

"I'll let your boy explain the long of it," she said. Once the glass was empty, she scooped the little fox into her lap and sat with me. "But the short of it is you've been asleep for a week, and we's all worried about ya. This is my second visit… I was hoping to introduce you to Jinx."

The fox looked up and yipped. It was adorable, with a black button nose and a triangular head that was mostly a big pair of ears. Its fur was fluffy and gray, with hints of the cream tones of adult illusion fox fur starting to come in.

"You two Linked?" I asked.

Wildcat beamed, which was answer enough. "Yes! I saved her from being trampled when the stampede started, and she must'a liked me."

I smiled and picked up Chance in my palm, pressing him to my chest. He curled up, letting just the tip of his nose peek out from under the cup of my hand. "It's a great feeling, isn't it? Congrats," I said.

I only just noticed I was wearing pajamas, and I recognized the pattern and fabric. Shauna must've changed me into her clothes while I was unconscious. "It's really been a week?" I added.

"Really really."

"What did I miss?" I blurted. "Did we make advanced?"

She bobbed her head. "Yep, both teams."

I nearly went limp with relief. I'd worked so hard for that. "It was worth it," I murmured, indicating myself.

"We ain't changing classes until the start of next year. But Sybella says we's getting new extra credit challenges next semester," she said.

I was going to need it, with how behind I had to be in all my classes at this point. "They's not mad I've been asleep?" I asked nervously.

"They's know what happened. It should be okay," she said.

I wish I knew what'd happened too, but I'd ask Vance for the details. Thomas came in shortly afterward with a bowl of soup for me, and she left, promising to tell Miss Barrios and the others that I was awake.

I spent the rest of the day in bed, cuddling with my little friends and dozing between visits. None of my siblings wanted to tell me anything of substance about the completed job, and there was a sense amongst them that Vance needed to explain why I felt like the melting stub of a candle. He'd been upgraded to "my boy" amongst my family for whatever he'd done while I was asleep.

Vance himself arrived the next morning, holding a bowl of dark broth. "I've been told this is very healthy," he said as a hello. I figured that was code for *this is disgusting* and was right. It was quite bitter, and the leafy things floating on top of it weren't for added flavor.

"What happened?" I asked for what felt like the twelfth time.

He put the bowl and spoon aside and dug the Eye of Acuity out of his pocket. I gasped upon seeing it, my eyes widening. *I need that!*

Wait, why? I was reaching for it, fingers flexing. I let my arm fall back to my bedside.

"Madam Morashi happened," he said.

Her name had me breaking into a frightened sweat. I'd waxed between excited and covetous to afraid within a couple breaths, picturing my frosty night in a jail cell with a shiver.

"I looked into her eyes..." I tried to focus on what'd happened next, but those memories were buried beneath the fog in my head. My face pinched with frustration. "...And now I'm here."

Vance sighed, fiddling with his fingers and looking down at them. "It was bad luck. I knew there was a chance you would meet her...but then you did and...I'm so sorry, Heather."

"We knew it was possible. Plus, she'd do much worse if she saw you." I was trying to reassure him, but I think it did the opposite. He tousled his hair with an aggrieved sigh while I spoke.

"She sensed my magic on you, though. She's the only formshifter who can smell another formshifter's work," he said, sounding miserable. "So, she started the process of stealing your vitality and didn't seal the wound she gave you. It...it's...it would've been fatal if I didn't find someone who could cast the spell to fix it."

I reached for him, taking his hand before he picked a wound in his fingers with how he dug at them. "You must've," I said, smiling uncertainly.

"Yeah. I watched what she was doing from the Eye and found a mage who could heal you. Chance helped you break the trance, but the other mage broke the compulsion. The madam...she sent you to kill me with a poisoned dagger and retrieve the Eye of Acuity for her."

"Vance, I would never," I protested.

"I know," he said gently.

"Where's the dagger now?"

"Fletcher has it. He's trying to develop a cure for the madam's poison, since the madam coated it generously." He cleared his throat. "You were so lucky. Look." He gently took hold of the long sleeve of my pajamas and drew it up to my elbow. Pink lines dotted my skin, and they crossed in shapes like...runes. Someone had healed me while I was out for the wounds to be so far in the healing process.

My forearm was coated in runes. Vance pointed out a series of five of them close to my elbow, cut in half with silvery marks already scarring. "She worked her magic on you directly. But a certain mouse destroyed enough of the runes to ruin her spell work."

"I bite bad marks on you too hard?"

My eyes welled. "Chance saved me."

"He saved *us*," Vance corrected.

He still wouldn't look at me. I tried to tug on his hand. "Vance. It sounds like you saved me too," I said tentatively.

"Someone else did. I just carried you to them," he mumbled. Releasing my hand, he stood and left the room.

I exchanged a glance with Chance and a cluster of his

siblings, who listened from their place next to my hip. None of us mice knew what he was going to do next.

Vance returned a few minutes later with a hand mirror. He looked like he was near tears as he held it up to reveal my reflection. "I'm so sorry," he repeated.

A near stranger looked back at me. I understood why everyone was looking at me funny and avoiding the obvious. The disheveled face in the mirror was mine in a couple of years. My cheeks were hollow in that familiar way that implied I needed several good meals...but that was my face.

Madam Morashi had stolen a couple of years of my life. Instead of taking from the back of the thread, where I'd die earlier in my twilight years, should I be so lucky as to see them, she'd snipped away what I'd be at fifteen and maybe sixteen. I was as unremarkable as an older teen as I was as a young one, but my features were more balanced now. My hooked nose seemed smaller, my lips more generous, and my brown eyes were still too expressive but not as prominent.

I didn't have a single spot of acne, but my skin was so dry I could see flakes forming. I needed to eat and drink, because my body had aged and probably eaten up every bit of fat and spare drop of water I possessed.

My gaze flicked from my face to Vance's guilty one. "This isn't your fault," I told his guilt. "I'm alive because of you. I'll adjust to...this."

I looked at myself again. It was sinking in that I'd been stolen from. Madam Morashi may not have killed me like she had some of my siblings, but she'd intended to. My life had not been worth more than a moment of casual cruelty to her.

Vance and I now shared a dubious dishonor: we'd both been victimized by the same monster of a mage. I got out of bed, standing on weak legs, and hugged him for a long time. Seeing how much he cared, I agreed with my siblings: he was my boy.

My energy came back once I started eating. Margot visited in the morning on her way to her job, with a delivery of as much food as the cafeteria would allow her to take. By midday, it would all be gone. As soon as I started moving around, she'd glanced down and frowned before gently asking if I owned any chest bands.

Margot also delivered clothes after that embarrassing conversation. I stayed at Little Wonders Pet Shop with the blessings of someone at RSI, probably Miss Barrios.

She came by on the fourth day with a packet of papers. We sat in what had been the prey room, which was now the only room the resident little wonders needed, as the vast majority had disappeared into the city with their families.

"The homework you've missed," she said, handing over the packet. "You're going to be in an evening remediation class once you return. Not for academics… Most of it can be excused. We'll need to work on your muscle strength after what you've been through."

Miss Barrios was doing the same thing I'd noticed everyone else falling into. None of us knew how to address my sudden aging, so we tiptoed around it in conversation. It was always "my ordeal" or "my loss" like a family member had died, not a few years of my youth.

"That makes sense," I said, setting my lips at an unhappy angle. I didn't enjoy a lot of the adjustments I was getting used to. It turned out my body had also taken the muscles that weren't entirely necessary to help me grow overnight. I was taller, but perhaps not as much as I would've been if I'd had the time to grow properly. That didn't stop my curves from appearing, to my dismay. A sneak didn't need padding. I'd be aging out of the role if I were looking like this in the Menagerie.

"Is Manny waiting for me to report?" I asked.

"When you're feeling better. May I look at your arm?" Her hand hovered over my right wrist. I was glad of the cool weather giving me a chance to cover up my forearm.

I nodded and slid my sleeve up. She tilted my arm to look me over. Since most of the wounds had been sealed by magic, they weren't scarring, but I had the shadow of a few marks here and there that were looking like they'd be permanent. The scars were just another sign of how Madam Morashi had taken advantage of me. The lines of Chance's bites were raising too, but I didn't mind those scars as much. They were a reminder of his lightning-quick thinking.

She tisked. "I'm sorry, Miss Mouse."

I nodded, still focused on the Spymaster. "Is he..." I bit my bottom lip. "Does he know about the two spies that died?"

She eyed me strangely. "A few died to complete the mission."

"A few?" I echoed in dismay.

"Along with nearly forty civilians, Morashi mages, and peacekeepers. Manny is happy, actually. He was expecting it to be much worse," she told me. "The gryphons of Wild Flight went berserk until they were reunited with their young. We knew there would be consequences to involve them."

I sat in silence for a while, and she didn't press me to share my thoughts. I just...I was used to sneaking in, taking, and sneaking out. No jobs had had *forty* casualties before.

"No one you would've known were amongst the deceased," Miss Barrios said eventually.

Shaking my head, I told her about the woman Madam Morashi had killed. "That sounds like Agent Pinewood. Her body was found after the fact with wounds around her throat but no vine," she said, patting my shoulder. "She was one of the most cutthroat candidates in her class, more assassin than spy. I imagine she's satisfied in the sun-washed lands, glad she died with a weapon in hand."

I imagined she'd be more satisfied to still be alive…but maybe that was just me.

"Maybe," I said doubtfully. "Did my crew report everything about the job?"

"I'd say so."

"Did they tell you what Sivana said as we were getting her ready?" I pressed.

She eyed me with a brow lifted. "Tell me what you think they may have missed."

I told her about the secret Morashi facility Sivana had mentioned, the House of the Unstable, with the experiments on battle beasts and pyromancers. Miss Barrios nodded along, looking troubled as I went on.

"Zizi," she repeated. "I know that name. Well, thank you. I will tell Manny to ask about it when you give your official report."

In the meantime, she reassured me I should stay here and regain my strength. I learned this was for my own good, so none of my fellow students saw "my condition" before I was ready to reveal it.

I hoped to put on weight quickly, falling back on my old thinking for the rest. *Maybe they won't notice anything different.*

CHAPTER 35

GRYPHON FRIENDS

It didn't take me long to learn the pet shop had a gryphon in residence. Thomas took me out to the stable attached to the shop. Since it had the bones of an inn, the family maintained the small stable to provide services for horses and other livestock.

And gryphons, apparently. Arimus was in the first stall, bandages wrapped around his torso and wing. He lay on his belly, letting the damaged wing extend to fill most of the space. He'd stretched his bulk into a long line and rested his head on his front legs, eyelids lowered over the yellow painted orbs that substituted his eyes.

At the sound of our voices on the other side of the stall door, he lifted his beak, making a questioning *craw*.

"Sorry, Ari. It's not time for lunch yet. I was just showing Heather that you're here recovering," Thomas said.

In answer, I felt Ari's emotions like he'd opened my head and stuffed them in beside my own. My lips turned down at the weight of loneliness that settled over me.

Thomas turned back to me, smiling like he didn't feel a thing. "He's had too much healing magic worked on him in the past, so he's immune to it now. We're looking after him until he heals from a few fractures naturally."

We went back into the shop soon after since I needed to sit down. But I was soon approaching Ari's stall with my book bag slung over one shoulder. He hadn't moved much but lifted his head and tilted it in my direction. "Mind if I sit with you?" I asked.

He patted the straw by his side with one massive set of talons. I went into the stall and set out my things. He nosed me with his beak and scooted until I could lean back and be cradled in the space between his good wing and muscled shoulder.

"I'm recovering, too," I told him, taking out a quill, inkwell, and the stack of parchment that grew with every delivery from Margot. "So, I have some homework to do. How are you with numbers?"

He clucked and sent a feeling of doubt.

"Okay. How about Lithosian?"

I had the feeling the noise he was making was laughter.

"Me too," I sighed, getting to work.

I wondered if everyone was too respectful of Ari to try sitting with him like this. Shauna's eyes just about bugged out of her head when she came by with fish for his afternoon meal. He seemed to tolerate me, at least, and we figured out how to communicate with simple yes or no questions.

When I wasn't eating, sleeping, or spending time with a visitor, I sat with Ari. He told me without words that he was lonely and bored, and listening to me labor over my homework was better than nothing. Especially when the Balenciaga family decided he wouldn't eat them. He clucked and rustled around as Chance's siblings and cousins scampered through his fur and feathers.

Tickles.

Through Chance, I learned he wanted me to read him a story to help pass the time. "Will a play do? I need to study my lines," I asked. The winter showcase was weeks away, and I hadn't glanced at *A Pinch of Nutmeg* in quite some time.

"He say yes yes," Chance said. The gryphon made a soft sound closer to a meow than a bird noise. "What you mean, one yes yes? I say what you say to Heather." Ari shook his head in amusement.

I cracked open the play and read the whole thing to him, with a terrible impression of the male parts and all. It took a while, but I had the feeling Ari was following along attentively.

"He ask which part you?" Chance reported.

"I'm supposed to be Nutmeg."

Ari clicked his beak in approval. He listened as I read back over my parts, repeating a few as I tried to get the emotion right in each. By the shifts of his emotions, he shared which deliveries he liked best.

I wished I had Ari's support when it was time to perform this for an audience, but he would be long gone in a couple of weeks. He was already moving around more and flexing his wing and leg.

Ari tilted his head. He seemed thoughtful.

The next morning, a letter arrived at the shop addressed to me. Thomas handed it to me, looked as confused about it as I felt, and I nearly fell out of bed in shock when I opened it and saw the signature:

Sivana Walker

Lieutenant, Gryphon Knight Corps

"Sivana wrote me a letter," I said. It sure sounded like there were stars in my eyes.

Thomas's mouth dropped open. "Well? What does it say?" he asked excitedly.

I scanned it and paraphrased the highlights. "She doesn't know if I work here but figures this letter will find me since she isn't sure if RSI kids are allowed mail." We were, but I was glad she hadn't written to me at RSI since there was a guarantee a spy would read the letter first. "She says thank you for helping her get her younglings back. The wild gryphons have settled down and gained some perspective on what kinds of humans are their friends."

That was all I told him, though there was a little more. *Genuine friends are a rare find, in my experience. I hope we can stay in touch. Regular correspondence only arrives and departs from Fortress Aerie once a week, and I live for mail drops,* she'd written. I was excited she still wanted to talk to me, but my more calculating side pointed out how beneficial it would be to strike up a friendship with such a powerful woman.

"You gotta write her back!" Thomas exclaimed.

"Yes. I'd better," I agreed.

CARMEN VISITED LATE THAT AFTERNOON, finding me cuddled to Ari's side again. I glanced up to find her frowning face on the other side of the stall door, taking in the scene. "I was thinking you'd forgotten about me," I said in a small voice. She was the only one of my crew that hadn't visited yet.

Fariq had recently spent an extended stay, helping me correct my homework and catching up over dinner. He'd mentioned some trouble at the forge with a meaningful glance but couldn't say more with Fletcher's family nearby.

Vance and Margot came to see me as much as they could. But Carmen? My first friend at RSI seemed to be avoiding me. I was relieved to finally see her.

"Yeah. I got a little busy," she said, avoiding eye contact. "Can we talk? Without you sitting next to a giant gryphon?"

Ari clucked and nudged me toward her with his beak. I left my homework and took her for a walk. "I'm getting better, but I shouldn't go too far from the pet shop," I warned her.

She led me wordlessly to a tavern, where she ordered a giant dinner for us both and eyed me from across the table. "You seem…okay," she said.

My brows drew in confusion. But I could see Carmen was struggling with something, so I let her approach it how she would.

"I thought you were dead," she explained in a low voice. "I thought…I'd failed to help you. It happened so fast. That guy had to knock me unconscious. Did you know that? I kept fighting him, trying to get back to you."

My stance softened with understanding. "I'm really okay. There was nothing you could've done," I said. "I'm glad he saved your life, because trying to help me in that situation would've been…"

As time passed and I grew more accustomed to the new me, my anger over what'd happened had blended with understanding. All the what-ifs led to death. Carmen, Vance, me, or that spy that'd saved her. There was nothing any of us could do. Our enemy was simply that powerful.

"Yeah. But that doesn't stop…" She gestured toward me.

I put on a smile for her sake. "I'll be coming back to school soon and doing some strength training in the evenings. I figured, if you weren't busy…maybe you would want to help? It won't be Tosh Zorena."

"It doesn't have to be. Of course I'll help," she said.

"But we'll work back up to it. I want to learn. I want to be stronger." *I want to be strong enough to do what's necessary if I have to, like Agent Pinewood.*

She tilted her head. "All right, pipsqueak. And no offence. You might be a bit bigger, but the nickname still fits."

I sighed playfully. "I wouldn't want anything less."

Toward the end of my stay at the pet shop, I asked a question that'd been lingering in my mind. It was strange, but I still asked it. "Do you have a wand?" I asked Shauna over dinner.

Because I could've sworn I'd heard Fletcher say, *"Thomas, go get Shauna. Tell her to bring her wand."* Yet I didn't know when in the mixed up haze in my mind that moment had occurred.

Fletcher and Shauna exchanged glances. She gave him a pleading look, while his lips tugged downward.

I fidgeted with my fingers as Thomas joined the nonverbal discussion. Their lips moved and they gestured toward me. "What's going on?" I asked uncertainly.

"This is a family secret and…I would like to share it with you, if you would agree to a vow to keep it to yourself. After everything that's happened, it has felt wrong to keep it from you," Fletcher said, drawing his wand.

I eyed the length of wood and asked, "A blood vow?"

Wizards like Miss Barrios could swear magical oaths like the one I'd made to keep RSI and my status as a spy candidate secret. Healers could work similar magic, with different consequences. A vow sworn on my blood was easier to break because it wouldn't restrict my tongue, but it was a piece of magic that would live inside me and have fatal consequences if broken.

"That's right. Vance swore a similar vow when he learned the secret by accident."

I glanced toward Shauna, who nodded in encouragement. She wanted me to agree and looked like she was straining not to say anything in the meantime. With that input, I agreed and put my arm out. Fletcher worked a brief spell and touched the glowing tip of his wand to my wrist. "I vow to keep the Archer family secret to myself," I parroted.

The line of one of my veins turned green for a moment, traveling to my heart, where the vow would remain.

"First, my real name is John. Jonathan Archer." He put a hand on his chest. "I've been hiding from my former cult for over a dozen years."

Then he turned his wand on himself. His features shifted to that of a different man, and a layer of magic left his hand. A familiar ugly snake tattoo hissed from its place on his skin. It coiled around his wrist to bare its teeth toward his knuckles.

"You're a Morashi mage," I said in disbelief.

"*Was*," he corrected. He pointed his wand at Shauna. A green Tulari mark took form on her cheek. It wasn't complete yet—the skin was still peeling around the bottom of the rune which marked her as a mage.

I gaped at her, too. "I've wanted to tell you *so* badly," she blurted. "Dad couldn't work the spell to save you, but I could. I did!"

"You did?" I echoed, before I launched myself at her for a crushing hug. "I was wondering who…thank you! Thank you so much." Vance had avoided telling me who he'd found with the capability of fixing what Madam Morashi had done to me, and now I knew why.

Fletcher watched us, smiling gently. He'd given his fake face more flaws and made his appearance more nondescript and older. The real him, John Archer, couldn't be a day over thirty. I trusted the *former* part of his declaration. No one wanted to be more haggard in appearance unless they had to be, and besides, Fletcher didn't seem capable of the cruelties of someone who followed Madam Morashi.

I was glad to know someone who understood the depths of her depravity was the one with the poisoned dagger, developing a cure.

"What happened to you?" I asked.

"Now that is a long story," he answered in the way that said he wouldn't actually answer. "Vance told me you know about the cult."

"I probably know too much," I said honestly.

"My ex-wife and I married young, as the madam requires of her followers. When Thomas arrived and didn't develop a Tulari mark, we were offered Shauna instead."

My eyes widened with realization and alighted on Thomas. Madam Morashi would've consumed his life force without a second thought, except...

"I cut ties to keep them both. Madam Morashi believes John Archer died for his audacity." He lifted his wand, formshifting himself back to his false appearance with a few flicks and erasing his snake tattoo. "So, let's keep it that way, yes?"

I gave Shauna one last squeeze as he hid her Tulari mark. "Yes," I agreed.

"Ari tells me you have a play performance coming up," Sivana said a couple of days later.

She'd arrived on Sunset's back and immediately gone to her gryphon's side...just to step into the stall and find me there too with the last of my homework. I was scheduled to return to RSI tomorrow, and when I'd told Ari that, he'd given me the feeling that today was the day for him. And it was.

Ari had crowed with delight and stood, rushing in her general direction. Sivana sidestepped into his path, intercepting him and pressing her forehead to his. They spent a long time like that while she ruffled the feathers and fur along his neck. After they were done greeting, he moved around her to press to Sunset's side, and now the two of them were grooming one another while I sat next to the gryphon rider on a pile of hay.

"Oh, yeah." I scratched at the back of my head. "He's caught me practicing for it a few times."

She leaned over to nudge my shoulder with hers. "When's it going to be? And where?"

I blushed up to the tip of my ears. "It's not going to be very—"

"Ari wants to see it." She tapped the side of her temple. "Because of our Link, he can see through my eyes sometimes."

Oh, in that case…I told her about the winter showcase. She looked over at me as I spoke, making a little hum. For a moment, I wondered if she was going to make a comment on how I looked or sounded older. "We'll be there," was all she said. "In the meantime, I offered you a ride on a gryphon. How do you feel about a joyride?"

I lit up, surprised she even remembered saying that. Would it be a dream come true? Absolutely. "Oh, yes, definitely. Now that Ari is leaving…maybe I should too," I said, thinking aloud. "Do you mind if I go grab my things?"

"Not at all. I should check in with Fletcher anyway," she said.

We went inside, and I headed upstairs. As I packed away my clothes, I took in the little friends who had made my temporary home here theirs too. Lucky, the silver rabbit, and Smoky with her kittens. Flicker, who had said goodbye to her "little embers" as they swiftly left the stage where they needed their mother's care. She was ready to meet Fariq at last and maybe make a home in the forge where he worked.

Then there was the Balenciaga family. I kneeled down with Chance in hand, saying goodbye and petting all the mice I could. They were going to stay here, with Fletcher's blessing, as long as they didn't scare off the customers. All the various siblings and cousins promised to find professions around the pet shop, but Chance would be the only spy amongst them.

Lucky and Smoky were staying, too. As would Wils, who was grateful to have some space to himself again. I would see them all when I came to visit for Sunday dinners, but I'd miss falling asleep cuddling with most of them.

Then I found Thomas and Shauna, saying goodbye with a hug for them both. Finally, I went to Fletcher, who reached up to take both my hands in his at the back of the public portion of the shop. He pressed several coins into my palms. "Some belated payment for helping us during the crisis," he explained.

Gold and silver cloret coins glittered in my palms. "You've already done more than enough for me," I protested.

"Nonsense. Take it. And…" He cleared his throat. "Someone at RSI finally bothered to reply to my letters. They will not release you from the school, unfortunately."

I nodded, completely unsurprised.

"But the shop has been invited to join their apprenticeship program, as long as I pay you in the hourly rates of the Farrier Guild." He folded his hands over Edgimus in his lap, who released an encouraging squeak. "Which should not be a problem. How do you feel about becoming more than an honorary employee around here?"

"I…yes, of course!" I exclaimed. After my convalescence here, the pet shop felt more like home than the school I was about to return to. "I should be back this weekend, then."

He smiled warmly. "Until then, take care."

I left the shop, heading back into the stable and securing the money he'd given me in my pocket for now. Sivana was kneeling under Ari, securing a few straps to his underside. He stood perfectly still, except for his wings. The reddish-brown feathers quivered with his excitement. "I brought his old tandem saddle, just in case. Don't mind the scorch marks. It's seen war and survived, just like the rest of us," Sivana said without looking up.

Now that she mentioned it, the second seat had patterns of darkened leather. If she wasn't worried about it being damaged, then I wouldn't be either. She checked the complicated-looking series of straps by tugging on each, then went to his head to adjust the bit in his beak and the fit of more straps that crisscrossed his face.

"Is he going to be okay, carrying both of us after his injury?" I asked.

He answered with his emotions. *Yes, Heather Mouse.* At some point, he'd started saying my name by showing mental pictures of a field of heather or a scampering mouse. Sometimes he would flash those images multiple times, almost like a test to see how much gryphon communication I could take before I grew overwhelmed.

"Yes, he's all healed up. He's *much* stronger than he looks," she answered after him.

She went to Sunset and retrieved a second set of goggles, handing them to me to wear. She gave me a boost onto his back next, explaining that I needed to be tied to the saddle at the speeds we'd be flying at. There were two sets of straps for such a task, and she laced me into the back pair before vaulting onto his back and lacing her set on. "You did that fast," I noted.

"Academy training," she said with a chuckle. "We had to mount and tie ourselves in within thirty seconds and were timed until we got it right. Put your arms around me."

I did as she said after adjusting my book bag so its straps were looped around both of my shoulders. "That sounds stressful," I said.

"You know, it wasn't bad to be held to high standards. Many of the things I learned at the Academy helped save our lives later. Plus, I made some amazing friends." She lowered the goggles from her hairline to over her eyes and took up Ari's reins. There were two sets that she wound around her fingers and gave a few testing tugs. He snorted softly but responded to each tug, turning his head up and down, left and right.

With a nudge of her knee, he began to walk, turning naturally to the tug of the reins, as if he could still see where he was going. I could feel his muscles bunch and push in a feline lope. He felt strong, solid, and warm from where my legs pressed to his sides.

"So, I'm dropping you off at RSI?" she asked.

"Yeah, if you don't mind."

"We'll take the long way. Ready?"

Ari scratched at the ground with his talons. When I said yes, she snapped the reins, and he surged forward into a run down the market street, wings unfurling. I leaned over her shoulder to see where we were going, mouth open in an excited grin.

Ari pushed up with his legs and down with his wings, beating the air into submission with a heavy *whump*. We hurtled into the air, steadily leaving the ground behind with each powerful flap of his wings. I left my heart behind somewhere in between with a sensation that was half exhilaration, half terror.

But when we leveled out several stories over the nearest buildings and climbed further into the air at a smooth pace, I forgot to be afraid and whooped. Wind pummeled my face and whipped my hair behind my head wildly, screaming in my ears, but I still heard Sivana echoing me and Ari screaming with happiness I *felt*, the kind of elation that only came after being helplessly earthbound when you were meant to fly.

Sunset screeched as she passed us as a maroon streak, disrupting the air around us for a moment. "Faster?" Sivana shouted at me.

"Yes!" I shouted back.

She leaned over, and I followed suit, the two of us flattening as much as possible as Ari stretched out his long body and tucked his limbs. He scooped the wind under his wings, accelerating until everything streaked around us.

The clouds, the city, and even the bright spot of the sun

elongated and lost their meaning. All that mattered was that Ari caught up with Sunset, and something passed between them, mind-to-mind. They flew at the same pace, weaving around one another in a midair dance that must've looked effortless from below. Wings nearly brushing at places, Ari remained upright while Sunset flipped around him. There was no hesitation that he was blind while she wasn't. They trusted Sivana's guiding hand completely.

Ari's heart beat against my legs like a great drum, fast but steady and strong. There was no pain, only love for the open sky, his rider, and his mate. Yet I was welcomed into this moment, too.

We spiraled around the city, lapping the outer edge with its high walls and bell towers, looking as small as toys from this distance. The palace could've been an expensive play set, and RSI a smaller, more affordable replica that we inevitably headed toward at the end of the joyride.

Ari touched his weight down lighter than I expected, though the straps around my legs pulled taut as Sivana and I leaned with the momentum before being pushed back into the saddle. We slowed before the front steps of the school as Sunset touched down behind us, and several passersby stopped to stare.

"Just ignore the crowd," Sivana muttered. She dismounted and helped me out of the harness and off Ari's back. I stumbled, my legs numb from the trip. I did as she suggested and tried to tune out the surrounding whispers.

Chance poked his head out of the neckline of my shirt, where he'd hunkered down for the ride. As much as I wanted to go back up, he hadn't enjoyed the trip as much as I had. Mice were meant for the ground, after all. I wouldn't be getting a gryphon of my own, but I could still admire the two huge beasts who waited for Sivana to return to them.

"Thank you for the ride. That was incredible," I said. I let myself be envious for a couple of moments that she had this experience every day. No wonder most of the times we'd met, she'd seemed so windblown. "I suppose you need to go back to Fortress Aerie, huh?"

"I suppose so," she echoed. First, she pulled me in for a hug. "It's not goodbye. Just see you later. Good luck." After we released one another, she looked up at RSI's ivy-shrouded walls. "Hope you are released from this place soon."

Musty devils, she was too nice, just like Fletcher. RSI was still the proper home for a spy candidate like me.

CHAPTER 36

GROWTH

I DEBRIEFED with Manny shortly afterward in the privacy of the headmaster's office. I shared everything I could remember, and he jotted a few notes down, unsurprised by everything I was saying. When I was done, the only sound in the room was his scratching quill and then his breath blowing over the ink.

"Well, then. It will be nice to finally file this mission away as completed," he remarked. Then he placed the parchment aside and looked me up and down. "You're older."

"Yes, sir." It must be pretty obvious, now that I'd eaten enough to regain a normal body shape.

"Does this upset you?"

"I'm not mad because I look older. But *how* I lost those years, yes, I am angry about that. I'm upset because I don't remember it happening. Madam Morashi didn't even break a sweat. She meant to kill me." My hands balled into fists in my lap. I hadn't put up a fight…hadn't even had a chance to do so. She'd just reached out and plucked my vitality from me like it was nothing.

"Good," he said.

I blinked in surprise. What part of any of that was good?

"Never forget that feeling, Miss Mouse. Let it motivate you to succeed and grow until you are the one making the likes of her sweat." The edge of a smile graced his mouth. "Due to the nature of your recovery, you have already heard that Five & Chance is an advanced team, I presume. Congratulations. You have been here less than a year and have already achieved a promotion many don't attain in five plus years of attendance at RSI. I've been holding on to these for you."

He passed me two clorets for the Wall of Achievement, already engraved with my heather and mouse symbol.

"One for leading your team to the advanced tier, and another for your completed, successful mission," he narrated. I smiled and put them away, already planning where I would place them. "My other gift to you has been this time to recuperate. Time is always a luxury, though few seem to understand that before they're already aged and tired."

"Thank you, sir," I murmured.

"Things will be more difficult for you and your team going forward. Next school year, you will be honed into the sharpest agent we can make you." He leaned back in his chair, steepling his fingers as he spoke. "Beginners experience mild pressure, intermediates experience consequences, but advanced students…they experience failure. Expect to get to know it, Miss Mouse. Picking yourself up no matter what and thinking on your feet is a life skill."

"I understand," I replied.

"Do you?" He raised a questioning brow. "You've come here with more skills than most and succeeded in raising my expectations for you toward the sky. Do you have what it takes to scrape yourself off the cobblestones if you were to, say, fall from those heights?"

I took a heavy swallow from the doubt I heard and saw from him. My eyelid twitched at the inevitability that I would one day run into a job my crew couldn't complete with the skills we had now. Hells, the last one had nearly killed me.

"We will have to see when the day comes, sir," I answered.

"So we shall." He put an affable smile back on and gestured toward the door. "Go, catch up, have fun. We will revisit this discussion when it's time."

I nodded and got to my feet, gathering up my bag. As I left to do as he said, I couldn't help but wonder…what had I really gotten my crew into, pushing us into the advanced tier so soon?

THE SPYMASTER WANTED to see growth from me, but if he was watching at any moment in the next few weeks, I didn't know about it. He melted back into a mysterious driving force no student saw, though we often talked about him and what he wanted, or didn't want, from us.

Five & Chance debuted on spot number thirteen of fourteen on the advanced team list, right above SHAINA. The moment it happened, the kids around me started looking at me and my crew differently. A bit of respect sometimes, but more often sized up as a threat. The meanest glances of all came from Davit's Day, who emerged from whatever hole they'd been hiding in to shoot mean looks and the occasional shove my way. But they weren't as obnoxious as they used to be. Was it because I'd taken my team to advanced and they knew their bullying tactics weren't going to work?

Who's to say. I didn't have time to worry about what they were plotting when I had to dive headfirst into my classes, every moment of my free time gobbled up by remedial studying, strength training, and dress rehearsals for *A Pinch of Nutmeg.*

A series of semester examinations crashed into my life with the force of a charging bull. But at no time was I alone when I studied for them. Fariq helped me study for Innovation's practical and Lithosian's oral exam. Carmen gave me the hands-on treatment for Self-Defense each time we hit the mats during class and my strength training sessions.

Margot and I held long conversations in Uncommon to prepare for the Language test. Sybella and I raced on the rock wall for Agility—she always won—and Ned helped by quizzing me on Craft basics.

Finally, for Theater, Vance would read every part except for mine until we both had *A Pinch of Nutmeg* memorized. He teased me about how overprepared I was but never complained when I wanted to go over it "one more time."

With their help, I passed my classes, even though some of my grades scraped the edge of failure. I avoided those theoretical cobblestones Manny thought I would fall to from the heights where I'd risen. Maybe next semester.

EPILOGUE

The day I'd once dreaded arrived: the winter showcase. *A Pinch of Nutmeg* was the third play of four to run on the first day, and the theater was teeming with people by its mid-afternoon time slot. I looked out at the audience from behind a side curtain, already dressed in stage makeup and my costume as a young baker with a flour-stained apron. The backstage crew had had a little too much fun staining the apron, I thought, but it needed to be seen from way far away, so maybe throwing off little drifts of flour every time I moved was appropriate.

I knew I was about to be disappointed. No one had mentioned gryphon riders or their beasts while I'd been busy prepping for my stage debut. And there was no sign of them out in the crowd. Sivana was probably being polite in asking about when and where I'd be performing.

"Attention! Everyone, gather around!" Miss Stone exclaimed. The Theater teacher was usually so put-together, but when I turned, I was taken aback by how harried she looked. She'd probably been pulling on her hair out of stress, which I couldn't blame her for when she was in charge of the whole winter showcase. I joined the other actors and helpers in making a semi-circle in front of her.

"There has been…an unusual request made of the theater's space. Headmaster Radcliffe decided to grant it, but it will require *A Touch of Nutmeg* to be the last show of the day," she explained. A few of the kids groaned, and I suppressed the urge to echo them. We were all made up and ready to go, after all.

Then, she told us why we were being delayed, and I was seized by a completely different set of emotions. Miss Stone had to hurry off, calling orders to get the backdrops changed out and the next play in motion. I sat with the crew of *A Pinch of Nutmeg* out of sight to watch the performance.

My heart beat, and my fingers trembled in my lap as my excitement and anxiety met while the other class performed their play. There was motion in the sounds of the crowd—folk in certain seats were discreetly being asked to move to the standing area and told why. Miss Stone had mentioned that the ushers were used to taking care of such tasks, so it would be a seamless transition to make room for our special guests.

Once it was our turn, Miss Stone fixed her hair and stepped out in front of the closed curtain with a magic rod designed to amplify her voice. "Good afternoon, everyone! We are about to have an unusual addition to the theater today. Do not be alarmed, but a group of gryphons heard we were going to have a performance of *A Pinch of Nutmeg* and wanted to see it for themselves. These are friendly beasts under the authority of the gryphon knight corps, but if you would like to avoid any close encounters with them, I suggest you either move to the standing area or leave now."

I couldn't help it. I had to take a peek out of a side curtain to see what was happening amidst the murmuring crowd. A group of folk were leaving, but not as many as I expected. Once the murmuring crowd settled, the double doors leading outside were held open and the first gryphons filed in. Sivana walked amongst them, gesturing toward the spaces emptied out for them.

Sunset, unmistakable from the brilliant reds of her fur and feathers, split off from the group and walked straight up to me with a murring sound. I froze in surprise upon seeing her approach, but she bowed her head and pressed her softly feathered forehead to mine.

Heather Mouse. She projected images of both objects, as Ari had started doing. But more thoughts, emotions, and pictures entered my mind behind them, mixing together in a feeling. A message I think I mostly understood.

I hugged her around the neck. "I wasn't the only one who worked to save your baby," I whispered.

Her talons tapped the wooden step below her. *No,* she seemed to say. *All gryphon—see play—celebrate you. We see Heather Mouse.*

"All of you?" I echoed in surprise.

Riders too, she answered, butting my chest with her massive head gently enough that she didn't throw off my balance. *Bye, Heather Mouse.*

"Bye," I said, just standing there in awe for a few moments before I shook myself off. Several other kids crowded the side curtain with me after she left, watching the crowd too.

The sound of massive wings beating echoed around the theater as a whole flock of gryphons found places to settle. More than a few of them gathered on the nearly invisible catwalks that ran across the ceiling. I hoped those were built to handle the weight of several gryphons.

The bulk of the group lined up on the second-floor balcony, piling on top of each other. The ushers had been expecting this—the first few rows of seats had been cleared out to put a safe buffer between them and the folk who hadn't expected to be sharing their theater space with a gryphon flock. A few of the large beasts took advantage of this and stretched out across multiple emptied seats.

The front row behind the orchestra pit had also been cleared. Once the beasts were more or less settled, the gryphon riders sat up front instead. In the center was Sivana, her arm entwined with Acton's, though she leaned toward the girl seated on her other side, who wore a big pair of spectacles and gestured grandly with fine-boned fingers. Puzzlebox had laid her white, fluffy bulk over their feet. She rolled a wooden toy around in her beak and seemed quite content.

There were more riders and a few companions, though I only recognized Noah amongst them. In the limited space between their feet and the orchestra pit, several gryphons had piled on top of one another.

Ari rested his head on his feet, sitting between Sunset and another female gryphon who gleamed with golden feathers. His red youngling, who I'd learned was named Novali, lay on top of a male gryphon with a prominent scar through the fur on his side. She played by trying to bite his taloned feet while he flexed them toward and away from her beak. He seemed a lot more interested in her than anything else, his tufted ears tilted back toward his skull.

Ironfeather rested out on his belly, chin pressed to the ground. His mouth opened occasionally to reply to something Chance had squeaked. My mouse didn't even clear the point of the bigger animal's beak, but they were chatting away like dear friends. *That explains where Chance disappeared to…*

A common rule of Theater was: if you can see them, they can see you, and I'd gaped long enough to be noticed. Noah waved, then the woman next to him with the glasses. Sivana looked up, grinned, and flashed a thumbs-up before tapping next to her eyes. She was watching for Ari to finally see what all the fuss was about. And she'd clearly brought friends.

I waved back and then ducked out of sight. My heart beat

rapidly, but I took a centering breath, blowing it out slowly. *I can do this*, I told the nerves which threatened to make my eye twitch without pause. I'd give the folk of Kaiamear *and* the gryphons of Wild Flight a show.

After everything I'd done in a few short months, I could go out there and perform the lines I now knew like they were inked in my brain. The gryphon riders weren't the only ones here to see me, I reminded myself. Carmen was in the crowd with her aunt and cousins, and Margot was here on a date with a gentleman spy. I hoped they were hitting it off.

Thomas and Shauna were also in the crowd somewhere, and Fariq and Vance were backstage crew for the production. As Miss Stone declared we were ready to go, I spotted my two crewmates over her shoulder. Fariq gave a thumbs-up, while Vance cupped his hands over his mouth. "Break a leg!"

"Okay!" I replied, grinning. Yes, I could definitely do this.

When the curtains rose and a specialized magelight spotlit me center stage, there was a "whoop whoop!" from someone in the crowd, accompanied by a few young-sounding gryphons sounding off with a set of *scree* noises before the elders shushed the sound.

Musty devils, they're looking at me. Eyes on all sides, even from the beaked faces peering out from the sides of the catwalks.

No. This is a reward. I kind of earned this. I swallowed and decided to have fun rather than let my anxiety leach away the joy of the moment. I was a far cry from an actress, but as a spy candidate, I assumed the identity of Nutmeg for a couple of hours and delivered the best performance I could for this mixed crowd.

I wouldn't have gotten to this moment if it weren't for my friends. And it wasn't just for saving my life from Madam Morashi's trickery. They'd been the driving force motivating me to succeed and bring the crew a chance to rise to advanced, where we belonged.

A year ago, I'd been a girl cowering in the shadow of the Gladbeck Mansion, there to steal a valuable necklace, just to be framed for its disappearance. I'd already grown from that into the girl who convinced a Hero of Altare to help us and the girl who didn't give up until her little wonder was reunited with his family. How much more growth could I push myself to in the next year? And the next?

RSI was the best thing that could've happened to me. Even something I'd felt was far past my comfort zone, this performance in a leading role, was something I'd adapted to succeed in. The energy of the audience and its reactions made all the practice and worry worth it.

Once the play was done, the curtain rose one last time on the cast taking a bow to thunderous applause. Gryphons screeched their delight, and several folk whistled and whooped.

I looked out without seeing them, dazzled by the stage's magelights. True spies were rarely applauded for their deeds and accomplishments. I soaked it in while I could.

Tomorrow, I would step back into obscurity, an unremarkable face amongst many in the city. I would continue through this year and beyond, counting the days I grew and improved. Someday, I would become the girl who made Madam Morashi and other monsters of her ilk tremble. My friends, and the Spymaster, expected nothing less of me.

Heather and her crew's story will continue with Royal Spy Institute 3: False Royalty! Publishing date TBD.

Interested in more? Join my newsletter as one way to get access to a bonus scene from this book! Sign up on my website.

Stay up to date with Royal Spy Institute and the Altare world by joining my Facebook group: People of Altare! In this community, we'll talk about fantasy book releases, share fun posts, and have the occasional giveaway.

Please remember to review! Reviews help other readers find stories they may love. Consider leaving a review for Royal Spy Institute 2: Five & Chance on Amazon and other websites.

ALSO IN THE ALTARE WORLD

GRYPHON RIDER ACADEMY

Are you ready for a high-flying adventure on gryphon-back? Join Sivana as she becomes the first female cadet at the highly competitive Gryphon Rider Academy after the blind gryphon Arimus chooses her as his new rider.

Dragon Riders of Pern meets Song of the Lioness in this YA fantasy series in which a pair of underdogs rewrite what's possible in a formerly all-boys military academy.

- See Gryphon Rider Academy on Amazon -

ABOUT THE AUTHOR

Elise Hennessy is an author of young adult fantasy full of adventure and found family. She holds a master's degree in journalism and enjoys crafting unique stories. When Elise is not busy writing, she's trying to reduce her prodigious TBR list. She lives in Texas with her family and is owned by two cats.

Find out more about her books at: www.elisehennessy.com

www.ingramcontent.com/pod-product-compliance
Lightning Source LLC
Chambersburg PA
CBHW031641200726
48289CB00004BA/1087